ORLUVOQ

BENNY HINRICHS

ISBN 978-1-7371064-0-1 (Paperback edition)

Edited by Austin Gragg (@austingragg)

Front cover art by Abel Klaer (@superstarfighter)

Released 22 June 2021

https://www.bennyhinrichs.com

Asanninnermut kusanartumut akigisaq tassaavoq anniarneq kusanartoq.

The price we pay for beautiful love is beautiful pain.

PART I

NUNAPISU

8 YEARS OLD

1

PAARSISOQ

T he Watcher sat at the end of the earth; he sat at the start of the sky. Today he watched errant flakes of snow drift over the edge in apathetic gusts of suicide. It was one of the few dances his eyes would never tire of, their ambling drift shimmering before a backdrop of inexhaustible darkness. If his luck held, that would be all he watched today.

As idly as the snow fell, he pondered over what happened to the spirits of those forsaken flakes. Did they, through some mystic means, return to earth, or were they consumed entirely by the void? A younger Watcher—and indeed not yet then a Watcher—would have contested against the cruelty of the nihility at the end of the earth. But such were the customs of naivety.

Today's Watcher knew frailty. He knew nullity. He knew reality. The knowledge lodged in his skin much as humans lodged in the earth's hide. The snowflakes were gone.

Gone...

The thought guttered out as the candle beside him tugged at his innards. He gathered up the glim in his gloved hand and focused on the swaying flame, the other dance his eyes never tired of. The distinctive odor of burning alicorn wafted into his nostrils and his eyes slid shut. An indistinct gravity flittered behind his spirit. He damped his breathing and released himself from the world.

The gravity consolidated. There she was, a mile east, the thrum of her quavering within him like the lowing of calving glaciers. He tracked the pull of her paltry procession toward Nunapisu, the end of the earth. Today he would watch more than snowflakes.

The Watcher's eyes cracked open and he groaned to his feet, stretching his back once he arrived. He took a brace of exploratory steps to check that his snowshoes needed no adjusting, then embarked.

Twenty minutes later, and silent as a dead fox, he trailed mere paces behind on her approach to the edge. Her feet carried her to the brink then scuffled to a halt. They always stopped at the edge.

He slid in beside her and resumed his observation of the dying snow. "What do you see?"

She sucked in an acute breath, jumped back, and turned to appraise the newcomer. A portion of her hackles settled as she decided who he must be. "I don't need your words, Watcher."

He stared into the neverending, arms crossed over his chest. *Few may* want *my words, sister, but all need them.* "What do you see?" he repeated, nodding to the dark.

A frozen moment passed before she shook her head. "Nothing. I see nothing."

Nothing. That was true enough. But two decades had taught the Watcher that much could be wrung from the inky abyss. "Nothing? If that's so, then I don't think this is the place for you." He pushed some of the warmth from his candle onto her.

Her breath flickered in preparation for weeping. "Everything, Watcher. I see everything." A gulp. "I see everything behind me and realize that everything is nothing now. I see nothing before me and realize that nothing is everything now. I am nothing. And so, nothing must become my everything."

He waited, turning over half a dozen replies in his mind. "Who do you run from?"

"Who do I... It's not that simple. I..." She sniffled. "My mother has disowned me." A sob tremored her body.

The Watcher turned to behold her for the first time. Matted hair clung haphazard about her face. Dull eyes weary of being squeezed for tears regarded him. She was somewhere around his age, mid-forties and holding, and from the state of things, it appeared the age of her spirit might be near his as well.

"Loss is not friends with ease, I know," he said. "Even more so when the one you're deprived of *chose* to become lost." He let the words hang in the air, then continued when she made no reply. "And what of your husband? Your children? Do none of them claim you any longer?"

She wiped at the fresh tears on her contorted face. "My husband is a quiet man who fears talking against anyone. He would never dream of confronting Mother. My children are... Well, Inneq has always hated me. He was glad for the change. And Silaanoq—she's too young to sway things either way, but she's always been more like her father. It wouldn't matter if she were older."

He nodded at the revelation. Some took longer than others, but all wanted to spill their story at least once more. "And so, everything has become nothing, and nothing has become everything." Both of their eyes were drawn to the glinting flame in his hand as silence set in. After a minute, he broke the quiet. "Here you've come, unable to resist the draw of Nunapisu. That queer hope offered by this gulf of eternal nothing. You resisted many miles of hungry ice for the chance to cast yourself beneath the sky."

Her gloved hand pawed at more tears. "What does it matter to you? You don't know me. What if I deserved to be forsaken?"

"There is always somebody who cares about you. Today that person is me." He lessened the amount of heat he was drawing from the candle so he could funnel more to her.

She scowled at his pronouncement and took a step to peer over the edge. A shiver gripped her body, and the Watcher discerned other telltales of a fever.

"Infinity gets smaller with each moment that you stare at it," he said.

"What does that mean?" she eventually replied.

His gaze disappeared into the expanse. "When you look into the stars and imagine how far away it all is, it makes you feel a tiny piece in the midst of greatness. Not so for the void. The longer you stare, the more you realize that there's nothing. You could fall for a thousand years and never see a difference. And when all is the same, it doesn't matter how much there is. It begins to shrink around you until you're pressing your arms and legs against it, and then the nothing swallows you."

The woman picked at a fraying seam in her caribou coat. "Then I must jump."

His candle burned lower than he would have liked. He thought about scaling back the heat he was channeling, but her preservation was worth more than some narwhal tallow and horn. "When I came, I thought the same. I reasoned I was bred from oblivion's stock and was through with my sojourn in existence. Time is the only thing that can heal these wounds."

"No. This wound will fester with time. Better to cut it off and save myself the pain." She shuffled closer to the edge.

"I'm not here to tell you what to do with your life; it's in your hands." He underscored his statement by grabbing her hand. Sometimes, they hadn't known the touch of another in so long, mere contact could pry them from the edge. It had kept him back often enough. "I'm here to beg you to give your body to the ice. Let it be preserved forever instead of disappearing, and your spirit along with it. Give me your name, and I will remember it. Give your spirit a chance. You may be filled with sorrow now, but you'll have all eternity to find joy."

"Which is the same as saying that I'll have all eternity to be miserable." Her fevered face reflected her belief in the words.

"Unbound by present cares, you will find misery tiring." He pontificated from his own musings and the words of elders from his youth.

Her breathing increased to an angry rate as she snatched her hands from him. "Do you know what I see? I see a fool at the end of the earth who doesn't understand why people come here."

Her words spoken in a tangle of emotion twanged hollowly against his heart. "You're right, of course. A score of years on this lurch sweep has shown me nothing."

The woman's face distorted with grief again. "How could someone I love so much cast me aside so easily?" An unintelligible moan racked her body. "Where did I love you wrong, Mama?"

His heart quickened at her sudden change in humor. "It's not always—"

A rustle of movement and a wail of despair cut him off.

The Watcher stood at the end of the earth; he stood at the start of the sky. Today he watched an anguished woman throw herself over the edge in an irrevocable thrust of suicide. It was one of the few dances his eyes would never watch while dry, her miniscule form sprawled before a backdrop of inexhaustible darkness.

His luck hadn't held. She was gone.

Gone.

Gone...

Gone.

2

Orluvoq loved when the ship stopped and she could get off and play on the ice. Though the boat was vast and full of crannies for stashing herself away in, the ice was endless and full of life.

But not today. Today Orluvoq watched the men lower her mother's corpse to the ice. She shook from the cold and the hideous ache in her gut.

It's not fair. She can't be gone. A fresh gout of tears froze as the wind shouldered by. One of the ship's women, Kitornak, laid a hand on Orluvoq's shoulder.

"I'm so sorry. No one so young should have to experience this sorrow."

The words stopped dead in her skin. Why did what "should" happen matter when it had nothing to do with what *did* happen?

The rest of the crew fanned around the funeral proceedings like a sail cupping wind, all mindful that it could be any of them atop their grave. Ribs of ice trickled up from the tundra and slowly cocooned the body.

Captain Naalagaa pulled his hood from his head,

turning to the grieving girl. "Your mother was a good, hard-working woman. Your parents were a valuable contribution to this vessel, and we're all sad to see them go. But soon they'll be reunited at the end of the earth." He examined the fur on his glove. "You'll have berth with us until we can take you back to your clan. Sorry to both you and your parents, but we just can't care for you."

"I'll care for her," Kitornak interjected, hand returning to Orluvoq's shoulder. Orluvoq wondered up at the woman maybe fifteen years her mother's senior.

Naalagaa frowned. "It's not just supervision I'm talking about, Kitornak. There's also the matter of supplies. The girl will grow, and where will her clothes come from? Also, this ship doesn't have enough candles for two angakkuit, as we've seen over the past years. Ikingut has been hard-pressed to earn his keep."

The word still had a strange ring in her ears: angakkuq —worker of candles. Angakkuit were supposed to be strange old people reserved to themselves, but she had first worked the tuuaaq candles two years ago when she was just six. She still hadn't quite acclimatized to hardened adults asking her to heal their cough or try to receive a vision for them. It sometimes embarrassed her they didn't go to Ikingut instead, but she secretly knew her angakkuq abilities surpassed his.

The woman vouching for her didn't reply to the captain. The matter was done. It wasn't right to eject a faithful crewmember just because something newer and better came along. Instead, she turned again to the exequies. "And look, your mother is gone to Nunapisu now."

It wasn't a revelation, merely a comment to fill the heavy air. Orluvoq had watched the ice consume her dearly departed inch by gelid inch, just as it had her father five months prior. If she ever wanted to see either of her parents again, she would have to travel north, past demons, to the end of the earth. Then came the climb spirits knew how far down the frozen cliff—the cliff which had no bottom, only depths. The cliff which held all the dead to ever die. Some devotees made the pilgrimage, but none returned with tale of success.

With the funeral finished, the crew re-embarked and set about preparing the ship for travel. Luckily, it seemed there was enough wind that they wouldn't have to hitch the dogs. Well, maybe it wasn't lucky. It was a predicament she had heard the captain gripe about multiple times. When the dogs pulled the ship, it went too slow. When the dogs were onboard, they were too much of an obstruction. Orluvoq always preferred onboard doggies, except for the time Ikik had peed on her.

"What was your clan again?" Captain Naalagaa asked as they ascended the ladder.

"Terianniaq." Orluvoq pulled herself over the gunwale and dogs bombarded her.

"Ah, that's right. Haven't been there in a spell." Naalagaa mounted the railing. "Let me see, we should be over that general direction in, say, a week. Week and a half at most. You'll be home with your people before you know it." He turned his attention to the crew, commands barking from his throat.

After the hounds had settled, Orluvoq hung over the side of the ship while the unfurled sails gathered in wind. Her body slid back as the boat kicked to life, sliding along the ice. When she bored of tracking aberrations in the landscape over and over, she headed toward her bunk.

Dead. First Daddy, now Mama. She collapsed on the poorly furnished floor she had called a bed for the last three years and wept. Above her rocked the hammock that her parents had shared. More tears came as she stroked it, remembering the times she had tickled Mama and Daddy through the thin bed.

How am I supposed to live? Where would her food come from? She didn't even know how to take care of her hair, much less herself. Orluvoq got up and crawled into the hammock, images of her parents playing in her mind. *Mama's just in the scullery. She'll be back in a couple hours. Daddy's just on deck, playing dice with Inuunu and Kakajik. He'll come and pick me up when he's done.*

The images faded into visions of her parents sinking into the ice. The cursed ice. Visions of them nuzzling heads as they floated, frozen in the cliff at the end of the world.

All they have to look at anymore is the forever blackness. They can't even turn to see each other.

Orluvoq curled like a rabbit in its hole at the first light of sun, not wanting yet to rise.

Helpless. The mechanism of memory could eke out no other time where she had truly been helpless. There had always been somewhere to turn. Not now. Toothless beneath the bite. Legless beneath the trample. It felt like she'd been rendered into an unquenchable candle and set ablaze, fated for eternal burning without even a hill to scream on. Helpless did not feel good.

Their spirits live on somewhere else. Maybe I can talk to them. Excitement tingled through her, a reprieve from the sobs. *I need to burn a tuuaaq candle and try to talk with them. Or maybe see if I can get a dream or vision.*

Remembrance doused her enthusiasm. The captain himself had said it earlier. Tuuaaq was no common object to be collected from the ice. Hunting narwhals inside the great green aurora in the sky to obtain their unearthly tusks was a difficult pursuit that yielded a limited amount of tuuaaq.

Her parents had let her stay up to watch a hunt had been two years ago as she began her angakkuq training. They figured she should know where the candles she'd be using came from. Watching the hunters fly into Arsarneq, the great aurora, with their kites surpassed anything she had ever done with the tuuaaq. She'd watch them every night if she could.

After a few hours, she wondered if she should eat. Thinking about food set her stomach swirling. No, no food. Maybe if she went long enough without eating the crew would have to lay her on the ice, too.

At least then she wouldn't be a burden. She could join her parents at the end of the earth.

An unexpected nudge rocked her cot. She looked up to see a pocked face and an uncomfortable smile. Ikingut, the ship's other candle worker.

"Heya, Orluvoq. I can't tell you how sorry I am about your parents. I know how you feel."

Hairs crawled down her skin. She couldn't remember the last time Ikingut had truly been friendly to her. He had been nice enough when her training started, but his disposition had soured as her proficiency had passed his own. Maybe the death of her last parent had finally made him feel superior again.

"I don't mean I know exactly how you feel, obviously. Only you can feel that. I mean rather that you're in the middle of a tragedy, and I've had plenty of those." Ikingut's voice rasped against her ears. "Do you need me to get you anything? Meat, maybe? Tubers? An extra blanket?"

Orluvoq shook her head and shut her eyes. Was there no one else in the sleeping quarters?

"I know I haven't been the kindest to you, little one," Ikingut continued. "It's my fault, really. If I were a better angakkuq we wouldn't have a problem. I've just felt so useless on this ship ever since you've taken up the candle." A sigh puffed above. "But I have no clan to return to. Well, none that won't kill me and eat my body. You have made me useless. Sometimes I consider taking a candle and running to Nunapisu and jumping into the blackness. Haven't done it yet though." He chuckled, though Orluvoq couldn't figure why.

"Anyway, do you know what I do sometimes when I can't feel any hope?"

Orluvoq cracked a red eye and shook her head. How could this strange man do anything to help her pain?

He removed a stem of tuuaaq from his pocket.

The milky curve reawakened thoughts of communicating with her parents.

"I just take a little nibble of our friend tuuaaq here. You thought burning it did spectacular things? Just wait until you have a bite of this in your belly. It'll absorb all your doubts and worries. Burning it in tallow can heal the body. Eating it can heal the spirit."

"Daddy told me not to stick it in my mouth." She tried to slink further into the hammock.

Ikingut waved a hand. "Of course you don't stick the whole thing in your mouth. That's how you choke or stab your throat. You really should try some. Your problems are big. That calls for a big solution." He broke off a shard and offered it in her direction.

She shook her head again. "I don't think I want it." *Please just leave.*

A scowl bent his face. "Orluvoq, I didn't realize you were such an ungrateful girl. Do you turn away help from all who offer? As an angakkuq, you yourself know how valuable this gift I'm offering you is. This is from my own private stash. You disgrace the memory of your parents by rejecting the hands that care for you when they cannot."

Anxiety swilled through Orluvoq's chest. It didn't appear Ikingut was leaving anytime soon. And what if she *was* disgracing her parents? Besides, he was an adult, and an angakkuq at that. He knew things. Maybe trying tuuaaq would help her deal with her loss. It certainly couldn't be bad, could it? It did so many good things when in a candle, and it came from creatures that lived in the aurora.

"What exactly does it... do?" she asked.

"Oh, it makes you feel better. So much better," he rasped. "Everything that you thought was a problem, you'll realize that it actually isn't. That life is amazing. I can promise from personal experience."

"So," she took an elastic breath, "when... you feel helpless?"

He nodded. "I always have somewhere to turn if I need it."

Somewhere to turn. No more toothless. No more helpless.

Orluvoq swallowed hard and held out a hand to accept the bit of bone. "Do I just chew it? Or swallow whole?"

"Oh, no. Chew it, please." He clipped out a laugh. "Wouldn't do any good to choke and die."

She furrowed her brow and turned the tuuaaq over, feeling the curves and ridges. The deadness in her stomach curdled. What was she about?

Ikingut nodded with a pressed smile and a gesture of the hand. An uncontrollable tremor ran through her body, then she popped the tuuaaq in her mouth.

Though she was missing a couple teeth, it crumbled

easily enough, turning to a chalky paste on her tongue. She had to swallow several times to get the majority of it down. As she ran her tongue over the last of the grit, she waited.

"When will the good happen?" She shifted to get a better position.

"Give it a minute. Your body has to process it."

Orluvoq waited, listening to her heart in her ears. The pulsing grew more distinct, and her hearing fuzzed. *Is this the good? All the hurt is still here.*

A gust of euphoria blasted through her body. It hummed in her chest for the briefest of seconds, then exploded into her head. It shrieked into the tips of her fingers and toes. It tore through every unexplored nook she possessed. It glided under her skin. She fell to the ceiling. Falling, falling, but never getting closer. She tried to voice something, but it came out a blur of word vomit.

She had no problems.

Nothing in the world could ever go wrong. Whatever she attempted, she would accomplish. Life was hers.

Ikingut smiled and departed with a, "Have fun."

Fun. There was absolutely nothing in existence that had been or could ever be this fun.

I am perfect.

Her eyes rolled back into her head. That would be a good place for them for a while.

THREE DAYS LATER, Orluvoq finally fell asleep. She sunk into the black depths and lingered there for who knew how long. Sometime the next day, she woke up full of evil spirits. Aches wrenched on every corner of her body. The fists of a thousand sailors squeezed her stomach into senseless shapes. Unrefined hatred pulsed behind her eyes and under her scalp.

But worse of all was the thirst.

All the water in the world had been thrown off Nunapisu. Her throat begged for release from its shriveled self. Her tongue hogged too much space in her mouth. Just a drop. If she could feel one tiny drop dribble onto her swollen tongue. One little flake of snow. Or maybe she could cry and drink that?

The rage for water warred with the barrenness of her spirit. Where there had been the impulse to gambol about the ship, confabulate with the sailors, and play with the dogs, there existed now only a listless vacuum she couldn't fill if she tried.

She quivered. The malicious mishmash of maladies ablated any memory of the high ride the tuuaaq had taken her on. Why had she listened to Ikingut? Sticking tuuaaq in your mouth was an awful idea.

The rippling pain from her throat finally overcame her lethargy and other infirmities. She struggled to her feet.

Where am I?

Oh. Dogs.

Her eyes darted past the lazing hounds piled around her. *There.* She ran to the water bowl and plunged her face in, draining gulp after gulp. The water hurt her stomach, but it felt like the aurora itself spilling down her throat. When she pulled her face out, it was attacked by dog tongue.

"Ah, Ikik." She patted the hound's head, then pushed it away.

With the thirst problem addressed, her other issues battled for the forefront of her mind. Seek out food? Fetch a candle and implement some healing? Curl up and disappear?

Last the best.

She laid herself among the pack and passed out again. A fistful of hours later, she roused in the dark of night and realized how good it didn't smell in the den. Sticking her face in the water bowl had proven a horrible idea. Her cheeks, nose, and forehead felt—well, that was the problem: they didn't really feel like anything. The time had helped her lifelessness, and she thought she might finally be able to service her tortured stomach.

The green, waving light of Arsarneq guided Orluvoq's footsteps to the scullery as the ship bumped along the ice. She pilfered some raw meat and filled her mouth. Had she eaten at all the past four days?

"Orluvoq."

She jumped, dropping the caribou meat. In the hustle to reclaim it and some pride, she glanced back to see Kitornak standing behind her.

"You've certainly been bustling about the past few days. I can't tell if you're just taking your parents' deaths exceptionally well or if you've cracked." Kitornak reached out to smooth some of Orluvoq's hair from her face.

Orluvoq flinched at the touch, headache still polluting her skull. "No, haven't cracked. Just trying not to think about life, I guess." She brushed off what dirt she could and took another bite of meat.

"I suppose we can excuse a little girl whose mother just died for climbing up the mast thirteen times in a row."

"Was that me?" The memory jumped into her mind. *Yes. Yes, it was.*

Kitornak nodded. "You could have almost gone to the start of the world and back with all the hurry. I was also worried when you stared at the passing ice for six hours straight."

"I, uh, needed to make sure we were moving. Going to my clan." Orluvoq's head and body aches needed candle ministrations, preferably soon. Couldn't Kitornak quiz her another time?

"I know everyone has their own way of handling grief, but I can't say that I've ever seen anyone run with the dogs while they pull the ship."

Orluvoq's eyes sat wide with innocence. "I, um. I needed to make sure the ship was moving."

"If I didn't know you better, I'd be tempted to think you had eaten some narwhal tusk. What do you think?"

"Uh... Yeah, that would be weird." Orluvoq tried to swallow. She'd have to watch her behavior more sharply the next taste of tuuaaq.

"Mhmmn." Kitornak tapped her chin. "Have you even eaten before just now? I tried to give you some food two days in a row."

Orluvoq shrugged. It just hadn't seemed important. A few non-replies later and she was able to extract herself from the conversation. The demand to banish her pains with a tuuaaq candle bawled up her body, but she didn't think she could sneak through the captain's cabin in her addled state. Instead, she stole to the sleeping quarters and climbed into her painfully empty cot.

DAYS ROLLED on as the ship glided over the ice, stopping to trade with a clan or two. The negative effects of the tuuaaq faded away. The negative effects of life faded back in.

Despite the crash at the end, the tuuaaq had done exactly what Ikingut had promised it would. The initial half day had been the purest bliss ever to embrace her. For five days, every problem she carried had been blown away like dust-snow under a stiff hunting wind. Definitely better than going around crying about her parents being consumed by the ice.

Two days after it was all over, she couldn't help but think how nice it would be to try a little more. Something to push back that creeping helplessness. To scour out the slow rot to toothlessness.

Captain Naalagaa came to her and asked her to divine some directions. After she provided a bearing he said, "Thousand thanks. We spent a fair bit more time with the Ukaliussaq clan than I had planned, but that's alright. Good business was done. I reckon we'll be at your Terianniaq clan in about four days."

With that information, she hatched a plan. She would go to Ikingut and ask if a poor, distressed orphan girl could have another nub of tuuaaq to help with her problems. That way she would crash right when she reunited with her people. They would see her ailments and take special pity on her. Perfection.

After being asked to heal a few cuts and aches while she had the candle out, she set off in search of the angakkuq. A short inquisition found him leaning on the prow, watching the dogs run. She tugged at his sleeve and he turned.

"Ah. Little Orluvoq. How nice to see you." His rasp was almost lost in the grinding of the boat skis against the ice. "I hope you found your tuuaaq experience close to what I promised."

Now that the conversation had started, she wasn't sure she wanted to be a part of it. He was still being too nice. She shrugged off the unease, remembering her goal. "It was incredible. Everything you said." She didn't want to mention the bad part at the end. That might make him think she didn't like it. "But now that it's over…"

He wheezed a laugh. "Now that it's over you can't understand why it ever has to stop. You wish you could capture that feeling for all time."

She nodded. "Exactly."

"Mm. The wonderful thing about tuuaaq is that you can always eat more—if there is more. It's not like friends who turn backs, or some special moment you experience, one that's there for a couple hours then gone forever. No, tuuaaq is always there, ready to help you heal your mind."

Yes.

"You may have noticed a bit of a crash at the end. That's where the true beauty of the tuuaaq comes in. You can just burn a candle and take away all the physical pains—the price you pay for removing the mental pain. Then you'll wonder how anyone ever lives without it. It's truly a magical life. I can't afford it myself, but you're more talented than me. People will throw tuuaaq at you in exchange for menial tasks."

She cleared her throat and squinted as she looked off the boat's head. "Do you think… I mean, I don't want to be a bother, but… That is…"

The older angakkuq clapped her on the shoulder. "You're here looking for another little dose, aren't you?"

She nodded feebly, shrinking at his touch.

"One thing you should remember, little one, is that everything has a price. Like I said, the price you pay for mental healing is taken out on your body. The price you pay for food is work. The price you pay for murder is permanent exile."

Her heart fell. She had nothing of value to trade.

"But me?" he continued. "I'm your friend. I can give you

a little tuuaaq now and then for free, because that's what friends do, right?"

She nearly nodded her head off her neck.

"So. So, so." He reached into his pocket, Orluvoq's eyes tracking every move. A slightly shorter curve of bone than last time appeared. She had to stop herself from reaching for it.

"And yup. This is her. A little bit of the sweet tooth." He broke off a shard. "And this little bit belongs to Orluvoq."

She snatched it from his hand, heart fluttering, and resisted popping it in her mouth right then. "Oh, thank you, thank you." She wrapped halfway around him in a hug.

Ikingut patted her on the head. "Have fun."

She promised she would and ran off to her bunk. The first part was the most intense and would be much better spent somewhere she could lie down. Right before she tossed the white magic to her teeth, she reminded herself of one thing: water.

Having briefed herself on all the necessities, she ground the gritty nub into pulp and washed it down with a drink. After a minute of her heartbeat growing more distinct in her ears, it happened. The wave of ecstasy.

Orluvoq drowned.

A PALL of clouds swirled overhead as they pulled up to the Terianniaq clan. Deep winter had yet to set in, so ample sunlight still filtered through to light their arrival.

Orluvoq wished it were deep winter. The wicked sun, filtered as it was, spun calamity into her head. At least she had followed her own advice and hadn't woken up drier than old bones. Hadn't Ikingut said he just burned a candle to get rid of the aftereffects? She hadn't considered how suspicious it would look for her to just grab a candle without telling the captain why. It appeared she would have to pay the price for her mental healing.

Clan archons—matriarch and patriarch both—greeted the captain and his mates, engaging in the traditional series of salutations. With the way her legs shook on the ladder, Orluvoq feared her face might soon be engaging in some less than traditional salutations with the ground.

Once fastly on the ice, she steadied herself against the boat and overlooked the settlement. Bulges of snow lead to the interconnected caves that housed her kith. Children played some game she didn't know. Men and women gutted and dressed a narwhal fresh from last night's hunt. Something other than tuuaaq warmed Orluvoq's heart. Somewhere to turn.

All thoughts of how strange it was to think she wouldn't be reboarding the ship, how strange it would be to live under-snow, and how she wished her parents were with her vanished when she saw it. The glorious twirl of tuuaaq. An ensign stabbed into the ice that took all her effort to not sprint toward.

The young angakkuq had forgotten just how big the tusks were. Including the part lodged in the ground, it must have been at least twice as tall as her—taller than even the tallest man! The potential mental healing the one bony lance contained crammed her body full of giddiness. *If I can become the clan's angakkuq...* A spontaneous shudder shook her.

And why wouldn't she? She was more gifted than the ship's angakkuq, and he had been working the candles for at least fifteen years. Doubtless she could match whatever shaman this clan had to offer. They would be dumb to prevent her from using her gifts.

She licked her lips. Were they really chapped again? Her mother would have never let that happen. Breaking from her tuuaaq reverie, Orluvoq strolled over to the people carving, lugging, and cursing. Might as well give some sort of homage to Mama's memory.

"Hey," she said to a lady with blue diamonds embroidered down her parka front. "Do you have anything for my lips?" She stuck them out to display their chappedness.

The whale dresser pulled off a work glove, knife still in the other hand, and rubbed her eyes. "Are all ship's children as cute as you?" She opened her eyes and looked at Orluvoq. "Here, take some of my wax."

Orluvoq smiled at the compliment. She accepted a swipe from a pouch the woman pulled out of a pocket and smeared it on her lips.

"Sorry, but I'll have to ask you to run along." The woman gloved her hand. "We need to prep this narwhal before you all sail off again. GET OFF THAT!"

Orluvoq startled at the outburst before realizing the worker was shouting at some of the ship's dogs. "Ikik! Tala! Malit! Come here."

The brutes turned away with only a strip or two each of fat in their jaws. "I won't be sailing off again." Orluvoq petted the dogs, just now realizing how short her time would be with them.

"Oh?" The butcher raised an eyebrow but not an eyeball, as both of those were fixed on the carcass. "You're planning on building your own igloo and settling right down?"

"You think they would let me have my own igloo?" Living in a dwelling of her own edged out the dogs, pains, and tuuaaq.

The blue diamond woman huffed, the breathy laugh pillowing into a thick cloud in the moist air above the narwhal. "Sure, sure. And the king at the start of the world will come help you build it."

"Orluvoq!" a voice called.

She turned to see the captain ushering her over. With a yip, she packed her way across the snow, careful to not jar her head. Too far away from that bone beauty transpierced in the ice, she reigned in her tender trot. A dizzy spell of fatigue made her plant her butt on the ground.

"Ah, here she is." Captain Naalagaa motioned to the panting girl. "You of course remember Orluvoq, daughter of Nataaq and Anaava, two of our finest workers. Or, that they were, right up until recently. Nataaq went to Nunapisu some five months ago and his wife joined him just a couple weeks back. A terrible loss for all of us. Though we have many orphans on the ship, they usually don't come as young as poor little Orluvoq here. As much as we love the girl, her life will improve much by waxing among her own, among Terianniaq."

The archons turned their wizened faces, gauging her with dark, deep-set eyes. Something about them simultaneously inspired comfort and trepidation, not unlike death itself. Times of judgment. Times of death. Of steamy nights in a dark lodge. Memories forked across her mind then faded to lambent afterimages, like lightning in a sunless heaven.

"The Terianniaq are ancient and venerable, roots reaching deeper than the frosts themselves. We will be happy to receive one of our own, Naalagaa," the crone said. "We only require to first see her token of kinship."

The captain froze. "But you're the archons. You were

there at her birth, as she cut teeth, at her *parents'* birth. She is Terianniaq and belongs with her kind."

"Her token, Captain," the patriarch said, unmoved.

"What's wrong?" Orluvoq asked. What was so important about this token thing? They knew her.

As usual, the adults paid her no heed. "She is one of the most skilled angakkuit I've ever seen. Any clan would be delighted to have her work among them."

"Then produce her token, Captain, or find another clan who doesn't care so much about blood." The wrinkles framing the matriarch's mouth cut deeper as she pursed her lips. "But if your grand claim is true, one wonders why you're so eager to rid yourselves of the girl."

Naalagaa's wispy beard quivered. "Look, we forgot to salvage a token from either parent. You know how us clan-less can be when it comes to those matters, and you know her fate should she become clanless."

There was no way they could reject her over such a small oversight, right?

"It is not you who are at fault, Captain," said the patriarch. "Orluvoq's parents failed to provide her with a token of kinship. This is either because they didn't think she was yet worthy of the title of Terianniaq, or because they no longer considered themselves part of this noble breed. Either way, we cannot accept the girl into our lodge."

"Or because she's eight!" The captain waved his arms in the air. "Don't tell me the Terianniaq undertake the Rites of Waxing when you're still wet from your mothers' bellies."

"What sorts of herbs do you haul from the sea, Captain?" asked the crone.

The sudden change in conversation confused Orluvoq.

"The girl rejoins your lodge."

"We will discuss no more of this." The patriarch's words

bit through the air. "You will respect our decision, clanless one. Now, what do you haul from the sea? We have fresh narwhal to trade."

Captain Naalagaa worked his jaw muscles over. "Orluvoq," he said at last, "go tend the dogs."

"Wait." The archons' words began to sink in. Orluvoq looked the matriarch in the eyes. "You're rejecting me?"

The crone refrained from blinking for a prolonged moment. "We do not expect a child to understand the gravity of blood."

"Yet you expect her to bear it," Naalagaa responded.

"There may be some wisdom in you yet, Captain," said the old man. "For who among us understands life? And who among us isn't called to bear it?"

The captain cast a scowl to the horizon. "Run along, Orluvoq. We will speak later."

Her own igloo, playing with her cousins, and becoming the clan angakkuq—all stained foul by those fold-faced ancient ones. Head still pounding, she hobbled off to find some water and the wombic embrace of her cot. First her parents, now the rest of her family. The ship didn't want her either. No one did. She choked on sobs, each heave inflating the pressure behind her eyes.

3

PAARSISOQ

26 Years Prior

Paarsisoq would normally have cursed the wind, but tonight he needed it. His hands balled around his kite grip and spear haft as his nerves balled around his stomach. Arsarneq, the great aurora, pulsed preternaturally in the sky, its emerald waves raining light onto the ice.

The clan's sky watchers had spent almost a week scanning the heavens for the shimmery inklings of the aurora. The summer was almost dead, and their stores of meat and tuuaaq were all but gone. Blessedly, the long day of desolate skies ended with the dark of tonight. The hunt had arrived.

"I hope I'm not too frosty," Arpap remarked, hood down low to shield from the elements.

Several of the men grunted their agreement.

"I hope that each of us fells a narwhal," Sinik said, rolling his spear in one hand.

"I hope the wind spirits see fit to bear us all the way to Arsarneq and back," said Aallaaniar.

"Never fear that," said Arpap, "they always..." He trailed off, casting a wary eye toward Paarsisoq.

Yes, thought Paarsisoq, *always. They always bear the hunters, except for when it's my father.*

"Don't worry." Arpap tried to reassert some peace. "Your father was the greatest of us. He could fell a narwhal with one spear. He rode the winds as if his mother were the sky and his father the air. You'll do just fine. He would be proud to see you behind a kite."

Paarsisoq said nothing. What could he say? Nothing the older clansmen wanted to hear. Instead, he ran his tongue over chapped lips; their stock of lard had depleted a few weeks prior. The last hunt of winter had been his father's last, the great hunter's body dashed against the ice along with Paarsisoq's vigor.

"Look," said Sinik to the dozen gathered men, gesturing to the ribbon of light overhead. They tilted their heads in unison to scry the sky. A pod of dark dashes cut through the green.

"Heya!" shouted Arpap. "To Arsarneq we ride." He cinched his mouth flap against the coming blasts, held his kite skyward, wind ruffling the edges, then let it loose.

Paarsisoq watched the other men follow suit, sliding across the ground on their skis, until he alone remained. The kite reins shook in his hand, and not for the cold nor the wind. His hands slid around too easily inside his gloves. There was too much moisture on his mouth flap, turning it to ice against his lips. He was sure his feet weren't strapped well enough into the skis.

He crouched down and buried his face into his knees. *Why did you have to go? Why wasn't it me instead? I needed you... Still need you. I know I can never be you, but I'll try. Just please, please don't let me fall.*

He waited a moment after sending out his prayer before extracting his face. In the distance, the first hunter departed from the ground and began the ascent to their prey.

Alright. The boy stood and rose his kite above his head with a tremble in his hand. The wind gripped and tugged at the sail. Once his fingers slipped off the line, his chances at remaining ground-bound vanished. *Just like the training runs.* With a shaky breath, he unraveled his fingers, and the reins ran wild.

The line snapped taut and nearly pulled Paarsisoq onto his face. Heart thumping, he kept afoot as the elements drug him across the ground. The ponderous pace didn't last as long as he would have liked. Before he even had enough presence of mind to grapple with it, he was clipping along faster than a bear at full trot, wind screaming in his ears. He might have preferred facing the bear.

The rest of the party were aloft and well on their way to Arsarneq. Already his skis took little skips away from the ice, his stomach ricocheting with each jounce. He knew what that meant. It was time to fly.

But his skis didn't venture more than a foot from the ground. No matter how many times he played the motion of him yanking the kite in his mind, he couldn't bring his arm to do it.

"Father!" he shouted into the wind, breaking his lips from the freezing mouth flap. "I cannot do it alone. Help me rise."

With that, something switched inside him and he jerked his kite arm heavenward. The sail wrenched him from the earth.

Panic flashed as his fingers struggled to remain fast. Paarsisoq reached up with his spear arm and wrapped his last three digits around the kite grip. Only after a frantic minute in the air did he finally look to see where he was headed. He had stopped ascending and was shooting off parallel to the ground. A tug of the kite remedied the trajectory, and he turned to find his comrades.

The agile pack of hunters plowed through the aurora above, already swirling in battle with the whales. A narwhal corpse pluming with spears plummeted past him on his final ascent. He readjusted so he could once again grip with only one hand, the other fast around his spear.

Breaching the aurora cut mischief into his mind. The howling of the wind snapped off into a burbling approximation of silence, haunted by the indistinct moans of the narwhals. All that reached his eye was drowned in the ghostly green. Beastly bulks barreled past him, threatening to spear him or his kite. Their maws gaped, pocketing as much of the aurora as they could before being forced to swallow.

Where were his clansmen? Paarsisoq had been warned of the odd way that air acted inside Arsarneq, but firsthand navigation spun his head dizzy. Questing this way and that, tugging on the kite to get it to do *something*, he pitched into the consuming green.

"Heya," he called. "Arpap? Allaniar?" The words seemed to jump a few feet from him, then fall out of the sky. His gut descended to a new level of unease. A narwhal brushed his skis, throwing him into a twirl.

In his precarious pirouette, a scuttle of humanoid motion caught his eye. He jerked on his kite until it tugged him in that direction.

At last, he did something right. The hunters had almost felled another narwhal, several spears sprouting from its hide.

Okay, grip it like so. Not too far forward, and... Oh, no.

Too fast. The freakish light sucked him along far faster than he had anticipated. He was going to skewer himself on the horn of the beast.

His kite hand twitched and his body jerked to the side as he cast his spear. He sped past his clansmen, desperately trying to tame his kite with both hands. He swung it around and shaved off speed.

The shot had gone wide. A lot of help he had been this hunt. *I'll never be you*, he lamented. As he approached, he could see the other's mouths moving but couldn't hear their words. There was no need.

Dangling between the free arms of two hunters was Sinik, spear lodged perfectly between his ribs.

No.

Paarsisoq stared in raw horror at the dark liquid gushing down the man's coat. The spell broke and he jerked the kite in any direction. Away. He *must* away.

He burst from the eerie calm into the wind that screamed as it tore. Assailed from outside and in, he swerved for the ground, trying to implement what little landing training his bereft mind could muster.

It's not possible, he panicked. *I couldn't have killed him.* But there was no other way that spear could have made its way into Sinik's heart. *I set out to become a hunter of narwhals and instead became a hunter of men.*

A minute later, he landed heavily on his side, face ramming into the snow. Wild flashes of color lanced through bitter stings of cold as he rolled to a stop atop the ice. Pathetic tears froze to his cheeks along with streaks of blood. Killed a man. He had *killed* a man. Slayer of kin. Darkest memory of ice and sky. Good for nothing, save to be devoured by a tribunal of his kin.

I'll never be you. He sobbed into the snow, wishing for the world to leave him. *I have killed and too must die. But I could never face you in the hereafter. But neither can I face the clan again.*

In the midst of his wallowing, he opened his eyes and saw tiny kite shapes angling for the ground.

"Tiaavuluk," he swore and spat out blood. The horror of confronting his kinsmen beguiled his spirit into abyssal inaction. To face the men of the hunt was but one tribulation. The greater trial lay in confessing to Sinik's wife and children. No matter how deep he looked inside, he could not find the words, "I killed your father." His fingers only closed on bile and blooded shadow. And after his vain struggles to testify of his sins, the clan would open his throat and eat his flesh.

So Paarsisoq would flee. Had to flee. But where in all the ice could he find haven? A merchant ship? A bear's cave? He traced the far above river of green to the horizon. Somewhere long past where any sane man set foot, past demons aplenty, was a cliff where it all ended. Where he could end it all. A place that could eat his body and his spirit, to become what the ice forgot.

That is where I must go, he thought, gaining no relief from his resolution, stomach still flush with bloodborne sick. *To the end of the earth.*

He stood shaky legs upon his unbroken ski and took one last look toward the igloos of his youth. Nothing. Darkness all, save the sky flecks of downward tacking hunters. He turned to face a deeper darkness, pitted kite against wind, and let himself be dragged toward high north.

Orluvoq spent the entire trade in her sorrows. Nothing seemed less interesting than the barter banter, the playing children, or skimming for moss on the ice. There would be no mother calling her back from her strayings. No father poking her and asking whether she had found a new boyfriend. As unbearable as that was, it was unavoidable and therefore almost understandable. Daddy and Mama never wanted to leave. "I'll watch you until you join us," Mama had uttered in one of her last fevered, wet breaths.

Until not so many minutes ago, Orluvoq had imagined she'd been hit with the worst. She'd vested her hopes in one final refuge—more than hopes, her kin were her reality. They would assimilate her back into the life of igloos, feed and clothe her, teach her how to dress caribou and narwhals. They would assume the role her parents could not.

It was a lie. They hated her. Whatever she was, she wasn't one of them. Her very existence abraded against theirs. Yes, her parents were gone, but they were taken. The rest of her kin had *chosen* to leave her. Chosen to leave her clutching helplessly at snipped strings. No, not entirely helpless. She had *something* she could turn to. If only she could get her mitts on a little...

The jerk of wind catching the sails startled her out of her woeful abstractions. Were they not going to spend the night moored up here? She uncurled from her cot and pattered to the deck to assay affairs.

"Tiaavuluk!" the captain swore, shattering a chunk of ice against the deck. "That Terianniaq whore and her wrinkled scab of a husband better never see the end of the world. I'll eat them myself, piece by nasty piece. Then I'll puke them back up and let the dogs devour the vomit."

The gathered crew watched him rage in front of darkening clouds.

"To do that you'd have to sail back there and stick 'em yourself." Siulleq, the first mate, grinned. "Shall I schedule a return trip?"

"Return?" Naalagaa spat. "Terianniaq will never see our sails again. I hope they starve and have to resort to eating each other. Hope none of them ever see Nunapisu. Their spirits can die along with their bodies."

He caught sight of Orluvoq's wide, red eyes. "Ah, buck up, lass. If they've rejected you so swiftly, you never wanted kin like that anyway. We'll find you better company, sure enough."

"But not the ship?" Orluvoq asked, eyes no less wide and no more white.

The captain scowled and glanced to the sky. "Wish we could keep you, but circumstances and whatnot. Don't worry though, we'll find you a good home soon enough."

A voice barked from the women gathered sternward. "You're not—you can't possibly be thinking of taking her to Atortittartut or another one of those filth dens." Orluvoq perked up at Kitornak's objection. That sounded like the name of a clan her mother had once condemned.

Naalagaa waved a dismissal. "Her angakkuq skills will serve her wherever she goes. But you know the options for a clanless girl, and few they are. What else could she do? Give herself to the ice? Go north and play with demons?"

It must have been a trick of the light, but Orluvoq saw darkness draw around the woman. "Yes, we're perfectly familiar with the options accessible to a clanless girl, Captain." Kitornak spat the last word. "More so than you. I often wish I had just been given to the ice rather than turned over to Atortittartut. Can you look at this ruin of a girl," she flung her hand at Orluvoq, "say that we have no room for her when the only other option will destroy her last shreds of life, and call yourself an honest man?"

"Enough with the histrionics, Kitornak. I don't keep you on my ship to make me headaches, but food. You think I'm any happier about it than you are? If I ran a charity among all the Nuktipik peoples, we would trade for smiles and handshakes alone. The world is crueler than the ice that covers it. I'm just a man who's trying to avoid seeing Nunapisu as long as possible. If you can't handle the truths that flow through the aurora, that fly through the air, that fall in the snow, that die in a rancid puddle of their own vomited blood, then the ice awaits. The ice is always hungry."

"You miss the storm for the snowflakes, Naalagaa." She pushed black hairs mingled with a silver or two beneath her hood. "This is much bigger than—"

"Tiaavuluk, woman!" Fists clenched to match his jaw. "If you really wanted a child so much, then why didn't you keep one of the bastards you whelped?"

Kitornak's jaw clicked shut. Orluvoq recognized the

deep, melancholic longing mingling with the rage in the woman's eyes—recognized it like she would her own mother. After all, it was all she had since the one had replaced the other.

"Where's Ikingut with that forecast?" Captain Naalagaa turned from the stern and squinted against the wind at the gathering storm. "Not that we much need it."

"Oi," called the angakkuq, climbing out from belowdecks, candle in hand. "It ain't so hard to notice, but there's a regular squall ramping up. Sailing in it would be a mighty unfine idea. Probably lose a couple dogs to the drafts if we threw them out front. I'd say batten down. Spirits whisper it'll be a few days at the least."

Naalagaa scowled, wind rustling the ice in his mustache. "Tiaavuluk. Well, men. Let's get those sails furling and those anchors planting. I don't want her to tip over while we're all entranced."

The crew piqued at the mention of entrancing. "Cap," said Siulleq, "you sayin' we're gonna batten down then all get tranced up?"

"Aye, mate. I'd say we're about due for a vacation."

Excitement buzzed into a cheer. "I reckon it'd be a much better vacation if we were up by Atortittartut," shouted one of the men. His suggestion was seconded, and thirded, and twelfthed.

Captain Naalagaa fixed his gaze on what must have been Orluvoq's spirit. "Don't worry too hard, lads. We'll be there before you know it."

A dusty shiver ran the length of her back and she turned to run to her cot.

"Orluvoq," called the captain, "be so kind as to entrance us, would you? You and Ikingut can argue over who gets to stay awake."

She wavered. On the one hand, the putrid dialogue that slipped just above her comprehension made her want to run and bury herself under the dogs. On the other hand, if she put all the sailors under trances, she alone would have access to all the candles she desired, and that meant...

An opportunity to fight the helplessness. A *new* opportunity.

"Yes," she said. "Get some tuuaaq and tell the men to go meditate in their cots. Ikingut, too. I don't really want a trance right now, anyway."

TWO CANDLES BURNED in the ship's hold, one of tuuaaq and one of a mundane wick. Orluvoq sent the sailors into trances one by one as the weather gripped and ripped at the bones and the hide enclosing them. Once entranced, they would caper through limitless waking dreams for at least a day before waking.

She wondered if Kitornak and some of the other offended women would spurn the trance, but they were just as eager to be rid of the chores, pains, and worries of life as the men were.

"Orluvoq," Kitornak whispered as her cot gently rocked in the shadowed light. "The Captain is a hard man. Don't worry, I'll bring him around. I wouldn't want anyone to suffer the same life I had, and you're much younger than I was."

The young angakkuq frowned, not wholly clear on what the older woman meant. "Don't worry. I'll be fine." She glanced at her candle. "I have a plan."

"Oh, and what is your plan, my dear?"

"Can't tell you, it's a secret," Orluvoq whispered back.

"Every plan needs helpers. Let me be yours."

The girl shook her head. "No, this plan can only have angakkuq helpers. And I don't think I want to tell Ikingut about it." Her thoughts fled to the angakkuq's strip of tuuaaq and pilfering it from his entranced body. But no, he would know who did it. Better stick to the plan.

Kitornak eyed her then the candle, the dance of the flame almost entrancing enough without the help of the spirits. "Well, let me know when you need help. And don't do anything dumb while we're all entranced."

"Okay, I have to get the other people, too, so you have to start meditating."

The woman, who'd apparently led a more interesting life than Orluvoq had assumed, nodded and let her eyes close. Orluvoq tapped into the flame and mumbled a mantra about dreams and trances and spirit dances. A minute later, Kitornak's breathing metered out and she awoke inside a dream.

After eight more sailors were nestled snug in their berths, sporting through visions of fancy, the young angakkuq paused by her own hammock. The cot pulled on her harder than gravity. The need to succumb to its embrace suppurated from the lesions of her dismembered spirit.

No. She drew in a measure of heat from her candle. No, if she laid herself to sleep now, that might be the end of hope. This was her only chance to escape from whatever fate the captain had planned for her, and her only chance of overturning her clanless state. If she didn't push against desolation now, how many years would her sojourn in it be?

She nodded to herself and turned from the bed. Checking to make sure that she still carried the extra candle in her pocket, she slipped out the door, latching it as quickly as possible again.

Had summer still reigned, night would be yet a far dream. But with the shortening of the days in winter's inexorable approach, darkness lay over the ice already, aided by the angry sky above. Orluvoq trickled heat from the tuuaaq, careful not to draw too much. She smiled as she watched the snows and winds assail the flame in ceaseless assaults, yet the bucking light held, never dimming.

A needle of panic lanced her through when she realized she had been belowdecks as the ship took its bearings away from the clan. The mounting slurries threw an impenetrable curtain all around the boat, robbing her of sight.

No, where is it? She ran to the gunwale and tried to penetrate the storm. The faintest of green glows touched the clouds above, but the aurora's light didn't make it to the ice. She drew on the tuuaaq, forming a stormless dome around her, then expanding it as far as she could. Even if her talents exceeded average, she couldn't push the umbrella very far beyond the confines of the ship.

Well, no angakkuq can control the entire weather. She huffed and let go of the storm shield. *Oh. I'm stupid. I can just ask the candle.*

Orluvoq refocused on the tuuaaq and muttered a string of words about seeking the Terianniaq. A second later, she felt a tug from the starboard side of the stern.

Disembarking, she looked through the stormy pall between her and her rightful clan, rubbing the vestiges of headache still plaguing her.

Wait a second, I have a candle in hand now.

She tapped into the flame, and healing washed over her. The power of the burning tusk extinguished the debris of the eaten tusk still afflicting her. *Wow.* The whipping winds faded to the tune of vanishing maladies. She snapped back to reality upon seeing how much tuuaaq the healing had chewed through. Not even a finger joint, but far more than she hoped to use in one stunt.

Alright, now to run. Windwalking angakkuit stirred up trails of tales wherever they ran. In dire times, clan archons would instruct the angakkuq to windwalk between clans, carrying messages or healing. Outside of that, windwalking had no allowance, as it burned through too much tuuaaq. Orluvoq herself had never seen or tried it, but how hard could it be?

She breathed to center herself, dropped into a light level of meditation, and emanated words that could only be heard by that with no ears. Words that spelled out the way she was to walk with the winds; the way she was to slip through all obstacles unscathed; that she was to be a breath from the heavens above, streaking across the realms.

Motion. Her feet flurried forth, pitching her into a mad career across the ice.

"Whoa." She struggled to maintain concentration, the world a maniacal muddle clawing for her attention.

"Gah!"

Her feet flew not like wind but like narwhals hunted out of the sky. She tripped and tumbled across the ground, frost infesting her face, ramming down her throat, robbing her of breath. Skidding to a stop, sobs racked her body. She may have dwelt in the cold all her life, but she couldn't restrain the weeping in the face of a face forced with frost.

A minute later, emotional stability regained, she stood and cast about for the candle. Through the snowy press, a good span off, she spied it. Tears came again as she ran to it, overcome with joy that the wick had stayed lit. If it had snuffed out it would be like, well, finding a lump of off-white wax in a nocturnal snowstorm.

The young angakkuq centered herself, then lowered

herself into a shallow meditation. This time she spun words into her mantra about how she was to never slip, though slippery the ice may be.

Her feet took to motion, and the world once again became a neurotic splodge. The slipping clause seemed to do the trick, though the pandemonium rushing by threatened constantly to wrest concentration from her and send her crashing across the cruel cold again. Windwalking simultaneously vivified and terrified. She imagined herself hunting narwhals in Arsarneq as she ran.

From the midst of chaos came a point of clarity: igloos thrusting out of the snow, weakly illumined by an oil lamp. She reined in her gait a small way off and hid the candle behind her back. Two men were outside doing something— maybe with the narwhal meat? But it seemed the rest of the people had taken refuge below.

My people. They will be my people. They are my people. I am Terianniaq. I am their angakkuq.

She looked around in the meager light for the beautiful lance of narwhal tusk from earlier, but couldn't see it anywhere. *That will change soon enough.* Shadowwalking angakkuit left rashes of rumors wherever they slunk. In times of perfidy, they would take up the tuuaaq and skulk, leaving corpses, taking possessions, discovering gossip, covering scandals. If the archons could substantiate claims of shadowwalking, severe punishments ensued for the angakkuq. Orluvoq herself had never seen or tried it, but how hard could it be?

Maybe someday she could achieve such feats with barely a thought, but tonight the young angakkuq took a deep breath and meditated. Words poured forth, speaking to the ever listening tuuaaq. Words that clarified the way she was to twist and vanish with the darkness; how the shadow was to eat any sound she made; that she was to be one with the shade, and all things cloaked made clear for her eyes.

She cracked her eyes open, and the shock of a suddenly bright world rattled her from concentration. All fell dark save the twin flames of the oil lamp and the glim in her hand. *That was dumb. Of course it was going to be brighter.* She regained the shadowwalking state, now unphased by the rush of lucidity, and crept toward the clutch of igloos.

"Meat's half frozen already."

She perked. The wind battered the man's voice, but enough of it reached Orluvoq's ears. Shadowwalking in the dark of the night storm, she could have stood anywhere, but her sneaking instincts told her to huddle around the corner of an igloo.

"Don't know why we're the only ones out in this storm."

"Oh, what are you so worried about, Upippoq? That your wife will already be asleep, and you'll suffer from having one less shag in your life?"

She watched as they sectioned off meat and blubber, then wrapped the cuts in skin. The spike of tuuaaq was nowhere visible.

"Look, Oqarusiut, I fully recognize that everyone has to take their turn doing hungry ice work, but it seems like the archons are constantly giving me a face full of frost. Guess who had surface duty last storm? And what about the one before that?"

Orluvoq couldn't remember a plethora of names from when she lived in Terianniaq, but the faces usually weren't so distant. She sidled around to an angle where their faces came into view, risking herself in the light of their lamp. Realization struck her. That was Oqarusiut. He had always talked with her mother.

"Alright, alright." Oqarusiut waved him off. "But you

know who really got a face full of frost today? That ship girl, Nataaq's daughter." He got quieter. "Anaava's daughter." He cleared his throat and set back to his work. "By rights, she should live among us. But by the saggy archons' decree she ain't got no place here."

"Yeah, well, you and I both know that. Nearly everyone living under this patch of ice knows that." Upippoq sniffed. "It's a joke saying that just because she doesn't have a token, she doesn't have a place. Spirits know she has the blood, and isn't that what's truly important?"

A yearning burned inside her. They wanted her. If the token was really so important, she would get a token. She would travel to the end of the earth to get a token. They *wanted* her. Somewhere to turn.

"You ever think of doing like they did?" Oqarusiut asked. "Getting away from this patch of ice, seeing the world?"

"Forsaking the clan? Never."

"Come now, you know there was no forsaking that happened. They always planned on coming back. Anaava said it would only be for a clutch of years. But with our matriarch and patriarch, can you really condemn their departure?"

Upippoq wrapped the last of the fat, slamming it on the sled, then stared his coworker in the eye. "Let's just get inside. I have too few toes for this type of weather."

Orluvoq followed the bob of their lamp toward freedom from the biting cold, careful to stay far enough from its watchful eye. Anticipation tickled her insides as the sled reached the larder. Tuuaaq awaited.

She danced back and forth on her feet, waiting for the light within to fade. When it finally did, she rushed the hold, nearly crying to be out of the wind. Not that she needed to—the gelid gusts had whipped tears out from her eyes constantly the past quarter hour. She almost regretted the choice to not make a windbreak or to sap heat from the candle, but a glance down at how much her wind and shadowwalking had burned through sobered her up.

Suppressing a giggle at how clear everything was to her in a room with no light, she set to searching the store. Skins, fat, meat, moss, trinkets, antlers, clothes, knives, a body—where was that stupid tusk? She scanned again, but her superior eyesight revealed noth—

Wait.

A body?

"Tiaavuluk!" she uttered in her best impression of the captain. Behind a pile of skins lay the woman she had talked to earlier that day, the one dressing the narwhal. Her coat with the sewed-in blue diamonds was brittle with blood.

The sight rattled Orluvoq from her meditative state and pitched the world into darkness. The feeble light of the candle hardly filled the room at all, the corpse now an indiscernible bundle of shadows.

She tried breathing deep but couldn't get centered. *Someone's going to notice me.* The thought only amped her anxiety, dragging her further from the calm the tuuaaq required. She wanted to drag a cluster of skins over her and cry in a bundle until sleep took her. But she also wanted to be in a room that didn't house a dead person.

No. I can bear this. Then once I have the tuuaaq, I can get all the mental healing I need there. A lot of mental healing. And after that... She brushed aside worries about part two of her plan. Her fingers quivered at the thought of swallowing the chalky substance, and suddenly the thought of rooming with a corpse wasn't so important. Or present whatsoever.

The thought—no, the need for a nibble of tuuaaq provided her with an amazing level of concentration, and before long, the world was thrown again into light. She stole out of the larder and began her raid through the complex of igloos. She marveled at how she could walk right by people and they wouldn't even spare a look in her direction. *I should do this more often.* Frustration pricked through her otherwise calm state as she unsuccessfully searched her fifth room.

Wait a minute, I know where it'll be. She racked her memories of the igloo catacombs, seeking to pinpoint the chandler's room. A bearing in mind, she trod through shadows until she stood outside the light flickering out from his quarters. She gulped, peeking under the flap of skin that covered the doorway. *It'll have to be quick, this candle's almost dead.*

The old man sat facing the door, setting strips of tuuaaq into melted tallow. About half of the tusk remained, the rest already sitting in candles. The desire to ingest some mental healing almost pushed her over the threshold right then. Reminding herself twice that she couldn't shadowwalk through the fire's light, she tried reversing the heat flow trick she usually did, leeching heat from the man. The chandler frowned, rubbing his arms. As he stood to retrieve his parka, Orluvoq ghosted into the room.

She stayed behind him, turning as he turned, muttering words, words he couldn't hear. They weren't meant for him. The tuuaaq heard every word.

The chandler's eyes fluttered, and he fell onto his bed. Orluvoq grinned, then the room dropped into darkness. Panic followed suit.

Wait. She angled her hand to better see in the weak light. All that remained of her tuuaaq candle was a mess of wax down her glove. She cursed herself for letting it go out without first lighting the other one and fumbled to bring out the spare. Worry snowed down upon her that someone would walk in inquiring after the chandler. The sight of all the unguarded tuuaaq on the floor blew the worry away.

She shook off a glove, snatched some heatmoss from the chandler's supplies, and rubbed it onto the tuuaaq between her fingers until it sparked. The world illuminated again as she regained her shadowwalking state.

Orluvoq gathered up what candles she could fit into her pockets, along with a few strips of raw tusk and heatmoss, then skulked her way back to the surface and windwalked into the storm.

WIND and furious snow molested the boat unceasingly, testing the anchor pikes' stabbing prowess. Orluvoq lay clutched in the hide hammock that held all her spilled memories and tears, the vesicle of her crucible. The windwalking, the shadowwalking, the dead woman, the sleeping chandler—already the thrill deliquesced in the burdens which ratcheted her spirit.

She could do it. She could just lie there forever, taking bite after bite of tuuaaq until she could bite no more. They'd eventually figure out she hadn't moved in too long and feed her to the ice. Then she'd be with Mama and Daddy at Nunapisu.

Or she could take one last big bite of tuuaaq and jump off ship, off into the storm, and feed herself to the ice. The sting of the frost would be hardly noticeable with all the mental healing the beautiful little tusk would pour out upon her. Maybe in her elevated state she could even make it back to Terianniaq and die there. Then they'd really feel bad they rejected her.

She worried away at the end of a strip of tuuaaq with her

teeth, grinding a delicate patina of powder into her mouth. The dryness hit the back of her throat, making her gulp by reflex, and the dusty delight slid bellyward.

Half a minute later, rhapsody bubbled into her little frame. It was nothing like the full euphoric flood an entire bite offered, but her concerns seemed terribly unremarkable.

Enough sulking about, she quoted Mama, then dropped out of her berth. It was time for part two of the plan.

It took little time to gather her few possessions. She gave the dogs a brief goodbye, wishing she could take them all but knowing she could care for none, then scurried to the scullery. Between bulging candles and twigs of tuuaaq, she tried to fit as much meat and fat as she could. If only she were older, then she would have bigger pockets for more food.

"A late-night snack, is it?"

Orluvoq jumped at the voice and whipped about to see Kitornak. The sounds of the storm had masked her coming. "Angakkuit get hungry now and then," said Orluvoq, "even us little ones. Why aren't you in your trance?"

The older woman sighed. "Even in my waking dreams, I couldn't help but think of you. I found no rest in the trance. I thought I might talk to you, and your empty cot told me that would be an option."

"That's very nice, but I can't talk right now. Busy."

"Busy? Dear, we live on a merchant ship in the middle of a storm-blown ice waste, and you're an eight-year-old girl with no chores now that everyone's asleep. I promise you're not busy."

"I won't live here for long," Orluvoq asserted, "and you can't come with." Hm. Why had she said that?

Kitornak's eyebrows jumped to all kinds of heights. "And where might you be going, child?"

"To get a token." She said it like the winds had been howling the same fact all night.

"A token... Orluvoq, I don't think that clan Terianniaq will be very excited to see you again." The maid planted her gloved hands on her hips.

"Not without a token they won't." The girl smiled.

"Which you don't have." The woman frowned.

"Right, but I will."

Kitornak studied her the way a caribou might study a slippery patch of ice. "But where will you get a token of kinship if not from the clan itself?"

"Mama or Daddy, where else?" She shrugged, colored carefree by the tuuaaq.

The woman stared for a long time.

"Daddy said if you didn't blink enough your eyes would freeze out of your head."

Kitornak blinked. "You're going to climb down the ice cliff at the end of the earth to find your dead parents?"

Orluvoq giggled. "Yep. And you can't come."

"Now listen here, you little—" She cut herself off. "You can't leave. The ice will consume you and you'll be at Nunapisu a lot quicker than you planned. Unless some demon gets you first. You know they say the north is demon country."

The young angakkuq nodded. "Either I get the token and my clan takes me back, or I rejoin Mama and Daddy. In the end, I'll be with my family."

"I'll be your—" Kitornak cut herself off again. "Look, I understand the desire to reunite with family, I really do." Her eyes glistened in the nearly nonexistent light. "But eventually you realize they can't always give you everything you need. Stay here. I'll look after you."

Somewhere to turn. Orluvoq burned to believe her, and the mental healing the tuuaaq provided almost allowed for it. But, like the captain said earlier, she was learning the only thing that never lied was the ice. Cruel though it may be, the world was crueler. "What about when Captain takes me to that one place, Atortittartut or whatever? Will you come with me and look after me there, wherever *there* is?"

Words scraped out Kitornak's throat then died in her mouth.

The need for mothering clawed and yowled inside Orluvoq like two foxes fighting. She desperately wanted to break and shout, "Please, Kitornak, hold me close and let us start our own clan, just us two." She sensed something genuine in this scullery maid, not like the other ship's women who saw that she was cared for, but not that she was loved. The bereavement of her parents had scored a deep trench of love-longing across her heart.

But her mother, who had loved her more than she had loved anything, was torn from her. Love, it seemed, meant little when the world was crueler than the ice that covered it.

No, I can't love her. That's the way you get hurt. Love was just the precursor to helplessness and pain.

"If you were an angakkuq, I would bring you," said the girl. "I would tell you to come run with me. We would find the token together."

"I'll—I'll get skis." The woman dropped to her knees, taking Orluvoq's gloves in her own. "You can pull me along as you windwalk. I'll see that you are sheltered and fed, that no one takes advantage of you."

The young angakkuq leaned forward and kissed

Kitornak on the cheek. "I love you." *Oh. I said it anyway.* "Maybe we will see each other again someday."

Kitornak pulled her in tight and wouldn't let go for a long, long time. Orluvoq felt something break a little inside. She clearly hadn't taken enough mental healing. The other woman's sobs racked her. They might have even squeezed a tear or two out of her.

Finally, they pulled apart and Orluvoq pulled out a candle. Kitornak kissed her on the cheek, then stood. The young angakkuq rubbed some heatmoss together and lit the glim. Without another word, she stepped out into the storm and ran toward death.

SNOW BURNED ORLUVOQ'S FACE. She jerked her head up and gasped for breath, wincing out a scream. Light came from a horizon, but she couldn't guess whether it was morning or evening. A gentle breeze caressed the ice. Her hands were far too cold. Was that even cold she was feeling?

Wait, where are my gloves? Oh, tiaavuluk! Worry boiled inside. Five puffy lumps of rigid black sat instead of fingers on each hand, the darkness spilling over into her palms. If she could see them, she was sure her nose and ears wouldn't look too different.

She fumbled for a candle and propped it between her legs. Like catching a pesky fly, she gripped heatmoss between the flats of her hands and rubbed until it ignited. It burned her hand, but the pain didn't register.

Ah, can't even think. Her whole body shook as she watched the flame flutter. It took another minute before she could extricate some tuuaaq from her pocket and get it crunching between her molars. When the mental healing finally came, she almost cried for joy. No bother from her hands or face anymore.

After half an hour of watching the glim flicker, Orluvoq remembered that her hands were frostbitten. *Right. Should probably do something about that.* In response to the musing, she laid on her side and closed her eyes.

Spirits only knew how long later, she woke to night. The tuuaaq's mental healing still washed over her, though not as strong. Her frame shook with such violence she thought the sky was falling.

Finally, bringing her eyes down from the top of her head, she saw the candle, nearly a nub, still aflicker. *I sh-sh-sh-should p-p-p-pro—* She didn't even finish the full thought, instead funneling her energy toward talking to the candle.

Warmth.

Ohh. Ohhh.

Tears dripped from her face as she finally stopped convulsing. How long had it been since she left the ship? Seven days? More? She had tried to die more than once, but it was too hard. Every time she woke up halfway to Nunapisu, she couldn't resist healing herself.

Hands.

She drew from the candle and watched the blackness slowly retreat down her fingers. About the middle knuckle, the flame guttered to nothing. She pawed for another, then finished her banishment of the frostbite.

Her stomach foundered. She took another nibble of tuuaaq, knowing the meager bits of tusk couldn't take the place of a strip of fat.

I need to find food, or else I'll never find Mama and Daddy. She looked around while waiting for the euphoria to hit. None of her attempts at vision had brought her parents' spirits calling. *Of course, there's an easier way to find them.*

Two spirits warred inside her, one dying to live and one dying to die. She found that she feared them in equal measures. If she lived, she would have to suffer life. If she died, she wouldn't get to enjoy life. If she danced with one spirit beneath the aurora, she frolicked with its antithesis beneath the sun, ever teetering, never toppling.

But that only applied when she wasn't elated by the tuuaaq. A wave of bliss swamped the young angakkuq. She found it much easier to not worry about living, dying, or anything in between by maintaining a constant state of mental healing.

The fresh surge of energy boosted Orluvoq to her feet and put her in motion across the ice. After following the light of Arsarneq for some time, her stomach complained enough to get her to ask the candle for directions to... somewhere. Food, shelter, no bears. She couldn't remember quite how she worded it, but she was sure the tuuaaq would take care of it.

Brimming over with impatience and brio, she leapt into a windwalking jaunt. The ground flew by faster than a summer falcon overhead. She laughed at the tiny forms of narwhals swimming in the green light above. Before the sun made its appearance, she came over a rise and felt the navigating tug of the candle pull behind instead of in front. She ditched windwalking for mundane snow walking and turned around.

Following the tug of the tuuaaq, she saw... nothing. Just a hill of ice. She ambled around the rise in the tundra for a few minutes, but she found no food, unless snow could fill a belly.

Discouraged, she took another gnaw of tuuaaq and cut some ice to melt in her mouth. Querying the candle again, it pulled her in the exact spot she sat. Stupid spirits.

Wait, it's not pulling here. *It's pulling* down.

Re-encouraged, she clambered over the hill and down the other side. Sure enough, there gaped the maw of a cave not twice as high as her. The tuuaaq in her system took her into the cave at a nice stroll, no worries about whether hostile beasts might inhabit it.

Immediately, something pierced through her mental healing. Tinged it like a leaky chamber pot sitting in one corner for too long. Rustled it like a breath on the back of the neck when walking in the pitch of night. Stained it like finding blood in your bed and knowing it wasn't yours. She damped her pace, now acutely aware of every scuff, puff, and drag her feet clanged out.

Around a bend, in the belly of the cave, flickered a light. A pale blue light. It glimmered with a cold colder than the darkest shadow in deepest winter. It wicked the heat from her small body, stealing the warmth she gleaned from the candle in hand. A faint, high-pitched wail stung her ears.

She gulped. What demon emitted frigid, blue light? Tariaksuq? Kigatilik? Ijiraq?

Perhaps if no tuuaaq flowed inside her, fear would have paralyzed her. Perhaps she would have had enough wits to windwalk in the opposite direction for as long as possible. Or perhaps the spirit that was dying to die would have taken her by the hand and led her gently into the light, as it now did.

With measured steps, she rounded the corner.

Five tuuaaq candles rested on five gray stones encrusted with thick gushes of tallow. The votive pillars burned bleak blue, and as they burned, they screamed. In the middle of the damnable display lay a man, his frost-coated lips babbling soundlessly.

Amid her shivering, Orluvoq shuddered.

The scene transfixed her for some indeterminate time. How could the candles take heat instead of give it off? Then again, how could they burn blue? Her own candle fluttered dangerously low. It was either time to get a new one or get out. Maybe both.

Maybe neither.

Many demons looked like humans, but she had never heard of one that could work blue candles. A sprig of hope twitched inside her. If she could take one of the azure flames, then the powerful demon magic might actually allow her to find her parents.

She strode forward. Heat, happiness, and coherent thought sucked from her as she approached the perverse flames. It was as if she had never eaten tuuaaq in her life.

I don't want this. She whimpered. Her jaw ached from clenching.

But some vestigial force from her earlier decision to take a candle carried her on. The candle in her hand died. As she reached out to grab the candle on the small pedestal before her, she watched frostbite run black down her hand, then arm.

Bad, bad, bad.

Orluvoq's senseless fingers touched the candle.

The demon's eyes split open, a jet of blue light spurting out. His head whipped sideways, and his glowing blue eyes lanced her through with cold. He shot to his feet, bolted to each of the candles faster than her eyes could follow, then windwalked out of the cave.

Orluvoq fell to the floor, her shivering turning to quivering as the warmth returned.

What demon was *that? And why am I still alive?*

She relit her candle with a scrap of heatmoss and

pushed the frostbite out of her arm, burning a precarious length of tuuaaq.

But... why would the candle tell me there was food here?

She decided to ask the candle. A stitch in her gut tugged her to a sack against the wall of the cave.

Ah.

She slumped down beside the small stock of meat and fat and stuffed herself with as much as her face would allow. Stomach on the mend, she stared at the stones in the weak light, wondering who had dug how deep to surface such marvels.

If she was running into demons, her travels must be actually getting somewhere. Then again, maybe not. The high north was a plane for demons. On unlucky days, so was the south.

Starting to run out of candles. And tuuaaq. I should probably get to Nunapisu before too long. No reason not to.

With that thought, she took a bite of tuuaaq, blew out the candle, and promptly passed out.

IT TOOK several more days to find the end of the earth, but not for lack of trying; it was just that far away. Twice she had diverted her route because of bad premonitions from the candle. That was as close as she came to another demonic encounter.

The most she had ever learned about the compass was that Arsarneq flowed from the north. How far east or west she might have been from Terianniaq, she couldn't say, but she trusted in the track of cairns she had found. How someone had pulled so many stones from close to the ocean all the way out here befuddled her. They'd even taken the time to stack the rocks in humanoid postures, arms jutting out. Inuksuk, she thought they were called.

In the dying light, she noticed the most curious thing. An igloo sat almost right at the edge of the world. That could be none other than the infamous Watcher's house—the man Mama thought was brave and Daddy thought was foolish. Nunapisu was endless, and yet she had managed to land smack dab on top of its only inhabitant. How was that for luck?

Beyond that lay the true spectacle: nothing. Absolute zero. Like the universe had yawned one day, then misplaced its mouth. As she came upon the end, she edged forward on her knees.

Now *there* was a drop.

It went down, down, down. Farther than stacking the aurora on itself a hundred times. Farther than if all the Nuktipik peoples ate a giant serving of tuuaaq and then crashed. To crash there had to be something to hit.

"Tell me."

Orluvoq startled. Grateful she hadn't been standing, she glanced up to see a stout man.

"When you look out into the darkness that has no end, what do you see? Beauty? Terror? Hope?"

She shook her head. "It's not the darkness that I came for."

A smile quirked onto the Watcher's lips. "No? Of course not. One so precocious, hardy, and dedicated as you couldn't possibly have come to feel the void's embrace. Not at such a young age."

She waited for him to continue or become impatient, but he simply watched the emptiness. "I've come for my parents," she volunteered, wiping some snot off her face. She should probably find somewhere else to paint with mucus, but ever since losing her gloves, her sleeves had acquired many stripes.

"Indeed? An orphan, then? Or were you hopelessly thrust from each other, their final words an anguished, 'Meet us at the end of the earth?'".

"Nope, just an orphan." She peered down the face of the cliff, trying to discern the identities of the few body-shaped blurs visible from this angle.

"Mm. I've been half an orphan most of my life. Can't blame you for looking."

She looked up at him. "Is that why you came here? Because your Mama or Daddy died?"

The Watcher paused. "That's close enough to the truth that I think I can say yes."

She nodded. "And did you ever find them?"

"Find my father?" He sighed. "I've only looked for him once. But no, I didn't find him." The man's eyes drifted again to the void.

"Oh, sad." She coughed. "I'm going to find my parents. Or at least one of them." *Or maybe fall off trying.* No, she didn't actually want to fall off. She either wanted to be with her clan or with her parents again. Falling off would be the end of her body, spirit, and name.

"Your ambitious quest across the ice and down the cliff to dangle above the void would be satisfied by finding just one parent?" The Watcher raised an eyebrow.

"Yeah, I only need one token."

"One... Oh, my dear, what is this business? You seek a token of kinship from your deceased parents? Your clan won't accept you, I take it?"

Orluvoq nodded. "They know whose daughter I am, whose blood I have. Once I have a token, they *have* to accept me as part of them. I don't even need them to love me. Just accept me."

The Watcher was quiet.

"Watcher—"

"Please, my name is Paarsisoq."

"Paarsisoq, will you help me find them?"

The silence groaned over Nunapisu as Paarsisoq watched errant flakes of snow drift over the edge. It stretched on too long.

He doesn't want to help. His job is just to watch for people who are going to go over the edge, not worry about those already gone.

He turned his gaze to the girl in the snow. The seconds ticked by, then something in his visage cracked. "Child—"

"I am Orluvoq."

"Orluvoq. I can tell you with the highest surety right now that no amount of searching you can do will ever lead to you finding them. There are numberless droves of bodies in this cliff. You could climb straight down for weeks and still be seeing new faces."

Her heart fell. That was the exact news she had been fearing on her journey out; the reason she wouldn't mind a nice death on the ice. She would never see her parents or her clan again.

"But," he continued, "I will help you."

Her heart jumped. That was the exact news she had been hoping for on her journey out; the entire reason she came.

She scrabbled to her feet and wrapped her arms around her new friend. "Oh, thank you, thank you. I always knew Mama was righter than Daddy."

A slow, sturdy smile spread across Paarsisoq's face. The Watcher dropped to his knees and returned the embrace.

"Your mother sounds like a wise woman. I hope that we find her."

There, before the unfathomable nullity of the universe, two negligible silhouettes hugged a particle of healing into one another's heart as the first wisps of the aurora played to life overhead.

25 Years Prior

Paarsisoq fumbled the bone needle, cursing himself for not having practiced with it more. That seemed to be one of his main activities these days, upbraiding the laxity of his past self. He'd never properly learned how to skin or gut a caribou or narwhal, much less hunt one. Never learned how to distil oil or render tallow. Never learned how to use candles. Never learned how to make tools. Never fully learned how to hunt. Never truly learned how to live.

He couldn't describe what had kept him land-bound that day he had showed up at the end of the earth. His intentions to jump were wings, his guilt updrafts. But as he had stared into the consuming murk, something inside had told him to wait. Perhaps it was cowardice. Nevertheless, another pilgrim of nihility had shown up the next day.

"You here just for the view or did you come to meet the void personally?" the man asked, removing his gloves and digging into his sizable pack.

Paarsisoq stared slack-jawed through squinted eyes. When his mind registered that it was another human, he tried to dredge up the proper protocols for interacting with something other than ice. "Uh, I'm going to, well, I'm here for my own business."

"A man after my own heart. I don't mean to disrupt your important business, but perhaps I could interest you in some narwhal meat." He pulled a bundle of waxy leather from the pack.

Paarsisoq grunted and accepted a hunk of red flesh.

"You been here long?" the newcomer asked. "I didn't notice you ahead of me on the ice."

The prospective suicidal shook his head. "A day." He finished masticating his mouthful. "What about you? Have you come to, um, jump?"

The traveler chuckled. "Not in the sense you're thinking. No, the spirits know I won't see the end of the earth after I die, so I thought I needed to see it in person." He slipped the pack from his shoulders and pulled at his coat where the straps had rested, peeling away the sweaty leather. "You wouldn't mind looking after my belongings for a moment, would you? I promise to pay you."

Paarsisoq slowly ran his eyes over the environs, ending with a raised eyebrow on the strange man. "Where..."

"Where indeed," the fellow remarked, removing a tuuaaq candle from inside his parka. "I suggest you don't follow. Actually, that would depend on the nature of your business here."

His eyes slid shut and breath seeped in through his nostrils. When the man seemed he might pop, his eyes shot open, and a sharp breath smote the tuuaaq wick. Fire flickered to life.

Paarsisoq radiated disbelief. The man merely nodded, then ran over the edge.

What the? Paarsisoq rushed to follow him with his eyes. Looking down the unending cliff, he watched the stranger *sprinting faster than should have been possible. Admittedly, the sprinting should also not have been possible.*

There might be more to this world than I thought. *The incredible feat twisted his mind into knots. A few minutes later, the man grew on the vertical horizon below until he popped back up over the edge with a flourish. Seemingly unwinded, he snuffed out the candle and dug into his pack.*

"What do you need? Food, clothes, tools? Ooh, candles? I bet it's candles."

"Um."

The angakkuq selected two tuuaaq candles from his overcoat and handed them to Paarsisoq. "There. You have a knife?"

The boy touched his hip and nodded.

"Well, maybe we'll meet again. Perhaps at the start of the world next time." *The man grunted as he reshouldered his pack.* "What was your name?"

"My name is Paarsisoq. What did you just do? I've never seen anything like it."

"I wish I had time to explain all. Suffice it to say there was an object that needed retrieving and I was the one to do it." *He smiled, the first Paarsisoq had seen in weeks.* "Farewell."

"Wait, what was your name?"

"Hm," *he tutted,* "call me Nalor. Unless you're overly concerned with formalities, then call me Nalorsitsaarut." *Another smile and he turned to the great white expanse.*

Nalor's nonchalance in helping a stranger and performing great angakkuq feats had pacified Paarsisoq's fatal urges. In the year since, he had wished plenty often that Nalor would never have shown up—that he would have just jumped upon arrival—but the fluky encounter had firmly planted one foot in the present, though the other often toed the grave.

He had used the tuuaaq candles to summon caribou for

meat. His knife had faced trial by ice when constructing his
igloo. He received incidental supplies from people come to
jump. Some inquiries turned into genuine conversations
that fogged over the reason they came. Seven different
people had boarded with him for seven different stretches of
days until finally they turned their backs on the void and
returned to the ice. Three of them had invited him to join
them on boats. He had almost accepted the first until he
realized that he felt something he hadn't felt in a while. He
felt good.

"Paarsisoq."

His hands jerked, and the needle pricked his thumb.
Who on earth's white face would be calling him by name?
He turned to the doorway of his igloo and his jaw fell.

"Mom?"

Her round, worried face bloomed with relief. She
dropped her hood, her other hand flying to her mouth as
tears flowed. "It's true." Pack slumping to the ground, she
ran to him and threw her arms around his neck. "My baby."
She trembled above him, then collapsed into his lap.

Paarsisoq couldn't find words to match his feelings, so he
just hugged her back as she heaved unfettered into his chest.
The last person he had expected to see had traveled weeks
to find him, and she was *happy*.

"How did you find me?" he ventured at last.

She sniffled. "Word whistles over the ice farther and
faster than you might think. It was maybe six months ago
we first heard of the one who lodged on Nunapisu, chatting
with the forlorn and bringing them back from the darkness.
I tried to quell any hope that this watcher might have saved
you. Fools hope, sages wait.

"But then a ship came by the clan and one of them told
us the story of how he was saved by this strange, young

watcher. 'So few years for so much wisdom,' he said. The other line I'll never forget that he said was, 'I tried to convince Paarsisoq to join me as a sailor, but he insisted Nunapisu was his home.' You can't imagine my shock.

"'Who?' I begged him to tell me.

"'Paarsisoq, my dearest friend,' he replied. I almost couldn't contain myself. I blasted him with endless questions about you and knew that I had to come." She took his face in both her hands. "And here you are."

And here I am. It still shocked him that his mother didn't hate him. In fact, it seemed like she still loved him. "But why? How could you come after what I did? Why couldn't I just be dead to you?"

Her smile tarnished over with a melancholic matte. "My dearest one, my asasaq. I know your spirit, and I know your heart. Killing is not the way of Paarsisoq. The first hunt is always a time of trial and accident; yours just more so than most. Your father didn't fare so well his first time around either." Her smile dropped entirely, her voice a feeble diminuendo. "Or his last."

The words jabbed a bone into his heart. "Mother, I apologize, but I'll never be like dad. I tried so hard in the months after he died, but I can't." The doubts and inadequacies of a year ago came creeping back in, and suddenly the Watcher became the watched.

"You needn't be your father. The only thing that must happen is that I must be your mother, and you will always be my son."

Now it was his turn for a pair of wet eyes. How could she still love him? He was a killer and a disgrace. Not worthy of a spare thought, and especially not worthy of a trek to the end of the earth.

"Come home, Paarsisoq."

He looked at this woman who wouldn't give up and turned away. "Mom, I can't. I'm so sorry, but I can't. I have no place there."

"Of course, you do. You are one of us, and you always will be." She squeezed his arm, then looked away herself. "I need you."

The three words broke his heart into a million pieces and threw them all off the cliff. "You don't understand. I have finally found my place. Here, at the end of the earth. I... I can talk to people and make them alright when all is wrong—usually. I can't explain it, it just happens when the conversation starts. This is my lot."

The strongest woman he knew surveyed him, her dark eyes peeling back the layers of his soul. "My asasaq. You realize that no matter how much you do, no matter how hard you try, how much of your heart you give them, many of them will still perish?"

He nodded. "Of course, Mama. But if I do nothing, then they all shall perish. If I watched and waited all my days and turned back but one soul, not a day of my life would be wasted."

She looked as if she might cry again. "There. I told you I knew your heart. That is the way of Paarsisoq." She leaned against him.

"You don't know what it's like to stare into that void and realize that your only hope is hopelessness." His mind jumped to his dead father. *Or maybe you do...*

"If you are certain that this is where you belong, asasaq, I won't force you away."

Paarsisoq sighed a bittersweet sigh. "Thank you, mother."

"But I will be staying two weeks."

A smile took over Paarsisoq's face.

"Hand me that needle and let me show you how to sew so that you won't have to do it again in a month."

Orluvoq's lips were a battleground devastated by the wind's unremitting forces. As soon as she healed them up, they tore into a thousand craggy pieces again. Her eyes felt like a bone pole left out to dry for too long. The spots on her thighs where the harness gripped had needed a break for the past three days. All that could quickly be forgotten by providing herself with a little mental healing.

"Ah," Paarsisoq barked. "Keep that in your pocket."

Orluvoq whimpered, tuuaaq trembling in her hand. "But I need it."

"As far as I'm concerned, there's nothing about hanging above an endless void that calls for dulling your senses by getting stewed up on the crooked horn." The Watcher hammered in another piton above somebody's frozen face. "If I would have realized how much of an addict you are, I would have made you leave all your substances up in my igloo."

She tried to figure out a way to take a bite without him noticing. That had proven pretty hard with the only life for miles being their dangling bodies bopping into each other.

"No, I said put it back."

"But just a little nibble," she pleaded. "That's all."

"You don't need those 'maintenance morsels' as much as you think you do." He motioned to the nearest set of corpses in the cliff wall. "Any of these look like your parents?"

The girl shook her head and curled the tusk toward her mouth.

"Hey," Paarsisoq called. "Cut that out. You can just hand over the tuuaaq to me and we don't ever have to have this conversation again."

She stared at the beautiful sprig of bone before finally pocketing it again. The movement was like watching the sail unfurl first thing in the morning, slowly pulling it apart from its frosted self. "Can't do that. You'll just throw it down there." She pointed at nothing.

"I already promised I wouldn't." The Watcher sighed. "You remember a couple days ago when you took a bite? Then suddenly we found your mom, I spent spirits know how long digging down to her, only to have you point at the next one over—who was a man—and say, no that one's my mom? And the next one and the next one was your mom, too. I said I'd help, but how can I help if you're polluted on tuuaaq?" Another sigh brushed by his lips. "If you'd rather, we can return topside, and I can turn you to wander strung-out on your favorite snack."

"No! I need to find a token." She wiped at her raw nose. "If I don't have that, I don't have anything." The face of a person long dead, this one with its eyes open, sat a foot from hers. Paarsisoq had said it was only unsettling for the first few hours. That had been six days prior, and she was still waiting for the 'first few hours' to pass. *Oh, I know how I can make it better.* Her hand drifted to her pocket.

"Orluvoq."

She pulled the hand back and lowered herself down the cliff to reach the Watcher's level.

"I think it's about time to head back up, anyway." He sucked some snot into his throat and spat it into the nullity below. "We need to restock on food, and these harnesses aren't doing much for my legs either."

"But we haven't found my parents." Even with the Watcher, even with the tuuaaq, even after her trek across the ice and encounter with the demon, she had gotten nowhere. Maybe if she couldn't make the right decisions, she should have just let the captain decide.

"Quite true, my child. If only Nunapisu was a little more sequential in how it deposited bodies. We'll take a respite, then make another expedition." He offered a conciliatory smile and pulled himself upward. "If we start now, then we won't have to sleep on the cliff again."

The young angakkuq noticed he said nothing about 'before dark', just about sleeping. As much as she wanted to see her parents again, taking a little break to see the sun wouldn't offend anyone. Being on the cliff, she decided, was like voluntarily entering winter, just with fewer storms.

After a few hours of climbing, she heard Paarsisoq stop below her. The stopping itself wasn't unusual. Both of them initiated their fair share of breaks. The hand on her heel was.

"Orluvoq."

Was he about to congratulate her on not taking any tuuaaq in the past while? Because she had definitely taken some about an hour ago when he wasn't looking. She wasn't even sure why he was so upset about—

"Look!"

She cast her eyes up to the left and leaned back on her

leg straps. "Did someone jump?" A dark form dropped rapidly down the cliff.

"Not if my intuitions are attuned," Paarsisoq answered. "I believe we're looking at an old friend of mine whom I haven't seen in a couple years. Can you light up a candle and tug him to come this way?"

Could she? Maybe? Trying wouldn't hurt anything. Candle in hand, she sparked some heatmoss. In the deftness of inebriation, she tried to light the tuuaaq wick and ended up hitting Paarsisoq in the face.

"Ah! Did you just drop the candle?" It was the first time genuine anger had tinctured in his voice.

"Sorry. Didn't mean to."

"Wait, are you on tuuaaq right now? Tiaavuluk, we don't have time for this. You need to call him over. Nalor!" he shouted.

She tried to redouble her concentration and pulled the last candle of the expedition out of her pocket. With the utmost care, the candle flared to life and she tapped into it, sending a summoning out across the cliff.

Paarsisoq cried out in triumph when the man who was somehow running down the cliff changed his course toward them. "Perfect, I knew you could do it, Orluvoq. Just try to burn the tuuaaq next time instead of eating it. Resources do have their limits."

The girl watched the figure approach. As he neared, her fear ballooned. She needed to be anywhere except for there. Claw her way up the cliff, cut the cords, anything. This was something more than windwalking, and it was almost upon her. When his face came into focus, her fears crystallized. She had seen him before.

In a cave.

He ran up alongside them and stabbed a pick into the

ice. He made hanging there look like the most natural thing a person could do. "Paarsisoq, a pleasure. I was wondering why I didn't see you at your typical post. And... oh my. I do believe we've met, but I can't admit to being properly acquainted. The name's Nalor, or Nalorsitsaarut for the stuffy, formal types. You know, when they talk about hanging yourself, I don't think this is what they usually mean. What has provoked you to throw the old trope on its head this fine day?"

"You're not a demon?" blurted out Orluvoq.

"That seems like a very contextual question," said Nalor.

"A deep pleasure, as always, Nalor," Paarsisoq said from below. "This is my new friend, Orluvoq, who would do well to show a little more respect. We're on a quest to find her dead parents."

"Oh, I do love a good quest, Paarsi. You'll have to try and swim up Qilaknakka next. Maybe the king will even go with you." Nalor gave a wink. "Any luck so far?"

Orluvoq tried to pinpoint what was unsettling about the probably-not-a-demon man. Definitely something about how evil he seemed in the cave versus how confabulating and friendly he appeared now. What were those blue candles, and why wasn't he using one now? Oh well, the tuuaaq she had eaten a while ago gave her enough mental healing to not worry about it too much now that he didn't seem like an immediate threat.

"You know, it's the strangest thing," Paarsisoq said. "No. Not a single parent has turned up. Even though Orluvoq here is an angakkuq and we have her working the candles to search for them, they've evaded our search so far."

Nalor tutted and rubbed his chin with the candle in hand. "Most curious. And an angakkuq, you say? Hm, yes, I seem to remember something about that from our previous meeting."

"I know you're a terribly busy man, Nalor, but do you think I could convince you to lend your abilities for just a day to aid a poor little orphan girl in a quest that will give her life meaning again?"

Orluvoq didn't much fancy spending a day above oblivion with the lord of blue candles, but if he taught her how to run on the cliff, it might be worth it.

"You know, Paarsi, I can't. I'm absolutely booked. I'm here on a small forensics mission, then I have a four-day windwalking excursion to get to a very important meeting."

"Completely understandable. We'll leave this orphan to while away her days chewing toward the crash at the end of her tuuaaq addiction, which will likely throw her right off the cliff, another soul claimed by Nunapisu."

Nalor stared at the Watcher. "You know, what's a day, really? Spirits know I've done worse things with my time."

Orluvoq looked down to see Paarsisoq smile. "Would it be too much trouble to give us a hand getting topside?"

"It would be my honor."

Orluvoq kept her eyes trained on what was not a demon, just a sinister angakkuq, while Paarsisoq sat entranced with a candle trying to call a caribou for dinner. How could this Nalor character be so baleful and threatening, surrounded by dark powers, then be so chipper and cozy? When a man wore two faces, neither could be trusted.

"What were all those blue candles?" she asked him.

He pulled his gaze from the incipient wisps of

Arsarneq's light. "Hm? Oh, those? Those are tuuaaq candles."

"Great. Why did they burn blue, and how were they so cold?"

"Perspicacious questions, my little tuuaaq fiend."

She scowled. Paarsisoq had taken away her tuuaaq upon reaching the top, and a headache was already setting in.

"Those candles you saw were nothing more than simple tuuaaq—though tuuaaq itself isn't so simple. We've been trying to get to the origin of Arsarneq for years with no success. However, the candles in the cave had one small difference from the tuuaaq candles your talented self employs. The tusk inside was used to murder someone."

Orluvoq's stomach sank into a huddled clump. "Murder?" she whispered. "You've murdered someone?"

Nalor's lips curved into a smile. "You say it like it's a bad thing."

She scooted away but kept her eyes trained on him. "How could it not be?"

He laughed, the sound of frolicking frost. "You're right, of course. It's a very bad thing. But with a life this hard, the only true option is to be harder."

Oh, spirits, he's killed people. "How... how many?"

"I don't kill very often, and only when they deserve it." His grin burned with an impish hue. "Of course, in that case, I'm the one who decides whether they deserve it. If you decide to ever come away from this cliff, you might well find yourself being a decider for someone else someday. With a life this hard..."

The girl shook her head. "Never. What does the blue flame do? Why can't you just use a normal flame?"

"Have you ever heard of tirigusuusiit?"

"No."

"It's an old word. 'Things to avoid.' You consider the things you can work with a candle to be marvelous? Wind and shadowwalking, bonding creatures, healing maladies, drawing warmth, weather forecasting? No more marvelous than coloring the snow with your morning piss. The tiri-gusuusiit are a whole new set of awes."

"Like what?"

His smile faded. "As an angakkuq you can receive visions. As a tirigusuusik you can leave your body and travel across the world. As an angakkuq you can walk with the wind across the ground. As a tirigusuusik you can walk with the wind across the sky. As an angakkuq you can create a storm shield. As a tirigusuusik you can call down vengeance of ice and lightning from heaven. And whoever said that the dead cannot walk has never heard of the tiri-gusuusiit."

She sat stunned, trying to process all the implications of the tirigusuusiit. Where skepticisms crept, the memory of the cold of the cave ravaged. "Wait, if the dead can walk, then why can't we just bring my parents back with one of these tirigusuusik candles?"

"Now that's something I would absolutely not recommend." Joviality boiled back into his demeanor. "For one, they would fall into Nunapisu. For two, you would find them a bit... different than you remember. Much less enjoyable company."

"So, they'd still be dead?"

"Mhmm."

"I thought you said—"

"I said they can walk." Nalor held up a scolding finger. "I didn't say they could hold intellectual conversations or they were capable of love. Not that that makes them horribly different from most sailors I've met."

Orluvoq heard that all too clearly. "Alright. Well, uh, why did you have to have five candles? Seems like a waste."

"Ha." He balled a bit of snow and pitched it over the edge. "One candle is usually sufficient, unless the task needs a little more oomph. What if I just wanted to dream of somewhere a bit warmer? You can imagine that would take at *least* five burners."

She rolled her eyes at the joke. "I've never even tried using two candles. If the tirigusuusiit are so much more amazing than normal angakkuq stuff, then what could possibly need five candles?"

Nalor's eyes bounced around her face, his own maintaining a slight smile. "If you really want to know that, you'll have to wait another eight, ten years. Talented though you may be, experienced you are not. Find me then and I'll teach you everything."

"I don't want to kill anyone."

"The ice is cold and hard. The winters are dark. Ten years and you may find your soul has become all three."

Headache percolated through her skull. The words sowed unease, but his general manner captivated strands of her spirit. This was not a toothless man. "Nalor? Do you ever feel helpless?"

"Helpless?" His eyes untracked from the present, gaze flying through both girl and wall. "Not for a great many years."

If the things to avoid could embolden the powerless, how strictly should they be avoided? The frostbiting chill of the blue flame pentacle goosebumped its way through her memory. She shuddered.

"Ah," exclaimed Paarsisoq, coming out of his trance. "I've pulled a caribou out from its herd and made good progress getting it to head this way. Let's go meet it."

Orluvoq hurried to the Watcher's side, head pains disregarded, and headed away from the end of the world.

ORLUVOQ PEERED OVER THE EDGE, the darkness beyond cast deeper into shadow by the sun behind her. Cravings to chomp her way through a stick of tuuaaq scorched her from the inside. Who was Paarsisoq to take away her tuuaaq? "Are you sure I can do this?"

Nalor waved a hand. "Absolutely. And if not, well, it's only your eternal existence at stake."

She frowned up at him. "Not funny."

"My dear, when you're dealing with robbing the dead and the chance of slipping off into Nunapisu, you need all the humor you can get." He flipped back his hood and ran a glove through his hair. "Now, take a bite of this. And don't tell Paarsi when he gets back from doing whatever Watcher rounds he's doing." He held out a nub of tuuaaq.

Orluvoq's eyes bulged, and she pounced on the piece of mental healing. It wasn't enough to really do damage, but it took the edge off.

"Alright, you feel it coursing through your body? Good, now I want you to tap into it and light your candle." He motioned to the glim in her hand.

"What?"

"Watch." His eyes rolled back into his head and air poured through his nostrils into his lungs. After Orluvoq was sure he couldn't breathe anymore, his eyes shot forward and he spat onto the candle in his hand. The tuuaaq flickered to life.

"What? How did you do that?" She glanced from his flame to her dead wick.

"I don't know. It's like explaining what cold feels like. All you can say is that it's not warm. But what if the person you were talking to had never been hot or cold? You couldn't explain it. You just have to *feel* it burning inside. Then blow the candle to life."

"I don't get it. How can you burn tuuaaq inside you? You already ate it. Is there going to be a fire in me?"

"No, nothing quite so fantastic. In short, I can't tell you exactly how it works. We feel like we'll know a lot more once we get to the start of Arsarneq, but that still seems a long time off. Just know that it does work."

She tried to burn the tuuaaq inside her. "Wait, why can't you just use the blue candles? Didn't you say last night that tirigusuusiit are a lot stronger than normal?"

"I am first an angakkuq and second a tirigusuusik, young lady." He put his free hand on his hip. "Now hurry and tap into that tuuaaq before it's all wasted on you getting a buzz."

"Okay, so how do I—"

"Once you can finally feel it, then concentrate the feeling in your mouth. Let it build up for a bit, then spit it onto the candle."

She nodded and tried to do what he said. The tuuaaq in her system helped her stay calm when she still hadn't found it five minutes later. "It's not working."

"Not yet. You just have to keep looking. Reach for the light of Arsarneq inside you. The narwhals feed on it and the residue builds up in their tusk."

Five more minutes and the evasive tuuaaq inside couldn't prevent her from frustration. "It's *not* working."

He shrugged. "Worth a try. Let's get windwalking, then."

"What?" She squatted down. "You're supposed to teach me how to walk the cliff. I can't just go over!"

"Oh. It's just normal windwalking, except everyone else I

meet is too scared to point a different direction. Do you still say mantras with your candlework? Still meditate before?"

"Uh..." She looked at the cliff and wondered what mantra could save her from slipping. "Yes."

"Then I suggest you cook up some tasty lines and pop another one of these." He palmed her two more chips of tuuaaq. "Save the other for the trip back up. That can get trickier."

She received her prize with reverent glee and looked up. "You're so much nicer than Paarsisoq."

"Yes, well, since we're about to be tethered running down the most dangerous piece of ice in existence, I need you as alert and energetic as I can get you."

The pieces were a fifth as big as she'd have liked. She chomped one and reluctantly pocketed the other.

Nalor pulled her up and batted her back. "Right-o, shall we get a little more horizontal?" He paused. "I'm glad you're not old enough to realize the unintended implications of that statement."

She ignored whatever he said about implications. "So how are we going to get my parents out once we find them?"

He gestured with the candle. "Apply a little heat and soon you have a lot less ice." He picked up the rope and began to secure it around himself. "This will keep us together. You have that ice pick I gave you earlier?"

She patted her side in reply.

"Good. Keep that in your dominant hand." He tied the rope around her. "This rope will hopefully keep you from seeing too much of Nunapisu, but do try to stick that beauty in the ice. You can windwalk and navigate at the same time, yes?"

"Yeah." She thought back on stumbling into his blue cave.

"Good girl." He straightened after finishing his fastening. "Well, I'm ready if you're ready. Lead us."

"Wait." Panic stabbed through the modest mental healing inside her. "What if the rope comes undone?"

"That," said Nalor, "is where the blue candles come in."

A jitter of excitement shook her body. It almost made her want to fall just to see what would happen.

Orluvoq exhaled to center herself, then wove a web of exactly what she needed the tuuaaq to do for her. Slipping and falling were both off the table. Super speed was encouraged. A direct route to her mother—simpler than 'parents'—was also in the clear. Her gut tugged down to the left. Putting some finishing garnishes on her mantra, she opened her eyes and ran over the cliff.

Her stomach got tangled somewhere on her spine. She was falling. She was running. She was flying? She was *living*. But she was definitely dying.

"We're going to die!"

"I can't really hear you," came Nalor's voice from behind, "but isn't this great?"

Yes. It was incredible. Life crammed her full, and for the first time in a while, helplessness was nowhere to be found.

They ran on for some time in the cold shadow of the wall, Orluvoq following the tug of the tuuaaq. Bodies and pale faces flickered by beneath their feet. She was glad she didn't have to look at them anymore, like when she and Paarsisoq had crawled across the cliff. Now lower than she and the Watcher had ever gotten, she threw a look up at the sky. The ridge cut the sky what must have been miles above, showering her with a spritz of vertigo. Better to look down. Into the abyss.

The tug changed to pointing toward the sky. Orluvoq switched course and scrambled against the icy wall. Her progress came to a halt. Fear scrabbled against her innards as she scrabbled against the cliff. She slid backwards.

"Tiaavuluk!" shouted Nalor.

He slammed his pick into the cliff and beckoned for her to do the same. She came level with him and pierced the wall. The combination of candle and pick made it surprisingly easy to hold herself steady. She stared at the dead woman in front of her with terrible brown teeth.

"Right," he said. "Which way then?"

She pointed with her chin up and to the left. "There. I don't think it was so far back."

"Hm. Let's climb with the picks then."

Orluvoq followed his lead as he swung the pick, took a couple steps, then repeated. The candle kept her from sliding long enough to spike the pick in again. "Wouldn't it be easier to just take a little tuuaaq and run up there?"

"With your level of control, this will get us there a lot quicker than doing laps around your dead mother." He breathed a little harder with the exertion of the climb.

A dozen pick hikes later, Orluvoq gasped. There, beneath less than a foot of ice, was her mother. Her beautiful mother. She leaned forward and pressed her chapped lips on the ice above the dead woman's face. "Mama."

"A hit?" came Nalor's voice from above. "Excellent." He lowered himself back to her level. "If you got your mother's looks, then you'll be a pretty sight when you get older. You ready to look for this token?"

"Yes." Orluvoq didn't hold back the tears. A ripple of shame rotted her insides green. *Oh, Mama. I want to be strong and good like you. You and Daddy said not to eat the tuuaaq, but I did. I'm sorry. I'm sorry.*

Just a minute ago freedom had coursed through her. But her mother's corpse abraded away all artifice. The tuuaaq.

The Watcher. Nalor's running. All of it was just a flimsy scaffold to keep up the pretense that she lacked nothing. That she didn't need parents or a clan to become strong. But she didn't have parents or a clan, so how else could she do it?

The ice separating mother and daughter dribbled away as Nalor worked his candle. "I know this is quite a moment for you, but please try not to lose your connection with your candle. You'll quickly find the pick a lot slipperier than you thought."

She nodded and tamed her tears. When the last shard of ice melted from the corpse's face, Orluvoq passed her candle to the thumb and forefinger of her pick hand and reached out to touch her mother.

Water dripped onto her face.

"What?" said Nalor, glancing up as water hit his face.

Her gaze followed. On the ice above them crouched a body. Ethereal blue trailed out of its eyes. As soon as their gazes brushed it, the thing let go of the wall.

"Tiaavuluk!" Nalor shouted and tried to move.

Orluvoq's hand flew back to her candle and she cowered. She glimpsed blue diamonds embroidered down its front before it thumped against her and growled. They tore off the cliff. Its hands latched around her throat. The rope snapped taut, wrenching an excruciating grunt from Orluvoq's gut.

Wait, it's the woman I saw back at Terianniaq cutting up narwhal—the one whose corpse was in the storage room.

"Nalor," she gurgled.

"It's a bluebody," the man cried out. "Tirigusuusik." When it quickly became clear that he wouldn't be able to pull the rope up with one hand, he started swinging it, hoping to bash the bluebody into the abyss.

Flickers of light that Orluvoq couldn't follow appeared

in her vision, tracing and dancing to an unheard tune. The rope cinched too tight at her waist.

Through some trick that she didn't quite follow, Nalor must have whipped out a different candle and lit it off the first. A blue flame burst to light, its birth drawing out Orluvoq's warmth. The flickers danced harder.

The pressure around her neck disappeared, and the tension around her middle lessened. Her vision returned, and she watched the woman skitter along the wall. The— what had Nalor called it? Bluebody's movements were the grotesque scuttle of a fleshy puppet, snicking its way over a field of cadavers.

Nalor grunted, and the woman halted, staring shards of blue hate back into him. He stared back just as hard, and the air between seemed to jellify into a faint blue. The ice cliff wept, and corpses poured forth.

The flame in Nalor's hand pulsated, and a series of liquid pops sounded from the bluebody. Suddenly, the woman's head and spinal cord ripped off her body and flipped off into the void. The blue light in her eyes died and the rest of her slipped off to follow.

All was silent on the face of the cliff until Nalor broke into a laugh. "A bluebody. Tiaavuluk. Someone sent a bluebody *here* for *us*. Must have crawled from wherever the ice slotted it."

Orluvoq groaned and tried to right herself, a difficult task as she lacked both pick and candle. "What was that?"

"I think it best we explain topside. No need to leave ourselves vulnerable for what else might be lurking Nunapisu."

"Wait." Panic poured into her. "Did my mother fall off during the fight?"

"No, she wasn't in the danger zone, luckily." He doused

the normal candle, then transferred the blue flame to his pick hand. "And this," he pulled off a bauble crafted of bone from her mother, "means that the mission was a success. I'll carry you since you look a little rattled. And lost your candle."

"AND THEN YOU threw it off into the void?" Paarsisoq popped another cube of fat into his mouth, the steady sway of an oil lamp casting light on his features.

"Precisely, Paarsi." Nalor followed suit and fed himself some more.

"I've seldom heard talk of bluebodies, and now they're in my domain?"

"It's not a particularly common topic of discussion outside of certain circles."

The Watcher turned to Orluvoq. "And to think, that could have been you and me instead of you and him." He laughed. "We'd both be getting better acquainted with darkness right now."

I guess he did save my life and help me get the token. She massaged the new bone carving strung around her neck. *Maybe he isn't all bad. Even if he does kill people.*

"What we have to figure out is who sent the cursed thing," Nalor said. "And was it for one of us, or just coincidence?"

"It was for me." Orluvoq rubbed at her snotty nose.

Nalor faced her. "How can you be so sure?"

"The bluebody. It was a woman from Terianniaq. I've seen her before. And... and I've seen her dead body before. She had a stab wound over her heart that could have been from tuuaaq, now that I think about it." She squinted at the memory not of her first dead body, but of her first murdered body.

"Hm, interesting indeed," Nalor mused. "So, from that I think we can conclude that someone from Terianniaq is the perpetrator. But who? Whoever this tirigusuusik, I don't like him. I think that very soon he won't like me either. He should have avoided the things to avoid." A shadow that made Orluvoq uneasy passed over his face with the last pronouncement. It vanished with a smile. "And are you still set on returning to your old home? To your rejectors?"

"Well, I don't have anything else."

"Someone there did just try to kill you."

"I..."

"Don't worry, I'm sure it was a happy accident for them." Nalor rocked his head with strokes of the chin. "The ice decides where to place a body in Nunapisu. That tirigusuusik must have sought a vision of you, then buried the body when he thought he had a chance. I would bet that bluebody would have come after you wherever you settled in."

"You could stay here," Paarsisoq offered her. "I mean, I talk with someone at least every other week, but it can still get lonely."

She shook her head. "Thanks, but I need to be with my clan. It's my blood."

The Watcher looked a little defeated, but he quickly brushed it off.

"I assume you don't know the fastest way to get back." Nalor devoured a slice of meat.

"Windwalking?" she responded.

"Oh, so close. I'm talking about the sky. Arsarneq."

She frowned. "Arsarneq? I'm supposed to fly in the aurora?"

The older angakkuq grinned. "The aurora is a thing of

beauty. It's where we angakkuit get our powers. It's where the narwhals—a main food source of all the Nuktipik peoples—live. And inside Arsarneq, your angakkuq powers are amplified. So, you may not be able to skywalk anywhere else, but you can in the aurora. The hunters prowl Arsarneq with their kites. The angakkuit reign inside it. There you can run faster than anywhere else. Skywalk back to your clan."

"Wow. Could you go all the way to Qilaknakka?"

"Could I?" He chuckled. "Sure. Just strut up to old King Qummukarpoq at the start of the world and stay for some fish and leg wrestling. Could you? Not a chance."

"Okay. And... how am I supposed to *get* up there? It's not like there are any kites lying around here." She anticipated his response with glee. She had always wanted to be a hunter.

"Well, one way is to make yourself extremely light. That has its ups and downs though." He laughed at his own joke. "Another, as you have aptly named, is riding a kite. We don't want to bother ourselves with either of those methods, though. The last option is to use a blue flame."

Her eyes widened. "You're going to give me a blue candle?"

"Has it been ten years yet?" He smirked a chuckle. "No, I'm going to ferry you into Arsarneq's holy light."

Orluvoq's jaw dropped. She put some fat in it. "And then I can skywalk to Terianniaq?"

"Yes. But it will have to be tonight, because I have places to be. You won't fall asleep on me, will you?"

"No, sir." She swirled her finger around her empty pocket, wishing it contained more tuuaaq. She'd eaten the last gift from Nalor on the trip back up Nunapisu. Fake strength. She knew it was false, yet she needed more of that counterfeit. Didn't that make her more helpless?

"Right, then. The sun will be down in a couple hours. Have some fun until then." He considered. "Or sleep."

Two hours later, as Arsarneq snaked across the sky, Orluvoq said her goodbyes.

"Here." Paarsisoq offered her a stick of her tuuaaq. "But only if you promise to only nibble at it. I know that going off it completely can be pretty severe."

"Oh, I will," she promised, overjoyed at the feel of bone in her gloved fingers. The shame from meeting her dead mother surged and wrapped around her heart. How could she take joy in dishonor and weakness? She wrapped the Watcher in a soft hug. "Thanks for helping. And watching and stuff. I'll miss you."

He smiled and stroked her hair, other hand pressing her tight to him.

She pulled away and turned to Nalor. She still wasn't sure what she thought of him. No, that wasn't true. She thought he was good, but scary. "Thanks for not killing me and for helping me find my mom."

"An absolute pleasure." He made a grand bow. "This side excursion has proven more beneficial than any of us could have anticipated. Light your candle."

Despite her shame, she nearly choked on resentment putting Paarsisoq's tuuaaq gift away. Orluvoq pulled out a candle and a scratch of heatmoss, bringing the wick aflame.

Nalor gave a satisfied smile. "You know, I've known angakkuit who had worked the candles for ten years and weren't as good as the little I've seen from you. Look for me when you're older and I'll have some very interesting work for you."

"Will I have to murder people?"

"I believe I answered that question earlier. Now, are you ready to skywalk?"

"Wait," she interjected. "If being in the aurora amplifies my angakkuq powers, then how strong is a tirigusuusik up there?"

A grin dripped onto his lips. "Talk to me in ten years and find out." He lit his blue candle, the flame sucking away her warmth.

"Spirits," said Paarsisoq huddling into himself, "that's quite the demon you carry."

"Alright, Orluvoq," said Nalor, "whatever you do, don't drop that candle."

"Okay, so—"

He grabbed her under the arms and exploded into the sky with a whirl of legs. Small minutes later, he dropped her into Arsarneq and vanished toward the distant ice.

THE WIND that tore at Orluvoq's ears and face evaporated. Ghostly green usurped control of her mind, bleeding in through her eyes, weeping in through her ears. Silence both austere and imposing cloaked her, spun her in a languid circle.

Arsarneq.

The light that she could almost notice when she consumed tuuaaq streamed all around her, swaddling her in power. She bit at it, but her teeth came down on nothing. How did the narwhals do it? The itch to fill herself with mental healing burned like a thousand candles in the face of a luxuriant, untouchable stream of the stuff.

Oh, wait. She took out the piece of tusk the Watcher had given back and took a bite—not a big one, though. Neither her resources nor tasks ahead could support that.

The young angakkuq centered herself and issued a

volley of words at her candle, though less than she was wont to. The glim responded, and she shot off down the tunnel that was full but somehow hollow. Her footfalls connected with nothing, yet she ran. No wind assailed her. Her clothes rustled somewhat but didn't flutter. The aurora devoured what little sound they made, and everything clipped off after a few feet.

The ground far below shifted more slowly than she had thought it would. But wasn't she going unbelievably fast? How could she be running faster than she'd ever run before, but the ground looked like she was just walking over it? She tried running faster.

Hours later, Orluvoq's eyelids wrestled to remain apart. She'd try closing just one and hooding the other. She even tried holding one open with her fingers, but it just defocused and wandered around.

A low, disembodied groan reached her ears. She jolted awake. Narwhals. She dropped close to the bottom of Arsarneq and avoided the dark blurs. If just one of them was pointed north, her sleepy southbound body could get a bellyful of that tusk she so coveted.

Then maybe Nalor could use it to make bluebodies, or whatever it is you do with five blue flames. Or wait, does that only count if you murdered someone with the tusk? Can the light of Arsarneq tell if it was just an accident?

She decided that green light probably couldn't discern the intent of a particular killing. Then she thought about it some more and decided that maybe it could. She'd just have to remember to ask Nalor the next time she saw him, in ten years or however long. Or maybe she could just accidentally kill someone with tuuaaq before then and find out herself.

No, better just wait. He'd probably visit soon to talk to the tirigusuusik anyway.

A finger of unease poked her heart, indicating that she needed to redose on tuuaaq. Someone from Terianniaq had killed this woman, then possessed her body, sent her to Nunapisu, and then—planned or not—commanded her to attack Orluvoq. That person was going to be there when she arrived. That person was still going to want her dead. They'd probably turn her into a bluebody and send her to kill someone else.

She slowed her skywalking. *Maybe I should just turn around and run back to Nunapisu. They'll kill me if I come. I would have realized that sooner if my head wasn't full of tuuaaq. If I was strong, like Mama.*

But wasn't that what she had wanted all along? To die? Hadn't the whole point of her excursion been a final fling at hope? Or more appropriately, a final fling *with* hope? One last affair with hope before immutably resigning her spirit to hopelessness?

If so, what would completing this journey do? What would it be?

She stood in the sky, buoyed up by a green phantom, surveying the world below and her life ahead.

It would be the end.

Dead father. Dead mother. Clan reject. Tuuaaq addict. Clueless girl. Helpless girl. Hopeless girl.

She nodded and licked her chapped lips.

I'm ready for the end.

Orluvoq queried the candle for directions to Terianniaq then resumed her pace. They would take her token, then eventually her life. But this time, she was ready. This time, they wouldn't take her hope, for she had none.

PAARSISOQ

16 Years Prior

The days grew longer, stretching like a white bear stirring from sleep and sticking its nose toward food. Before long, the sun would show its face throughout the night and the great narwhal hunt would be off. Paarsisoq liked to imagine that sitting there at the end of the world, he could still see the green glow of Arsarneq in the deep void to the north when the sun hovered a finger above the horizon to the south.

Ten years at Nunapisu had brought many surprises, the greatest of which might have been the fact that he had survived. Survived the storms. Survived the times when he called to caribou or rabbits with the candles, but none came. Survived the torrents of heartbreak he had taken upon himself—and those lingering breakages he had no choice but to suffer. The loneliness so cold it burned. The urges to thrust himself into somber oblivion.

There was something both intoxicating and sobering

living at the end of everything; knowing that you could end your being at the merest flicker of whim, trusting that you possessed the strength to do exactly the opposite. Sometimes the Watcher wondered why he stayed. Ships aplenty would take him in. A few clans would accept an able-bodied man as a laborer. But every time he wondered, someone came along and reminded him. He was the final shred of hope, the last defense. He was the one for the ones who had none.

He stared off toward the line dividing something and nothing. Not the line dividing life and death, for even death was something. Contemplations floated through his head about which side he felt closer to today. He hadn't been able to save that teenage boy two days ago, the one whose clan had eaten his father in recompense for a murder. The one who had wailed that if he couldn't be with his father, then he couldn't be.

Today, Paarsisoq leaned toward nothing.

Sounds of anguish came sailing over the ice, pulling him from his ponderings. Without even looking, he knew it was a woman, and she wanted to die forever.

He followed the sounds with his ears until he could follow the woman with his eyes. Tiaavuluk, she was beautiful. He directed his pace until he strode alongside her. She calmed her cries but didn't stop the tears rolling down her face. The Watcher waited until they were close to the brink to break the silence.

"Before you go, please share some of my caribou. I've just recently killed it and can't possibly finish it all by myself."

She turned to give him a quizzical look. He tried not to react to the bruises purpling the left side of her face.

"It's a long way to the bottom, and I can't imagine falling all that way on an empty stomach."

Her brow stayed plastered in a pained frown until at last she gave the slightest of nods.

"Right this way." He hooked a gentle hand under her arm and led her toward his igloo. After directing her to a seat carved of ice out front, he set about preparing the meat.

"Beautiful, isn't it?" he asked as she stared into the darkness beyond the door. "In its own strange way."

"I suppose."

Wow, she really was a spectacle, albeit a laconic one. But beauty was not the ultimate ward against hardship.

"That's why you're here, no? You find more beauty out there," he motioned to the abyss, "than out there." He motioned his other hand at the ice. "You'd rather jump and forget you ever existed than spend another day with your tribulations."

"I suppose." She took the meat he offered.

"Well, if you need a few days to consider, then I have plenty of room and extra blankets in the igloo." He took a bite himself.

She swallowed then paused in bringing the next bite to her mouth. The woman licked her lips and tried twice to talk before finally getting words out. "Will you... will you just hold me?"

The Watcher quirked an eyebrow, then scooted around beside her and took the distraught girl in his arms. She returned the embrace and shook with sobs. He ran his hand across her back until the heaving dwindled to staggered puffs.

"I don't know who you are," she said, "but I know what you are. You're a miracle." She shuddered out a breath. "I've heard stories about you. The Watcher. A man I met told me you not only saved his life, but his existence. After my daughter... after she died, I realized that I either wanted to get a new life, or I didn't want to exist."

"A new life? And what did your old life consist of?" He pulled back to look at her. Tiaavuluk, bruising notwithstanding, she had him stunned.

The woman shook her head. "Please, I'd rather not say. I think that goes against the principle of getting a new life. Do you mind if..."

He drew her in again, and they sat swaddled in the mile-thin hush of neglected eternity. Their twinned breathing quilted the air with a patchwork of truths unuttered, resonances that heavy spirits needn't—or couldn't—speak. Minutes brushed by like eyelashes batting flakes in a soundless storm.

"I can't tell you how much it means to be held by someone who doesn't have any preconceptions about who I am," the woman whispered after a spell. "I can't remember the last time I actually felt loved, but I'll never forget this. I don't quite understand it, but somehow I can feel that you love me even though we've just met."

Paarsisoq nodded. "I love everybody that is driven to the end of the world. I can't help it. That's why this job is sometimes hard—harder than I imagined, at least. Every time I fail, and someone casts themselves into the infinite nothing, I feel like a piece of me is destroyed with them."

Her gaze lingered on him. "You're a good man, Watcher. I wish I could say that about most of the men I've met."

"How'd your daughter die?"

The woman's face distorted with grief and anger. "She... I don't... it was at the hands of some of those not so good men from my past life. And that's all I really can say about it at this point."

The Watcher laid a hand on her knee. "Say no more." He looked to the void. "Do you still plan on taking a hop out there, or do you fancy a new life?"

She smiled. "It's very hard to think of anything positive, but you've given me hope that if I can find someplace that doesn't know about my past life, and that will take me in, I can regain some happiness."

He chuckled. "Am I really that potent?"

She took him by the shoulder. "You really are."

His heart sputtered, and words failed him.

"Is the offer to stay a few days still open?" she asked.

"Absolutely."

Three sunrises later, the pair stood once again at the edge of the earth, staring into the oblivion that could have been.

"Paarsisoq," she said.

"Hm?"

"I can't thank you enough for the love and hospitality you've shown me. It's been many years since I've received such kindness."

"Anything to keep you from the edge."

She granted a smile. "I—I want to tell you about my past life. Partly because I like you, and partly because I just need to tell someone."

He wanted to tell her to stop. Tell her he didn't need to know who she had been, just who she was and who she was becoming. Under that rode the fear that if she told him about her old life, then he could never be a part of her new life. He would forever be just a stepping stone. But he didn't devote his life to watching to be served, but to serve. So, Paarsisoq listened.

"I was a whore. I hate to even say it out loud. It was never my choice. When I was fourteen, my clan had a really bad hunting season and were starving. They decided to sell a girl to Atortittartut, and I was the lucky one. I was always plotting ways to get away from that life, but nothing ever worked out. The pimp is a hard man. He stopped everything I tried and beat me to make sure I wouldn't try it again.

"I've had six children. Three didn't live past infancy. Two of the healthy ones were boys. I still don't know what happened to them, whether they're alive or not today. They just disappeared one day. The only one that's always been by me is my little girl, my Issuaq. I loved her so much it hurt my bones. But I knew what they were going to do with her. Prostitute her out once she was old enough. That's what they do with all the bastard daughters.

"They usually don't start them till at least twelve, but a man with a lot of money came through and demanded a girl under ten. They tore Issuaq from me. My precious daughter, hardly even nine years old, forced to do that. I don't know exactly what the man did, but whatever evil that disgusting cur worked on my baby, she didn't survive.

"I killed him. Strangled him. He kept punching me in the face." She motioned to the blotted contusions. "But his punches got less and less powerful. Eventually he stopped moving. Then I ran. I had—have—nothing left. Didn't even have the will to live left, but you helped me with that."

Paarsisoq didn't know what to say, and he suspected that nothing he could say would help, so instead he wrapped his arms around her. The world held its breath as they slowly rocked back and forth at the start of the sky.

"You could make your new life here, you know."

She swallowed. "I know. But I have this settled feeling that I need to see what the world has to offer me. I can't stay in one place for too long after what happened with my daughter. It makes me too anxious. But I'll be back, don't worry. I love you, Paarsisoq."

"I love you too, Kitornak."

They pressed a kiss on one another's lips, then Kitornak turned and headed south.

Today, Paarsisoq leaned toward something.

Orluvoq touched down a mile outside of the Terianniaq enclave. Making herself light had been much better than winding up as a red splat on an igloo, but it gave the wind a lot more say in which way she went. Miraculously, her candle was no shorter than when she entered Arsarneq. She would have to try skywalking again if she made it past the next couple days. Maybe she could volunteer and be the one who skywalked to the origin of the aurora.

Actually, that seemed like a much better plan than waiting to get murdered by someone who dabbled in the things to avoid. She looked at the fading trail of green up above. Skywalking would have to wait, and she would need to be taken up by a hunter anyway.

Well, and no one knows how far it is to the start of Arsarneq. I could go up at the end of the earth and skywalk all night, and then it could just disappear, and I would fall into Nunapisu. Maybe getting killed is better.

She affected some healing on her lips, then set off toward the igloos, sapping heat as she went. Walking would keep her from showing up too soon. Nervous excitement built in her stomach. She took off a glove to clutch the totem beneath her parka. Still there. It was time to become Terianniaq again. She briefly wondered if whatever Captain Naalagaa had planned to do with her would be preferable to getting killed by an evil angakkuq.

Orluvoq pulled up to the igloo cluster's main entrance and waited. She made sure to only leech the barest amount of heat in case she needed the candle later. The odd nibble of tuuaaq helped in that department as well.

After what seemed like years, a middle-aged woman came out the igloo's mouth. A look of censure flooded her face.

"Girl, what are you doing out—" Her mouth dropped, and she rushed forward. "Who gave you permission to take a special candle?"

Orluvoq jerked away as the woman tried to grab it.

"Give it here."

Orluvoq shook her head. "It's mine."

"No, it's not." The woman reached for it and missed again. "Whose are you anyway? My memory can't be going bad already."

"I'm the daughter of Nataaq and Anaava. I've come home."

The woman's expression cycled between anger, confusion, shock, and finally fear. "You—you're Orluvoq?" She turned back to the door. "Wait here." And she was gone.

A moment later, the creased faces of the archons emerged one after another. Orluvoq couldn't tell which was uglier. She didn't think that it mattered, though, after reaching a certain amount of ugly. Surprise painted the two ugly faces. More faces, much less ugly, filtered out of the igloos.

"Orluvoq," said the matriarch. "You have returned, though we are not sure why. We are happy to house travelers for a few nights, but—"

"Last time I was here you said that you'd be happy to welcome one of your own into Terianniaq. I am one of your own." Orluvoq battled equally hard to keep defiance and despair out of her voice, losing on both fronts.

"Child," said the patriarch, "of course we said that, but you forgot to add that we must see a token of kinship."

Orluvoq reached around her neck, removed the bone trinket, then proffered it for their aged eyes to see. A subdued gasp moved through the small audience. The archons' eyebrows rose in tandem. The patriarch reached out an ungloved hand to touch the token.

"It seems you have indeed acquired yourself a token, Orluvoq. But how can we be sure it's not a forgery?"

The question hit Orluvoq like an open-handed slap. Tears pooled in her eyes. "Please. *Please*. There's no way it can be a fake. I have traveled to Nunapisu and seen the darkness. I have climbed down the wall of the dead and found my mother. I *found* this. I am Terianniaq!"

"Well, now we know the token isn't real," said the matriarch. "No one can scale the neverending wall and find one body among the many."

Orluvoq fell to her knees and held up her candle. "Please. I'm an angakkuq. I used the candles to seek her out. What more could you want?"

"Patriarch Inupaj, Matriarch Arnaqqua," a man broke in. "I may not be the wisest among us, but I think this can be determined quickly by fetching Sauneq. He's been carving our tokens for many decades and knows his cuts better than I know my children."

The archons hesitated, then Matriarch Arnaqqua nodded. "Bring us Sauneq."

A minute later, a man almost as old as the archons, but not as ugly, was turning the bone carving over in his fingers. "Mm, yes," he mumbled to himself. "Cut, slick... stagger. Yep. Flourish..." He coughed and looked up. "Archons. I carved this token myself. Fourteen years ago, if I'm right. I think it went to that Anaava girl. Where has she been?"

Relief washed over Orluvoq.

Whiteness crept out from the archons' pressed lines of mouths. "Thank you, Sauneq." The patriarch motioned for him to give the token back to Orluvoq.

"So, Orluvoq," Patriarch Inupaj continued, "whatever you did and however you did it, you do indeed have a genuine token of Terianniaq kinship. However..." He looked to a man in the crowd. "We can't accept those who work the blue flame, and you, Orluvoq, have been dabbling in the things to avoid."

Orluvoq's face folded into almost as many creases as the man addressing her. "What? I've never used a blue candle. Where would I even get one? I'm not a murderer."

"Ah." The patriarch smiled. "By the very fact that at your age you know what it is, you are implicated. But that is not all." He nodded at the man in the crowd.

"I, the angakkuq of Terianniaq," said the man, "have cast myself into visions of you at the archons' request. The visions do not show all, but I saw scraps of you in a cave with five blue flames alight. I then saw you at the end of the world with a blue flame."

"Thank you." Patriarch Inupaj nodded at the angakkuq then turned back to Orluvoq. "You leave with nothing. You come back with your mother's token, robbed from her resting corpse. No one else has done such a thing. No one, except the tirigusuusiit, those wicked workers of the blue flame. The tirigusuusiit are vile creatures, and are never welcome among the noble Terianniaq, no matter what blood they have." He leaned in close. "And they usually have more than just their own."

Orluvoq shook as she cried and sank to the ice. "No. Please. I'm not a tirigusuusik. I've never touched a blue candle or killed anybody. I'm just a girl with no Mama or Daddy. I'm just a girl with no Mama or Daddy." The last line was nearly incomprehensible, garbled by sobs and snow.

The gathering spoke no words and moved no muscles. Only the sounds of a weeping girl filled the air. Slowly, the people disappeared until only the archons stood before her.

"We have spoken twice, Orluvoq," said the matriarch. "Go. Do not return to Terianniaq. If we have to speak against you a third time, you will not get off so easy."

The words registered in Orluvoq's brain, but they didn't find her spirit. She thought she had no hope left they could take from her. Clueless girl. Helpless girl. Hopeless girl.

They must accept the token. She hadn't expected them to find some loophole around it. Why was it so hard for them to take her back? She was just one little girl who could work the candles. No one in their right mind would consider her a burden. They couldn't actually think she was a tirigusuusik. Unless the angakkuq was weak and his visions unclear.

I hate me. I hate them. She lifted her head, but no one was there. *I hate them.*

Not helpless.

She stood, took a big, gritty bite of tuuaaq, thoughtless for the crash it would bring, thoughtless for the shame she brought her mother, and began chanting to her candle. Her legs ripped into motion and took her windwalking through the igloo complex like an angry white bear. The tuuaaq within her effervesced into gleeful rage. Ceilings and walls melted at her passing. Screams. Everywhere she appeared, screams clawed the air. She crashed through the hound room and the dogs went wild.

The high north was a plane for demons. On unlucky days, so was the south.

"Stop her!"

She laughed pure scorn at the one who shouted. *I am more powerful than any of you will ever be.* She barreled a woman off her feet and sent her through the wall.

She bit off another heaping chunk of tuuaaq. Artificial euphoria swirled around the natural joy of wreaking havoc. The fresh burst of elation almost knocked her off her feet. She slowed to a stop and looked around her. People cowered, covering their possessions and loved ones. Others approached with hands held up to guard or grab, whichever turned out to be necessary.

Orluvoq gazed at the heat gleaming inside her.

Heat. Tuuaaq. Inside. Nalor. Burn. Ignite.

She funneled it all into the flame. For a moment, she would have sworn it flickered blue. Heat erupted from the glim, brushed her by, and slammed into everything else. Bodies flew back, and the entire igloo enclave flowed down at her feet.

Screaming. A lake of it.

Orluvoq swayed woozily and opened her eyes. Yelping dogs struggled to stay afloat. Fur parkas dragged people down as they flailed in chest-deep water. She stood on the surface of the lake, watching their struggles. How many would make it to the shore, and how many would freeze and die after that? Already ice crept along the edges. A child struggled through thickening slush.

Seeing that her not-blue candle was almost gone, she queried it for the location of the closest tuuaaq. She followed the tug in her gut until she could see a cluster of candles under her feet. Trying something new, she commanded the water to swirl until the candles rose to the top. She snatched them up and looked for the archons.

"You." She pointed to Patriarch Inupaj who was trying to remove his coat and make it to dry ice.

He looked up at her, his ancient face stricken with fear. "You've destroyed everything and killed three people!"

The news made her feel a little sick, but she carried on. "I have spoken once about clan Terianniaq. If I have to speak against you a second time, you will not get off so easy."

Before he could respond, she broke into a run, wind-walking back onto the ice and into the depths of the wild.

No.

Orluvoq stumbled across the ice. Having left off the windwalking an hour before, she called on the candle for warmth only.

No. Everything was wrong. Her mother was dead. Her father was dead. People that *she had killed* were dead. But she wasn't.

The tuuaaq wasn't doing a good enough job. How could she feel so good and so bad at the same time? Where was the mental healing? All it did was make her feel good, not happy. Made her feel strong, not be strong.

She needed more.

Even though she had taken a bite just half an hour before, she set the tusk between her molars and snapped some into her mouth. Too much. No, not enough. The granular paste threatened her with nausea, but she didn't care. It needed to be in her stomach.

It almost came back up when she swallowed, but she doubled over and made it stay. Half a minute later, a whiteness purer than the freshly driven snow exploded into her vision and she was lost.

Orluvoq awoke. That wasn't good. It meant she was alive. She still felt good. But she still felt bad. At least she hadn't felt anything for a while.

Why can't I die? I know how to do it. She hated that she couldn't do it. Hated that little voice—that stupid survival instinct—that always kept her above the ice. *Just take off all your clothes and go to sleep.*

Couldn't.

Stop drawing warmth from the candle.

Couldn't.

Summon a white bear and command it to tear you.

Couldn't.

Don't melt down any snow the next time you're thirsty.

Couldn't.

Burn yourself alive with the candle.

Couldn't.

Cry until you have no more tears than hope.

That she could do.

She rocked back and forth, huddled over her candle, tear-blurred vision blocking the horizon. *I have nothing. I am nothing. I was never anything. It was my parents that were something.* For a scintillating moment, she hadn't been helpless. She had reigned, grander than the king at Qilaknakka. But her self-help had been worse than her impotence. What good was the strength that could only destroy?

Maybe she could go back to Paarsisoq, but could she

really live like that, just staring into darkness all day? She could try to find Nalor, but he said she couldn't join him for at least eight years. The only other option was whatever Captain Naalagaa had planned for her, but that—

Wait.

She rubbed and blinked until her eyes were mostly tear-free.

It was a person. Someone was running across the ice toward her. Who on earth could it be? No one ran between clans alone. At the very least, they took a couple dogs. The only solo runners were—

Angakkuit.

Her pace picked up. This angakkuq came from the direction of Terianniaq, and a substantial amount of money said that he brought wrathful spirits with him. Not that the Teri-anniaq angakkuq could do anything to her she didn't want him to. Unless he had blue candles.

Even now I want it to be someone scary that will kill me, but I hope it's someone coming to save me. She scoffed. *I still have room for hope? I thought I was done with that.*

She squinted at the sprinting form. It wasn't exactly sprinting, though. More in the range between loping and scrambling. Lurching. A tingle of fear tickled down her spine, percolating through the brume of the tuuaaq.

She stood and clutched her candle closer, trying to engage in light meditation just in case. The movements rang familiar. The unnatural gait...

Come on! she shouted at her tuuaaq-addled brain. The forbidding figure was four or five seconds off when she noticed the glowing blue eyes.

Oh. Her blood iced over, and she breathed a quick invo-cation to her candle. The ice sped by underneath her as she bolted into a windwalk. *I'm actually getting kind of quick at that.*

She looked behind her at the thing that towered over her. The conjure-bound corpse kept pace but gained no ground. *Spirits! He has burns all over. Did I do that?*

Yes, she had provided whoever the tirigusuusik of Terianniaq was with fresh bodies to make blue. It had to be the angakkuq, right? Unless someone was very good at hiding their pastime.

So, what now? Do I just run until either it or I run out of candles? There were certainly less exciting ways to go. *But what if it eats me?* The thought sent a shudder through her, and she almost tripped. *Then I'll never be with Mama and Daddy.*

What did Nalor do back on the cliff? I think he tapped into its mind and then tore its head off with his mind. He also had a blue candle. Nonetheless, allowing for her to have one of those wouldn't give her enough time to reverse engineer Nalor's methods.

Could I burn it with a burst like I did back at Terianniaq? That was probably her best option. If it failed, then she would go quickly, though likely not painlessly. Then she could stop worrying about all the cruelty and hardness of life.

All out of naked tuuaaq, Orluvoq took a candle out of her pocket and bit off the wick at the top. She checked over her shoulder—still safe—then felt for the light inside her. She watched it bloom and prepared to funnel it to her flame.

She swiveled around and drove all the light inside to the candle. The blast of heat once again swept her by and ripped the bluebody from the ground, tossing it like a snowball in a storm. This time she *knew* she'd glimpsed a flash of blue before shutting her eyes. Where had she gotten this candle?

She slid to a standstill and watched the desiccated form. Watched it right itself and retake the pursuit. Her heart slid to a standstill. The man's clothes fell off as he charged her, his entire frontside charred to an unrecognizable black and red—all except the eyes, which oozed a lustrous blue.

No. How is he not dead yet? The obvious answer was that he *was* dead. Orluvoq had killed him. Nalor's voice came to her, *"You would find them a bit... different than you remember them. Much less enjoyable company."*

Exhausted by overdoses of adrenaline and tuuaaq and an underdose of sleep, she spun about and pitched back into windwalking. *I need to keep doing that until its eyes stop glowing, or until there's not enough of it left to chase me.* She denuded the tuuaaq in her left hand of its wax and took another bite. Timing everything so the bluebody's distance and her channeling of inner light lined up, she swiveled and let off another burst of superheated air.

The scorched cadaver flew backward, crashing across the ice. Orluvoq stopped and waited, breaths coming almost as quickly as her heartbeat. The twiggy black body struggled to its feet, hobbled out a few steps, then collapsed. Cautiously, she approached, slipping in another bite of tuuaaq.

The thing still vaguely resembled a human. No one could have convinced her to try healing it had they brought it to her. It reached up to her with its devastated arms, eyeballess eyes still seeping out the lambent blue.

She sat down a small way off from the laboring remains. *Alright, I need to finish it. I have to make the lights go out of the eyes.* But as much as she told herself that, she couldn't. In the heat of the moment, she did what she did, but sitting here in the relative calm she couldn't help but think of it as a person.

Stupid. You already killed him. You need to show him the proper respect by ending this connection so he can be taken by to Nunapisu. Why was it so much more different—

The corpse heaved up from the ground and threw itself on the girl. She screamed and tapped into the tuuaaq light filling her body, venting another discharge of heat. The bluebody flew into the air and crunched back down. A look at the eyes told her that, finally, it was just a body.

She slumped back and let sleep take her.

ECHOES BOUNCED around as though in a giant ice cave as the ground rocked. The echoes got louder until Orluvoq opened her eyes.

"Hey."

Her vision came into focus and the voice found an identity. Nalor.

"Can I just say that I'm a huge fan?" He chipped off a laugh. "I mean, I thought you were going to die. Thought to myself, what is she going to do, just run until she runs out of candles? 'To burn this candle to its end is to burn this candle to no end,' and all that. And then you flip around and land a solid, concussive heat blast. Amazing!"

Orluvoq scowled at the man silhouetted against the night sky above. "You were there? Why didn't you help me? I was about to get eaten by a bluebody."

"Ah, yes, I can see why you would be confused." He pulled her to a sitting position and gave her some fat to eat. "I used a tirigusuusik trick to cast my spirit out of my body and find you. Like a more powerful angakkuq vision. I was belatedly worried that you walking into the den of whatever evil tirigusuusik had already tried to kill you might not be the best of ideas. At any rate, by the time I found you, the bluebody was upon you. No amount of skywalking, even through Arsarneq, would have gotten me there. So, I resigned to watching. And how fantastic you were! A girl of —how old are you?"

Orluvoq finished the fat, then accepted a drink from him. She finished her quaff with a smack of the lips. "Eight."

"An untrained girl of eight, single handedly taking down a bluebody in the Nuktipik wastes. That's a spectacle that has a hard time finding its equal." He shook his head, smiling to himself.

"Did you, um, see Terianniaq?" She drew shapes in the snow, not meeting his eyes.

He tutted. "Did I see Terianniaq, indeed. You've made a hot mess of your old stomping grounds. How does that make you feel?"

She shrugged. "I don't know. Bad, I guess. It felt good at the time. They ruined my life forever, so I ruined theirs for a while."

"A while?" Nalor quirked an eyebrow and flitted his eyes to the ghastly remains. "Death certainly does last a *while*, you cheeky supreme. But better them than you, in my opinion. I believe someone in your old clan had something of a feud going with your parents."

She chewed on his words, particularly the part about death lasting a while. She would have preferred chewing tuuaaq. "What happens now? Do I die?"

The question plucked a deep laugh from Nalor. "If that's your wish, you'll get the dish. But after seeing all the trouble you went to to not be killed by a bluebody, I suspect that's not what you truly desire. What do you think?"

She grumbled something indistinct, unsure how to correlate her thoughts, feelings, and actions.

"That bad, huh? Well, just to tame any errant thoughts you may entertain: you can't come with me. As fantastic and talented as you may be, I can't care for a child."

"For someone who can't care for a child, you sure have gone far out of your way to care for a child," Orluvoq shot back.

"Ha, right you are." He poked her collarbone. "But I'm not looking for anything permanent right now. Think of it more as... securing my investments."

"Okay." Whatever that meant.

"So. You don't have a clan to go to. You can't come with me. How'd you like to return to your old ship?"

"Not a whole lot."

"Not a whole lot, she says." He gave a close-lipped smile. "And I assume child prostitution is off the board? Right. I think that leaves the only option as becoming Watcher Junior."

She groaned. "But I don't want to stare into the darkness for the rest of my life. And Paarsisoq doesn't let me eat tuuaaq."

"Well, you've convinced me. I'm leaving you here." He stood and lit his blue candle.

"Wait, no." Orluvoq grabbed the hem of his coat despite the drenching cold. "Please, take me to Nunapisu. I'll stay there for a while, then figure out something else to do."

Nalor grinned. "As you wish." He threw her on his back and skywalked northward.

❄

ORLUVOQ STARED into the black expanse. The end of the world. Nunapisu. The place where the aurora and narwhals and tuuaaq came from. The place where she could go eternally with one big step. Her parents had died. Her clan had rejected her twice. She had *killed* people. And she couldn't even go a whole day without eating at least some tuuaaq.

Every day she better understood why Paarsisoq was so against it. It wasn't as fun as it used to be. She used to eat it because it took her to a new plane of existence. Now she ate it because life without it was a torturous slog. She ate it because she had to remain on that new plane of existence. False strength. It locked her into helplessness rather than liberated.

The last couple weeks at the end of the world had bored her terribly. Paarsisoq made her use the candles and tuuaaq sparingly, as they were never sure when they would be able to get more from travelers. But at the very least, she had concluded that she wanted to live.

Of course, the next day she had decided that death was the finer option. A few hours after that, life took the lead. The life-and-death struggle had continued ever since.

The subdued crunch of snow told her that Paarsisoq approached the cliff. She didn't particularly want to talk to him, but there wasn't much else to do.

"What do you see?" he asked.

"The darkness that has no end. It's like staring at a representation of my life." She flicked her thumbnail off the tuuaaq in her pocket.

"You know, it's kind of silly. I once loved a woman who lost a daughter about your age. When you came to Nunapisu, a clanless orphan, it reminded me of our love and I fancied I might raise you in memory of her. It would be a broken version of the broken family I never had."

"What happened? Between you and the woman?" Orluvoq broke off a crumb of tuuaaq in her pocket and discreetly slipped it into her mouth.

"You know, I've helped lots of people in my days, but she's the person that's helped me the most. She was only in my life for a short time, then she had to leave. I haven't seen her since, and I often wonder if she ever found happiness."

Something twitched in Orluvoq's heart. *I'm not the only person with problems. What sorts of problems has Paarsisoq had? And how many people has he helped? That woman was only with him for a couple days, but she helped him more than anyone. Maybe, just maybe, I could try to help him. Try to be like her.*

"Where will you go now, Orluvoq? You are a nearly peerless angakkuq, especially for your age. You could go anywhere, except for Terianniaq, I suppose."

She noticed that included the option of jumping into the abyss. "I—could I stay here?"

He turned to face her. "You want to stay with me? An old man who's spent most of his life away from people? A middling angakkuq? Someone with many acquaintances, but few friends?"

She nodded. "Because you accept me. A broken family is better than no family."

Paarsisoq's careworn face cracked into a smile. "Shall we make our own clan? Call it the Watchers?"

Orluvoq giggled. "Yes, please."

He snatched her from the ground and spun her around. "Well then, my *daughter*, how about clan Watcher has its first official meal together?" She agreed, and they entered the igloo. She spent the rest of the day fighting the urge to eat tuuaaq and only failed one little time.

Evening came early. Winter was yawning and soon it

would swallow them whole. Before the sun had completely bled out of the sky, clan Watcher heard the approach of footsteps crunching over the ice. As proper Watchers, they hastened out to greet the traveler.

Paarsisoq exited first and Orluvoq watched him stop dead in his tracks, jaw slack. She hurried out behind him to discover who or what could be so enchanting. Her face broke into a smile and she ran forward. "Kitornak!"

The scullery maid from the ship laughed as the little girl jumped into her arms. "Oh, my dear Orluvoq, I've been worried to, well, to Nunapisu about you. I'm so happy to find you alive and well." She put the girl down and turned to the Watcher.

"Kitornak," he whispered. Orluvoq saw a tear track down his face.

"Paarsisoq," she whispered back.

They rushed forward and encircled one another in an airtight hug.

"You came back," he said.

"I told you I would. I told you." She sniffed. "And I meant it."

Wait, Kitornak is the woman Paarsisoq was talking about?

"I waited. Sixteen years. What finally made you come back?"

"Orluvoq started it. We lived on the same ship, then she ran off to here. It wouldn't work out of my consciousness, letting a little girl roam the ice alone, so I finally left the ship to see if I could find her and... and maybe be a mother to her."

The pair pulled apart. "Well, you've come at just the right time. Orluvoq and I have decided to start our own clan. Clan Watcher. Would you like to join us?"

A smile as wide as the cliff they stood on spread across Kitornak's face. "I would want nothing more."

Orluvoq pulled her hand out of the pocket where she had been toying with some tuuaaq and grabbed Kitornak's hand instead. The urge to take a bite of the tusk prickled inside like mad, but she pushed it back down this time. Real strength?

She turned and watched the crystal dance of flakes glitter orange before the darkness of infinity. In the midst of the tractless expanse, a spine of green and purple lanced forth. Stars winked awake. Her other hand reached up and found Paarsisoq's. They stood like that a long while, watching Arsarneq crawl through the heavens.

Most of her wanted to be happy, but a darkened nook of her murmured cold imprecations against getting comfortable. After all, love was the precursor to pain. She decided to ignore her darkened nooks, at least for tonight.

When a yawn took over Orluvoq an hour later, Kitornak suggested they retire for the night. Two parents tucked her in. Two parents kissed her cheeks. Two parents snuffed the candles and sang softly of times before and times beyond.

Finally, she was home.

The spire of tuuaaq leered at Orluvoq beneath the midnight sun. As heaven's fiery ball sipped the horizon, amber dribbled out across the world and splashed against the white tusk. She twirled it slowly in her new mitts, sized for thirteen-year-old hands.

Skimming for moss. That's what she'd told her parents she was off to do. Not standing on the deck of one of the abandoned ship carcasses a league from home. She needed the two elder Watchers untouched by worry. The best remedy for staving off worry was cluelessness.

For years Orluvoq had followed Paarsisoq and Kitornak's admonition against partaking of the crooked horn. Holding the itch in denial. Tonight, she would answer a question that had been strafing her all the while. How could she be strong if she only hid from challenge?

The tusk mythologized strength. It filled her breast with an empire of hero-strummed notes, and so wreathed in the echoes of valor, she fancied that the song had been hers. And as it curried her with its sleight, it twined its fetters about her in climbing, cloven knots which she had no prayer of loosing. While she wandered a vagabond in the tusk's mythology of strength, it purpled her face with its grip.

Helpless. Whenever she locked horns with the tusk, she proffered open invitation to helplessness. Or, she had nearly five years ago. Tonight, she commenced on the path of the conqueror. Before the nights grew dark, she would be able to devour her oldest antagonist without it devouring her. The days of hiding from challenge were over.

She raised the stick of tuuaaq to her lips and snapped off a chip. Boils of nervousness, tumid from years of anticipation, burst in her gut like coughing stars. In seconds, the old effervescence would shatter through her veins in liquid maelstroms. It wouldn't break her. She would command. It wouldn't—

It clapped her like the cupped hand of a lightning storm to the ear, and she stumbled from the abandoned ship deck. She fell to the heights of Nunapisu and back. The midnight sun rolled, circling her head like a halo. Snow pillows burst into glamor after golden glamor of speck and sparkle. She led the birds in a choir of laughter.

The euphoria put her memories to shame.

Underlying the entire unearthly moment was the song. That immortal after-hum of gallantry unrivaled. In her head. In her head. It rang of power in her head. It must have come from *her*. *She* was the hero the notes proclaimed. Slayer of demons. Savior of peoples. She was Orluvoq, and she could do all.

No. It's not. It's not. She managed to inject a thought of her own. *It's the tuuaaq. It's fake. It's all fake. I can do this. I will do this.*

So, she struggled. Euphoria embrittled her mental grip

each time she built it up. Hours rolled on. The sun peeled away from the far horizon and climbed.

She practiced talking. "Hello Mom and Dad. It's just me, your daughter, out late or early or, you know, just sort of out and doing stuff, not really important, but fun. Definitely fun. Way fun. Do you guys do fun? It's night but the sun is up, and that's fun, but not fun because no aurora and no narwhals, and what if we run out of tuuaaq? Not fun. But still fun. Ha-ha! That's good. We're good. I'm just great. Been out late, maybe early. Been fun."

Right. *That* wouldn't make them suspicious. She tried again, pacing round and round, until she could almost say just one sentence at a time. Until almost her thoughts were hers. Until, capillary by capillary, she almost reclaimed her brain. Beneath the ecstasy, she exulted in the victory, incomplete as it was.

Strength. Real strength.

Not helpless.

She fell to the snow, laughing through the morning frost. Not helpless! She could be stronger than the tusk. No more stumbling across the tundra, letting her hands freeze black. No more fighting the itch. No more hiding.

Her laughter rattled on far longer than someone not on the sweet tooth would have shaken for.

THE SPIRE of tuuaaq stared at Orluvoq beneath the midnight sun. Should she have been trying it again so soon? After the first success, how could she not?

The bite nipped her tongue with its bitter, chalky pulp, but to her it diffused sweetness through her throat. After the initial explosion of sensation, she set about her exercises of normalcy once more. Walking, talking, sewing, eating, drinking, packing snowballs, rolling down hills, chasing foxes, scaling the abandoned ship masts. She mostly motored through, only going too fast on—well, on all of it. But that was fine. She floated on the cloud of tuuaaq-supplied giddiness all the while.

Finally, finally she was becoming someone who she could rely on. She could scarcely remember a time she felt so optimistic. The urge to run and tell her parents leapt within her, but she knew time must be bided. Unless she could exhibit complete control, they would be horrified if she told them. They would have to be clueless a while longer.

As the high dropped and the hour of her parents' waking neared, she held the raw tuuaaq in her gaze. She could take a smidge more. Just enough to ease her into the day. It would help her appear less tired to the two archons of the Watcher clan.

No. She wasn't strong enough yet. Perhaps soon.

THE SPIRE of tuuaaq smiled at Orluvoq beneath the midnight sun. "Hello to you," it seemed to say. Eight nights over the past few weeks she had taken up the struggle, and eight nights she had grown in strength. Her thoughts were largely hers. Her words were often hers. Her movements sometimes bore jitters and spasms. But either this time or the next, she would return home under the spell of the sweet tooth. This next challenge, passing undetected before her parents, she would not hide from it.

When morning came and she made the trek back, she pocketed the tuuaaq with great reluctance and no new bites.

Not quite ready. But soon. Definitely. She smiled as she trotted. Simply choosing was its own act of strength.

The day ambled on and her mind wandered to the time when she'd next battle against the crooked horn. Maybe that night? She'd already kept wide eyes through one night. Another likely would do her little good. But she needed the practice. She needed the tusk. The turmoil fed into itself again and again. When her mother asked her to look at mending some snowshoes, she snapped.

"No! You fix the stupid shoes. I have more important things to worry about." She stomped past the igloo at the end of the world.

"Orluvoq," said Kitornak. "What has gotten into you?"

Nothing, she grumbled to herself. *And that's the problem. Nothing in me right now.*

Night couldn't come soon enough.

THE SPIRE of tuuaaq beamed at Orluvoq beneath the midnight sun. Finally, she could put her time to good use. She bit down and lost herself in the work. When she finally revealed her newfound power to her parents, they would be so proud. Beaming, just like the tuuaaq. She went hunting for hares without a candle to guide her.

THE SPIRE of tuuaaq twinkled at Orluvoq beneath the midnight sun. She chewed her chunk and danced her glee. Daytime did nothing but drag. Dullard's delight. She could have flung herself into the abyss just to escape the inanity. Come the hour of her parents' sleep, come the hour of her strength. Perhaps she should just start sleeping during the day, then rise in the evening to pursue the heights. She smiled at the thought as she ran along Nunapisu's edge.

THE SPIRE of tuuaaq laughed at Orluvoq beneath the noonday sun. Finally, not limiting herself to nocturnal haunts, for what were limits but weakness? The point at which you became helpless? If she couldn't take the tusk whenever, then who was the true master?

It was said the king at the start of the world had mastered the art of the angakkuq, but had he mastered the tusk itself? With power over both candle and tusk, who was to say *she* couldn't run south and become queen?

THE SPIRE of tuuaaq cackled at Orluvoq beneath a gray pall of evening cloud cast. "We are the best of enemies, are we not?" it told her. She bit her assent and cavorted away.

THE TUUAAQ CALLED to her from within a dream. "Come test me," it said. "Are you strong enough to break from your sleep and fight me?"

She roused from her slumber and answered the call.

THE TUUAAQ PULLED her wherever she sat. It pulled her from between her parents. It pulled her from the caribou hunt. It pulled her from the suicidal wanderer headed for the world's dark end. Pulled her Watcher's eyes from what they ought behold. Pulled her anywhere into the white wilderness that it thought she might follow. The tuuaaq pulled.

THE TUUAAQ KNEW.

THE TUUAAQ *KNEW.*

THE SPIRE of tuuaaq leered at her beneath a clear sky of morning blue. Orluvoq held it before her mouth, but she could not bite, for she, too, knew. She was not strong. She was not able. These past months she had courted delusion. It was all false. She was still broken.

Still helpless.

She twisted her hands in sweat-soaked gloves around the crooked horn. She had tried, and she had failed. Like the havoc she'd strewn when she'd tried to rejoin her clan. There was but one path left for her.

Hide.

She gripped the tusk as hard as she could, then wound her arm back and slung it sailing off over the tundra. A shallow drift of top-snow swallowed it without a puff of noise. Time held its breath as she stared at the distance where it had vanished.

The tuuaaq pulled. It guggled between her scalp and skull like air gulping water.

It knew.

The taste fuzzed the back of her tongue.

It *knew*.

Her body shivered in jagged convolution. She had to hide.

Orluvoq turned and began the walk back home. Slow, heavy, empty.

THE SPIRE of tuuaaq nodded to her as she clawed it out from the wet snow, inklings of aurora feathering the sky. Two days it had pulled. Two days she had pushed. Two days it had spat, and two days she had swallowed.

Tears striped her face as she lifted the tusk to her gritted teeth. Hunched over the frozen wastes, she punched the ground. She punched it again. Hard packed ice broke knuckle skin through gloves. She shouldn't be here. How could something that felt so good hurt so much? No matter how much she took from it, it took more from her.

Yet here she'd come again.

Orluvoq screamed between sobs, and after the scream, she chewed.

THE SPIRE of tuuaaq leered at her before Nunapisu's inked-out depths. It knew she was too weak to fight it. It had always known. Through every "scrimmage" it had been smiling behind a hand.

She wanted to run as she'd done years ago, but this time to the southron reaches. Find Nalor. Beg him to unfold to her all the esoterica of his mastery. She loved her parents, but neither of them was truly powerful. These five years, she hadn't found the strength she *needed* from them, though they'd given her much.

Five more years until that day she could sip from Nalor's cup. Almost half a life. In the meantime, she stood here with the crooked horn.

It knew. As she raised the cursed tooth, it knew. From the tremble of her hand to the tightness around her eyes, it *knew*. It knew she was helpless. It knew—

She threw it. Flung it as far as her muscles would fling. The tuuaaq screamed as it tumbled into the black of forever, profaning her name in the plunge. She watched it disbelieving until there wasn't a scrap left to watch, then she collapsed at the edge of it all.

It didn't know everything.

There would be no more. She would tell Dad to sleep with their tuuaaq. She would only use candles with her parents around. Stricter curfews. Meditation. No more clueless parents. She would become the best hider. For what could she otherwise be, save for the best slave? A hider could at least choose the place of her cowering, but even the best slave could only choose where to die.

She shivered, this time from cold. She hadn't a candle on her to quell the chill. Maybe she should crawl back home, fall asleep, and do as Nalor had suggested all those years ago. Dream of somewhere much warmer. She did just that.

From the plummeting chasm, the tuuaaq pulled.

Orluvoq didn't answer.

She was hiding.

PART II

QILAKNAKKA

18 YEARS OLD

Decades Long Dead

Tendrils of lightning lashed against the storm's bowled back, and the storm bellowed back against the lacerations lining its tender gills. Nubivagant ribbons carved brighter than any aurora through the weighty gray, and the witless cries of wounded clouds bulled long over the tundral moors.

Puigor sat in the doorway of his igloo, eyes snapping to sticks of lightning as swiftly as they did manifest. His heart snapped just as frenetically, but to a different rhythm. In the corner of the snow shanty, his mother murmured tuneless tones of a song, an old lay reserved for seekers of consolation amidst desperation. The singing had gnawed hours.

The forks of electricity that wrecked into the ocean worried him most. Somewhere out on the white-capped sea pitched a boat. Maybe. And in that boat clung his father.

Maybe.

Twenty days gone, Piukkunna had voyaged south with the clan patriarch to ensure safe passage as Angakkuq

Preservant. Seafaring craft hauling and laveering across the main needed all the preternatural aid they could muster. Eight days to the royal island, three days of council, eight days back. The king never let the assembly run overlong. Two days the thundersnow had been spitting and fussing. Too malign for coincidence.

Puigor rolled a candle between his palms, ever tempted to light it and jaunt off across the squabbling surf and regain his strayward father. If only windwalking the sea didn't consume so much tuuaaq. If only his aptitude for working the candles was better than his fourteen years would suggest. If only the sea didn't consume so much life.

How fleeting. How fragile.

"This is it."

He started at his mother's spoken words which broke her monotonous song. "Mama?"

"Your father. He's not coming back. This is it. I feel it in the storm." She stared past him, mundane candles throwing bitter shadows helter-skelter across her face and the curves of the igloo.

Puigor turned and frowned, his face rimed by a pallid flash of lightning. He had little respect for the premonitions of a non-angakkuq, but he wouldn't openly disdain his mother. Besides, he had begun to amass similar misgivings. Every time he lit a candle and quested out for Piukkunna or the clan patriarch, it felt like grasping at dream filaments. They existed in memory only.

"I'll... I'll give the candle another go." He reached behind and held the narwhal tusk wick against one of the hutch's flickering flames. The glow spilled into his heart as he connected with the tuuaaq. His eyes slid shut and he pushed his perception southward.

Ells and furlongs and miles and leagues he quested into

the whipping blackness, probing for his father's thrum. Stretched to the fringe his skills afforded, he felt...

Blackness. Only blackness. No pull any which way. No kernel of life for a lure before his mind. The desolate leagues grated deeper the groove of his misgivings.

Then what of the patriarch? Puigor recalibrated his dour thoughts and sought for the clan archon. Ells and furlongs and miles and—

A pulse. A pause. A pull.

The old man was seafaring and homebound. The upper crust of Puigor's heart lightened, but the bottom darkened to a snow-bitten black.

"Mama." He licked moisture into his lips, eyes jumping open.

She lifted slowly her gaze from a rhythmic flame, like a hundred spirits pulled her eyes toward the earth.

"It's Ataasengut," said Puigor. "He's returning."

"And—" A flash-boom deafened them for long heart-beats. Her chin quivered as the thunder abated. "And... and your father?"

Puigor held her stare for as long as he could bear, heart frozen fast in his chest. Even bidden, the words pronouncing the potential demise of her husband wouldn't cross his lips. He finally shook his head and puffed out the tuuaaq wick. "He's some hours out still."

"Probably more than a day."

The correction from one who didn't work the candles pricked his patience. But she was right. The candles discerned afar, and no vessel would make good time in the throes of inclemency. Their alternatives to waiting were scant and imitated insanity. That was all one could ever do in this wasteland. Wait or embrace insanity. When would *he* be the one they waited upon? He despised the suspense.

So, they hoveled in like bedding bears and awaited the dawn, the storm break, or the patriarch's homecoming, whichever event led.

As Puigor lay twisted in his bedroll, old childhood fears of being prematurely consumed by the ice and frozen alive in Nunapisu returned to plague him. Freezing teeth knifing up from the ground to gobble him with greedy verve. Snickering, disembodied mouths dragging him through muricated tunnels, ice spines scarifying skin and flaying the lids from his eyes so that he mightn't look anywhere but into the crush of champing terrors. Then they left him in the middle of the earth and denied him death, his spirit unable to withdraw from his body, and returned to tear at his flesh for millennia.

He at last broke from his slumber, but kept his eyes sealed for a time, basking in the pleasure of willed darkness. When he reached satisfaction, he clad himself and ducked out the igloo.

It was morning. If not here, somewhere on this bleak scrap of land. The lightning taskmaster had retired, at least for a time. A dainty spread of flakes drifted from the yet shadowed firmament. He voided his bladder then lit the tuuaaq anew.

The pull of the clan archon bumped into him immediately, much stronger than the previous attempt. It wouldn't be more than an hour now. He prodded his mother awake, and they roused the rest of the village and clustered near the shore.

Ataasengut ran the catamaran into the bank with a dull thud and gingerly lowered himself off, sail already stowed. His wife, the matriarch, stepped from the clan huddle and draped his arm across her shoulder to support his creaking bones.

"That," he said, shaking his hanging head, "was the worst voyage of my sour life. I thought I was a dead man more times than is worth numbering."

"What news do you have of my husband?" asked Puigor's mother from the crowd of thirty.

The patriarch eyed her from gaunt sockets without raising his slumped head, a strand of gray hair cutting across the left pupil. "Piukkunna," spoke he with measured anger, visage as an eel leering out from its grotto, voice slick with rheum, "has been taken by the king."

A murmur oscillated the clansfolk.

"Taken?" came her tremulous reply. Puigor gripped his mother's hand. "What spirits can tell me what that means?"

"I know not what it means." Ataasengut rolled his deteriorating teeth over one another. "But I know it means he's not coming back. He is a dead man."

Racket flared in the quiescent morning snowfall.

"What?" a clansman exclaimed. "He was our only angakkuq. How are we to survive?"

Puigor frowned. "I'm also—"

"The king can't just take my brother," shouted his aunt.

"Why didn't you stop him?"

"We're going to die!"

"We will make war on the king!"

Ataasengut endured the clamor until his brows had nearly swallowed his eyes. "Enough!"

The clansfolk quieted. Waves combed the tense silence.

"I haven't the smallest clue what we'll do. Yes, Siooraneq, perhaps we will die. At this moment, I haven't the smallest care either. I'm going to go lay myself down for a long spell. If I'm lucky, the ice will take me before I wake. If you're lucky, too, because if I actually wake up from this sleep, I'll be mighty surly. Good day." He strode right through their midst and off to his igloo, wife assisting his stumping gait.

He didn't even acknowledge me. Puigor stared at the gray surf.

His mother wept.

Another thought rose, hot like runner's breath. It grew hotter still as he watched his mother's tears.

I am going to kill the king.

She dreamt of ice. Of what else could she dream? Ancient ice, primordial odors dead in her nostrils. Barrow ice, interred by heaping centuries as land sought to caress the auroral ribbon. She took a new lungful of senescence and sensed more than stale air within the tombic walls.

Spirits congregated in the long-sealed catacomb. And though cold it might be, frigid it was not. No winds to scathe and castigate the noble and abominable without partiality. No stars to wheel the heavens over in their villainous, warmth-wicking swirl. She didn't think spirits could feel such things, but perhaps memory alone was caustic enough for them. So, the phantasms clustered in their cloister unseen... but not unheard.

Hints of syllables teased her straining ears. Utterances unknown emanated from the aged walls, from the floor of frost, from her very forehead. An ineffable pressure, as when someone enters your quarters in pitch night. It clung around her as she advanced through the tunnel with faintly crunching steps.

Unhewn stones of deep-colored translucence, the likes of which her imagination had never conjured, jutted from the path in regular intervals, laid by some unnamed ancestor.

Unnamed? Could that be so? Such would imply that whatever long-dead artisan who here plied their craft existed no longer. Body, spirit, and name. Without one, the other two might as well cast themselves from Nunapisu's precipice. But who would still be repeating this ancestor's name? They must have died the final death. Unnamed.

She halted and crouched low to observe the nearest stone. A meticulous string of characters unrecognizable crowded the most prominent facet. She probed its strokes, stems, and spurs for a shred of significance, tried to tune herself to its tenor. The fist-sized stone remained taciturn. Its meaning was not meant for her.

As she gave it one last pass with her eyes, a bodiless voice solidified from the ghostly gauze around her.

"Ujarak."

A man's name. She repeated the word.

So did the spirit.

"Ujarak. Ujarak. Ujarak."

The babble. It was the spirits reciting their names in a desperate essay to guard against extinction. The stones were not artistic endeavors, but mnemonic cairns. She spake forth the word again with an added measure of reverence. "Ujarak. I shall not forget you."

"Kingippoq. Savik. Ikuallan. Annilaarti." Down the cramped corridor she made her procession, kneeling in deference at each stone until the spirit pronounced its name. Each ancient appellation leaving living lips for the first time this epoch as she articulated the premonitions. She wondered whether mayhap her first parents would kiss her ears with whispers of cherished, unforgettable names.

But no. This keep was not theirs to haunt. This reliquary of names; this elaborate effort to append oneself eternally to existence. Whatever sum had been boundlessly named for some to be boundlessly named, her parents had not paid it.

She rolled the ritual along, giving due obeisance at each memorial, speaking once more things that above all mustn't be forgotten. "Sorsuttar. Uisuk. Aliasunneq. Naassaa."

"Orluvoq," said a formless voice.

She froze, and not for the fact that the voice had called her name. That was no effete spirit who had named her. Her eyes flickered up the tunnel.

Or was it?

In the unaccountable light stood a figure, at once wholly a man and wholly an apparition. Taller than most with a face that spoke of eighty years' wisdom packed into a body of forty. His eyes managed a convergence between sportive and sad.

"Nalor," she said, subconsciously continuing the ritual of names. Years had transpired since their last encounter, yet with each meeting something he exuded tugged her interest tighter. "Do you walk my dreams, or have you spawned from my mind?"

"I do more than walk, kuluk. I have prodded you here."

"Prodded? What is this place, then?" She motioned with a gloved hand. "And is it real, or does it only exist in the dream?"

"You stand in the Warren of Immortality." He plucked up a stone and gazed into its depths. "Memory is a fragile hope we humans hold fast to. We laden children with the names of six, eight, ten of their ancestors and content ourselves that those ancients will not die the final death. But what of them who lived a thousand years ago? Two thousand? Who bears their names? Who among us could identify a single ancient body in Nunapisu's reaches?"

Nalor's replaced the pellucid stone. "Call it a temple if you'd like. You stand within the final remembrance."

Her jaw fell open. "Incredible. I have always wondered about being forgotten by the far future. But how are you connected to all this? What is this place to you?"

He met her eyes with a look of tired amusement. "I am one who remembers."

A chill jittered in her spine.

"These halls are not full, Orluvoq," he said. "Your talents are immense, worth remembering. But to carve your name into a gemstone is not an honor doled out with absent-minded disregard."

She nodded. "I wish to be remembered."

"And remembered you shall be. Ten years it's been since our first meeting, and now the time is upon us." He took a step toward her, head nearly brushing the ceiling. "Come find me, Orluvoq. Greatness awaits you, the likes of which will put your dreams to shame."

Nalor faded from sight until he was no more than a pair of staring eyeballs. Then those, too, blinked to nothing.

She woke frosty with excitement under her blanket, and no matter how she sought, she could find no sleep. But a sluggish few hours and dawn would break upon the day of abandonment.

KITORNAK SWALLOWED the raw caribou meat. Pale dawn crept through the igloo door, striping her chin and nothing else. "You will be harshly missed, sweet girl."

Orluvoq ducked her head in acknowledgement. "Yes, Mama. I'll miss you too, you know that. It's not like I'll stop thinking about you two."

"Ten years. Ten years?" She reached out and ran a finger across Orluvoq's cheek. "The person you've grown into in ten years—it'll take the rest of us fifty to catch up. You were completely lost in the sweet tooth, and in nine years you've only slipped up a few times."

Orluvoq grimaced inside. Nothing to bring on a good mood like reminiscing about her most regrettable moments. Thankfully, she'd avoided another slip-up as severe as her thirteen-year-old fiasco, and she'd been using candles solo for three years again. But while she *had* grown, there was a piece or two—at least—that hadn't quite grown to fit.

"It will be quiet." Paarsisoq's eyes lingered on his food.

The air sat heavy while the trio broke the fast. Paarsisoq spoke again. "What exactly is it you'll be doing? It's not that I lack respect where our friend Nalorsitsaarut is concerned, though I can't say his methods fill me with confidence either."

"I... I'm not certain." Orluvoq kept her expression calm, trying to instill the surety absent in her words. "But I am certain it's greater than anything I could do here." Regret stabbed her innards. "Uh, that is, not to say that our clan isn't noteworthy. We do wonderful things that are very important. Uh, but there might be greater."

The words tasted stale, a breath held too long, not at all like the names she nurtured in the night. "I mean no disrespect, I love you both, but, you know, the world ends here —" she gestured north, twenty paces to the endless cliff "— and the rest of it is there." She extended her second hand southward. "And I've been here forever, and I hardly ever see anybody else, and—"

"Orluvoq."

Her tangle of words finally snagged. "Yes, Dad?"

"Go."

A pained tautness pulled at Kitornak's mouth, but compassion shone in her eyes. "We will always love you. In a perfect world, you would never have to leave. But you know just how perfect this world is, kuluk. Especially living here for a decade. At the end of the day, we are Watchers, not keepers. Have you known us to force someone to stay when they truly desire to go?"

"Oh…" Orluvoq's words had tangled even more. She had anticipated more pushback, but now facing the moment, she wasn't sure why. Could there be found more docile souls than her parents? Her feelings tipped from audacious to melancholy. Perhaps she had *wanted* more pushback, and so had indurated herself against it. Bereft of a battle, her ice determination turned to wash. A tear streaked out into the cold air. "I really will miss you."

Kitornak shook her head and sobbed out a laugh, then leaned forward and took Orluvoq against her breast. "We know. It's been our privilege to raise you, even when you knocked your father's new spear off Nunapisu. We've always known we couldn't keep you here forever. I hope that doesn't mean you'll keep away forever. You know where we are."

Paarsisoq ran a hand over Orluvoq's hair. "Yes, your mother could stand a visit now and then."

"Oh, hush now." Kitornak batted at his hand. "We all know who the bigger doter is."

A self-incriminating grin curved across the old man's face. "Well, I suppose your father wouldn't mind a visit here and there too."

Orluvoq laughed and wiped at her cheeks. "Will you get along without my angakkuq help?"

"I'm not the most adept worker of the flames," said Paarsisoq, "but you do recall that I somehow survived two decades without your talents. Not to say they won't be missed."

"You're right, you're right. I've been thinking of this day for so long, and now I just feel clumsy in my goodbyes. I guess I haven't had much practice."

Kitornak clucked. "No, that's true. I hope we soon find out how good your hellos are."

"Of course, Mama."

"You're a Watcher. It's in your blood now. Think of all the good we try and do here. Maybe it's time to export a little of that to the rest of the world."

"I know you will make us proud." Paarsisoq's voice hitched. "You already do every day."

Orluvoq crawled out the door and stood before the endless abyss she'd gazed into more than half her days. A silly nostalgia snuck into her at the thought of not seeing this gaping maw of nothingness for months, if not years. Slowly, the same giddiness of the sleepless night suffused through her and she turned to the south.

The day of abandonment had arrived.

ESCAPE. The fluid movements of windwalking broke through bindings that had held her for ten years, crisp sun and brisk air splashing over her with equal relish. Not that those bindings had been objectionable, merely that every child flexes against familial fetters, peeling off the parental collar that once fit so safe and snug.

The past handful of years had seen her windwalking the ultimate coastline, Nunapisu's verge, regularly, seeking self-styled wastrels come to embrace nullity. Her angakkuq prowess augmented Paarsisoq's enterprise of salvaging lives at the end of the world beyond what he had allowed himself to hope. How many had she talked down from the infinite precipice?

Reproofs nagged incessantly as she ran farther from home. Her journey-seeking was self-serving drivel, and scores would worse than die from her disregard for duty. Her parents would fold themselves over and over with worry, both for her and for the suicidals they couldn't reach. And for what? So she could go rendezvous with some murderous, dark shaman, the tirigusuusik? So she could become exactly that herself?

Orluvoq focused on the candle in her hand and the streaming landscape around her, letting the accusations slough away. Mostly. Deep longing and a touch of unembellished curiosity drove this expedition. She would see herself unbroken, and Nalor was the one to show her. Once she had had her fill of the world, she would return to Nunapisu better equipped to help others. And there was no curiosity potent enough to drive her again to the depravity of murder. That much was absolute.

She exulted in the simple fact that her course led neither east or west—or north, for that matter. The pulse that was her candle-fed intuition of Nalor's location drew her down to the heartland of Nuktipik, and perhaps on to the sea.

Eleven years had gone since she'd last frolicked in the damp, warmth-wicking air of the south; since she'd watched puffins and cormorants spar with kayakers for fish. She pushed the memories aside. Those jaunty days were too fraught. Too full of her first parents.

The young yet adept angakkuq ran until a star winked on her left and the sun spewed orange and red on her right, plating the earth in auroral antithesis. It was then, after burning through wellnigh an entire candle, that she spied him atop a hill, limned by the ruddy refulgence. Gentle anxiety clutched in her chest. After all the years of constructing her own mythos around him, what would she really see in those eyes? What would she know, come the dawn, to shatter her conceptions?

She slowed out of her motion blur and walked the remaining twenty paces to his side. Nalor didn't turn at her footfalls on the ice.

"Not the worst thing you've seen, eh?" He motioned to the bleeding sun.

Orluvoq searched for good words, something to impress her expectant mentor. "Once I saw a caribou give birth to twins and die while the second was halfway out."

He slid his eyes to her, head still forward, then back to the horizon. "You know, you're probably the least sheltered, most sheltered person I've ever met. Never been to a party. Melted a whole village."

"We had some parties when I lived on the ship."

"Oh, my apologies. How quickly I forget your storied years of carousing with sailors, gobbling down tuuaaq every spare moment."

Her brow dipped down, trying to determine what level of gravity his words carried and pick out a response that wouldn't offend. It would be quite the dispiriting to be turned back here for an aberrant tongue.

Nalor grinned. "No need to be a fussbudget. I jest. Glad you came so swiftly. I was tiring of standing on this rise."

Orluvoq relaxed. "Have you been here all day?"

"What I do on my own time is my own business, thank you." He took off a glove and examined his nails. "How's the old man?"

"Paarsisoq?" She examined his nails too, bemused at the sheer elegance in the splay. Who was he cleaning up for? He wore gloves. "Um, good. Or he was when I left. Maybe he accidentally fell off Nunapisu since then."

Nalor clucked his tongue and reinserted the hand. "Sounds like he hasn't changed since the day I met him. And your... mother? Is that how you're referring to each other these days? Mother and daughter?"

"I call Kitornak mother," said Orluvoq. "But what mother just says daughter? Don't most parents usually use their child's name? That's what I remember from my small years."

"My mother liked calling me daughter, but we can swap treasured childhood memories on another occasion." His eyes skipped her up and down several times, then he puffed a petite sigh. "I told myself I wouldn't say it, but it seems my self-control is less than I esteem it to be. Look how big you've gotten! Is this really how time works these days?"

She gave him a commensurate appraisal. "It would appear not, looking at you. Is that some trick you've learned working the blue flame, always looking the same age?"

"No matter how many times I extol the virtues of skin care in this harsh, dry, windy climate, no one dares take me seriously."

"Skin care? Like what, rubbing pit sweat and blubber on your face?"

"No, mostly just working the blue flame."

She reached up and shoved his shoulder, then froze. Too familiar too fast. Not skipping a beat, Nalor chuckled wryly, and Orluvoq slowly untensed. She laid a mental finger to her nose in reminder that however convivial he seemed, he had killed before. Or had he? Maybe he had a blue candle supplier the same way some people have a coat supplier.

"Can I ask a question I've been wondering for *years*?"

He heaved a melodramatic sigh. "I will bear your interrogations if I must."

"What were you *really* doing with five blue candles in that cave?"

"That's almost the start of a good riddle," he said. "But in this case, the answer is simple. I was controlling a *very* distant bluebody."

"You—what?" She screwed her head back and forth. "I thought you didn't like them?"

"Well, not when other people send them scuttling down Nunapisu after me."

"But *five* candles? What for?"

"Have you ever wished all the ice covering the world just disappeared?" He flicked his gloved fingers toward the horizon. "Sometimes I like to look into those possibilities."

She made to reply.

"Anyhow," Nalor cut her off, "you've scurried a long way —I'm sure for something more than a spot of frivolous repartee. Now it's my turn for a question." He leveled a calcifying gaze in her direction. "Do you know Qummukarpoq?"

"You mean the king at the start of the world, as far south as you can go? I've heard of him, of course, but out at Nunapisu he's more of a fairy tale. Why?" Every sentence she strung together was stitched with the foreboding that she spake nothing but the wrong answer.

"You outdo yourself, Orluvoq. King at the start of the world indeed, icy carven castle nestled before that great wall of water that reaches upward forever. Fire in the skies and he is the arsonist! An iridescent bow flexes across the heavens and he has limbered it! The stars and vapors he sings from the heights and spools them into his vesture! The host of the gallant array themselves in queue, and lo! there he stands first, and lo! there he stands last!"

Orluvoq left her mouth agape, wonder flowering in her bosom. She ran her tongue through the gap where a baby eye tooth had fallen out three years before with yet no mature canine to follow. "Is he really so magnificent? I've never heard any stories like that. Just that he's a good angakkuq."

Nalor shrugged. "Rumor likes to sing songs it does not know. But he *is* one of the greatest angakkuit the Nuktipik have seen since the ice began."

She tried to dampen the tingle of jealousy at the thought of an angakkuq greater than her. "You're saying that his abilities aren't just rumor, then?"

"I am a curious creature." He tossed a bone knife up and down, torquing it with dazzling twirls. "And an envious creature. I couldn't just take someone's word that there was a greater worker of the candles than myself. I have been to the castle at the base of Qilaknakka, that wall of water stretching forever upward. I have seen him bend the very aurora to wreathe him in its radiance."

Jealousy relented, and awe abounded. "The aurora? That's, well, incredible at the best. Impossible at the worst." The things you could do when directly tapped into the aurora. Assuming you *could* tap into it. Gleaning anything from it was hard, even while walking through Arsarneq burning a candle.

"It *was* impossible. Until Qummukarpoq did it." He caught the knife and it vanished somewhere into his coat.

"Has word of his plight reached you in your northern retreat?"

"His 'plight'? No, what's that all about?" Is this really what it had come to? She had to run across half the world in order to fetch a scrap of news?

Nalor rubbed his mustache, veiling a thin smile. "He seeks to work a great wonder, greater than has ever been seen. So marvelous it will make bending Arsarneq look like bending your piss stream."

"But I don't—"

"Pee green? It's relieving to hear your relieving is clear. Nevertheless, no one knows exactly what wonder he wants to wreak, but it involves the great wall of Qilaknakka, and it will change the world as we know it."

"Is there any work of the candles so great it could change the world? Unless you mean a bunch of little works." And what would such a thing look like in relation to Qilaknakka? Did he mean to bring it down on the world, washing everyone over the edge of Nunapisu and leaving only a necropolis embedded in the end of the world?

"No," said Nalor, "not little works. A single great one. My best guess is it has to do with what lies *beyond* Qilaknakka."

"But... beyond?" Orluvoq squinted though the sun had descended. "It's the start of the world. How could there be anything beyond? Is there anything beyond Nunapisu?"

"Where does the aurora come from?" He grinned. "And where does the water of the ocean come from?"

"From... from..." She couldn't command an answer. "From..." But she dearly wished she could.

"Every few decades someone will take the odd foray deep into Arsarneq, past Nunapisu, and proceed to never return. Perhaps they'll all pop out at once, very confused."

"Pop out from Qilaknakka?"

Nalor's laugh gaily painted the air a deep puffy orange in the last embers of the sunken sun. "All sodden and sputtering. I like how you think. You're saying it all wraps back on itself, the world some perplexing circle."

"Wouldn't it make sense?" Orluvoq asked. "There are whales and other great fishes in the sea. Maybe the narwhals live in Qilaknakka and swim out each night to feed."

"I would love that," Nalor said, his eyes gazing so far away his vision wrapped around eternity and emerged inside his soul.

"Wait." Orluvoq scrunched up her face. "Does he think there's something beyond Qilaknakka that would help, um, get rid of the ice?"

Nalor shrugged. "Who's to know? Haven't talked with the fellow in decades. Does this thing interest you? For I believe it's something of this very nature King Qummukarpoq desires to discover."

She nodded, anticipation stretching her taut. "What's stopped him from wreaking this great work?"

The bare curve of a smile settled on his lips. "For reasons known only to him, he cannot work this the greatest of works unless he has wed himself to the most beautiful woman in the world."

The tensity held her breath in her chest, save for one syllable. "Why?"

"I have my suspicions, but the true reason is unknown to all but Qummukarpoq himself. Some quirk of the tuuaaq's power. The bond between powerful people acting to amplify, or somesuch. What are the three parts of a person?"

"Name, body, and spirit."

"Right. I think that he's looking for the most perfect person—in name, body, and spirit—to compliment him, which will give the highest chance of success. Orluvoq." He finally stopped his long gazing and looked to her. "Do you wish to be interred in the Warren of Immortality? You remember the dream, yes?"

"Of course." Her breaths came quicker, like the days of an old woman's life.

"Then," he said, "you must marry the king."

Blood pounded through her veins like a pack of foaming bears. Her legs were as tallow trailing the side of a candle. "Marry the king? But how can I... That's—it's—it's not possible! You can't just hop across the sea and be wed to the most powerful man there is. I'd be thrown out right away."

Still, the thought thrilled. Collected her mind in a cruse and sloshed it to warm froth. This might have been worth leaving the north for. An expansion of powers unreachable at the end of the world. How could she be stronger than as queen of the Nuktipik?

"Women from the world entire come to petition the king, to proffer their beauty. Qummukarpoq holds court and measures their worth. None have been chosen."

"And what makes you think I'll do any better? I've used the candles to see myself in vision. I'm less beautiful than other women I've seen, and I haven't even seen that many women. There's not a chance I'm the most beautiful woman in the world."

In the dark of the dying dusk, she hadn't seen a candle find its way to Nalor's hand. Hadn't seen what sleight he employed to light the tuuaaq. But in the man's worn glove flickered a baleful light that sucked the warmth from her back through her chest.

Shadows pooled in his unblinking sockets; shadows contrasted by the dance of that fell blue glow. Eyes locked to hers, he uttered.

"Not yet."

THE SHADOWS of the azure flame seeped through Orluvoq's skin to sway intoxicated on her heart, like the spirits of sea-buried sailors wandering through forsaken depths. Yes, the shadows convened—but so did the light. A mind-stunning admixture of horror and glory, as pathways to greatness tend to be.

She looked to the blue flicker, then back to Nalor. "But... I can't work the blue flame." Though she spoke one part of her mind, the other part yearned for him to brush aside her worries.

"And why's that?"

"Because you have to murder in order to make them. I'd like to have a spot in the Warren." She hesitated. "But I don't think I could kill to get one." One murderous spree had been enough.

A grin tugged over his serious expression. "*You* don't have to murder to make them."

"I don't care who's doing the murdering, I don't want a part in it."

"There's no offing in the offing."

"There's no what?"

Nalor barked mirth from his mouth, eyes nearly swallowed by his laughter. "No one gets killed. That's only what I say to people. The shroud of mystery is fantastic fashion."

Expressions weltered across her face. A decade of preconceptions uncloaked as misconceptions. Not a murderer? "You lied?"

"Ears ache for the taboo; lustful morsels they can turn over and over in their hearts and bring to their tongues for another taste when they find themselves near other aching ears." He watched the spirited blue in his hand. "It's easier to tell people what they want to hear than to try and convince them of raw realities. Besides that, I didn't deem you in a state to hear the truth."

"And what is the truth?" It came out more defensively than intended, but the overcautious regret of earlier didn't follow.

"The truth..." He took a step forward, the cold coming closer. "What is the first rule of being an angakkuq?"

A girlhood riddled with tribulations had taught her that lesson too well. "Never eat the tuuaaq." She had only slipped up a few times since her eight-year-old escapades.

"Just so. And what," he said, "do you think is the first rule of being a tirigusuusik?"

A different cold than the candle's cast cooled her insides. Her breath fled her lips in blue haze. "I... I don't know."

The mélange of light and shadow muddled Nalor's face to an imitation of a corpse peering out through Nunapisu. "*Always* eat the tuuaaq."

Orluvoq reeled backward, a keen sickness skewering through her chest. "No. No, no. I can't. This isn't—we just—I don't want—sorry. I'm not the one. The king can find his own wife without any help from me."

"Of course he can. That's irrelevant. None of them are you." The eerie scraping of his boots scratched at her ears as he floated toward her, feet dragging like timbers. "You're the most naturally talented angakkuq I've met, beside the king. I can trust no one else to ensure that the king's magic succeeds. That all of Nuktipik isn't washed to Nunapisu. Then there's no one to remember."

She fell to her haunches, one glove to the ice and one before her eyes in warding. "Please. Please, don't make me.

When I eat the tusk, it eats me. Teeth the height of a man stabbing through my spirit over and over. Spit my name into the sea and feed my body to the dogs, but don't make me eat. I've been doing so good."

"I wouldn't ask it of you if I thought you incompetent. I've no use for a gibbering, insensate bag of blood and bones. I've summoned you for that very reason; you're equipped with firsthand knowledge of the vice. It's nigh impossible to train someone into a tirigusuusik unless they've roiled in the darkness of tuuaaq. They always twist into addicts.

"But you have inculcated a deep fear of the tusk into your mind. More than a fear. A hate. You hate the unbridled love you have for it. And that hate will preserve your life. More than preserve, it will elevate you to unclaimed heights."

As he spoke, his voice detached from his body, thrumming from everywhere save above the feet dangling against the ice. Visions refracted across her mindspace. Lurid sleeps with puffy fevers. Saliva and sweat seeking egress. Throbs of ecstasy compelling her into ardent servitude. A girl entranced by an infinitely contracted world.

"No, I'm not what you think." She still avoided his eyes. "I'm weak. So weak. I'm—I'm broken." Broken. No matter the time, no matter the healing, she was nonetheless a medley of fragments waiting for a master puzzler to banish her chaos. Her voice dropped to a croak. "I'm broken."

"And why should being broken hold you from changing the world?" Nalor asked.

"I couldn't change the world even if I wasn't broken."

"If all is as all should be, then the only changes one can make are negative. Sitting on a pinnacle, the sole place to go is down. Good can happen only when things aren't perfect.

Will you lie alone in the world's grim desolation and let the imperfections pulp you? Or will you rise and lift the world as you do so?"

She sniffed an effete laugh. "That's a whole lot of words to convince me to do drugs again."

The omnidirectional voice swept around her and coalesced in Nalor's mouth. "Orluvoq."

She inhaled, dropped her hand, and raised her gaze. Lambent eyes locked on hers.

"I have walked every inch of this world in your boots, and when they broke, I walked back on blackened stumps. I have wept in the ice fens for father, in the sterile moors for mother. I have ransacked the hovels of sleeping wizards, sweeping the floor with my tongue in search of tuuaaq crumbs, fingers frozen to witless stubs. I have stood in Arsarneq's sidereal belly, clutching and unclutching the candle, disputing whether to throw myself headlong into the dark earth. Gaze upon me with your deepest eyes! Am I broken?"

From his visage streamed glories, a countenance carven from embers blue and embers green. From her nether regard, his shoulders braced the heavens, gathering the drizzled light of the aurora like a dusting of snow. Resplendence and dread dwelt in but one realm, and here stood its lord in the midst of the air.

"No." It came as a whisper. "I don't know if anything could be farther from broken."

"And that is because you only gaze upon me and not into me." He motioned to his spirit. "Within you'll find only pieces, and none that seem to fit. Edges that never lose their sharpness, no matter how much they grind one against the other. I will not accept that the broken have no part in shaping the world. Orluvoq. Greatness awaits you, the likes of which will put your dreams to shame."

The words touched the innermost motes of self floating around her core, and they would not be still. Vibrations pulsed and her particles aligned into something greater than roamed her flesh before.

"So you're saying that you're broken, but strong? That you can be broken but not helpless?"

"I have been broken for just slightly longer," he raised the candle, "than I have been strong."

Hiding. She had been hiding so long it hurt her brain to envision stepping out into the open. To face the devourer once more. Yet she'd anticipated this day longer than any other. If not now, as she stood in the presence of a master, then would she ever rise?

She placed both hands beneath her and raised her head level to the cold flame, neck tilting up to look at the hovering man. Her spirit stepped into the open.

"I'll try it. I don't know if I'll succeed, but I'll try."

Nalor quirked an eyebrow up but said nothing. A shudder ran up the inside of Orluvoq's spine. Lightness puffed up beneath her ribs. This was it. She was doing it.

"Now," she continued in tones of mounting boldness. "There's been so much talk about whether it's going to happen that I'm not even sure what's going to happen. Exactly how does burning a blue flame make me the most beautiful woman in the world? Is it just a secondary effect?"

"Ha." Nalor eased his weight to his feet. "If things were that easy, I'd look a lot less like twice coughed up weasel vomit. No, beauty's one of those things that you only get about as much as you're born with." He smirked. "Unless you steal it."

Her confidence of the moment grew old with the moment. "Uh. Steal it?"

"From pretty girls."

"But..."

"I suppose you could steal it from ugly ones as well. Same work less gain though. They *are* less likely to be hurt than the pretty ones, if that's weighing on your mind."

She murmured his last few words to herself, eyes not quite focused on anything.

He snuffed the candle. "No time like the present. Let us be off."

Tonight? He wants me to ransack someone's life tonight? It took her feet a spell to overcome inertia, then she mutely plodded down the hill, the hand of perturbation rummaging through her insides.

Decades Long Dead

Puigor grumbled and the sea grumbled back.

"I wasn't talking to you," he said.

"And you think I was talking to you?" it sloshed.

That was hopefully just the hallucinations. The rigor of keeping the keel pointed down and the hull pointed south had transcended his initial estimates, even with aid from the candles. He wanted enough wick left to issue him a visa back home should the weather turn too ugly though, so he had left the candles mostly be, and enervation had nuzzled into his creases.

With his feet on the shore, absconding with a ship and sailing southward had seemed a thing begotten of wisdom. On this, the eighth day, he suspicioned that idiocy had been the one stumbling into that assignation. The patriarch likely had been less than pleased to wake to the seaside scene of one less vessel. Maybe he'd even shouted a curse that the fourteen-year-old thief might die of ineptitude.

Puigor spat at the sea and the sea spat back, though with

a much more convincing cataract. He swore and the sea merely bobbed a nod. It must've appreciated hearing its native tongue.

A month of malaise had hazed by since the patriarch's pronouncement of Piukkunna's incarceration—if indeed it was incarceration that had befallen Puigor's father. Omens burbled in his belly, speaking direful words, insisting a greater corruption than captivity had its claws around Piukkunna. He scraped the tiniest wafer of tuuaaq off a candle wick and slipped it between his teeth.

Oh, tiaavuluk, he thought, clutching the gunwale to avoid being lifted into the sky. He felt his feet leave the boards but looked down and saw them planted firmly as if they'd frozen.

Of course it had been stupid popping the first flake in his mouth three weeks ago. Of course it snubbed the years his father had spent hammering his head flat with remonstrances against it. Of course it was stealing valuable resources from the clan. But he couldn't bring himself to trudge despondent through every moment, to fold himself thick with worry. Scraping tuuaaq was scraping happiness. And it's not like he took so much he couldn't function.

Settled into the high, Puigor cast his eyes over the bow and locked them on the unfathomable wall of water reaching skyward. Qilaknakka. Four days past it had first come into view, a fluff of mist grazing the horizon's expanse. Now it towered; thundered at his eyes. There wasn't a height it didn't attain. It made him feel... diminished. Like it might at some moment decide to fall, and no matter his speed, he'd be swallowed and deepened.

And finally, there at the base of the boundless skywall, he espied an island. *The* island. The august edifice at the start of the world puncturing humid air. It was said that the ice of the sculpted keep never grew, never varied in its form. Come damp, come wind, come slurried sleet, all harm sloughed off in swarm.

An hour more of plashing in his vessel's solitude and hull finally found shore. Puigor tumbled over the confines of his world and pressed his gloved hands to the cold, white earth, drinking up gulps of rigidity. Eight days. Too long for committing oneself to the elements and not a spirit with which to share the waves. Some would come through such an ordeal feeling sanctified. He couldn't help but somehow feel less holy. A shoddy sailor and tawdry savior were what the ocean had spit upon the strand.

He tried to shake the inebriated intuition that he had come to fail and raised to his feet.

Before him stood a man—a boy?—garbed in white furs and other snowy finery. Puigor's heart skipped when his eyes lighted on the fellow's head. A silvery diadem set with alicorns ascending from back to front hugged his brow. The king? No, the king was a heavyset man of many decades.

"You're not supposed to be here," said the prince, his accent harsh. He squinted with only the bottom eyelids.

"I—"

"But that is alright." He couldn't have been more than five years Puigor's senior. "You wouldn't cross an ocean for no reason. Tell me, boy, what petition brings you to Qilaknakka?"

Any misgiving that the prince was a boy and not a man evaporated along with any surety that Puigor was a man and not a boy. "I... It's my father. He came here more than a month ago for the council, but he never returned. I have come to bring him home."

An amused sneer crooked the prince's lip. "I thought it might be you. Tell me, what is your father's name?"

"Piukkunna. He was our angakkuq and we desperately need him back."

"Piukkunna." The prince tutted. "Shall we go see him, then?"

Puigor's spine whipped straight. "Yes. *Yes.*" *Not dead. Not dead!*

He followed his unexpected host up a long, straight acclivity and into the mouth of the fortress. Capacious, pristine halls robbed him of his attention and left him nearly charmed. The halls of home made him feel like crouching, and he had at least one more growth spurt in him. Back home, he bathed lying in a steam room with a roof mere hands above his face. His people's abodes were dolven from the ice so that they only needed to cast a ceiling overhead. No worry for walls. He didn't understand how a structure like this could exist, but he wanted to walk the halls of one every day.

Twice he opened his lips to question why his father had been taken, and twice he'd sealed them again. He should probably hold off on melting that bridge. One misplaced sentence and Piukkunna might never come home.

They passed entire tables of stone, a wall studded with a gem mosaic of Arsarneq, a hanging collection of profanely big sea monster skulls, a fleet of wooden ship miniatures. Too many wonders for Puigor to keep track of. He'd never seen so much woodwork in one place.

The one thing that never showed its face was people. The end of the world contained all the dead, and the start of the world contained none of the living? There had to be a metaphor in there somewhere.

It felt like the dream that stole into his head on occasion, the one where he walked to clan after clan and found every warren of igloos a mess of vacant halls. A choking absence that made him detest the bones in his skin. Upon him, earth's final man, rested the onus of remembering every name. He, the final strand that connected hide to carcass. He, the end of the world who held all the dead, and no living to inhabit the beginning.

Their feet found the top of a tower and the prince heeled before a doorway that opened to the air. Puigor gaped at the plummeting height. Terns wheeled far off, needle pricks in the blue. His boat not even a fingernail held at arm's length. A wobble weaved up his stomach and around his skull.

"You are angakkuq, yes?" asked the prince, not even out of breath.

Puigor nodded, nerves lighting up, his hit of tuuaaq all but gone.

"We will windwalk to the room. It's just around the corner. After me."

"Wait! I've never windwalked on... on a *wall* before."

The prince produced a candle. "That is of little consequence. There's one way to your father, and I will not carry you." He turned, paused, then dashed out the door. Puigor watched him streak across the castle wall, legs a blur, then disappear in a projection farther down the wall.

He squirmed before the opening and its drop. Where was the king in all this? Was there no seneschal? Just the prince and his whims?

He rubbed an ungloved finger over tallow, the other hand reaching for heatmoss. He pulled a lump of gray lichens out of a pocket and ground them between thumb and forefinger. The reaction took and he dropped it on the tusk. Smoke wisped. Orange flashed. Flame jumped to life at the end of the wick, and the familiar pull grabbed him.

Here we go.

Spirits. Guide me. Or catch me.

His legs whirred into motion, and the floor slipped away. He lurched down. In every bet was a fool and a thief; he the fool, gravity the thief. The ground rushed toward his face while his feet refused to do anything but glide.

He pedaled his legs like an elk in burning breeches and sucked on the flame with such zeal the tusk shot sparks. Feet finally finding purchase on the face of the castle, he banked upward with the ground less than a second away.

Piss on a fish and call it a vacation, I'm not dead! Perhaps one could be both the fool and the thief.

A stretch of ports pocked the immaculate castle's side far above. He angled for the one nearest where he'd exited, teeth a-clench, tears whisking into the wind. *Please, please, please.*

Darkness squeezed the corners of his eyes. Jelly fidgeted its way into his stomach. The shot was too dangerous! He'd thrash his ribs to splinters on the ceiling. He'd burst his skull to shards on the far wall.

Like slow thunder from a moiling storm, a roar poured from his throat, swelling as it ran its ire. The door soared toward him, nearly blending into a single white sheet with the rest of the wall. One final thrust up and he flew into the chamber, clipping a foot and tumbling, tumbling to *crack* against the back. He whimpered and clutched his shoulder.

"Extravagant, boy."

Puigor looked to the prince, then to the man hurrying through the thin room toward him.

"My son!" said his father, helping him up. He didn't look too haggard, but not too fit either. "What are you doing here? You need to be at home with your mother. The clan. Not chasing after a forsaken man."

"He came to save you." The prince stared, then looked toward Puigor. "What was it you said his name was?"

"Piukkunna." Puigor wrapped his good arm around the man he'd journeyed so long to find.

"Piukkunna. Yes." The prince slipped something into his mouth. His candle had been choked cold, opposed to Puigor's burning on the floor. "I'm glad you came to Qilaknakka, Puigor. I don't know if I could find use for you as an angakkuq after seeing your display. But I have been very curious about something, and I think this is the perfect opportunity to test it. What did you say his name was?"

Puigor frowned. "Piukkunna. Whatever you want me to do, I'll do it. I'll... I'll make your food, I'll clean. We'll pay more tribute. Just let me take him home."

"Son..." said Piukkunna. "Don't."

"No, this is tribute enough, thank you." The prince motioned to Piukkuna.

"No. I—I demand to speak to the king," Puigor stammered. Why were words so hard to find?

"The king hides from the sun in the sky and his son in the castle. He cares little for this world anymore and only does anything perfunctorily, and then only because the habits are in his bones. Whatever emotion you hope to stir in my father, you won't find it in him. It is I alone you treat with, boy."

The candle in his hand jumped to life, and Puigor's blood drained away, *away*. Anywhere, so long as it fled that frigid blue glow. Piukkunna clasped a hand around Puigor's good arm.

"Say it again, boy. Say your father's name."

Puigor's skin pricked with an ugly cold. "P-piuk-kkunna."

The prince snicked his eyes shut, heavy breaths fuming

out his nose. Somewhere within the confines of Puigor, something unlatched. The sensation made him sick.

Standing taller than the other two, the prince opened his eyes and twisted his lip into an azure-grimed grin. "Now. Tell me."

Puigor swallowed.

"What was your father's name?"

Puigor tried. Reached for it, the same place it had always been. The fingers of his mind came up empty, grasping snowflakes that melted with the grasping. "What have you done? It's gone! I do not know the name of my father!"

Piukkunna snarled. "This is too far, Qummukarpoq! Imprison me, deprive me, use me, but don't bring terror on my family." He turned to Puigor. "My name is q̃ jøktumkʃi, ⸱o⸱ qq̃q."

"Wha... what? Father?" The coldness seeped beneath his skin. "*Father*?"

"I said my name is pāq̃h̃tg̃ ꝛẽq̃pg̃nʲi."

"No. No, no." The sickness hadn't receded. "I can't hear it. I cannot remember your name!"

His father's jaw hung stunned. Dread sewed the windows to the man's spirit shut, leaving tears but no light in his eyes. "No..."

A bend from Qummukarpoq's crooked spirit pressed against his lips, curling the corners. "This is a most promising beginning to my test."

What was that blue flame? WHAT WAS THAT BLUE FLAME? Some instrument of demon hypnosis that scorched reality cold, brought to bear by this humanoid abomination. How could he *smile*?

Tears puckered in Puigor's eyes. "What have you done! Take it back now! Or I'll—I'll—"

"You," said the prince, "will return home and bring them a message: I am coming."

Puigor had no response. Pikkunna had no response. The prince—the king?—had spoken, and thus it was. They had no weapons for war and no chits for bargaining.

Qummukarpoq motioned to the still burning candle upon the chamber's ice floor. Numbly, Puigor knelt to pick it up, then walked to the edge. A single glance backward, then he tumbled from the verge.

He kicked his legs along the building side, though not as fervently. His chaotic descent would have earned backward praise from the prince. The man no doubt was saying something to that tune right now up above. Puigor thumped down several spans from his boat and groaned at his flaring arm. He lay there a moment, then got up, placed a shoulder against a gunwale, and kept windwalking.

Once far enough offshore, he vaulted into the ship and set some sail. Then he retreated to the stern, broke off a knuckle-size chunk of tuuaaq, and mashed it between his teeth.

O rluvoq squinted through the dark at the miniscule piece of tusk in her ungloved fingers as her legs ferried her along. Two beasts prowled her innards. One demanded she bite down and claim the skies. The other hissed and spat at the monster in her hand.

She pushed the chalky crumb into her mouth.

Bliss bubbled into her head and shame sank to her navel, oil distilling from water. Nalor was right. She hated how much she loved it.

"Alright, alright," chided the man himself. "Don't get too hung up on it. You've got a job to do." He took her by the elbow and pressed a lit candle into her hand. "Burn the tuuaaq *inside* you. Feed it to the flame. Maybe you'll have more success than the last time we tried."

She tried not to ask anything witless like, how do I get it into the candle if it's in my body? Then she remembered. "I've already done it."

"Oh? You've done more partying than I thought, have you?"

"When I... last visited my former clan. There was a flash

of blue. I thought it was because the tuuaaq I was using had killed someone."

Nalor shook his smiling head. "More talent in a sneeze than most angakkuit have in their whole bodies. Well, let's see you do it again."

"I'm trying! It's not easy." The tusk in her veins shoved her brain faster than her mind could keep up. Nevertheless, she honed in on the suffusive warmth and prodded at it.

Out. Out. Out? Oouuuuut!

Uh. There? There. There, there.

No. Um... Candle. Candle. Cand—

Whoa.

The glim in her hand flickered from orange to indigo to sky blue. She laughed out loud. "Nalor!"

A generously cut grin held his face. "What did I just say about your angakkuq sneezes? Let's see if your tirigusuusik sneezes are equally impressive."

Like a hundred windblown strings pulled taut between two hands, the tuuaaq's tantrum leveled out. The hero's thrum had ceased to blare, instead rolling softly through like worn-out thunder. The consonant constancy astonished more than the intoxication.

Her thoughts were hers. *She* was hers. And she wasn't hiding.

The tuuaaq didn't know everything.

A new glee inserted itself beside that of the tuuaaq. *My life isn't a shambles yet. Holding this blue flame just feels so... powerful.* She quivered involuntarily. The fire gusted an air of potency right through her ribs, as if multiple spirits resided inside her. This pleased her. It pleased her deeply. *This might not be so bad.*

Except for what was to come—what *might* come. She had cast no vows. But it *would* be exhilarating to see the start of the world. Ruling it might not be too shoddy either. What all that might demand, she couldn't say. But for certain it paid dividends of power that would hold helplessness in abeyance. All she needed to do to get there was...

Steal beauty. Her mind hadn't been able to compass it yet. What ramifications held hands with the act? For her; for them? What did her beauty mean to her? It didn't occupy the majority of her thoughts, to be sure. Then again, she hadn't the chance to live around men as a woman. But if it really was of little import, why was she considering stealing it? *Was* she considering it?

She shook her head to repress the discord. "What now?"

"The magic of the blue flame is that any typical act you'd do is now some magnitude more effective, *and* you've access to previously untouchable acts."

A frayed image of Nalor recumbent in a bone-cold cave, ringed by five abominable flames, unfurled in her mind. "Like what?"

"You already know about bluebodies from our previous adventures together. Cavorting corpses." A fond smile lay on his lips. It quickly turned down. "Stealing memories. Manipulating emotion. Yes, you can force someone's love to focus on you. But it recedes as soon as you let go. The healing will make you wonder why everybody doesn't heal with blue flame at all times. With a normal flame, you can call animals to you. With a blue flame, you can possess them.

"But memories aren't the only thing you can steal. Health. Youth. Beauty. Those attributes you can't quite tally, but you can see, nonetheless. Is your liver failing? Steal the function from theirs."

"That's a little terrifying. Someone could just come along and drink you dry at any—" She stopped, a frigid realization cutting into her high. "You steal people's youth. That's how you look the same after years."

Nalor spread his hands before him. "As charged. I am a product of the blue flame. But. I don't just steal years off someone in a single bout." He smiled. "I take it a day at a time."

Comfort wrapped around her worries. "You mean I don't have to steal it all at once?"

"You're free to do as you choose. If you can choose. However, who knows how long the king will wait?"

"Can..." She watched the cold fire's tilt. "After it's done, could I give it back?"

"The blue flame is very good at taking. It doesn't know nearly as much about giving."

"Ah." Her eyes slid shut. "But... none of these people— they don't deserve it."

He regarded her. "When a clan is low on food and the angakkuq can't call any beasts, who gets the food?"

She gnawed at her lip. "The hunters."

"To get the greatest gain, the clan must sacrifice. One step back so that they might take two steps forward. You've done great things at the end of the world, but think how much more you could do were you the queen at the start of the world."

She nodded. *I could do this. Just a bit at a time from a hundred different women. No more damage than a couple late nights would do.*

Blue flame leapt to life in Nalor's hand. "Alright. Let us be off, then."

"I definitely have to try this tonight?" Her lips spake protest, but her heart wished for a moment to ply her newfound mastery over the tusk.

"You'll be fine. You're a natural."

"Maybe…"

Well, she thought, *how much damage can actually be done if beauty is only skin deep?*

THEY SLOWED fifty paces outside the random clan and doused their candles, guided only by the aurora on high. It had been but a few minutes' windwalk. Her first blue windwalk. A taste like over-cold ice tainted the back of her tongue.

"So how is this supposed to work?" asked Orluvoq. "We just go in there asking their hospitality, and I sneak into a room or two at night and steal some bits of beauty?"

"That's more or less the posture of affairs, with one or two modifications."

"Is there anything I should know?"

"Just play along," Nalor answered. "It's more fun that way. And remember that exceeding expectations might open the door for your parents to enter the Warren of Immortality."

She glanced a question at him, but he kept his peace, footfalls dampened by a fresh fall of snow. Her parents? Could she see her dead parents again? Or was it limited to the yet to be deceased?

Friendly licks of light stuck out from beneath the warren's door flap. They ducked inside. The antechamber buzzed with candlelight despite the late hour. A woman in her fifties, cheeks brushed artificial red, smiled and pushed herself heavily from floor to feet.

"My good sirs, we are so—oh, one of you's a lady." She giggled, fidgeting with several ivory rings. "Hey there, sweet thing. Have you come to stay the night? No, no need to look all nervous if that's how it is. We got girls who don't mind a minute."

Orluvoq glanced another, harsher question at Nalor as she pushed off her hood. He swept forward and took the lady by the hand.

"Madame. I met the pleasant, young Oqupip several villages back. She told me about some... setbacks that she's had recently and is looking for a change of pace. I told her what you're about here, and she expressed interest in working with you for a few months, perhaps, just to see what it's like."

Orluvoq's main goal became avoiding cardiac failure, never mind the gaudy flush priming her cheeks. A brothel. Nalor had taken her to a brothel. Revulsion in a dozen shades spewed through her.

The lady perked up with every sentence from Nalor. "Oh. Oh-ho." She walked over to Orluvoq and grabbed her by the shoulders. "The face isn't terrible, a little plain, but no matter. Let's get you out of that coat and see what's going on."

Orluvoq froze as the Madame began fussing with her parka's fringe. Ribbons of shame coruscated up and down her body as she was stripped not only of her outer parka but her inner atigi and trousers.

"Oh, come now," said the Madame, peeling Orluvoq's arms away from her chest. "No need to be shy. It's just old Atsa. And your gentleman friend, of course. There."

Orluvoq tremored, and not for the cold—though her skin stood like gooseflesh. The need to sprint into the frigid night throbbed in her core. Some random woman's eyes raked over her exposed anatomy like a clan archon appraising merchant's wares. A man of queer morals about whom she knew nearly nothing gazed on impassively. She was being... sold? into prostitution. Even if it wasn't happening, the motions were the same.

It rattled terror into her bones.

Only last year had Mama explained that when Orluvoq came up clanless years ago, their old captain Naalagaa had designed to sell her to Atortittartut, a den of slatterns no different than this. The selfsame whore clan that Kitornak had been fettered to. The boon of spirit strength granted Orluvoq by the blue flame froze brittle in her blood.

The Madame paced a circumference, clicking nails against her rings. "Good. Good. I like what I see, sweetie. I think you'll fit right in. And you have a good shy, demure thing going on. Lots of men go cross-eyed for something as tender as you."

Orluvoq snatched parka and atigi from the ground and shoved her torso inside like an imperiled hare leaping into its den. The trousers followed just as quickly.

The Madame laughed. "You really are tender, aren't you? Have to know what we're working with, sweetie. Some men are very particular about shapes and sizes."

"Uh. Okay." Orluvoq's heart thundered. She didn't have a clue how one handled herself in these situations. "Am I, um, a good size?"

The Madame waved a dismissal. "Don't get hung up on it. Lots of men don't care if it's just for a night."

It surprised Orluvoq how much the comment stung.

"Let's get you settled in, then."

Stomach a wreck, Orluvoq didn't move. "Am I supposed to... work tonight?"

"Oh, no, sweetie. It's a slow night for us. We have ten girls just lounging about. Seventeen total. Eighteen now." A petite laugh blipped out. "Let's go introduce you to the girls. You too, sir, come on back with us."

The Madame's hands resting on Nalor's arm, they elbowed through the fish skin flap hanging in strips at the end of the room and into a much more sparsely lit hall. The rooms they passed were empty, occupied by sleepers, or occupied by people very much not asleep. *Does sex always involve so much shouting?*

Happily, she would not be finding out for herself tonight. She would wait till things quieted down then skulk the rooms, sipping glimmers of beauty from these whores like time itself. Then she and Nalor would be off into the fading night, and he better have some excellent answers, because she had some excellent words waiting on her tongue.

She tried to hold her disgust under her skin. No woman should have to live like this, especially not one as good as Kitornak. Taking beauty from one of them might be enough to get the 'lucky' woman out of this life. It had worked well enough for her mother.

They took an ancillary passage into another hall with rooms, the same candle-pricked darkness clinging there. The Madame called and nine or ten girls filtered out of rooms. Most of them wore ridiculous thin shirts that baffled Orluvoq. Why would anyone waste on making something so useless? The thin trousers too. It wasn't *that* much warmer in here than in the receiving room. It was like they were *trying* to—

Oh. Right. The necklines determined to hide as little breast as possible. The pant legs clinging to hips. It was all... packaging.

As the Madame made her way through the sultry intro-ductions, Orluvoq realized the names were more for Nalor's benefit than hers. Was he *shopping*? Her cheeks burned.

He brings me here to work candles, to do something terrible

*and difficult, while he blows the time sleeping with whores? I
should leave right now. Leave this moron to his women. Leave the
king to rot old and alone in his castle across the sea.*

She looked from girl to girl, taking note of the comeliest
ones. And was that a child poking its head out of a room?
But of course, here of all places, children could be found.

"Oqupip."

It took Orluvoq a handful of seconds to realize the
Madame was referring to her. "Yes?"

"No one here cares much where you sleep unless you're
with a client. Most of the girls sleep two or three together to
keep things a little warmer. And not in the way you're thinking." She winked. "If a baby starts crying and you get up to
tend it, there's not a soul here who'd complain."

Orluvoq nodded, forcefully aware of the unnatural jerki-
ness of the motion. "Thank you."

Satisfied that the new girl had been taken care of, the
Madame made a show of allowing Nalor to choose one of
the girls. He in turn made a show of lamenting that though
all their beauty deserved boundless attention, he could pick
but one. Then he picked the one with the largest posterior.
The man who had thrust Orluvoq into this misadventure
gave her a wink as his selection led him back to the first
hallway.

Desperation and confusion clouded together. This was
all a game to him. A horrid, mismatched game. She absently
followed as one of the girls invited her in to sleep and gave
her an extra blanket. Her thoughts slurred beneath the
strange roof, among strange folk.

How had things gone so south so quickly? After seeing
them face to face, how could she steal their beauty? Justice
unearned doled out by a hand unworthy.

If she didn't, the king would work his great magic

without her. She would be forgotten along with her parents. Clan Watcher would die at the end of the world. And more than that, she would remain broken. Unless she actually harnessed the blue flame, the novelty of her power would dim. Before the world could forget her, she would forget herself.

If she did become a face thief... what? A girl or two would be less pretty. Could there truly be a crime found in there? Of course there could, and she would be the criminal.

Hours passed in that near febrile state, each thought piling more muck into her mind. Each circular twist in logic leading her back down the same abandoned paths.

One most salient image in the haze was that if she didn't do it tonight, she would be expected to whore herself out tomorrow. Just like Kitornak. Where would her strength be then?

She could run and hide. There was always that. But regardless where her legs might carry her, Nalor's legs could follow. She wanted to scream, but she settled for crying.

When her subdued sobs had subdued, something in her settled without further argument. She pushed the blanket aside and stood in the dark, candle coming to one hand and tuuaaq crumb to the other. Heartbeats later, she held the flickering blue.

And it felt good.

Orluvoq was done hiding.

SINNGUP SHIFTED IN HER HALF-SLEEP, unsettled by the weight of the four-month fetus in her abdomen. The other girls loved to tell her exactly how her pregnancy would be. So far, they were all about sixteen percent correct. Why had no one warned her about the constipation?

The past few weeks, sleep had been like stepping into fog and eventually stepping out. You couldn't see where you were going, you didn't really want to be there, and when you finally got out, you weren't sure what the point of the whole event was. A part of her longed to be with a client tonight. That would have at least given her mind something to toy with other than quasi-sleep.

Pressure built up on her consciousness. Something she couldn't put her tongue on. Something dark and cold. Something...

She drew in a sharp breath and cracked her eyes open. A light leaked in around the door flap. A blue light.

A blue light?

"Innang," she whispered, scooting toward the corner of the room.

The woman in the bedroll next to her stirred. "Hm?"

"Look at the door. Do you see... blue?" Sinngup drew the blanket tighter around herself.

Innang made a sleepy moan, then gasped. "What is that? Sinngup?"

It grew. Stretched from thin, incorporeal fingers to meaty, sapphire talons knifing through the gaps. The faint padding of something stalking prey with balletic grace dripped beneath the door.

"I... don't..." Sinngup swallowed. The thing in the hall halted outside their room. She and Innang looked at one another, tongues lashed to the floors of their mouths.

A naked hand cut into the gap. It peeled back the flap like a northern wind stripping the skin from a disavowed skull. Then in rolled the cold. Like an ancient cavern of ice belching black flies in clouds beneath the midnight sun.

Sinngup cringed as the cold crept beneath the blanket and crawled across her skin.

In floated the candle that burned the baleful blue. Around it a hand coated in skin too smooth. The air pricked Sinngup's nostrils like chains of fractured ice dragging down into her lungs.

Her mind sat frozen behind her eyes. Blue light? The heavens unwaveringly threw down displays of Arsarneq's green and purple, of the sun's albine brilliance. From man came fire's amber glows. But blue? To capture the ocean in a flame? To reach down nature's throat and wrench her inside-out? What froward lunatic had made a pact with abomination and pulled it into this world?

Then came the face. Adorned only by sweat-slick hair and jumping with shadows of blue. The girl who'd come in just that night. Veneer of innocence melted to dust. Beauty amplified beyond imagining in the feeble light. She locked eyes with Innang. No one spoke. Perhaps no one could.

The rest of her body slid into the room and the door fell shut behind.

Sinngup curled her legs against her stomach, putting something substantial between the manifestation and the baby. What manner of monster stood before her? Tariaksuq? Kigatilik? Ijiraq? Yes, it must be an ijiraq come down from the end of the world, the border between death and living. And the only reason a shapeshifter would leave its cursed haunts was...

"We have no children here," Sinngup croaked, arms clinging around her belly.

The demon's head turned toward her, and finally its eyes turned too, snapping into place. It regarded her in viscous silence. "No," it whispered, "nor, I fear, shall you have."

Sinngup's head spun. Was this creature going to tear the baby out of her? "What? What do you mean? Have you—"

She choked on frigid air. Breaths came slow and ragged and left her as they came. No sounds could she produce save the strugglings of a child drenched by the ocean. In her incapacity, she could only watch as the ijiraq returned its gaze to Innang.

The womanish thing leaned, tilting over the quivering Innang, face alight with crooked hunger. Its heels came off the ground and it dipped beyond reason until its face hovered above Innang's. In a tight circle it wove the candle, illuminating each of the girl's angles. "Mm, you are a pretty one."

Sinngup could see Innang fighting to scream, but the same cold constricted them both. She made to stand, to flee and fetch aid, to shriek the halls full of working women and their clients. Nothing came to her limbs but the chill and its shivers. Blood of sleet and bones of ice. Breath of cloud and flesh of snow. Pinned in her bed by the candle's hateful glow.

Then Innang's face bulged. Not in the manner of puffed cheeks and high-flung eyebrows, but as if hooks snagged her by a dozen different barbs and tugged outward. Sinngup's already flailing heart convulsed harder.

Tiaavuluk! What thing has crawled from Nunapisu's black depths? Why can't I move? Please!

The skin stretched further from Innang's face, little gaps tearing in the sides. Innang's expression was too warped to read emotion, but the twitching of her body and desperate, retching vocalizations supplied every intimate agony. A lustrous, blue-tainted mist seeped out of the holes in her face and flowed up into the ijiraq's mouth and eyes. No, not an ijiraq. This was beyond any demon Sinngup had heard of.

It sucked at the woman like a starving man sucking the marrow from a fresh-found bone, drier and drier. The moment dragged on; the entire world shrunken to the confines of the room suspended in this disaster. Sinngup tried again and again to break away, to draw a regular breath, to stop shivering. Every effort shattered like the thinnest glaze of ice. She would die, become her child's frozen tomb, even as Nunapisu would soon become her final home.

The demon drew back.

Innang's head hit the pillow. Sinngup squinted over at her. Something was wrong, but the light was too weak to tell what. The labored breathing said that she still lived. Sinngup looked to the unknown terror looming.

Its eyes fluttered closed and it released a stuttering sigh, a thing of practiced pleasure.

Please. Please be done. Just leave. Just let me breathe *again.*

The eyelids didn't tarry. The thing returned its gaze to Innang, and the struggling woman's breaths evened out.

Asleep. It had just thrown sleep over her like a blanket. But... sleep? Not death? What demon *was* this?

Sinngup looked again to her bed mate. The light caught just right, and she was struck. Ghastly. Though no sign of the holes that had torn remained, the once comely Innang was wrapped with a grotesque simulacrum of what her face should be. Sinngup threw her eyes back to the demon and her cold stomach froze solid.

It's a beauty snatcher come to ravage us.

She tried to run, this time from the impending destitution. Anywhere into the night would do. Anywhere that might not be shared by this unheard-of monster. To the end of the earth, if she must.

The demon's eyes locked on hers, and she was immobile. Not for the cold, but for the pure shock its preternatural beauty jolted into her. The single most perfect face Sinngup had ever seen looked down upon her as the sun looks upon a morning fog. There smoldered a hunger that would soon know satisfaction. Her shivering intensified.

Slowly, the demon tipped until its face hung above hers, eyes and candle making their circuit.

"I will savor you," was all it said, face bathed blue by that odious flicker.

Sinngup told her arms to twitch up, to push it away. They held their jittering grip on her belly. She told her tongue to scream. Her teeth wouldn't be pried open.

It started as a tickle, then grew to an itch. Her vision blurred. Too many tears in the way. Her breasts, her stomach, her hips, her legs. But most of all, her face. They itched and buzzed like a blizzard scratching the land, all traveling in one direction. Pain pierced through as her face tore and the first wisps of beauty leaked out.

She screamed, but it ended as frozen gagging. Tears poured beneath her skin, across her muscle, and flowed out through her open wounds. She gagged and gagged and gagged.

ESSENCE OF PULCHRITUDE flowed into Orluvoq bit by luscious bit, and nothing in her power could staunch it. The atrociously stretched face and the girl below blurred behind the fog. Orluvoq tried to sever the stream, to amputate the parasitic communion. She failed over and over.

As she had with the last ten girls.

She couldn't remember why that was supposed to be bad. She was trying. Everybody loved triers. She would just take a little more, then cut it off...

Oh. That didn't work. I thought for sure it would work this time.

Strange. Why wouldn't it work? She was a good angakkuq. Maybe the best. How could she fail so many times in a row at something as simple as not ripping the beauty from another person's body? That's why it was bad. She should be better at working candles than this.

The flow of the glamor glow slowed. She made another push and severed the tie. Quicker than last time! She was getting better. Even the best had to practice now and then. No one was perfect the first try. Those were just the facts of life.

She floated back to her feet and shuddered at the settling influx of virtue. It coursed between skin and muscle like rivulets of summer water reshaping the land. Glissading on the substrate of tuuaaq in her veins, it felt perfect. Like her body was the most well crafted glove ever. Like her skin itself was skywalking the aurora. She ran the backside of a finger over her cheek. Smoother than seal skin.

A sound pulled her from her reverie. She looked down and briefly wondered why the woman half covered by blanket was making those constrained panting noises. Ah, right, Orluvoq had issued forth a stifling cold minutes earlier.

She fumbled with her mind on the candle, and the girl's breathing leveled. Orluvoq didn't know whether she had given sleep or taken consciousness. Did it matter though? She was trying.

A thought dispersed the choking cold, and she

wandered back into the hall, her blue light its only illumina-
tion. Her feet wandered aimlessly, but her hands wandered
passionately over her body and skin. Every morsel of flesh
curved in pristine proportion. Every modicum of skin
exhaled serenity like a field driven white by a soundless
storm.

Fit for a king. Perhaps too fit. Did that pompous cur
across the ocean really deserve her, no doubt the world's
most beautiful woman, not to mention most gifted
angakkuq?

Wait. Her hand stopped tracing. *Something seems off about
that. Isn't Nalor better than me? And isn't Qummukarpoq better
than Nalor?*

Her mind picked up as her feet left off, strolling down
avenues of perplexion. What was that off feeling? Should
she go find another girl to leech beauty from? No, the urge
didn't thrum like it had after the other ones. That last lick of
loveliness had imparted a sense of completeness.

Thinking on it, the memories of imbibing hung askew,
like a queerly angled bird cutting across the morning pale.
But why? Where was the lie?

A babe's cry broke the night, and Orluvoq's thoughts
scattered. She waited as the child wailed a few doors down.
Only a moment and mother's calming touch would caress
away the terrors of night and hunger. Yes, it would be but a
moment.

The cries dragged on.

Any... moment?

No one. Not the mother, not another. No soul rushed, or
grudgingly walked, to succor the child. It was as if this
whole side of the clan had been—

—*put to sleep. I did that. Right.* She wrinkled her brow.
Was it not frowned upon to send someone into deep sleep

unless they had specifically requested it? Yet she had done it. She had also—hm. Yes. She had also sucked the picturesque parts out of almost a dozen women. Would she really do something like that?

Annoyed by the bawling baby and the ebbing of her tuuaaq high, she sauntered down the corridor. The fish skin flap pressed heavy against her fingers as if she feared to see what lay inside. Had she not walked here mere minutes before? She shook her head and entered.

There. See? It was just two supine women and one wriggling baby painted dim blue. Nothing to be afraid of. She almost laughed at herself as she bent and scooped up the child.

She rocked it for a long moment to no effect. Mama had told her about inconsolable babies, but she'd had scant exposure. The image she'd slotted in her head had been too tame. This was a waking nightmare. It felt like high time to hand it off to the mother. She looked around, frazzled.

Oh. Right. Maybe I should wake her. Them.

No telling which one was the mother.

But if I wake them...

She refocused on their faces. Their wizened, year-stricken faces. Their sagging, pocked faces. Their grotesque, dysmorphic faces.

It... must be the light. The blue could make anyone look bad.

The baby's crying rapped against her ear over and over. The faces seemed to twist and droop into ever uglier pastiches of humanity.

I can step outside, then wake them up.

The light in her hand rippled and flipped to orange.

The gauziness coddling her thoughts broke. Effluent spewed out of her mind, chased by cataracts of understanding. Their faces. Their faces!

Tiaavuluk! I—I've ravaged *them!*

The memories stung clean as an ice-shredded breeze. That first girl. Orluvoq had tried to siphon off a smidgeon of beauty, the tiniest ounce, but it wouldn't stop! Why would it not stop? Infecting her mind with that unslakable, unbreakable hunger, pulling her from room to room.

She couldn't tear her eyes from the sleeping figures on the floor. The appalling countenances of her victims etched themselves into her mind along with their disheveled forms sprawled in exhausted disarray.

She clumsily set the crying baby down and staggered out of the room. Ceilings clustered violently and walls lurched from darkness as she wove down the hall. She knew she was making too much noise, but her thoughts were only noise. After searching and searching, she found the exit chamber, devoid of Madame and light.

Gracelessly, the monster Orluvoq fled into the night.

13

Decades Long Dead

The dark sky's oily streak of green waved ponderously, like a colossal sail in a gentle breeze, and its reflection on the landscape waved back. Miniscule shadows of hunters darted around the bigger pod-like shapes. Man and narwhal locked in the dance of generations.

Puigor watched the display wholly unaffected, huddled alone on a knoll. He should sleep, but he had no desire to lie in that tiny room made boundless by blackness. Lying, waiting for light, the darkness thickened by his mother's sorrow emanating like incense.

As angakkuq, he might as well be on hand to provide healing should a hunter get injured. And if he got to a kill before any of the huntsmen...

A narwhal flailed as it fell from the aurora, no doubt spraying its lifeblood to dapple the ice below in crimson constellation. Puigor's heart perked up and he hopped to his feet, groping for tallow and tuuaaq. Within a moment the flame was alive, and he jumped into a windwalk. No, the flame was more than alive.

It was blue.

He cackled as his feet whirled, pulling shadows around him. Normal angakkuq ways paled to white in comparison. The height. The power. It was divine.

Pure happenstance had colored the glim blue during that fated homeward voyage two months ago. A collision of substance abuse and severe weather. The unfettered wrath of sky and sea had inspired him with enough survival ambition to light up a candle whilst intoxicated. He still wasn't sure how he got the flame to flip, but he now knew he had been far too full of tusk. As soon as it had flickered blue, it had punched him into unconsciousness. Four times in a row.

When at last he'd burned off enough tuuaaq to handle the new color, he'd pushed a ring of tranquility out from his ship for spans and spans. Normal angakkuq Puigor could only dream of such weather control.

But he knew by some intrinsic provenance that the blue flame was not a thing to be shared and flared for all to behold. He must hold it jealously to his bosom, seclude it behind a clutching glove. They would spurn him for his aberration, more than they already disdained him for his failure of a rescue mission.

Few if any of his clansfolk believed the prince had actually stolen the name from Puigor's head. It had to, they mused, be a cover for the boy's ignominious return. No man —or demon—had ever stolen *names*. A man might as well try and steal a spirit. And the prince certainly wasn't coming for them, whatever that meant. Princes didn't do things like that.

Puigor dropped out of his windwalk as he neared the corpse, pulsing out to see how much time he had before company arrived. A hunter was kiting down, still a minute or more off. The dog sleds hadn't even reached halfway.

A piece had already cleaved off the narwhal's tusk from the landing. Fortunate. Knife marks weren't very discreet, and fresh tusk was a lot harder to break than dead tusk. With little effort, thanks to his blue candle, he probed and found the sizable shard fifty paces away before the hunter had touched down. Not that he would have worried much had it taken longer. His control over shadows exceeded any man's control over their eyes.

As he windwalked away, slick with glee over the tuuaaq tied inside his trousers, his thoughts turned to the prince. As they always did.

The day of visitation was not far off. That he was certain of. The regent of Qilaknakka would descend clothed in his awful might and... and what? Something dastardly. Something about rapine and the sovereign rights to one's own mind. Whatever it was, it would surprise the prince to find he wasn't the only wielder of the blue flame. Puigor's second encounter with him would resemble the first on no accounts.

The clan's sole angakkuq scuttled around the sparse forest convenient to the igloos, exercising his dominance with the tusk. In and out he dodged among shafts of lucent green that bled from sky through spindly tree fingers. He whiled away an hour of night in pursuit of whatever he could fold into his influence.

The clansfolk would have declared that luck ran companion at his side, for he avoided any demonic encounters alone in the groves. Luck. Yes, alright, let them nestle their heads against their claims so they might find sleep. Puigor knew it was the blue that kept all fiends at bay.

Here and there he ran across the carcass of some beast he had taken control of on previous nights. Why they refused to eat after he had relinquished control over them, he couldn't say. He should probably inform someone of the caribou meat in the morning.

Mysteries disregarded, his sport wasn't enough, swallowing shadows and conning his way into the minds of lured animals. He craved the next challenge. The human challenge.

He set his face eastward and skittered to the village.

Deep night clutched the igloos. The two narwhal kills lay in different states of carnage, left for morning butchering. An icy crust spangled the cooling corpses, creeping where steam had long since ceased to rise.

Puigor didn't trifle with tiptoes. The candle gobbled his scuffles with as much alacrity as he did tuuaaq. He rippled over the ground like a shrewd breeze. He stalked as does a tiriaksuq, glimpsed only in shadows cast, vanishing under direct observation. To where did he stalk? Where else?

He slunk inside the hovel where his mother lay.

She slept against a wall, curled like a wounded stoat. For a moment, despite the tuuaaq rush—or because of it?—he transmuted from wily, puissant lord of flames to anxious, sheepish lad of fourteen. Father gone. Father *taken*. Mother yearning to not awaken. All sympathy his clansfolk had held firm against their chests. Alone he stood, regardless of where, fragile skin stretched over his face. He durst not cry for fear that that face would shatter at the touch of the first tear.

He pushed aside the frivolous emotions. Prince

Qummukarpoq could arrive any day. It was moronic, perhaps suicidal, to become a melancholy dweller before then. Puigor must lose himself to preparation.

He bunched his brow and threw his focus at his mother's mind. His thoughts stammered like the hooves of a nervous caribou. All efforts at grasping the reins of her mind slipped and slipped and slipped. There was nothing to grasp. No hames, no traces. Or if there was, it was like infinitesimally flaxen strands purling in an unfelt wind, floating through each grasping finger.

The lemmings and the terns had been so effortless to claim. Shadows fell into file almost without him asking. The ground flew beneath him like thundering water. Yet a solitary woman could defy him from within the bowels of unconsciousness? What—what *witchcraft* was this? A fatal failing inborn in him? An innate resilience in her? An arbitrary governance on the candles?

He reached out and flailed once more. Nothing and nothing. Measured shock pumped through him. There must be something sacrosanct about the human mind, something the tusk refused to touch.

But the prince. He stole my father's name straight from my head. If you can take a piece of the mind, surely you can take the whole thing.

Again. Something had to relent. A covert crevasse concealing the entrance would reveal itself. A veil would rend. A fog would part. Something!

Screams scratched at his throat, but even under the influence of tuuaaq he had enough presence of mind to hold them down. A conscious subject would be far harder to insinuate himself into than the slumbering one before him.

Where *was* it? The... the *thing*. The thing that was so

easy to find in the creatures of the forest. The latch to pry open. He swerved and stabbed at her from a confusion of angles, whatever that meant. He didn't know. He only knew failing and trying again. Again. Again.

There. The spindly fingers of his mind wrapped around something slight, something gossamer. The portal to another's mind.

Ha, he cackled in his head. There it was. *There it is!*

He wove the strings into his grasp and gave his stoutest tug. But they didn't budge. No, whatever gangly cords leading back to his mother's mind he had ahold of stretched. More frustrations threatened to break out of his throat as he pulled and pulled. Just when he thought the ceaseless slack was coming to its end, the flame in his real hand jumped from blue to orange.

Ah! His mouth felt like it had been stuffed with furs for how dry it was. He should have topped off on tuuaaq a few minutes ago.

His eyes lighted on the sleeping bundle that was his mother. A fiery connection blazed through his mind, from her back to the animals of the woods he had ensorcelled, and the world slowly warped around him.

The prince had taken the name from Puigor and hadn't given it back. Puigor had taken control from the animals and hadn't given it back. That's why they just stood there until they collapsed. But what if. What if it *couldn't* be given back?

He snuffed the candle and clutched his soured gut. *Did... did I just nearly kill my own mother?*

The visions of insensate, frost-rimed animals swerved at him in lurid flashes, melting into the specter of his spirit-bereft mother. "Can't be given back," and, "can't be given back," rang through his skull loud enough to fracture the insides. He slumped down and pushed himself against a wall to await the pale of morning.

A sleepless hour later, restlessness drove him to light a tuuaaq candle. As it came to life, he toyed with a crumb, debating whether to eat the tusk. To don the truer power. The thought of a spiritless mother decided for him. Better to wait awhile. The blue flame gave magnificent power. But was there such a thing as a power too great? A sky too wide? A moment too momentous?

He wasn't exactly sure why he'd sparked the candle to life. Habit? Distraction? The need to prove he could work more than malevolence with the flame? Whatever the amalgam of reasons, he sent his mind a-questing toward the open sea.

The sea tugged back.

Rather, something—some*one*—seaward plucked a murmur on his mindscape. That shouldn't be there. He probed again.

Close. It was nearly upon the village. And—and it was coming from the sky? A meteor? The odd story about those hinted they could be sensed by an angakkuq. But no. It felt far too *human*.

He hopped up and ran outside, easy since he had neglected to remove his parka earlier. Lids peeled back as far as they would go, he cast his eyes to Arsarneq's green ribbon. Of course, he saw nothing other than the occasional dark smudge of a narwhal. Yet, letting his eyes slide shut and seeking outward, he felt it clear as noonday. A demon striding the sky straight toward the village.

Part of him begged for it to just pass over. What need had he for a night full of terrors from beyond his own mind? The other part of him needed it to come down, to show its brutish face. If he could trounce a roving demon, his clansfolk would have no choice but to put all stock in him as angakkuq ascendant.

But if it were to fall upon the village, and Puigor were to vanquish it, he would need witnesses. For who knew but that a demon's body might shred to scraps as it doubled over in defeat? Or if it were some warped man or woman—as he suspected—the ice might well claim their body to appease Nunapisu's gluttony.

Witnesses! He picked up his feet to rouse his sleeping kin. They were loath to shed their cocoons, but they had to give him *some* credence, as he was the only one among them who could commune with the candles. Eventually eleven men and five women had assembled, scowling and squinting in the harsh night air.

"So what exactly is it we're awaiting?" asked Puigor's uncle, hand on a harpoon. "What demon?"

Puigor regripped his uncomfortably short taper. "I'm... not really sure. But it's—oh, spirits, there it is."

From Arsarneq's glittering midst came a figure striding. Long scything steps that glossed the air. With each pace, Puigor's unease twisted further.

"Abyss take me!" someone exclaimed, hefting a spear. "It's a skeleton."

Two of the men began drumming, dancing, and singing in hopes their song might turn it away.

But onward it came, enrobed in a mantle of the purest white. Austere horns jutted from its head as if the thing had dislodged itself from a cavern ceiling and swept into the night. Unease huddled the clansfolk tighter together. Hunters sometimes returned from the aurora with tales of demons stalking their merry way through the glow. Puigor's fellows debated the nature of the beast and what malevolence it had come to wreak upon them.

Puigor needed no debate. He *knew*. A solitary flicker of blue escaped from its hand, held just so before its chest, and torment seized him by his chest.

"No," he broke their conversation, voice a crackle. "It is none of those things you say. We are being paid a visit by our esteemed prince Qummukarpoq."

The atmosphere between them tipped slowly then shifted its weight to a new disquiet. The horror that, perhaps, this boy they had so quickly discounted was more than the sum of a few tall tales. At the same time, it was a horror striated with relief. Not a demon from the heavens. Just a man with a candle.

That relief evaporated as one by one they espied the candle's hue. The thought rolled through each mind: what sorcery had the boy claimed the prince capable of? The men's song dropped to naught but hollow night, and the prince dropped to the ice.

Puigor fumbled a piece of tuuaaq into his mouth and shifted from foot to foot, awaiting the high. Ten paces away, the prince held his stiff gaze upon the gathered few. The clansfolk held spears and breath with equal tension.

"I applaud your ready reception of me," spake the prince, proffering no introduction.

Unnoticed by all, Puigor's flame jumped to blue. The high sloshed his brain from side to side. *Tiaavuluk. I might have taken too much tuuaaq.*

"Since you've all congregated so sanctimoniously, surely you know why I've come this night."

A few eyes in the huddle glanced askance at each other. No one savored the notion of being voice for the group.

"No reason? This is what I'm hearing? You think I've tramped over the ocean just to stare at a paltry audience of my subjects, then turn tail on you?"

Heads shook. No. Though he might have just declared their hopes, their hopes and beliefs belonged to different clans tonight.

"I assume this isn't your entire village. Go and fetch any sleepers."

A handful of people broke away, eager to remove themselves from the prince's presence, and Puigor snuffed his candle. A silence ensued, unnerving the more the longer it stretched. Qummukarpoq paid it no heed and twitched not a finger. He passed his stare over each of them as more clansfolk filtered in, pausing when he came to Puigor at the back of the sparse crowd.

"Ah, the man I was hoping to see. Have you informed your kin of why I'm here? Have you even figured it out yourself?"

Before Puigor could sift an answer out of his addled mind, his mother's cries cut into the night.

"Where is he? Where is my husband? What have you done to him? Why would you take him from me?" And on and on. She came running across the snow, course aimed straight for the prince. As she ran past the group of villagers, she extended her arms, claws curled for her target's throat.

"Bring him ba—"

She gasped and fell to the earth before his feet, limbs curling in around her body. The clansfolk shuddered as a wall of chill wafted over them.

"Let us dispense with hysterics," said the prince. "I'm going to release you, and you're going to go stand with your friends."

He struck no bargain, merely stated fact. Somewhere inside the too intense tuuaaq haze, Puigor cringed at his mother's actions while feverishly trying to gather a plan. A moment later, his mother gasped again, got to her knees, and crawled over to the clan as she sobbed.

Spirits. What sort of angakkuq power is that? Puigor thought, reconsidering his conviction in bringing down the prince.

"Is everyone gathered yet?" Qummukarpoq asked, not so much as a hint that he had just incapacitated a woman without touching her. With a nod from the crowd, he continued. "Then. I ask, what are the three parts of a person?"

After a quiet space, the patriarch cleared his throat and answered. "Body, spirit, and name." His demure demeanor was the white to the black of every irascible remark he had made about royalty over the past two months.

"Body, spirit, and name," Qummukarpoq confirmed. "And what happens when one of these dies?"

It was a child's catechism, but no one dared scoff at the simplicity.

"If one dies, the other two die," said the patriarch.

"Yes. Thus, Nunapisu. Thus, naming our children for a dozen or more ancestors. But I've long wondered, how true is this truism? This 'fact' so plain that any child of words can recite it? How do we *know* this to be true? Can any of you say for *certain* that a name forgotten is an ancestor killed? That a body dismembered is a murderer denied an afterlife? Is there any among us who can commune with the spirits so consistently to determine such a thing?"

The words worked on Puigor, but he couldn't get his brain to figure out how it all connected.

"I will know it. This is why I have come tonight. I have taken one of yours, and I will cast his name from this world. Nominal death. Once I have killed his name, I will watch his body die. Or not. And the world will know."

Puigor's spine wilted, and his mother wailed. He rushed to relight his candle. The clan tensed and a child joined its cries to the woman. Eyes jumped from face to face. Who would be the one to speak against this flagrant corruption? One of the archons? One of the hunters?

"Qummukarpoq."

The screaming stopped. Heads swung around, searching from under anxiety-knitted brows to see who had spoken.

Puigor took a step toward the tyrant. "Leave us be."

A single eyebrow on the prince's head quirked up as the people parted for Puigor. He regarded the blue flame in the young angakkuq's hand then let the eyebrow drop. "No."

Through the tuuaaq fog, Puigor's gut wrenched. A single syllable devoid of bluster, planted like a sky-scraping pillar that no eye might shy away from. The prince knew Puigor posed no threat, and he forced that knowledge down Puigor's throat with a word.

"Then... then take me instead. Let my father return home. The clan needs him."

"You seem to think I've come to bargain. I have not. Your offer amounts to another errand on my shoulders. However, if you wish to add your name to the list beside his, I will put it there myself."

Puigor's tongue clung dumb in his mouth.

The prince closed his eyes as if the matter were done. His nostrils pumped out thick breaths. The clansfolk passed around an unsettled look. Who had ever heard of a single man coming into a village, throwing out threats, then standing with closed eyes before the clan's hunters? Yet none of them moved to apprehend him.

A gasp sucked through the crowd. Qummukarpoq slid open his eyes.

"What was that?" asked one of the women. The question picked up echoes from the others.

The prince pointed to Puigor's mother. "This woman. What is the name of her husband?"

Several people drew breaths as if to make a pronouncement, then their faces crumbled to confusion. The prince smiled, a poison slash, and Puigor's mother broke out in inconsolable wailing.

Puigor stood stunned. He had gotten swept away in the rhetoric and hadn't even tried to stop the sorcery. What did he even hold a candle for? The light it gave was a pittance for the light the prince's took.

Qummukarpoq spoke to silence the people. "I want you to listen closely when I say gᵏɪ̃q̃ỹ ᵽóꞏꞏụ q̲ᵫ̲ᵗg̲ɩ̲p̲."

Gloved hands flew to cover ears. Some cried out. The prince allowed himself another small smile, then fixed his sight on Puigor, face a wicked playground of light and shadow.

"Now for you."

Panic stabbed into Puigor. "Wait, what?" The prince made no reply other than to close his eyes. Puigor flung his mind into the defensive, frantically dragging his name into his deepest bastion then throwing up as many walls around it as possible. Unknown instinct drove as he stood without a clue whether an angakkuq could even muster defense.

Another shock rippled through the clansfolk. Something pried at Puigor, but it quickly passed over. The prince opened his eyes.

"Your name," he demanded Puigor. "Say it."

"Um. Puigor?" *I did it!* Puigor thought. *I blocked him.*

His kin flinched. They flinched at his very name and backed away from him. His victory rung hollow.

Qummukarpoq's voice dropped low. "The next time you

come to bother me, Puigor, I will wrest your very name from you. Be happy I let you keep it now."

Puigor trembled and dropped to his knees. The last shred of tusk burned dead in his hand. The prince, the tyrant at the start of the world, turned in a flourish and strode into the sky.

Nameless. The boy was nameless to all but himself.

14

Bootfalls creaked through the whining wind that had arisen. Orluvoq didn't look up. There was no one else it could be. She remained on forearms and knees, head hung low.

"I can't hear their voices anymore," she said, trying to ignore the ringing in her ears. "I remember her saying once, 'Orluvoq, don't let the dog lick inside your mouth.' But I can't hear it. They speak to me no more. I... I don't even know if I can see their faces any longer.

"Where did they go? Does that mean their spirits are gone? Can you hear your mother's voice? See your father's face?"

She awaited Nalor's reply, but he never gave it. His silence galled her. She found her teeth gritted.

"After all you just did to me, you can't even grace me with a reply?" She raised her head, eyes level with his shins. "More fun. Remember saying that? It'd be more fun if I didn't know what we were walking into?" She pushed herself up. "I think that you—"

She stumbled back.

It wasn't Nalor.

"I should kill you right here." Orange candlelight played with shadow on the Madame's glowering face. "I should punch your ugly witch face until it stops bleeding. I—" she cut off, seeing Orluvoq's face for the first time. "*Tiaavuluk!* You... you're beyond beautiful."

Two tears spilled onto Orluvoq's cheeks, hot, then immediately cold. "I didn't want to do it. It was only supposed to be a bit. A tiny bit from each girl. But once it started, I couldn't stop. I drank it all. I want to give it back, but I can't. It doesn't work that way. I... I'm sorry. I don't know what to do."

The Madame's voice grew distant. "So this is what the beauty of a dozen women buys..."

Orluvoq scoured the barely lit face for signs. For traces of mercy. Was that awe commingled with... hate? Certainly none of the convivial air that bubbled off her back at the igloos.

Fingers flashed hot across her face, the sting of the slap mixing with the bite of the frigid air. Orluvoq recoiled to the ice.

"You," said the Madame, "are coming right back with me, and never touching a candle again." She thrust hands through Orluvoq's parka and trousers, extracting every tuuaaq taper she could find. Orluvoq watched in a numb stupor.

"Do you know how much business you've just cost me?" the Madame spat. "How many of those girls will *starve* now? No, your broken psychopath brain probably doesn't think past whatever prick of a man you think this little facade is going to land you. Let's go." She yanked on the stunned Orluvoq's hood.

When Orluvoq's bulk didn't budge from the ice, the

Madame lashed out another open palm. Orluvoq's head cracked to the side. Pain. Stupid pain that knocked her mind off her moral woes for a moment.

"Get *up*." The Madame pulled again. "Or I will slap your face until I get back every drop of beauty you took from my girls."

Orluvoq struggled to her feet, pulling her hood back over her head. Under the Madame's brusque guidance, she began stumbling back whence she came. The den in which the monster Orluvoq had been born.

How had it happened? She had held the reins to tuuaaq, but as quickly as she tried to direct its course, they were jerked from her. She wanted to try again—to prove that she was more than a single night of mistakes. Start with something a touch simpler. Simultaneously, she gagged on the thought of more tuuaaq slipping down her throat. The monster, she feared, would claw its way from the womb anew each time she bent the azure fire.

Perhaps she need not worry. If the Madame were to revoke her access to tuuaaq, like had happened five years ago, the monster would remain veiled. Perhaps the night of her crimes had lived its short life, and now was come the day of her repentance, to be spent ever pleasing hordes of faceless men.

After a couple minutes of walking, the Madame's constant dribble of curses dried up, and she pulled Orluvoq to a halt. She held the candle out in front of them, squinting at the dark.

"Do you see anything?" she asked.

Orluvoq strained to glimpse any anomalies on the barren horizon. Not so much as a flicker on the ill-lit landscape. "Nothing."

The Madame's mouth twisted downward. Her candle

was but a short burn from extinguishment. "Something's off." She slid her eyes closed to quest out with aid from the candle, Orluvoq intuited.

The flame sputtered cold; its meager but substantial light snuffed to nowhere. The Madame's eyes flew open, and she released Orluvoq in a panicked rush to relight the taper. Movement ahead drew Oluvoq's eyes away from the clumsy attempts at ignition.

Drapes of shadow unfurled before them in bulbous ripples, cutting through the aurora-tinged air like wrathful clouds severing earth from sun. From the bosom of the dissipating shadows stepped a man bearing a blue flame. Orluvoq relaxed at Nalor's appearance. The Madame tensed, puffing out a nerve-filled breath cloud.

"The girl comes with me." Nalor's voice flowed from the shadows curling around them.

With a pinky still wrapped around her composure, the Madame replied, "She—she owes me a great deal. She is mine." She succeeded in lighting the tusk, and just as soon, Nalor extinguished it again.

"I am not asking." He turned to Orluvoq. "Let's go."

Orluvoq tottered away from her captor and followed the man she had been despairing only minutes earlier across the tundra.

"No!"

Orluvoq's parka groped at her throat as the Madame grabbed her from behind. She let loose a choked cry, and Nalor turned.

"Did you not hear me? She comes with me." He made a gesture and the Madame dropped to the ice, hands distorting to clutch at nothing.

"Orluvoq," said the tirigusuusik. "Take her candles. Now."

She bustled to do his bidding, extricating candles with slightly more delicacy than the Madame had afforded her. She stashed the tapers in various pockets made for the very act and backed up to stand beside Nalor.

The Madame coughed a fit as he released her, glaring hatred at him. "You'll never be able to go anywhere again, *sir*. I'll tell everyone I meet about this. You will be hunted." She pointed at Orluvoq. "She may be a dumb wench, but that's all she is. *You're* the only mind her head knows. Don't think this ends with you walking away."

Nalor regarded her with pinched brow. "Tell everyone? No. No, you won't." His eyes shut. His breath pumped in concentration.

The Madame gasped, hands flying to her throat. Over and over she moved her jaw, but nothing save breath came out. Orluvoq watched with a turned head, as if she wanted to look away but couldn't quite detach.

Nalor opened his eyes and looked at the pathetic woman.

"What did you do?" asked Orluvoq.

"Our lovely hostess here expressed how eager she was to let her voice out, so I helped her."

"You took her voice?" she watched the woman beat the snow in anger, face awash with tears.

Nalor turned and walked.

In the mist-thin green light, Orluvoq stared upon the woman of ragged breaths, deliberating whether she ought do something. Frills of shame already buzzed along her bones from a night much lived. What was one more stripe?

She turned and walked.

❄

A FRESH SHEET of snow dampened her footfalls as she trod after Nalor on the forlorn plains. Thoughts pooled in her mouth only to drain down her throat. He walked with too much aplomb. Every step an ensign planted, averring that deference was his due. What could she say that he wouldn't discount?

A long while they walked, looking, Nalor said, for a cave they could bed down in. While caves evaded them, Orluvoq tangled with more conversation starters. Anything to extract a shred of closure.

"What would you do if I ran?" she asked.

The question slid off his back. Or it seemed. Several strides later, he spoke. "What did I do the last time you ran away, just now?"

Her stomach turned, the confirmation of her fears spilling in. She could flee, and he could follow. Their march continued.

"Orluvoq," he broke the silence. "I am not your captor. I won't chase you from Nunapisu to Qilaknakka and back. I won't compel the beasts of the ice and fowls of the air to harry you like common game. I won't tie the aurora around your ankle and reel you in to my igloo in the sky. If you truly wish to be gone, then make it so."

Breath poured heavy from her nostrils. Her hand itched for a tuuaaq taper. Run. She could hare until her sleep-hungry body gave out. Maybe she could make it back to Paarsisioq and Kitornak by dawnlight. It could all be over. Naught but a dream that ferried her through winter's long night.

But her hand made no move. Her feet gathered no speed. Her mind hovered between the here and the there. And in hovering, it chose the here. For somewhere slumped within her depths, she knew that if she resorted to hiding again, she would bleed away her vital years in the blackened heart of obscurity.

"You knew," she said at last. "You knew that it would take me over and that I'd end up sucking the whole place dry."

"I know a great many things, so I can see where your confusion stems from. But no. I did not know you would go and drain the whole warren."

She worked the muscles of her jaw. Truth, or convenient fabrication? And what could she do in the case of either? Just as she'd attested to the Madame, no length of tuuaaq would force what was stolen back into the dispossessed. What was done was done.

The contorted faces that had then seemed a trivial artifact of her satisfaction paraded now across her mind, dragging her through the quag of terror she had churned up. Skin deep. The flimsy justification she had propped up for undertaking the theft at all. But she had seen the truth on their faces. Beauty was skin deep, but its roots stretched into the spirit. She had torn it out of them with grace tantamount to ripping all their hairs out in one draw.

Her scalp crawled.

"I've been giving your condition a lot of thought." Nalor spoke as if he'd never stopped. "I've introduced a dozen and more people to the ways of the tirigusuusik, and not a one has ever reacted like that."

"Condition? You say it like I'm sick."

"Something like that," he responded. "Everyone is born with talent for the candles. Often that talent sums to nothing, but in cases like myself, the talent is something substantial. In cases like yourself, it's even greater.

"It is my supposition that you are not only sensitive, but hypersensitive to the aurora's power. So much that when you burn it both outside and inside, it's as if the aurora itself is using you as a conduit to join itself to life."

"And what does any of that mean?"

"I don't know. I'm still working on it." They made more footprints. "As the narwhals feed on the aurora, the excess they eat grows into their tusk, yes?"

She nodded, then realized she was behind him. "Right."

"But what really is the aurora? What is it made of?"

It hearkened back to their earlier conversations on the auroral origins, but she suspected it might just be a distraction technique this time. "That's not the type of thing people can know. Plenty of people have been inside it and still have no clue."

"You've forgotten one thing in your calculations. *I've* been inside it. And I think I know."

Her worries about scathed women, blistered feet, and abscessed morals lifted slightly. "Oh?"

"What are the three parts of a person?"

"Body, name, and spirit. You've already asked me that."

"Then let me ask." He turned to face her. "What are the three parts of all things?"

She halted before him, lit by falling green and rising blue. "All things have three parts?"

"What are they?"

Orluvoq looked around, searching the snow for any hints. "Body, name, and spirit?" The words didn't want to come out, but there they were.

"Precisely."

"Wait, really?"

"I believe that the world turns in an endless cycle. The first arc of its rotation is that." He gestured above to Arsarneq gleaming. "Void of all but potential. And the second arc is this." He swept his over his body. "The void given shape; body. Given identity; name. And given life; spirit. Snow and creature; ocean and air. All were once the same. But why do we die? What lies beyond the final heartbeat?

"As I said. It is the cycle that turns without surcease. Once this thing that is everything has become something, it desires to return to nothing so that it might cycle through again and become something greater. When it is nothing, it forgets what it once was and simply desires to be something. Anything.

"That is why we can work the candles. We burn the very fabric of life itself. And it is so eager to become *anything* that it becomes part of us; part of the world. And we become more than we could be alone."

He frowned. "But you. *You* seem to be more attuned to it than anyone I've met. I think with most people, it's like the essence of the aurora is running through chest-high drifts of snow. But with you, it runs as if over hard-packed ice. I haven't made sense of it yet."

Orluvoq had made far less sense of it. "So you're saying I shouldn't work the blue flame?"

Nalor grinned. "On the contrary. You may very well make the greatest tirigusuusik the world has known."

Her face twisted into a moue. "And what if I don't want to? What if I hate what I did to those girls?"

"Success rarely accompanies one's first trial."

"What if I hate what *you* did to the girls?"

His head pulled back. "And what is to be meant by that?"

"You took me there to do your dirty work, then you go and just take your pick of the flock and bed her down, mister *most distinguished guest*. And you didn't even pay!" She would much rather no one be in the situation of those women, but they could at the very least be compensated for their miseries.

"Appearances carry import. Do you know how they would have reacted had I insisted I sleep in the women's quarters?"

She flung out her arms. "You can cover yourself in shadow and walk unseen! You couldn't have come and, I don't know, chaperoned me? Kept me from going momentarily insane and devastating a dozen women's lives?"

His mouth pressed into a tight slit, keeping back his words—if he had any.

"No, you didn't even think of that. You were too obsessed with getting your jollies. Dirty old man." Anger at his actions spun knots with the fright of naming those actions to his face. A flame still burned blue in his hand, evincing a control and a power she couldn't match. His annoyance at her words could grow too great, and he could tear her voice from her throat just like the Madame. It was brittle ice on which she trod.

"Orluvoq," Nalor said after a measured pause. "Among us, who do you think is the better tirigusuusik? I could bend your emotions to fit mine like a glove and make use of your body over and over. And more so than you, I could do that to any ordinary girl with the barest of efforts. I could rape my way from igloo to igloo with no consequences, for I can hide where they cannot find me. Never once in all my years of being tirigusuusik have I done so. Yet here you are accusing me of corruption when I make a point of seeking willing partners."

And what was she to make of that? He had spoken no untruth. Yet his words made little headway in settling her. "She was only willing because she thought she was getting paid."

A foggy sigh puffed from Nalor's lips. "I left her with money." His voice bore the weight of an elder who had watched every last friend be fed to the ice.

Orluvoq's exasperation floundered with no good target to aim it at. "Oh," she said quietly.

"Ten years ago, you were almost killed by a bluebody. Why do you think another was never sent after you?"

In that moment, she knew the answer to a question she had always wondered but never asked. Nalor had gone and taken care of the tirigusuusik from Teriannaiq. How many times had he saved her now?

They stood eyeing one another in the low, blue luminance until Nalor swung about and resumed his trudging.

THE MOUTH of the cave drank midday light, and in the swallow, it tickled her eyes open. She sat up and walked out of the shallow cavity, laid a finger aside her nose, and emptied her nostril onto the ice. With a candid lack of dithering, the companion nostril was voided. Casting a leery eye about for Nalor or other undesirables, and none being forthcoming, she squatted and exposed her delicates to the churlish cold.

The first business of the day complete, she stood and refastened her trousers, then turned to see Nalor standing behind her, looking pointedly at another horizon. "Tiaavuluk!" she swore.

"Good to see you're up." He swiveled to reveal a piebald hare slung over his shoulder. "I've fetched a spot of breakfast."

"Were you watching me?"

"If I say yes, are you going to demand money?"

She scoffed in outrage. "I'm not a whore, despite you selling me off as one last night."

"And I'm not a voyeur, despite the Madame strip searching you in front of me last night." He swung the rabbit around and worked a knife under the fur. "I'm not so callow as to suggest we put all this bordello business behind us. But let us for a moment focus on what lies ahead."

"What lies ahead?" She planted her hands akimbo on her hips. "What makes you think I want any part in 'what lies ahead'?"

He splayed ungloved, bloody fingers before him. "There are a lot of places you could be that aren't here, yet you are none of those places. Why don't you tell *me* what makes you want a part in what lies ahead?"

Orluvoq looked away. She had been so close to being her own. No, she *had* been her own for those brief minutes of blue flame windwalking. Then she'd become something terrifying and helpless. Failed again. Like trying to rejoin her clan. Like trying to tame the tuuaaq. After both of those failures, she'd hidden. This time had to be different. A child no longer.

She put up a hand to shield her eyes from the glinting snow, wishing she had some goggles. Beside her desire for strength throbbed the onerous pressure of committed atrocities goading her to see the labor through. But what rhythm pulsed beneath it? Was it, "I must do something with what I have taken?" Or was it, "What's one more?"

They ate the raw meat in unrefined silence, then Nalor said, "There is good news, and there is bad news."

Orluvoq licked her fingers clean of blood. "How can there be *any* news? We haven't met anyone."

Nalor flashed a patient smile. "'What's the good news, Nalorsiitsarut?'" he said in mock femininity. "The good news, dear Orluvoq, is that thanks be your withering romp last night, we are heartily ahead of schedule."

"There was a schedule?"

"'What's the bad news, Nalor?'" came his girlish approximation. "How perceptive of you to ask, Orluvoq. The bad news is that, despite all your efforts, you're not quite there. The Madame's decidedly unladylike manner on the ice last night didn't help much either. Even after you heal that, we're going to need to affect a bit of touching up."

She angled her head sideways, eyes locked on him. "'Touching up'? 'Touching up' worries me."

"By the looks of it, it will be far less than husking another whole woman dry. I'll be present this time to ensure you don't go too far."

Her stomach clenched like it wanted to reunite rabbit and ice. *Not again. I can't do it again.* But it would be only a sliver. *Isn't that what I told myself the first time?* But Nalor would be there for this trial. *And I trust him?* That was insignificant. She needed to try again.

Nalor reinserted his hands in his gloves and clapped. "Let's be off, then. I think I know just the place."

THE SUN LOUNGED on the horizon as they quit their wind-walking a few hundred paces outside the village. No village she had ever seen aspired to distinguish itself much, to wax in both elegance and eminence until outsiders respected what a genteel people the denizens were. This cluster of igloos was no different in its functional design, yet Orluvoq couldn't help but feel it exuded a peculiar impression.

Nalor turned to her, grin set wide. "Here we are. Home, sweet home."

Her forehead frowned. "This is your home?"

"Don't be absurd, they hate me. But these people—" he swung a hand toward the village, then dropped it. "Actually, they probably hate me too. Regardless, I suppose I could see how you wouldn't be jumping and panting with recognition. After all, the last time you saw this location, you had turned the whole place into a lake."

"Oh, spirits."

"Yes, you did release some of those, if I recall."

"Can we," she said, stomach queasing, "take this somewhere else? Anywhere?"

His smile creased his face further. "Back to the prostitutes, then?"

"Nalor!"

"Are you really so worried about a little family reunion?"

"Family?" She jabbed an open hand past his jocose face and toward the igloos. "You think that Terianniaq is my family? I went to the end of the world and back for them, and they *still* rejected me. There is no one in this world further from family than them."

"Well." His mouth relaxed. "This sounds like just the place to be. Oh—" His eyes focused on an oddity off in the snow. "Is that..." He trotted over and Orluvoq trailed him.

The old angakkuq chortled aloud. "An unexpected boon!" Orluvoq expected him to jump in heel-clicking jubilation.

In the crust of the world lay the elephantine effigy of a man—or woman—carved out of the ice itself. It emanated spectacle in spite of its rough-hewn features, eyes shut, wrists crossed on the breastbone in a moment of eternal repose. Orluvoq could have laid down head-to-toe thrice and matched its length.

The snow above the head began folding in on itself, running to liquid and into the permafrost.

"What are you doing?" she asked.

"We're about to see just how deep our luck runs," Nalor answered, concentrating on the concentrated thawing.

"Meaning?"

He didn't oblige her an answer until he'd bored a hole deep enough to stand in and hopped down with a grunt. "Have you ever stumbled upon one of these before?"

"Uh..." She watched him prod the wall with a glove. "My stumbling usually isn't so fancy."

"Have you ever seen an inuksuk?" He seemed satisfied with his probings and began to work the candle again, the wall sloughing away.

"Yes. Pile of rocks made to look like a person. I *have* been north, you know." Markers for travel, hunting, and the like.

"Well, this marvelous monument is similar, except it marks death."

She scrunched her brow. "Mark death? The ice takes the body within half an hour."

"Not," he said as something dark poked out of the snow, "if you bury them in one of these."

A head lolled out of the vanishing wall, its browned teeth clicking like mud-caked rocks. Orluvoq recoiled even though she stood at ground level. She had seen death plenty through the wall of Nunapisu, but this open display twisted her gut. "What? How is this possible?"

"Who knows the mind of the ice?" Nalor replied, plucking some token out of a pocket and secreting it on the body. "It's said that the ice obviously won't consume itself, so if you hide a person behind a likeness of themselves, you can trick the ice for several days." With a boost from his burning tuuaaq he hopped out of the hole.

"What did you put on her?" Orluvoq was fairly certain it was a woman.

"Something to remember me by."

Orluvoq stared long and bemused at the man. "And what brain is she going to remember you with?"

"Oh, not for *her* to remember me by. For *me* to remember me by."

"For you to..." Her traveling companion had gone mad, and clearly not in the past day.

"Yes, yes, when I visit your humble home up north." He dusted flakes from his parka and swung his gaze back to the village. "Now then. Your mark for tonight. Any old scores to settle? Any strings of envy fairly thrumming with the lust for vengeance? Any self-absorbed step mincers that need to be taken down a peg?"

The riddle of Nalor and the dead woman clumped in her mind, and she came up short of an answer to his questions. "I suppose it's been too long, and I was too young."

"Alright, have it your way. We'll wait an hour, skulk about until we find a savory damsel, then you'll take a sip from her flask of youth and be on your way to Qilaknakka before you know it." He plopped on his rump and took a small bone flute from his pack, the sun's memory draining from the sky.

The dread clawed between her ribs again and brought its urges to flee and hide. One hour. One tiny hour, and she was to become the monster Orluvoq anew.

No. She now knew what she was up against. She could do it. She could brace open the jaws of the devourer.

❄️

WHEN WINTER SLEEPS, its dream is summer, as day is the
dream of night. When each awakens to reality, it finds
nothing as warm, nothing as bright. Winter huddles around
itself, railing at life with gales and sleets alive with death.
Night steeps in its melancholy, stringing lights through the
firmament to glimpse but an echo of its dream.

Orluvoq stole through night's sullen heart like illness
into tranquil lungs. Her tuuaaq taper's blue glow shone
only to her, clothed in the shrouds of shadow she hemmed
about herself. Nalor trailed after, prints in the snow the
only spoor of their arrival they left. The tusk within her
gently chirred its holy song. The power was hers. She
would take precisely what she needed down to the finest
mote.

They crossed into the igloo warren. They slunk through
the halls as demons unseen. They threaded through rooms
like nimble winds. They found their mark and began to
glean.

The woman's eyes jolted open just before Orluvoq sank
in her discarnate teeth. The pathos in her pupils penetrated
the rhapsody of the blue flame, and Orluvoq faltered. How
could she stand tall and ravage another woman? How
could she—

A fiber of beauty slipped through her hesitation and she
became the beast with the azure core. The woman's face
warped and peeled, a tiny sucking sound pinging around
the room.

Nalor held the husband and daughter under wraps of
slumber. The demon from the end of the world drank deep
from a woman who could have loved her. Sweetly flowed the
beauty from out beneath her skin as in her bed she writhed;
writhed in the strictures of the shaman.

On a fringe the demon heard her name. A tinkling from

a far-off land. It came once more, then came again. "Orlu-voq. *Orluvoq.*" A buzz of humbug that merited no heed.

Her head rattled empty, and she thumped against the floor. Smoke wisped up from her extinguished candle, limned by Nalor's flame. She hunched like a wolf about to die and worked breath into her body. The tuuaaq still in her veins propped up her lucidity.

Control had been in the tusk's hands, but less so than last time. She *could* do this. She *could* lay hold upon this ultimate strength, if only she would crawl forward and reach. However, she couldn't bear looking at her victim to discover the price of the crawl.

No, she turned her eyes to Nalor. He had looked. He had seen. He knew. The depth of her crime was writ large on his mind. She needed but one conciliatory look from him. A tacit confirmation that she retained some scrap of morality in her. That the crawl was worth the price.

Having pacified the beauty donor asleep, he watched Orluvoq breathe. He gave a nod so slight it could have been candlelight lancing with shadow, then said, "Let us be off."

She gathered her candle and a measure of wits, and they stalked back through the corridors, masked by Nalor's shade. Outside and away from the village, he turned and tilted her chin up with a finger. A smile stole across his face as he held his frigid glim almost to her cheek.

"Good. Very good. This is enough to convince any man —Qummukarpoq included—that you are indeed the most beautiful woman in the world. You are a marvel."

"A marvel?" she asked, eyes pointed at the ground. "I feel like wet clothes. I can't believe I did it again." Yet it was a lie. The crooked tooth must be straightened.

"A marvel," Nalor affirmed. "I've never met another who could accomplish what you have as quickly. Peerless. Prodigious. Marvelous. A woman of fable. Spoken of in fevered tones by men with hairs of gray. When lightning splits she takes a prong in either hand and rends it at the fork. Into separate abysms she hurls each fiery twig. The sky is her glittering promenade, her path lacquered green with the light of creation. Ware the glim grasped in her hand! Ware the visage she exposes! Both pulse with beauty and cruelest beguiling. What end awaits should one venture too near?"

She had not the wherewithal to process everything he said. His eyes said he knew as much as he continued on.

"And now your time has come to take your walk to Arsarneq."

"*My* walk?" She tugged at her hood, but it was as snug as it could go.

"The aurora is only out at night. If you leave now, you'll make it to Qilaknakka with time to spare."

"But, me? Just me?"

"You have the idea." An insouciant smile popped onto his lips.

She found her stomach twirling once more. Alone. She was to go alone. "But..."

"I would come, no doubt in the slightest, if it weren't for a diplomatic agreement between the king and I that myself stays off that quaint little island. You have enough candle to get you there, I presume?"

Her hand lifted toward her pack then fell. "I guess." But wasn't this what she wanted? To treat with the most supreme angakkuq and claim as much ability as she could grasp? "You know I'm not going to marry him. Well, maybe. But if I don't like him then I'm skywalking back to Nunapisu."

"Good, good." Nalor took her by the shoulders. "This has

been a most riveting outing, Orluvoq. I expect to be hearing good news from you very soon."

"How?"

He tutted. "Do you so easily forget our nighttime conversation of just a couple days ago?"

She grunted, recalling the dream talk.

He gave her one last clap on the shoulder and stepped back, motioning up to Arsarneq. "The world's finest footpath awaits the world's finest lady."

She sparked up her candle. Hesitation snagged her a second, then she chewed a speck of the sweet tooth and deepened the color of the flame. It hummed to her just right. Orluvoq took one last look at her old homestead and stepped into the sky.

Decades Long Dead

Puigor groaned at the air and the air groaned back.

In the hollow nights where bones couldn't hide from the cold—the cold that robbed the world of all color—voices carried for more than a league. Sap froze solid in mighty boles, straining until it sundered the pines in strident claps of thunder. Ocean breakers curled to solid spars of black, then the ice pressed down, gnawing ocean currents for its fare.

That dread chill of fearsome lineage claimed fast every nose. Should one not blink, it'd eat the eyes while sawing off the toes. No caribou cloak, no sealskin mantle, no hide of beast could stave that chill. Only rocking back and rocking forth could rob it of another kill.

Even warding the cold off with his blue flame, icy tongues licked past his defenses and swiped shivers into his limbs. The very air hurt his face. Why did the *air* hurt? He needed to scream, but he feared what frigid nightmare would sneak down his throat should he open his mouth too wide.

In his seventeen years, he'd never seen a more bitter winter.

Winter. The season where darkness conquered day, for no aurora hung in the sky, and day was dimmer than night. It suited Puigor fine. Fewer celestial lights, fewer nosy eyes. But *tiaavuluk*. It was cold. The sun's return would also suit him fine.

In the black of day, he stalked behind a man waiting to die. The elder had taken the final dignity and walked away from his clan to perish alone on the ice. Puigor had windwalked between villages for weeks looking for this very opportunity. He sometimes mused on returning to his home, but the pain of consideration was too great, let alone the pain of actually returning. No, this moment would have to be shared with a complete stranger.

He drew abreast the dying man, matching the moribund pace, and eased back the cloak of candled shadows from his face. "I am Puigor, and I see that your walk is lonely. Let me travel with you. Where are you headed?"

Saying his old name aloud dredged longing within him. If this man would just speak it, the name Puigor hadn't given in the three years since that night of visitation, then almost he could imagine the syllables falling in benediction from his father's lips.

Several halting strides trudged by before the old man answered. "Every step you take in life is another footprint on the same path. Though we walk side by side, I have found the end and you have only just lost the start."

The sudden keenness from a frame so frail stunted Puigor's thoughts. The old man hadn't so much as turned an eye toward him, the specter that had emerged from the darksome day. Time injected more and more of itself between each step until the elder finally stopped, huffing at the stinging cold.

"Let me be." The weight of every step of his life burdened the dying one's voice. "Leave me with my final dignity."

Puigor had finally regained hold on his thoughts. He kept his lips tight to fend off frigidity. "There is no dignity in death. Your bones slump in a heap. Your bowels release. Your mouth hangs loose, and you mindlessly eat snow until it eats you."

"It seems," said the old man, "there is no dignity in life, either."

Puigor kept his mouth sealed for several icy inhales, thinking on his dead father, then said, "No." He dropped the rest of his shadows and blue light sliced through the sunless day. The old man finally turned, fear peeling back his eyelids.

"Demon of the north. You've come to take my body." He took a tottering step in a futile escape attempt. When it was clear he had no hope of outrunning this boy holding the alien glim, he began tugging at his parka; to remove it so that the ice might remove him before the tirigusuusik did.

"I'm heartened to see you trying to escape this, but we both know that however quick the ice might take you, I'm quicker." Puigor broke out a toothy smile, illuminated blue from below.

"No," the elder despaired, still struggling with too-weak arms against his coat. "No, I've lived well. You can't do this."

"You can relax. You'll see Nunapisu before long. I only need your body for a few hours at most."

The man lunged a step back toward his far-off village. "You are a monst—"

But Puigor sucked the heat from his body and the word died in a rattle. A long life came to a short end; a man of stature bowed low by the element he had spent a life defying. The cold stole motion from his very veins. All went slack and he settled onto the ice, one leg bent under, the other cast behind in a gawky sprawl.

Puigor looped an arm around the deceased's torso—light with old age—and dragged him toward the cave he had scouted out. Who knew how long the elder could have walked for? Puigor couldn't drag him over a league to the cave. Needed him close. Still, stealing the old one's heat, his last moment... It sat askew on Puigor's heart.

Not that it should. Sending a man to his death mere minutes earlier than nature would be no crime. Nunapisu was riddled with babies that parents knew could not be provided for. The ice was cold and hard. Winters were dark. It was no secret that life was all three.

He huffed at the exertion, not quite pausing to rest once inside. No need to invite the ice to take the body. Where to put the corpse had consumed his thoughts. Pallet of wood? No, no thickets close enough. Table of stone? Even less of a chance. Sleds were too easy to track. The only way to ensure that the ice wouldn't take the body too soon was to lay the dead man on top of himself.

Puigor lowered himself and the body to the cave floor with the tenderness of a mother laying her dead child on the ice. The acerbic stench of the elderly pinched the air in his nose. He shuddered and his bones jittered in their sockets.

This was it. The culmination of more than two years' efforts. After an emotional, self-inflicted exile. After a fevered survival mingled with study of the blue flame. After sailing discreetly to the foot of Qilaknakka and sensing that his father was gone. This would be the first true step in exacting revenge on the prince.

He readied a fresh candle—his last—chipped a bit of tuuaaq into his mouth, and descended into a trance. The weight of the corpse, strangely, counteracted the discomfort of lying beneath a corpse. He rocked his mind back and forth like lazy ocean swells undulating a boat.

And into the body he went.

It came leisurely, like the first fleck of a long-awaited snow drifting its way from cloud to earth. A susurrus suffused with sidereal promise. A clamor of voices babbling in tongues the earth had never known. Drawn by the echoes into the void left by the elder's spirit, Puigor abandoned his bones and put on flesh anew.

It was... cold. Frigid to the marrow. Not that he'd expected much else from a bluebody, not when the weather cracked skin and took life without ruth. He opened his—its?—eyes and saw his stiff face twisted in concentration, tinged with blue. After a study of his own sleeping face, the person everyone else saw him as, he pushed the body to its feet.

It wasn't a perfect transference of consciousness, more an amalgam of mostly here and a little there. Likely a good thing, else the ice might assume his body had no spirit and port him to Nunapisu.

He ventured a few steps toward the light at the tunnel's end. All sensation came dulled save thermoception. The cold rang true like wind whistling through the field of ice flutes he'd found by the sea. He reached the cave mouth and pushed the body into a run.

The leaps and bounds came fluidly. Almost too easily. He steered the bluebody across the tundra at a withering pace, requiring but apathetic effort. His first windwalking experience had been far less of a silky jaunt. There might still be a trophy scar marking his skin from that adventure.

Corpse feet pounded, but the reverberations hit him like a wolf crying from outside a dream. He pressed the cold body for what fire it had to offer. Perhaps he could run it all the way to the ocean. Whatever the limits of a single candle, he would find them.

And the prince would die.

Puigor chortled, though whether in his cave-lying or field-sprinting form he couldn't wholly say. Perhaps both. Today marked the beginning of the end of Qummukarpoq's power.

A year prior, Puigor had finally met another who could work the blue flame. A seemingly simple clan angakkuq he'd boarded with for a week. At first blush, the words of the middle-aged woman had tasted foul to him. To arrogate a corpse and jerk it to and fro as his personal property? It was too much. The dead were Nunapisu's chattel, not the play-things of man.

But months had crept by. Days had grown long. Dull and lonesome aches had sharpened. And his father was no longer. No whisper of a name. No trace of a body. And no hope of a spirit.

The prince had vowed to end Puigor should they again meet. So, they wouldn't. Qummukarpoq would meet a dead man, and Puigor would guarantee him all the honors he had granted Puigor's father.

The old man's old form sped on without so much as a wheeze of the lungs. But speed wasn't all he'd need to strike the prince down. Puigor slowed up and took in the scene, what little he could discern in the dimness glazed blue. A... hill? A far-off stand of trees? A... No, that was about the sum of it.

He closed corpse eyes and quested out with his mind. Pleasantly enough, the searching centered itself at the blue-body and not his comatose form. Somewhere in his periphery, he nudged into a hulking presence. He flung corpse eyes wide and turned in a flash.

Empty. The few stars peeking through cloud gaps did more looking than luminating. The ghostly blanket spread over the ground in all directions held nothing save trillions of snowflakes. His heart pace quickened in the cave, and he leaned his mind back into questing.

There. Closer than before. It bulged obtrusively as an obelisk jutting from the tundra. What creature could be that massive? A narwhal wouldn't be moving like that. The sea was too far away for a walrus. Could be an ox. Was it—

His stomach fell somewhere along the invisible string that connected his two bodies. Was the thing *inside* the cave? What body *was* the feeling coming from?

He twitched.

Need to move. Need to move. Nothing that big is safe.

But his eyes stayed fast. His spirit still communed with the bluebody. He couldn't waste his last candle like this. Maybe... maybe he could run it back to the cave in time and fend off the intruder with the corpse. He opened the blue-body's eyes.

In the breath-thin light, the lusterless plain moved. The disorienting, blue-tainted image that played in his mind edged him toward nausea. The world, it seemed, shifted, but he felt nothing. It tilted again, translating in the other direction.

No, wait, that's not the earth moving, that's...

In the midst of the darkness, an even deeper pit of blackness gaped open. Puigor's mouth dropped as he finally reconciled the image before him.

A giant bear.

The bluebody rattled as a bellow from the belly of the bear blew over it. Puigor didn't have even a second to react before jaws clamped down on the corpse.

He jolted back into his body and lashed out on the cave floor in search of the candle. His glove latched around it and he immediately quested out for signs of danger. Nothing jumping out at him, he drew back into himself and blew out the candle.

He curled up and waited for his breathing to slow. Though he tried, he could direct his mind nowhere else: the elder would never see Nunapisu.

F ar below, the ocean pitched and yawed, but such details etched out their births and instant deaths beyond Orluvoq's perception. A river of green flowed soundlessly around her. Her candle pulsed its rhythmic orange. And she was flush with brow-creasing thoughts.

Now more than ever she could easily flee to her home in the north. One awkward conversation when Nalor came to retrieve that token he'd placed with the corpse, then she'd be free to live as she was wont.

But that would be like taking a mouthful of milk and never swallowing. The blushes of beauty she'd burgled had been the coup at the pinnacle of years of unrest. And after a coup, a new government must follow. So she strode to Qilak-nakka and its fearsome king.

She would see this great magic worked. That much she could do. Whether she stayed was another matter entirely.

And if Qummukarpoq desired to take her as his bride? Must she then remain the most beautiful woman, the scourge of the south that gobbled up girls ad infinitum? To grow ever stronger, the price of the crawl racking ever higher?

And if Qummukarpoq *didn't* want her? Then... then... Distended and detached faces bulged in her mind as she had sucked virtue dry. Plucking out a raggedy dirge on Nunapisu's unpeopled chasm strand. Hiding.

Could she content herself with returning to Nunapisu and simply loving her parents until they passed? Until the love turned to pain? Is that what came after Qilaknakka? More keenly than any point in the past decade, loneliness stabbed her through the core. Though the beauty of many adorned her face, it ran only skin deep.

She reached for more tuuaaq.

Her heart fluttered, and she stopped her hand.

I shouldn't waste it.

Ah, but it would be so lovely.

Her hand quivered.

I shouldn't take any more than is needed.

Though with a bite or two more, she could hasten her path. The ocean was long, and she must reach its start before night broke.

But I haven't tried more than a crumb. Is Arsarneq really the place to stretch my limits?

There was no place better.

The voice of denial made no reply. It stepped aside just enough to give hesitation a spectator spot. And where hesitation came, surrender followed.

As she marched through the green serenity scoring the sky, her fingers twitched their way to a naked spike of tuuaaq. The sweet tooth fit in her fingers like long-lost lovers finding each other's embrace. Out from the pocket. Up to the lips. Musky and dry the aroma ascended, dusting through each nostril.

Not too much.

The hiss of reason careered through her head as her eyes laid trained on the sallow tusk. She pushed it between her lips, sank in her teeth, and snapped off an over-generous lump. As the chalky chunk broke apart in her mouth, she broke Arsarneq's silence with something between a moan and a whimper. Orluvoq's loneliness evaporated, falling upward to dance with the moonbeams.

Orgasmic delirium curled her eyes back into her head while her legs kept pedaling on. The hero's song rumbled to the forefront of her mind. Oh, how she'd missed this.

HIGH AND LONESOME he stood above the world at its start. Through the castle's window, in the aurora's light, he gazed upon the water reaching ever the higher. That specter that had loomed over his back for decades upon scores. That custodian of secrets that had baffled his every questing and devoured every bluebody. But it couldn't stand mute forever. Soon, it would yield. Soon.

In his liminal angakkuq's senses, a beacon tugged from the north. He slid his eyes shut and tracked the pull with his mind.

It radiated undeniable power and moved toward the castle like plummeting icicles. Obviously careening through Arsarneq. Either angakkuq or demon. But what angakkuq announced his coming with such hue and cry? A demon, then, though none the likes of which he knew.

He must make ready for war.

Out through the window he stepped on the wind and hiked it to the castle's roof. Clouds content to linger hung above the green aurora. Softly plashed the ocean on the ice strand far below. Deeply groaned the sea wall stretching ever up behind. Darkly hummed the odor from the candle to his nose.

Though demons fell from heaven to best him; though shamans crossed the sea to worst him; he had laughed at every would-be. He had cast their flesh to ice then fed their bodies to the wall. Ever they came to vanquish, and ever did they fall.

But this thing. This *thing* in the middle of Arsarneq, it brimmed with untold might. With the power of the morning sun shaking off its slumber while sinful beaks of birds proclaim the coming of the light. This thing, did he fear it? He feared that he just might.

But no. He was Qummukarpoq, king of Nuktipik and all the world. Vultures' beaks broke upon his skin. Ice froze again upon his passing. The aurora bent the knee before him. In his belly wriggled primeval magics waiting to gush forth. He slapped distances flat with the bark of his voice, and as the hills re-echoed, they carved valleys to his feet.

No, this thing, he did not fear it.

It stayed its course and drew the nearer. The king readied him another taper and dashed more tuuaaq on his tongue. The wind reached round and grazed his skin, though he did not feel its fingers. The candle did its job on that front. Now to test its mettle in the job to come.

He steeled his jaw as the demon hurtled toward him straight down the belly of Arsarneq. It reached the apex above his head—

—and flew straight into Qilaknakka?

Water plumed out from the far-off impact, sprinkling as mist by the time it reached the ocean. The king blinked and kept all the steel in his jaw. Had that been a woman? Holding a flame of blue? If not a demon...

He rolled the possibilities and plausibilities over in his mind, then slipped another shard of tuuaaq into his mouth. This wouldn't be easy.

Once before, and only once, had he assayed a task so fraught. But on this night, it seemed his lot to bend the world to him once more.

He sank into a mindful trance. Felt the light above him slither. Felt the stolid wall of water and the periled girl inside it. That band of green with violet fringe became his only rival. That provenance of tusk was found his only worthy foe. He raised up feral talons and propelled them at its throat.

His wraithlike power tangled with the adamant aurora, throwing varicolored sparks into the frigid, darksome sea. His lips spat curses on the name of each of his forebears while the wind whipped up and stole the drops from every sweating pore.

And though it yowled in bastard tongues, the light began to budge. And though it frothed in motley hues, it listed when he nudged. In stitches he affixed his will along its nether side. Lastly it relented and untethered from the sky.

Hence and thence it slowly swerved, as is wont for behemoths. He stayed its weft, he held it fast, then rammed it into Qilaknakka. Like a great and laminar tongue, it wriggled as he fished within, combing to and fro to beckon forth the wandered demon girl. There he grazed her finding depths and swiftly compassed her with light; plucked her from the inky bowels and bore her into vital night.

Down he drew the emerald ribbon from its course on heaven's heights, sundered it from lofty haven, bent it low before his feet. Its luster glazed the castle over, blazed it to a radiant gem. Verdance spilled along the sides, pooled in fishes' wondering eyes.

Qummukarpoq released the aurora and doubled over. It snapped back home, and a growl of thunder followed. He looked down at what it had left—what *he'd* salvaged from death. Not a demon. A girl. A most beautiful girl, even in her deluged state. Might he say, a beauty with no equal? And a tirigusuusik at that?

His eyes fixed on the vast wall of water, then slid back to the woman. The most beautiful woman. For the first time in a great while, Qummukarpoq smiled.

ORLUVOQ HATED DEATH SO FAR. There was too much spinning. Would she always be this thirsty? Why was it still cold? She tugged at the blanket to cover her nipped nose. Eventually the furry dryness in her throat convinced her to look for water.

She opened her eyes to pure white environs. Not so different from life, save that every edge was cut with precision. She was loath to leave the exquisite bed. Never had she slept in one raised off the ground. Still, the itch in her throat wasn't leaving, so she peeled back the covers and sat up.

A man in snow white raiment entered a door she hadn't noticed. He wore an atigi with no parka, and a tall crown of tuuaaq ringed his brow. Like Nalor, his face displayed ethereal age. He had attained forty years, but whether today or decades ago she couldn't say.

"Is any of your tuuaaq high lingering, or is your system clear?" he asked.

The question and the authority behind it took her off guard. She reassessed the diadem adorning his head and attempted to remember anything other than plunging into that eternal wall of water. It seemed burning blue could only offset so much of the tuuaaq high. She ran his words through her mind once more and fingers of ice clutched at her stomach. She wasn't dead, and that was Qummukarpoq.

She swallowed at her withered vocal folds. "Um, I think it's gone." Just saying that made her wish it weren't so.

"Do you know where you are?" His eyes pierced like augers.

"Qilaknakka? Or, the castle in front of it?"

He made no confirmation. "You have come to be my wife."

"I—I suppose I have." Her voice sounded small to her.

"How many others do you believe have come to claim that title?"

She took another dry gulp. "Twenty maybe?"

"Some have come of their own accord, while others have been commissioned by their clan to come. All told there have been more than forty, and yet, I remain unwed. What makes you superior?"

Something inside railed against the unfairness of him asking such probing questions so soon after her waking. This was not a man who countenanced diffidence. Her reply must strike with sincere confidence. "Because none of them was as beautiful as I am?" She cursed at herself for turning the sentence into a question.

"The answer is tuuaaq." He drew closer to the bed. "Why do you think I issued the rumor I was looking to take the world's most beautiful woman to wife?"

Her faux surety departed. Everything she had done since leaving the north had been playing to the plans of a man she'd never met. Not a very good mark of strength. Betrayal's burn slushed through her, but it had no one to mark save herself. Her own fresh-faced stupidity had led her to this bed at the start of the world.

"That is right," said the king, confirming what she spoke with eyes alone. "The only woman who can ascend the echelons of beauty is an adept tirigusuusik."

"You mistake me. I'm not adept. I've only just begun working the blue flame a couple days ago." The words weighed heavy on her heart as soon as they left her mouth.

Qummukarpoq's lips itched a minute grin. "Then there is no further debate. You are my wife."

Such a slew of emotions rushed Orluvoq that she couldn't discern a one. "What do you mean? Why is it so important to have a tirigusuusik for a wife?"

"Come eat. Come drink. Come learn of the great things that await you."

Her vitals trembled as she beheld the majestic man blending so cleanly into the castle walls. His eyes were quick even when they did not move. Not a drop of poise spilled from his brimming cruse of a body. True, she desired strength, but he emanated an aura much colder than strength.

She longed for the empty expanse of Nunapisu. For the easy days when flames glowed orange. For the euphonic tones of her parents chatting through a morning. For the delights and distresses she had forsaken, perhaps for all time.

But. But she had succeeded. What had seemed a faint illusion spun by Nalor's tongue days earlier had transpired. Her transgressions bore fruit beyond ignominy. A king—*the* king, the peerless angakkuq of all the world—wanted her. Just then, she feared him more than she coveted whatever power he had to offer. She may very well leave after he and she worked a magic so great that...

That what? What if they failed and Qilaknakka fell, sweeping every man, woman, and child into Nunapisu's gaping maw? What if they killed Arsarneq, and neither aurora nor narwhal was seen among the Nuktipik peoples again? The hazards of the blue flame could not be avoided.

Figuring there was no other way to satisfy the curiosities, she pushed herself from the bed and followed Qummukarpoq into the corridor with a woozy sway.

ORLUVOQ SANK her teeth into the fat of seals, relishing the oleaginous chunks on her tongue. The viands a shade pinker than white brought her back to days with her first parents. Days when she could cling to the bowsprit and fancy herself a merchant lord as they sailed the ice. When she had hounds for bedfellows and hardened men doting on her and the sunbeams of innocence she cast throughout the ship.

The palace was much emptier than she had envisaged. No army of maids fussing over sullied nooks. No dignitaries pacing the halls with heads bent together in principled conversation, nor majordomo imposing order on orderlies. No detachment of hunters and fishers keeping the larder flush, nor faculty of angakkuit heating the castle proper. In fact, she had yet to see anyone save the king. Was his occupation so simple it could be executed by a lone man, or was the man so great that the task of ruling measured itself against him?

"What do you know of Arsarneq?" asked Qummukarpoq from across the wooden table. His eyes yet glinted with that same intensity.

She brought her eyes back from roaming the heights

and accoutrements of the hall. "It's the vein that gives life to all the Nuktipik peoples. The reasons behind its comings and goings are known only to the abyss." She wished Paarsisoq were here. He'd say something less obvious and more poignant.

"Some will tell you a great mother composed of seething blackness labored years a thousand up in the sky before delivering Arsarneq to the world. Or that deep within Nunapisu's guts is an upturned shadow mountain upon which stars fall like rain, and the runoff trickles through our sky.

"Then there are those who don't believe. They *fear*. They fear Arsarneq is slowly falling and will one distant day sunder the earth in twain. Or they fear that each manifestation of the aurora is a shedding from the great serpent Tisaruk. He slumbers in the summer, and when winter comes, he takes every occasion to gobble children up, growing and shedding. But his ever-expanding bulk takes an appetite to match, and his insatiety grows. One day he will swallow the world and thereafter go mad with hunger."

Orluvoq restarted her chewing after she realized her mouth had gone slack. "I've heard a couple of those. After being up there myself, none of those sound too likely. Except maybe the stars one. What do you believe about it?" Should she have said "know" instead?

"It is the essence of all things. Body, spirit, and name, these three come from that indefatigable source, and to there they all return in the end. Unless, perhaps, you cast yourself off the precipice of Nunapisu.

"I have, in times long gone, designed to probe the source. To walk right up its throat, find the head, and look it in the eyes. Yet there is no account of any ever returned from such a venture, so I will save those exploits for a later time.

Mayhap there floats transcendence within the grasp of every angakkuq. It shall be my final journey.

"But now that you are here, I can attempt exactly the opposite. My attentions have, as of late, been pointed toward the other end of Asarneq." He wiped a smooth gesture, presumably toward the south and the terrifying expanse of sky-snatching water.

It was the "but now that you are here" part that set Orluvoq's teeth on edge. The rest of the monologue enthralled her and planted miniature aspirations to charge down the aurora and into the abyss. "What precisely do you mean 'now that I'm here'? If your angakkuq powers are truly as great as I've heard, what use am I?" She attempted a coquettish spin on the last statement, but her anticipation twisted it timorous.

He regarded her a moment, lower eyelids hiking up. "The conduit."

Two words and thoughts of reneging on the marriage seized her mind. "The... conduit?"

"The conduit. The channel. The flume." He quirked a finger upward. "That formless cascade of essence yearns to speak as the world does, and through you it may attain fluency."

Orluvoq tried to let it sink in, but it merely swilled on the surface while malformed crumbs twirled down. She was to be nothing more than a mortal scepter of channeling? "What will happen to me? Will I... be burned to nothing?"

"I don't have reason to believe thus." Qummukarpoq's lips poised to amend the pronouncement. "But neither have I proof to the contrary."

Hold now. She literally might *die* for this? That was a sight more than she wanted to have truck with. Did Nunapisu's reach even extend across the sea, to this isle of exalted exile? Forget the Warren of Immortality. No archive perpetuated by shamanic crypsis could serve her a single scintilla if her body was consumed by the elements.

"Has your ingestion of tuuaaq ever resulted in injury to your body?"

"I don't think so," she replied. "Nothing that wasn't caused by my state of mind."

"Likewise, you have naught to fear from your role in the broaching of Qilaknakka."

She decided there was something wholly too immotile about his face. It stiffened where it ought supple. Froze where it ought flex. But worst, it pierced where it ought not perceive. His gaze flayed the seal from off her sanctum. Disembarrassed her of her confidence. She tensed to stymie a shiver, but it jittered past her stiffness and down her spine.

"Do I have the option of leaving?" Her voice parted from her lips in a diminutive parody of speech. None of this great magic sounded like her reaching greater heights.

"For your entire life, the option of never coming has been present and prominent. To walk across the firmament and prostrate yourself before an angakkuq of estimable power has never been the simple or obvious option. Yet now that you have gone to the pain of pursuing that path, you would squawk and squall for the option of never coming to be restored unto you?"

She shrank as though she'd drunk a draught of bitter poison. She could in no whit gainsay him. She never had to come—never *should* have come.

Never should have left...

Her every footstep, from the world's whisperless end to its awe-striking origin, was a slur on her character. A reproach on her intellect. Perhaps she deserved this. What had those women been to her but vessels of beauty? Could she count herself their better? No, in the taking she had cast herself below the most debased whore. Where the aspiration for survival spurred them to lustful congress, the lust for greatness seduced her into grinding their faces into the ice. So long as she stood taller, what did it matter if it were heads she stood upon? If she compounded the misery of the miserable?

No matter how she twisted it in her mind, the conclusion twisted back, ineluctable as winter's black dawn. She deserved to be nothing more than a vessel. Qummukarpoq's crawling came with a price, and she had come to pay it.

"Why is there no one else here?" she said in an attempt to shoo the future from her head. "Where are your hunters and custodians? Your, I don't know, deputies and what have you?"

King Qummukarpoq transpierced Orluvoq with his gaze for moments far too many. When enough time had expired for her to imagine every possible harangue, he spake between the silence.

"I am sufficient."

The terse return crippled her crooked conjectures. Truly, there was no pomp that propped him up. No porous pedestal of vainglory. He was as genuine as the hoarfrost riming the nostrils of every wanderer—and just as much cause for shivering.

He stood from the table and declined his chin toward her. "Rest until tomorrow's nightfall. We attempt to broach the wall at first black. If you require me, light a candle and call for me."

Before he could turn, Orluvoq posed a soft question. "You plan to get married after this ritual? Who will come?"

He regarded her, fingertips of his right hand barely brushing the table. "I am the king. My word is law. I have already declared we are wed." No reprimanding tone marked his voice.

"Oh…" Orluvoq's heart diminished inside her, her body deflating around it.

Qummukarpoq gave her a dip of the head, then exited the hall in a flourish of white.

She dropped her eyes to the remnants of the seal fat, unsure what emotion would first spurt out of the boiling concoction within her.

He had never even asked her name.

NIGHT at the start of the world came much as night any else-where, but it passed with greater unease. Orluvoq's mind warped in thrawn contortions.

Surely if she were to skulk on toe tips and peer around the jamb, she would behold demons of ungainly propor-tions dragging their nails on the hall floor, rictus grins shearing their faces wide. Or an interminable basilisk would slither out of Qilaknakka, torrents of water sheeting from its hide, and snatch her from her restless tossing. Or she'd tumble into some secret oubliette and come face to face with the faceless king, his skin cast aside for the night.

The air fairly prickled as she spun the litany of horrors; the dread of imagination that diverted her from the dread of reality. Strange that she should find respite in horror. But she had allied herself with dire straits and now scrambled any-which-way to forswear.

Dawn at the start of the world came unlike any else-where she had seen. Having met little success in her bid at sleep, she'd arisen before sunrise and found an east-facing vantage markedly removed from the ocean below. She plopped her elbows on the sill and watched the first scruples of dayspring leach into the heaven.

Stars vanished as if swallowed and ported to their own Nunapisu far above. Blisters of light coruscated through the august wall of water and gushed out in geometries of saffron and gold. She averted her eyes as tears blurred her vision—an artifact of the ascendant sun, no doubt. Nothing to do with ruminations over what else might burst from Qilaknakka in mere hours.

Running and staying jousted back and forth in her head, an unfair match, for she didn't have enough candles to skywalk north without Arsarneq. She paced from the highest corridor to the white beach. Back and forth, mulling and fretting. The day drug on like the oldest dog pulling the biggest ship, and when it was over, she found it had flown.

In the blear hours of gloam and star pricks, he found her with her cheek daubed by the sun's last hue. Rather, she found him. A presence with no prelude, a tickle with no touch. She turned from the window view of Qilaknakka to look at her... husband. The concept perched aslant on her mind. They hadn't even convened a paltry ceremony as would be had amongst the clans. The king's benediction alone graced their union, and that couched in nonchalance.

He'd made no attempt to bed her, or even lie in the same room, for which a small part of her couldn't help but be scandalized. Then again, she'd known nothing but the frugality of ship berths and igloos, where luxury was sleeping more than an arm's length from another. Perhaps a castle full of empty rooms demanded use.

"Are you hungry?" asked Qummukarpoq, ungloved fingers characteristically looped around an azure-gleaming candle.

She shook her head. Enough nerves twined in her

abdomen to sate her, vying against the urge to take a bite of tuuaaq.

He gave a measured nod as if he apprehended the true meaning in her mien. She watched the tall tuuaaq diadem bob and idly wondered what neck pains afflicted him. Did he sleep with the crown? Did he doff and don as sleep circuited through his body? Or, a better revision, *did* he sleep?

"Then we ascend to the roof to attempt the magic," said the king. "You have a candle?"

"Don't I have to prepare?"

"It is not you who calls down the sky. A candle will suffice."

The nerves redoubled their twining. She dragged a weary hand to a pocket and pulled out a half-consumed taper, watching it with doleful yearning. If she just champed down on the chalky wick, she could muddle herself to muzziness and postpone the impending ritual. Then do it again the next day, and the next day, and...

And die of starvation in the world's only castle. Queen for a day, whose sole undertaking was underwriting her inglorious demise. Not a word of her plight to her parents, which seemed grimmer than not securing them a place in the Warren of Immortality. She was more than that.

A considerable piece of resistance calved off her spirit, drifting away to melt in warmer climes. She would partake in the king's moment of transcendence, and her power would grow, whether in knowledge, in strength, or in sheer infamy. She had not come all this way only to hide. Orluvoq lit the wick a mundane orange and stepped through the window after the king.

He scaled the winds and she the wall to land amidst the many cupolas that hummocked the castle roof like an artful assemblage of igloos. Orluvoq took in the ice beneath her feet, wondering what hand had sculpted it, and indeed upkept it. Questions for another time. Qummukarpoq likely wouldn't welcome a sidetrack interrogation.

"This," said the king, "is an hour I've long awaited. A moment of no meager moment. Though we carve out but a spindle of time, it is on this spindle the world will turn hereafter."

His voice was still dignified, but it sizzled with a previously unheard élan. Orluvoq drew her parka hood closer around her face. It helped if she didn't have to look at his eyes.

"Eat this."

It took a few blinks for her to realize he was proffering something to her. She looked at his hand and her eyes flared like a caribou in the clutch of terror.

"That is a lot of tuuaaq." She didn't move to take the two fingers' worth of tusk, more than thrice as much as she'd ever eaten in ten years. "I thought you said this wasn't going to kill me."

"You are the conduit," was the simple reply. "This tuuaaq is not meant for you, but unless it passes through you, it will never reach Qilaknakka. This is the spark to start the flame."

She despised how level and routine his speech sounded. As if he weren't even attempting to convince her, for he knew she could step nowhere save along the preordained path. She pressed forward and took the psychoactive from his naked palm. Their intimacy reached a new zenith when her gloved hand brushed his bare skin, but she suspected it didn't even register next to his concupiscence for Qilaknakka. What was one girl when he was on the verge of claiming the maidenhead of the world's fountainhead?

"Break it up," he instructed. "I fear what might come to

pass if you don't eat all of it."

"What will you do once I've eaten it?"

He raised a hand toward the freshly fledged aurora. "I will pull the great light from the sky, pass it through you, and, once it's been concentrated, I will shoot it forth and pierce Qilaknakka. There is no greater event in human memory."

Her eyes ranged forward, scaling that empyrean escarpment, then falling to the talus that sloped to meet the ocean. If she blinked to find herself standing in her igloo at Nunapisu, she would almost content herself with the province of her parents. Almost. The tuuaaq in her hand knew it was stronger, but only half of her cared. The price of the crawl to see behind the wall. Half of her hated that she was willing to pay.

In a haze of self-loathing and determination, she piled the tuuaaq between her teeth and began to grind.

QUMMUKARPOQ WATCHED the queen chew and swallow, gentle anticipation aloft in his chest. Dalliances with jubilations must yet be held back, but the season was nigh. Exultations hovered in the hintermind, awaiting his exaltation. Today, he enfolded the skies into his dominion.

Though he had just taken him a wife, he impregnated something far greater. On this day of days, with his penetration of Qilaknakka, he pierced the mind of every child for millennia to come. This day, he begat legend. That offspring which out-breathed any human; which needed no eternal residence in Nunapisu; which lived in every body, clung to every spirit, and kindled in name on every tongue. Today, he became of an ilk with myth.

By and by the queen slouched into the stupefacient clutches of the tusk. A beatific expression treated with her ersatz beauty, the union more than enough to turn a thousand thanes from their harems entire. Were the moment any other, he may have entertained musings on carnalities and fornications, and they in turn may have entertained him. Were the moment any other, he might not be constrained to relegate desire to a murmur in the esoterica.

Almost in homage to the rescue of the night past, he tapped an extra dash of tuuaaq on his tongue, faced Qilaknakka, and embraced the trance.

Mold of mind he dashed to flinders, sent his spirit skyward racing. Guttling heights and ruckling night, he chased his mind to Arsarneq. At his touch, the holy ripple groaned aloud with scorn of green. Froth with loathing though it was, it could not but bend the knee.

Thin delight defined his lips. Even heaven knew its king.

Then he heaved the emerald mantle, tore it plainly from its sanctum, purged the sky of lymph and lightblood; darkness reigned the plane above. Seaward, seaward, fro the heights, pursing into spear of white; body, name, and spirit rendered to pearlescent furnace splendor.

When the spearhead met the girl, brilliance anchored in her bones. Porous skin bled blinding light. Quick her body jolted up. There she hung in fiery spasm, floating o'er the castle's roof. Tethered to a tributary longer yet than all the world. Qummukarpoq, with just a moment, nooked himself into repose. Then he drew a thorny breath. Now began the true travail.

In spectral semblance, bereft of guise, spirits limbered and tangilized. Like clouds congealing, clouds of shadow; shedding shadow, clouds of light. Seeping, flowing interstitial, licked the king's brain crease by crease. Choirs of ghost insinuations sang the worldsong in his ears.

Twixt tremulous girl and towering wall divided his attentions he. Shunned the chittering of the sea and ever-roving demons.

Yon wall, that soaring, olden chronicle, record of man's impotence. Yon wall, enraptured by its rank, a perfect portrait of hauteur. Yon wall, which beckoned all to come, then daunted them to flee. But Qummukarpoq had come to call. Anon, yon wall his thrall would be.

The queen, becloaked in power to the burning of her flesh. She, from heaven severed ragged, a garment of sidereal weft. She, auroral avatar, rendered limpid by its light. She, the daughter unpolluted, come to chasten Qilaknakka.

He grazed her spirit with his mind and paused before the forceful swell. With unexampled expertise, he pinched and drew him out a thread. Thread of silver like the tongues of merchant lords a thousand strong. Thread of body never moved. Thread of name pronounced by none. Thread of spirit never roused. Thread of every song unsung.

Coil by coil he moiled his moil; he bickered ever quicker with the wicker made of ichor. The blood of all that ever was and all that ever wouldn't be he spun into a halo for to tame the archon of the sea. Turning thus the helix grew, winding hence to Qilaknakka.

Had the world in throng amassed, gazed upon the deed unmatched, children's laughter would have ceased, staring taking place of sport. Wit of crones, their proudest crown, would have slid from crests to shatter. Ancient heroes, bold and bearded, would have fluttered from all minds. Youth vows would have been renounced for a newborn fealty.

Qummukarpoq with breath most bated watched the thread snake toward the water. In his gut sparked nerves to spare, an affair so rare the novelty shocked. Here the verge! Yea, here the cusp! Here the work of years' last thrust. Atoms reeled in giddy glee 'round fiery arrows of fate converging.

Then it burst, that gravid stound, vaulting through his lungs like thunder. Bowled his knees to viscous mush. Harrowed shrieks from air and sea. Snapped the queen to brisk attention, spine like hide stretched wide and dried. Lurid light of all creation, borrowed from the world's black end, wresting with the mount of water, fountain where the world began; where world began and sky found end.

In the thicks of his travails—teeth a-milling, tusk light drilling—chinks disfigured his composure; king of all began to buckle. Qilaknakka cared not yield, cared not bow to would-be king. Jealous warden that it was, secrets hoarded yond and deep. Palpitations tainted, seized the body of the wizard king, led him to the waters of submission, bade him drink till dregs. Yearning lips cracked in a slender gape to take defeat's sweet balm; to sing with every swallow prelude for the dark of failure come.

But lo, the incandescent lash, where it touched, the density doubled. Water froze to boiling glass panicked with auroral light, tightened into groaning glass, burst apart in riots of shard. Round it surged, a glutinous eddy, carving deep and chasmic bowels. Up and upward clawing, climbing, scouring secrets never lost.

The queen, the archetype of flow, allowed no slow, a vessel quintessent. With no cajolery from the king, Qilaknakka slurped the light. Long it chewed its crystal way and bored the mountain's belly through; gouged a great intestine belching guttural cacophony.

He felt it give like fragile snow, rupturing the head and quivering to toe. The thread he'd cast amain and away, become the fiber spanning worlds.

It was finished. It was done.

Qummukarpoq released his tuuaaq flow and dropped to his knees. It had worked. He let out one short breath, not quite a sob, and opened his eyes. Parting the face of Qilaknakka, a hypnotic maelstrom stirred and pulsed with night sky light. A hole rimmed by slowly spinning green, burrowing up into the wall. He didn't spare the queen a glance. There was more beauty to be gazed elsewhere.

In his minute of composure collection, the queen stirred upright and gawked at the channel. "We did it? We did *that*?"

"Whatever odds we were against," said Qummukarpoq, straightening his crown, "yes."

Her goggling continued a fistful of moments, then she seemed to remember herself. "Wait." She turned to the king. "There's no tuuaaq left in me.

He gestured with the mostly melted taper in his hand, the flame a banal orange. "Let us be grateful it needed no more."

She seemed to vacillate between marveling at the lack of tuuaaq high and the tunnel in Qilaknakka.

He dropped a tusk fragment in his mouth and lit a fresh candle off his old wick. "Let us make haste. It's impossible to predict how long the bridge will maintain its structure."

A vigorous rub of the eyes later and the queen was on her feet preparing a candle. That was well. After the breaching, he had no desire to repeat commands.

Once she nodded her preparedness, he walked off the castle and made his way through sky to Qilaknakka. As he passed into the green pulsing tunnel, exultations scrabbled to the forefront of his mind. He smiled so hard he almost showed teeth.

Decades Long Dead

Puigor chuckled and the wind chuckled back. His originated from that part of his innards—maybe the spleen?—that fostered the hylozoic fear that his mind was being watched. By everything. The wind's soft laughter derived from the hylozoic knowledge of everything sparking in Puigor's mind. He was sure of it.

Eight days past he had set sail southward to set the seal on his father's vengeance. After nearly four years, the prince —now the king—was mere hours from repenting stealing a man's name. How delectable that would be.

But...

He shuffled his eyes from the sea to the man sitting near the prow, aglow with the light of Arsarneq. Not an archon, but an elder nonetheless hearty enough to endure more than seventy winters. Pilliap had been once to Nunapisu and wished to see Qilaknakka before he was consumed by the ice, so Puigor had taken the man on as his ward. It would be fun to have some company on the trip anyway.

That animistic paranoia greased down his spine again.

"This has been worth every minute of the trip," said Pilliap, eyes fixed on the coming wall of water. The ponderously shifting wall that made you feel like you were falling backward regardless of your angle of inspection. "Thank you again for your invitation, Nalorsitsaarut."

Right. He needed to truly transition himself over to the identity of Nalor. Puigor was a weakness in all matters regarding the king. He'd been giving the name Nalor for two years, and he almost believed it when someone said it.

"Just wait till we actually come to the foot." Nalor rested an easy hand on the tiller. In the idles of his mind, he counted the rhythmic percussion of swells against hull.

Pilliap dabbed around his brow with a wet skin and tried to huddle tighter against nothing. His contrastive efforts at fighting the fevered aches that had stolen into his body two days past did nothing, Nalor was sure. The sorry old thing probably didn't have long anyway. *That* Nalor couldn't be more sure of. Probably.

Once again, he tried not to flinch at the twitch of psychosis, the off-kilter intimation that every spirit in every particle fed on his deep-thoughts.

He spent the next couple hours watching the flickering orange held in his lap and responding with light conversation to Pilliap's exclamations and inquiries.

"I am glad to see Qilaknakka after so long," said the old man as they came abreast the wall. "But might we not also visit the castle?" He motioned to the edifice in white leagues west of them.

Nalor feigned consideration. "It is conceivable. Though I don't know how well the king likes unexpected visitors. He didn't have an overabundance of hospitality for me when he was prince and I showed up unannounced. Who knows, perhaps he's changed since becoming king."

"Indeed, indeed." Pilliap kept his blood-webbed eyes on that far-off house and its peerless quietude. Was he among the men who longed to take part in the communion of ultimate solitude, or those who desired to bask in the monument's perceived greatness? Those of the latter were the type to gawk at a woman's toenail while missing her body and spirit.

While the elder traded glances between the castle and the wall, Nalor pulled his candle stock from a pack and arrayed them upright. All postures straight and sure, he concentrated on the flame in his hand and began rioting Pilliap's fever.

"Oh," the old man cried out and clutched at his shivering frame. "This ague is getting worse." He turned to Nalor. "Can you not use your angakkuq abilities to rid me of it?"

Nalor pulled his lips into a flimsy smile. "I've told you before, I was kicked out of my village for being such a poor angakkuq. I can hardly do more than a little warmth and seeking." He pushed more heat into the man.

Pilliap's eyes went wide, and he burbled in alarm. "It's—I'm—*help*!" He spun his hyperventilating face toward the inky sea.

"Stay in the boat," Nalor commanded. "I have an idea." He slipped a chunk of tuuaaq between his teeth. Euphoria bleached his veins.

"Wh-what idea?" The elder had little capacity for anything but shaking.

The flame in Nalor's hand chilled to a malignant blue.

"*T-t-tia-avuluk*! What are y-you doing?"

"Getting rid of that fever." Nalor shut his eyes and wrenched the heat out of the ailing man.

It came in a series of gasps and convulsions devoid of dignity. Pilliap slumped into the crook of the aft, head angled as if he lay in thoughtless sleep. Though regarded as the color of heaven, the green of the sky's great river imbued the corpse with an infernal aspect.

Nalor pulled his gaze away. His shoulders and spaces behind the eyes frosted hoary with paranoia. The king had sensed that. There was no other possibility. Nalor had spent nearly two years perfecting the act of masking his magical movements from other angakkuit, but his test subjects had been scant, and none could match the prowess of Qummukarpoq.

Best get on with it before the king could intervene directly, then.

He laid himself in his sleeping position, silently grateful that the weather was showing clemency, set his candle in file with the others, then carefully consigned his consciousness to Pilliap's pliant body.

First came the cold. That recalcitrant familiar who always suggested he make the full transition from life. He sat upright and observed the dull world through dead, blue eyes. For a viscid moment he stared at his own lifeless form, ringed by bright votives of a dark ritual. Such a fragile thing to leave in open ocean. With a forced blink and a push more adroit than he could have teased from his own body, he sprang from the boat and pedaled his feet across the sea's pitching surface.

Now came the truly tricky part. The *first* truly tricky part. A mad dash to the castle while skirting beneath detection. He hadn't an idea's shred of how deterrent his newly acquired shielding abilities would be against the king's candles, especially as the distance between him and blue-body increased. Howbeit, he bent his mind to each moiety of the plan, the cloak and the dagger.

He ate the waves as winters eat the echoes of happiness from a sunless mind, yet he felt the footfalls as through a word pinging off the shell of a dream discarded. In short order, he was upon the shores beneath the towers, then hastening through doors and halls. He didn't see the sense in seeking out the king with magic. Bifurcating his mind was risky enough business. He daren't trifle with trifurcation.

One empty room after the next streamed by. Given that sound came to him as though filtered through an igloo wall, striking a balance between silent and swift proved arduous. Though perhaps his caution was misplaced, and the king stalked the halls, bearing down on his position at the very moment.

On the third floor, he peeked behind a door flap and saw a lump in the bed. Leagues distant, his heart ticked up its pace. As far as he knew, Qummukarpoq had slowly rid the castle of servants during the last few years of his father's reign. The body could be none other than the wicked king himself.

Long ago, Nalor had settled to strike the king dead without hesitation when the chance arose. Gloating and observation could come after. He pushed the bluebody into the room, withdrew a knife, and strode over to the king's bed.

As he plunged the blade toward the man's throat, Qummukarpoq whipped his head around. The knife sunk into the bedding, narrowly nicking his throat. Nalor yanked at the embedded weapon. Qummukarpoq whisked a candle from his bedside, and it flared to life.

Nalor went for another pass, but the king windwalked to the corner of the room, and the knife bit air.

Tiaavuluk. Nalor drew back to the opposite corner near the door. The king had entered his own domain and cast black on the odds of any positive outcome for the boy angakkuq. He watched Qummukarpoq chip off a piece of tusk, raise it past the trickle of blood on his neck, and dash it in his mouth. Nalor pressed his brain for a plan.

Drop the body and sail north as fast as angakkuqly possible, or fight the king. The first appealed to the craven that crouched inside every man. But what then of the king? Would he not hunt—

Nalor grit the old man's teeth as he realized Qummukarpoq's lack of motion stemmed from an attempt to suss out Nalor's location. The boy in the boat scrambled to fortify his artificial stronghold. The king's questings unnerved as though rippling between Nalor's skin and muscle, but it didn't get any further than that.

Nalor laughed, likely a disgusting breach of silence coming from the bluebody. He could control the corpse well since he had initiated the connection, but his opponent tirigusuusik couldn't exploit the connection so long as Nalor held strong his shield. The distance was too great an expanse.

Realizing the same, the king cut off Nalor's chuckle with a charge. In the fraction of a second that Nalor noticed and processed the change in his mark's stance, he managed a gauche dodge characterized by more misplaced limbs than his first time with a whore. The king clipped his arm and met the wall thumping. As Nalor stumbled to right himself, the right plan tumbled into his head.

Run.

He shouldered his way out the door and bolted down

the hall, this time with significantly less discretion in the slapping of his boots. At the end, he wheeled toward a flight of stairs and caught vision of an angry angakkuq in blurring pursuit. Up he went, mind spinning for want of a bearing. He wouldn't outlive a castle chase, and it was wholly possible the king could divine at least a direction from the corpse once Nalor abandoned it.

A halo of auroral green tinted blue cascaded through a window midway down the next hall. Nalor urged Pilliap's body forward, then lurched at the window. Even through the bluebody's lamentable senses, resistance took him by surprise.

It relented immediately with a faint tinkling. He glanced back to see the opening encrusted with jagged shards. There must have been a pane of completely transparent ice set in the window. He tucked the factoid away to ruminate on later and pressed the body forward toward...

Toward Qilaknakka, he supposed. Not much else lay forward. A peek over the shoulder confirmed that the king had made it through the window. A little thrill spurred Nalor to refocus on running.

Here arose a flaw in his foresight. He hadn't undertaken any underwater trials. For all he knew, his connection would snuff like a candle when doused. The king would pull the body from the vertiginous wall of water and be upon him faster than he could wipe away the spittle of his sleep.

But perhaps that could be avoided.

He tilted his trajectory toward the gleaming path of Arsarneq. The dead man's hood whipped behind him, a flailing banner of the reckless. Had breath been required, the frigid scourges of wind would have chastised his lungs into piteous submission. As it was, the only blight he suffered came from the bluebody's endemic chill. Closer and closer he chased until he tore into the lush luminance, and Arsarneq dissipated his weight like an afternoon zephyr dispelling a dry morning snow.

Almost he thought he could see the green combing through the parka's fur, coating the backs of his hands, but it was just a more brilliant blue. Where all hearing had been muffled before, the aurora seemed to quake through to him with a changeless roar of silence divine. The air clumped like half breaths in the chests of Nunapisu's many.

He stayed the southward track, glancing back only briefly to ensure the king still had his trail. Before him came the crash into Qilaknakka. In seconds, he careered into the bulwark of water that scraped the realms beyond sky. The transition hit him like walking into a chamber forgotten from youth, but he slowed only enough to be noticeable. His corpse face split into a grin. Arsarneq would provide him safe passage in its hallowed corridor. He ran on.

After a minute of pumping his legs, he finally checked over his shoulder and his eyes went wide. Qummukarpoq had made short work of the watery thicks between them. Mere seconds separated them now. For some brain-dead reason, Nalor had assumed the sea wall would snuff the king's flame. He looked to the darkness that encroached everywhere save straight ahead. One last thrust, then withdraw back to his real frame and run like mad.

He tipped down and faced the abyss.

Leaving the solace of the light felt like a non-crucial yet beloved skin peeled off the bluebody at the aurora's edge. The ocean sucked and pulled at his limbs with far more tenacity than had the evergreen road, but he made sure progress down and downward. The light receded faster than he would have thought, though due to his haste or being eaten by the ocean's black he couldn't say.

He'd passed far too many fathoms by when he realized that his connection to the corpse hadn't died yet. Nalor floated to a stop and watched the unplumbed depths all around, spun up in threads of wonder. The king was nowhere to be seen. Must not have wanted to risk plunging into the infinite ocean so far from home.

Nalor pondered his next course of action and settled on swimming the complete opposite direction Qummukarpoq had seen him go. No knowing exactly *what* beastly brand of candlework the man might be able to conjure to hoist the corpse from the seafloor.

He flipped directions and stroked up, up past aurora, away from the castle of white. If windwalking was expedited striding, what was this tusk-aided transit he now made? Waveswimming? It was about as close to swimming as he'd ever prefer to get.

Up and up and up. He paddled his arms and legs so long that he eventually felt like they were moving of their own accord. His mind wound back through the days leading up to this attempted camisado, and it seemed that he recounted every wave that had bobbed the boat, matching them to strokes. Clever though his arrangement of candles was, he was amazed they hadn't burnt to nubs yet. The blackness was everything. He couldn't even say that he still traveled upward. Not that it mattered, so long as it was away.

Then it happened. The waters began to lose their dark. The occasional fish puttered by. Bits of sea debris floated to a current of their own. It was almost as if...

Life. He had found life.

Before he could reorient himself, his hand swiped through the air.

The air?

The bluebody popped out of the water and came back

down in an indecorous splash. He merely trod while he awed, borrowed body slack-jawed. Qilaknakka *had an end.* Or, a beginning? A top. And on that beginning sat...

Islands. Splotches of paradise dripped from heaven's ladle, swaddled in the light of their very own moon and stars. Thick with trees. Bulging with rocks. And—and—

The bluebody felt *warm.* This scene plucked from a wondertale somehow divested the corpse of its perennial cold. That alone was enough to deck him with chills.

He glanced between the three islands within his view. What... what *was* this place? And how could he bring his truebody here?

Finally, he gathered enough wits to force a blink and began stroking toward the nearest of the iceless isles.

The tuuaaq had all burned off in the ritual, and now she felt fine. Perhaps the price hadn't been as steep as she'd imagined. She still couldn't conceive of staying for the marriage. Qummukarpoq was too... inhuman. Now that he had what he wanted, she would head north after they returned from this far-flung fantasy.

As they ascended the glowing tunnel, Orluvoq finally made the connection to a decade ago when she'd melted her village. She'd eaten so much she should have been lost in delirium for days. But she'd blasted it out, enough to make a lake of the igloos, then walked off with a good showing of wits.

After an age of climbing, she and the king burst out into that patch of night sky they'd been watching grow. Her legs slurred to a standstill and she began to fall from the air as the sight hit her. She reasserted her slack grip on her candle and windmilled her arms as if trying to fling away her panic. Her legs found their groove again and she avoided committing her body to the sea by a margin of fathoms.

As she followed Qummukarpoq circumnavigating this

oasis atop Qilaknakka, she could only stare and blink, and stare and blink. Under moonlight alone, an obscene amount of green furred the clutch of islands before her. Green closer in kin to Arsarneq than to the coniferous trees that grew near the Nuktipik coasts. The scene glittered as if suffused with a light of its own; as if the spirit in every leaf couldn't contain its joy for life.

She wanted to cast off her gloves and run her fingers up branches until the sun rose. *Would* the sun rise here? That couldn't be a privilege only for those below Qilaknakka. What would it look like during the day?

The king led them to set down on a shore of moonlit pearlescent white. Orluvoq tested twice the way the sand sank into an approximation of her boot wherever she stepped, so like snow, yet so alien. A forest beyond the wilds of her imagination awaited them a few paces off. Flaring verdancy in every direction, leaves that dwarfed her head. Reds, yellows, blues, and purples spangled the green depths as if the otherworldly domain bled out a color for every mood.

She laughed. It was so *beautiful*.

And hot. Horribly hot. Her clothes had become servants to the all-enfolding oppression. She stuffed down the urge to disrobe. Who knew when they might need to flee back down the channel?

"Curious," said the king, rubbing a trickle of sand between ungloved fingers. "It was a physical ascension I needed to attain my mythical ascension."

A rustle from the foliage. They both snapped their eyes to the disturbance. The forest gave birth to a man, barely blued by their twin candles. His skin was darker, richer than any Orluvoq had ever seen. About his loins was girdled a skirt of some type of plant. A string of long, sharp bones enwreathed his neck, backdrop to a stone face on a cord. Complex bands of black coated his left arm from shoulder to elbow. The opposite hand gripped a club studded with serried rows of serrated teeth. His carriage bespoke a familiarity with murder.

Her first instinct bade her run into the sky and never look back. Whatever savagery they courted as culture in this molten paradise, they could do so without her. Her second instinct was to recoil at the ridiculous outfit. A small second lapsed before the punishing weather reminded her of her own ridiculous trappings.

Something approaching caution and touching on awe tinted his eyes. His ample lips parted and he spoke. "*He atua anei'oukou?*" It was obviously a question.

"We do not speak your language," answered Qummukarpoq. Orluvoq sighed inward relief that she needn't treat with the stranger.

The warrior pointed at each of the candles in their hands. "*Ke lawe nei'oukou i ke ahi polū. Ke hele nei'oukou i nā lani. Aole anei'oukou he mau atua?*"

She ransacked her mind to locate any hints that candlework could interpret tongues.

"This will take time, but I hope we can come to an understanding," said the king.

Excitement poked into the warrior's face. He babbled another senseless string punctuated by exaggerated, open palm gestures that they stay put, then he jumped into the forest and bounded away in vaulting arcs.

Orluvoq blinked. "Did he just jump higher than a man? From a standstill?"

Qummukarpoq, for the first time ever, showed less than complete resolution. "Whatever folk dwell on these heights might be fiercer than we're accustomed to. Have another candle at the ready."

She touched the pocket where her other candle lay, but a portion of her wondered if it would be enough. True, they had just carved through Qilaknakka. But the man's ferocious countenance and casual use of power—it unsettled her.

And fed her a heaped dose of exhilaration. The two emotions arrived like bickering sisters.

A short time of shifting her discomfort between feet passed, and a low thrumming like the morning stretch of a giant rubbed her between the ears. She tossed her head back and forth, seeking the source. The king did the same. Then in the sky, her eyes found a phalanx of figures swooping toward the beach.

She tried to keep her composure as twenty men plummeted past the treetops and planted feet on the nacreous sand. Their presence slapped her with an anatomy lesson on the potential of human musculature. Every one of them was attired similarly to the warrior of before but differed on matters of neckwear and tattoo coverage. To the man, the company had tattoos over most of their torso, arms, and face. Far more than the occasional chin or forehead tattoo she was used to.

The middle one, the only man unadorned by a stone face necklace, stepped forward and spoke in a booming voice. "Which one of you is the blue god?"

His effortless command of their tongue twinged Orluvoq's gut. Such foreknowledge was not an advantage to them.

"I would be called god by some, but king by all," said Qummukarpoq.

The dark-skinned speaker broke into a toothy smile, white glinting between tattoos, and laughed in puissant tones. "I have the same struggle every day! I am Ariki Haka'atu, king of Rapai'i."

Qummukarpoq inclined his head. "Qummukarpoq, king of the Nuktipik, and my queen."

Orluvoq smiled over her unease. The foreign king's mouth moved to a different yarn than the words that came out.

Haka'atu swung a broad gesture and stepped closer. "And look at her! She would still be called queen even if she didn't know you."

Her blush bloomed, though it contributed little to her heat-stoked cheeks. Everything about these Rapai'ians exclaimed grandiosity. Their entrance. Their hands. Their calves. Their lips. Their—at least *his*—voices. To say she felt out of her element would be too kind.

"You have obviously traveled far. Please, come to my palace and join me for an evening umu parehaoga. Yams, kekepu, swordfish, gu fish, mahimahi fish. A feast for gods. Even those of us who are only *sometimes* gods." He winked and cried out in laughter.

Despite her angst, Orluvoq laughed back, more at the hoot than the jest. Qummukarpoq supplied a diplomatic smile.

"Come! Tell me of your Nuktipik," Haka'atu beckoned with a meaty wave. "Do you need me to fly you?"

"No," said Qummukarpoq. "We manage just fine."

Three royals and one entourage took to the sky. The Rapai'ians' feet remained posed as if they yet stood, while Orluvoq and her king pumped their legs.

"Ha!" called Haka'atu after them. "Slow down. We want to get there when the food is hot, not still cooking."

They couldn't go any slower, so they resorted to circling round the honor guard, much to Ariki Haka'atu's amusement. The forest below enchanted more than her stolen face possibly could. The group took its time approaching an expansive building of tall stones slotted snug against one another. So much stone dazzled her. The Rapai'ian king pinged jibes off his warriors, and they slung back in kind. Or, so she assumed. All spoke gibberish save the king.

They reached the palace, snuffed their candles, and followed Haka'atu's lead inside. The majority of the building, it seemed, was devoted to the main hall. A score of women in clothing of woven reeds crouched before multitudinous stone pits, moving red-hot rocks with staves and turning foodstuffs. The king led his guests to a mat and enjoined them to sit. Platters of steaming food were before them before Orluvoq even had time to realize that the heat was *more* oppressive inside.

The nonchalance. The convivial conversation. The sheer volume of men and women all mingling around the stone cooking pits like oldest of friends.

"Do you eat with your warriors every day, Ariki Haka'atu? Or is this a special occasion?" she asked after a helping of food, but she already knew the answer.

Haka'atu grinned, chin slick with grease. "Of course! Where else would my matatoa eat?"

"And... their wives? Or are these just maids?"

"Their wives, of course. Who else would take the job of cooking for these scallops?" He motioned at his entourage. "The children will eat after."

"Another question. How is it that *you* talk to us, but no one else does?"

"You are turning out to be a very questionable lady." He laughed and pushed her shoulder. "Look upon their necks. You see the moai hanging from each person?"

"The stone faces?" Some of them looked too hefty for neck bearing. "The thing you lack?"

"You women, so quick to judge a man by what he *doesn't* have."

She was saved from saying something in her defense by the king's self-inflicted chortling.

"I kid, I kid. You made a stone face for a second." He screwed his face into frozen scandal, then broke into another smile. "Those moai. I have one too, only I keep mine under the palace."

Orluvoq furrowed her forehead. "Why would you…"

Haka'atu leaned in and raised a conspiratorial eyebrow. "Mine is ten times as tall as I am."

"Oh. Wow." It was a grand thing to someone who'd never seen a rock larger than a flagstone. "And… what exactly is it?"

Shock crossed the king's face, then he burst into a laughing spate. "It is your stone likeness cut from the inside of a volcano. And what does it do, I anticipate your next question to be. Why, *everything*. They tell me it will even draw my life out a thousand years. Many kings only make it to three or four hundred before going fishing the last time though."

"*A thousand*?" She glanced at Qummukarpoq to gauge his reaction. These moai seemed a greater magic by far from that alone.

The king of the Nuktipik sat mostly silent. He had never shown poor wit around her. His words struck true and undoctored. But in the presence of Ariki Haka'atu, he'd become most taciturn. Was he simply withholding information to maintain some upper ground, or had the king at the start of the world finally been outclassed?

"I desire one," he said, quiet and firm.

Haka'atu poked him in the chest with a voluminous finger. "A moai of your own, eh? Hah! Tell me, what is the origin of these candles? One of the other tribes, the Moko-mae, tells tales sometimes of a blue god that visits them from the deepest sea. Then here you appear bearing blue flames. I must know! I must!"

"Light paints our night sky in a green river. A special whale, the narwhal, swims inside this aurora. Their tusk is full of the basest of magicks. It is this tusk, this tuuaaq, we burn."

Orluvoq admired her king's concision. She would have mangled the explanation.

"Excellent, excellent," said Ariki Haka'atu. "I desire one."

"A trade, then?" said Qummukarpoq.

"Your tuaku for my moai? A seemly enough deal."

"Yes. I desire a moai as big as yours."

For the first time, something other than joviality crossed the dark-skinned king's face. "As big as mine? No, no. This is not the way of things. A moai nine times as big as me? Ten times as big as you? Fine and fine. But as big as mine? Suddenly we are evenly matched, except you have your tusks. It is, for me, a very bad deal."

"I see." Qummukarpoq considered a moment. "Then nine times as big as you."

Haka'atu's lips edged toward a smile once more. "It is a great thing you ask, but I think a trade can be. For this thing I will ask... hmmm... One thousands of tusks."

Qummukarpoq's eyes didn't open quite as wide as Orluvoq's, but his surprise showed, nonetheless. "It is a great thing you ask, Ariki Haka'atu."

"I would not expect them cast in one pile blocking my door." He laughed and stacked some fishbones on top of each other. "We can say, ah, fifty per year. Reasonable?"

A tense moment of calculation. "You would tell me this moai will take twenty years to make?"

Haka'atu grinned. "If you ever want a break from being king, come and keep my accounts. My moai took twenty-two years. I say we can do yours in twenty."

"What about nine smaller moai? Could you not make those in one ninth the time?"

The island king flopped a hand over his eyes as he laughed. "Nine! You want nine?" His fingers wiped at tears. "If it were as easy as chipping out some more rocks from volcano throats, I'd have a hundred thousand moai and own all the islands. That would be bad. Who would my matatoa battle? No, no, you can only have one moai. And unless you want a warrior-size moai, it's going to take twenty years. Is it a deal?"

Orluvoq watched her king think long and deep, and she realized she knew vanishing amounts about his motives. Would he snap at this dangling chance for power? Did he catch a noisome odor from this realm and wish to escape down their tunnel and seal it for good? Was he content to rule their world of ice, or had he seen the vitality here and coveted it too? After considering all the options, she finally understood that it was too hot to do any thinking and went back to watching.

A moment later, without any ceremony, Qummukarpoq, king of the Nuktipik and all the world, transfixed the large man with his stare and spoke. "It is a deal."

A splutter of dread painted her heart. Twenty years. That was a very long crawl.

And a very steep price.

THE NUKTIPIK FREEZE embraced her as she lighted through a castle window on the heels of Qummukarpoq. She'd never had cooked food before, but a belly full of it slowed her thoughts. There had to be something she could say, or a moment unguarded in which she could slip away. The magic had been wrought. He had no more need of her.

"Every power we can muster, we must." The king paced as he spoke, more agitated tonight than she'd ever seen him.

"What do you mean?"

He stopped and pointed a glove toward the island paradise they'd just left. "Were you not just with me? Those Rapai'i can decimate us anytime they so please. What is tuuaaq against moai?"

She sensed an opening. "Then let's collapse the tunnel. Send the world back to what it was yesterday."

"And how would they view that act of diplomacy?" His face moved more humanlike than usual, pulled by upheaval. "We know not the extent of their arm. They could burrow through as we have, or simply swim. We are known. Our only chance is to preserve an amicable channel until we have at least one great moai."

This was not why she'd come. Not the strength she'd been seeking. Now she saw that while she may have fancied ruling the world, she couldn't live up to protecting it. She couldn't even bear the weight of her own frail spirit.

"I can't..."

"And yet you must. We must." The blue of his candle nipped cold across her ribs. "How many pathways were open to you, and yet you chose to walk this one?"

"Couldn't we just tell them that we don't know how long the tunnel will stay open? They didn't seem that bad, honestly." How much of his sayings was truth, and how much was *his* desire for greater power?

"You heard him. They war with neighboring island king-doms constantly. Unless we keep a strong treaty, it won't be long before their eyes turn to our land."

"They didn't really have the clothes for it," Orluvoq said, mostly to her hood.

"There is another step we must take to bolster our position even further." He moved closer, and his features snapped back to that tense, inhuman calm. "I need an heir."

Cold flounced in her stomach. She backed up a step. Mother to the heir. That would certainly strip her chances of ever leaving. "An... heir?"

"The reasons I desired a strong, angakkuq wife are twofold. To probe Qilaknakka, and to produce a strong, angakkuq child." His dark eyes caught the candle's cast and flung it toward hers. "The first has been fulfilled. The second soon follows."

His face, grim, ghastly, unmoving. His stature, towering, thin, shadowed. The cold, inside, inside, inside. Needling her to run. She couldn't bear his child, for that would mean bearing him. Whatever strength she might have gained so far, it hadn't been far enough for that.

"I can't..."

"I am the greatest angakkuq the ice can remember. And more than that, I am the greatest tirigusuusik." His eyes narrowed, but only the bottom lids. "Emotions are but a momentary hindrance, whether mine or others'. If you feel your emotions are hindering you, it will take very little for me to make that not so. I am giving you the opportunity to choose. If you do not take it, I will."

She broke the eye contact and stared at his cold-oozing candle. Her gorge pushed at the bottom of her tongue. Travel to the start of the world to gain knowledge, she had thought. Become queen, become strong, she had thought. Can't hide forever, she had thought.

She had thought wrong. From tremulous knees to the ache in her scalp, she wished she'd seen plainer the wisdom of vanishing. How her parents would anguish if they knew what she had come to. Would they soon be seeing any of the girls she had ravaged? They had only ever loved her. Why must the price of love always be pain?

But then, she had no love for Qummukarpoq. Perhaps that made it safe. She could pin her lips up in smiles when visiting her parents to spare them. If the king might die, or might say to her awful things, it wouldn't hurt because there was no love.

As much. It wouldn't hurt *as much*. Besides, what other option lay before her? She had forsworn hiding, and now it had vanished.

Her gaze fell to the floor and she ground her teeth. Why had she come?

Why had she left?

She wet her lips and, in the darkness of the upper room of the ice castle at the foot of Qilaknakka, she spoke.

"Very well, husband."

O rluvoq watched her daughter play with the bone snow goggles, holding them to her face and pretending they let her see all the way to Nunapisu. Soon enough. Soon enough. She listened to the life of the castle —the various servants and angakkuit she had insisted they invite—and missed it already. Seven years and it almost felt like home. Not quite enough to keep her, though.

"Qaffanngilaq," she said. Her daughter didn't look at her through the goggles. "The aurora will be out in just a few minutes and we'll be off to grandma and grandpa's. How about we go give your father a farewell?"

"Okay." The six-year-old girl pulled the goggles away, wiping her nose in the same motion. She ranged ahead of Orluvoq through the halls, stopping to inform any passerby that she was going to run the aurora. She babbled the same speech to an itinerant Rapai'ian, and he nodded while understanding nothing.

The queen smiled a genuine smile as she watched her daughter frolic. Finally, she was going home. Sulluliaq— that's what they'd taken to calling the glowing tunnel through Qilaknakka—persisted. It had been over five years since she had sapped any beauty, and still it gaped wide as the day they'd carved it. After weeks of importuning, the king had finally acquiesced. She would be taking Qaffanngliaq for a months-long stay at the end of the world. And if she forgot to track time, well, it might just end up being years.

That last episode of beauty leeching had gone well, discounting her spirit screeching protest. It still hadn't been an unimpeded sweep of prowess, but she'd cut off exactly where she'd intended. Then came the begging.

"I'm as beautiful as I ever was before Qaffa's birth. Let us test Sulluliaq. If it closes next month, then I will take more beauty. But if it would stay open a year and we waste all our people's beauty in the meantime? There will be nothing left to open it again."

Qummukarpoq had nodded short agreement, and Sulluliaq had held. It presaged well. Orluvoq may never have to drain another sliver of beauty.

That was what she recited to the surface of her mind. Recessed in some slimy crease wriggled a darker knowledge. Despite every scoff of indignation, every lick of lament, she wanted more. Longed to feel that apex power flux of finally taming the blue; to glimpse again the surety her first parents provided. For though she still used the cold candles to better accomplish anything she would with the warm, she never quite strayed all the way into the things to avoid. All of that crawling came at the price of someone else, and recalling that always stole the sting from her strength.

So she avoided it, even as she needed it. As Nalor had quipped years ago, she hated that she loved it. Somewhere between Nunapisu and the last of the islands, there had to be something else. Some way to crush helplessness without crushing anyone else.

"Daddy." Qaffa ran up to the king as they reached the darkness of the high chamber.

He paid her an austere smile and a pat on the head, then turned his gaze back to the window and the sunset-depleted sky. "You're still set on taking her tonight?"

"Of course," responded Orluvoq. "It's been ages since I saw my parents, and I know they ache to see their grand-daughter."

"Of course." For a rare moment, he held no candle, flame color regardless. "If you want to begin her courtship with candlework, that would be very beneficial. If not, we will start her studies when you return."

"I will do what I can."

The king wanted their daughter to become a great tiri-gusuusik. Orluvoq wanted to keep the path of the azure fire far from the girl's feet. For seventeen years she'd heaved against the crooked horn, and never had it once brought true joy—unless one counted Qaffanngilaq herself. Qaffa deserved a better path.

"Very well." He tipped his crowned head toward the window, at the slender bough of green light ornamenting its way through the sky. "It would appear your pathway has arrived."

Arsarneq spilled out like a goddess's lost needle and thread, then lanced through Qilaknakka and settled into stasis. A low woosh followed its track. Qaffanngilaq clapped her gloves and began to shout a children's chant about the aurora.

"Alright, alright." Orluvoq pulled some leather bands from her ample backpack and held them out in front. "Come over here and strap in."

Qaffa trotted over, stood before her mother, and fidgeted through the entire battening down. Orluvoq might have been vexed, but she was just as antsy. All tassels cinched up, she stood with a grunt and pulled out a candle. Probably should have lit it before strapping a squirming human to her chest.

She turned her eyes to Qummukarpoq, the last interplay they'd exchange until the sunless murk of deep winter. "A few months, then."

"Even so."

The world broke into roaring chaos.

Orluvoq pitched to the ground. The king jumped to a crouch and a candle exploded blue in his hand. Qaffa squealed death.

As the drawn-out boom still shouted its ire, Qummukarpoq dashed to the window. For the first time, Orluvoq saw pain cross her husband's eyes, flickering blue in the dark. "No," he said, and jumped into the night.

She struggled upright as the roaring blended into a never-ending crash, like leagues long ice sheets plummeting from the sky. Finally, she pulled her face above the windowsill. Her heart began to burble in acid convulsions.

"Mama?" came Qaffa's voice. "What is it?"

Orluvoq's tongue would not be loosed. Spectral green burnished the wall of water at the start of the world, and where there ought sit a tunnel, there thundered a waterfall. Gouts unceasing issued from the ocean wall. Particulate mist ghosted across her cheeks and nose, thrown from where the torrent met the sea behind the castle. Sulluliaq had collapsed.

She stood up enough to pop Qaffa's head over the ledge. "My little asasaq. We might not be going to Nunapisu just yet."

Qummukarpoq landed on the sill and Orluvoq jumped back, eyebrows high. "Unfasten her," he commanded. "Sulluliaq mustn't remain closed. Quickly."

Her brain chewed on that for a stitch too long before she reached to undo the harness. The sooner it was open, the sooner she could leave. She called and someone came running to watch after Qaffa, and then she was skywalking to the roof.

The king landed amidst the hummocks and turned to her. "How much tuuaaq do you have?" Unearthly urgency pinched his face to stern angles. "Never mind, take this." He proffered a modest stang of the sweet tooth and she grabbed it.

She begged time to stop. To spare her a finger tally of breaths to make her own decision. That was a lot of tuuaaq. Time seethed forward. She crushed the tusk in her teeth. The king, not sparing a moment for the high to hit her, sank his eyelids shut and beckoned to Arsarneq with unnameable might.

It heard his call, yielded to his yank, and groaned revolt as it splintered from its nest of sky. Euphoria unspooled in her veins. Muffled soundscape. Lips drained numb. Speckled taste of shark blood. Silver string around her spine. Falling skyward. Knees hitting the roof. Candle following. Green. Greener.

By warp and woof he snagged the flaxen light of all creation and wrestled it toward the castle. He governed it into a narrow rill and thrust it upon the queen. Arsarneq collided with her hooded head and shattered. She barely noticed.

Emeraldine fractals chattered across the rooftop, etching rhomboid graffiti in every direction. Qummukarpoq swore, mental grip stuttering, and tried once more with what control remained. Green brilliance soared through the dark like an arrow loosed for the queen. It met her skull and dissundered into ten thousands of powdered fragments spewing up into the night. The king stumbled. Arsarneq tore itself from his grip and flew back toward its nesting grounds, howling its basso pique as it retreated.

The king coughed. "It's rejected you. Light your candle again."

Orluvoq's brain understood the intrinsic meaning, but the implications slipped by on frictionless skis. "What?"

"Get a blue flame going so we can actually speak." He bent to the roof, picked up her candle, and pressed it into her glove.

Her thoughts circled as she stared at it. Finally, she fumbled around with her mind, pressing against the flame. Clarity snapped into place. Or, some did. The high was too strong for the blue to offset entirely. "The aurora. It didn't work," she said, realization piercing deep.

Her husband took her eyes in his, greased by a veneer of blue. "It will. Hurry."

Within her danced dread clad in boots of glee. The need she had been trying not to want for years capered forward to meet the king's command. Tonight, she would steal again.

In a smoke of euphoria, fear, and longing, she skywalked back into the castle. There in the high room, two women stood with arms wrapped around Qaffanngilaq, and nerves wrapped around them all. Orluvoq pointed to the one on the left. "Take my daughter to a lower floor. Quickly."

The servant rushed to do her bidding. The other woman, finding herself alone with the queen, balanced a question on her brow, hoping the queen would take it up.

"Kinnugu." Orluvoq turned her attentions on the girl.

"When you came to the castle, you swore an oath to serve me. Correct?"

"Yes?" Kinnugu touched the tattoo on her chin. She couldn't have been older than Orluvoq's twenty-five.

"Sulluliaq has collapsed. The islanders will be angry, might see it as us betraying our agreements. Sulluliaq must be reopened. I call upon you to help me."

"What... do you mean?"

"Kinnugu." Orluvoq swallowed, not even knowing what emotion filled her. "I must take your beauty."

The woman's pretty face soured with fear. "I'm sorry?"

Orluvoq nodded. "So am I, but the king has commanded. Will you give it freely?"

"I..." Kinnugu's hand inched from her chin to mask her mouth. "What happens if I say no?"

The queen slid her gaze to the window and Qilaknakka beyond. "I cannot speak for the king."

"Oh." The puff of air blew so soft it didn't even fog the air. Kinnugu's eyes dropped to the icy candle in the queen's hand. Twin tears ran the course of her cheeks. "Then yes."

She fell to her knees, hands in her lap. Orluvoq drew nearer and stitched together spellwork in her mind.

"Will it hurt?"

Orluvoq's formulations fumbled. She looked down, realizing she would be the last to ever see the girl's face. Though, she suspected, not the last to see her tears. "No more than losing any other loved one."

Then she struck.

Inhibitions shedding. Chill regimenting outward. Skin slurping off the face. Muffled voice screaming around chokes. Gauze of blue misting from skin holes. Power sledding into the queen. Drawing. Pulling. Taking.

Living.

She wished it would surge on forever. But she held it in check. Bore rein upon its rushing. *She* was in control here. When she felt she'd had enough, she sliced the connection. Kinnugu's face slapped back into place, and the woman slumped into a weeping heap.

Orluvoq had done it, and never had she felt a greater confidence. No external hand to guide her. Five years since the last attempt. Hadn't taken a drop too much. All the years of her youth, this surety was what she had been in quest of. She loved it. Loved every gloried second.

And yet.

She flicked her eyes to the heaving remains of Kinnugu. The woman creaked her neck up just enough to peek out from under her hood. Orluvoq's chest seized at the ghastly visage.

The crawl. What price it bore.

Through the tuuaaq high, through the beauty high, through the power high, the thought struck once more her muddy heart. There *had* to be something more. In all the ice below and ocean above, there must be found a better path.

She pushed the burden aside. No better path would be found tonight.

Orluvoq skywalked back to the roof and landed beside the king. Having espied her coming, Qummukarpoq swayed in the thick of his parlay with the river of green. It broke from the heavens and careened toward them. Orluvoq's chest forgot its seizing of moments before and took to soaring. It was coming, cutting its trail of legato zigzags. When it struck her—

The past and the future flashed white, all incinerated by the thin, endless edge of the present. She saw the stars. All of them. She was in the depth of Nunapisu. She was in the reach of Qilaknakka. She was in the height of the wall of cloud past the islanders' ocean. Every name yet to be sung. Every body yet to be bent. Every spirit yet to be spun. It all snarled and yammered, begging for creation. Pleading for a mother.

She obliged. The hinge of divinity turned as she wedged open the door of life. The billion unmanifestations beguiling her brain burst from her chest and galloped into frigid mortality. Every rictus grin cackling as it finally became. It blasted forth like a congealed blizzard of sunbeam snowflakes. Electric white emblazoning its brief run at life in the immortal sky. Cascade after screeching cascade pummeled through the rigid queen. Her body no longer hers.

She collapsed and hit the roof.

The flood dried. Vertigo spittle flecked the top of her brain, pulling her balance just slightly upward. She wrestled to bring her breathing under control. But other than that, she felt remarkably fine. Orluvoq opened her eyes in time to see the last of the light leaking into Qilaknakka.

Into Sulluliaq.

"It worked," she said with a half-smile. Open again. The distant roar of Arsarneq slotting back into place rained down.

"So it did." Qummukarpoq, for his part, didn't have a hair out of place. "But its collapse raises some concerns."

The passion of the moment started to dissipate, and the worries started to reassimilate. It was coming. Another bolt flying from afar to take over her body, only this time it wouldn't leave.

"You will have to postpone your trip to your parents for a very long time."

There it was. The hope of escaping Qummukarpoq. Of finding a better path for herself; for her daughter. Vised into obscurity. The other hope—of reaping more beauty, of continuing the crawl—wriggled forward again. She poured her acid on it. Buffeted it with fists. Gnawed its ugly face. And still it stood, fast as stone. The price was too high, and the joy was always tainted. But—and there was always a "but" lurking blindsides the objections—it was more joy than anything else brought her.

"What are you suggesting?" she asked from the floor.

"You will need to be around for any future incidents, and incidents there will be." His regard only cared for the glowing ring of Sulluliaq. "The older one grows, the quicker one falls apart. The more it takes to put oneself back together."

"That's why you go north every month?" How much youth had *he* taken from the Nuktipik people?

"That is why you will stay here, and we will implement a beauty tariff on all travelers. In addition," he motioned to the castle below, "we will seek an exchange with Ariki Haka'atu. His son, Mahiahia, will come live with us, and our daughter with them."

A gap opened in Orluvoq's chest, and she didn't know that it could be filled. "Qaffa?"

"It is common enough with the islanders. Attempts at peace. Our position will be fortified should another, longer collapse happen. My heir will learn of the islanders' ways and tongue. It is wisdom."

She lay there unmoving. Love. Love was always followed by pain. She had escaped loving her husband, but she couldn't flee the love for her daughter. So, pain had found her. Perhaps it was for the best. She desired a new path for Qaffa, did she not? How much farther from the blue flame could one go than the ocean above? Qaffa could go flourish in her haven, and Orluvoq could crawl in her hell.

And crawl she would. The king had declared it.

The glimmer of a new path, perhaps at the end of the world, winked out. Orluvoq, it was decided, would be beautiful, and Qaffa would be safe.

She slid her eyes shut. "My husband. I see the wisdom."

PART III

SULLULIAQ

38 YEARS OLD

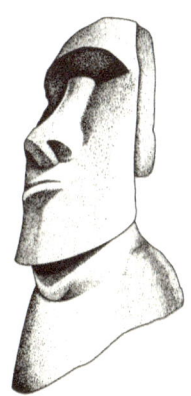

9 Years Before

"An age and an age ago warred the two zealous kings Kautoki and Nana'ia. Their moai were great, their rivalry greater. Ariki Kautoki's islands were flush with the hauhau tree, most adept of all the trees at becoming boat keels and pleasant incense. Ariki Nana'ia's islands grew forests full of the sweetest fruits man can taste.

"It seemed hardly a week could pass before they once again lined catamarans with their mightiest matatoa and sailed to battle. But they were not couchant kings; no volcano huggers were they. They built themselves monstrous vessels and cruised forth with their kingly moai as freight.

"What other king would dare such folly? It would take no more than faulty timbers or a savage storm to send their moai to the depths and all their rule be lost. Yet so bitter was their feud, they cared not that they might lose all so long as they had the chance to take all from their rival.

"While they warred, their people suffered. Oh, the

matatoa had chances aplenty to prove themselves in battle, but how many battles does it take until there's nothing left to prove? Slowly, their islands' populations began to diminish. Other kings observed their wrangle and clash, but what could they do that wouldn't involve more death?

"One day, Ariki Poriko, the king poor in islands but rich in wits, invited the two rival kings to feast with him. Same island, same day, different harbors. Of course, they brought their moai, but out of respect they left them in their boats. Poriko swore an oath on his moai to each of them that he would not kill them. Satisfied—and considering their host to be of the lesser kings—they each marched with their modest retinues into Poriko's palace.

"They feasted in separate halls, not knowing that the other did the same a mere room away. Once hours and courses had passed and they got up to stretch their stomachs, Poriko brought them into the same room then told them to remove their feast masks. Curses jumped into mouths, spears jumped into hands, and warriors almost jumped into battle. Almost, except Ariki Poriko's moai lay just beneath the floor. They were in his power.

"Kautoki and Nana'ia reached for their moai's power, but they were weak from the food. Poriko put them all to sleep. When next they awoke, the rival kings found themselves alone on a boat with no islands in sight. They couldn't move, for they were tied fast to their moai, and great cords wrapped the moai together. No matter, they thought, breaking bonds was one of the simpler things a king could do with his moai.

"But the ropes held fast. Poriko the clever king had enchanted their moai so each rock thought the cords around its king were part of itself, and who can break moai with moai? But the moai had no intuition about the other king's ropes. Parting the rival's ropes would have been easy as keel parting smooth sea. The zealous kings would have none of it. Ariki Kautoki tried to push the ship to his islands while Ariki Nana'ia tried to push it toward his islands. The boat would have none of it.

"A week passed, and a ship approached carrying a giant moai. A fellow king, then, but which one? Whose ally would they find peering over the side? Of course, it was none other than Poriko the clever king.

"'I see you are not done fighting,' he said to them. 'Otherwise, I would not find both of you here.'

"'Send Nana'ia to the deep and I will give you two islands!' called Ariki Kautoki.

"'Send Kautoki to the deep and I will give you five islands!' said Ariki Nana'ia in response.

"'I am afraid that neither of you deserves any of your islands,' said Ariki Poriko. 'I will watch over them for you. On the day you come to me as friends, I will give them all back. But if one of you comes alone, I will strike him down and keep all.'

"With that, Poriko waved his hand and their ship split right down the middle. Kautoki and Nana'ia both sank to the deep. Ariki Poriko lived until time had worn him to almost nothing, and never did he see the zealous kings again. On this day, at this very time, the rival kings sit on the ocean floor, each waiting for the other to free him."

"How are they still alive if Poriko died?" asked Qaffanngilaq, eyes wide at the foreign tale. She moved her gaze from the moai around a matatoa's neck to the floor, beneath which lay the king's gargantuan rock statue.

"Maybe the air dries us out quickly!" Ariki Haka'atu gestured wide. "That's why it's good to swim often, daughter

BENNY HINRICHS

of the ice. Or maybe Poriko was old before the story began. I know I was."

The answers were good enough for her eight-year-old mind, which was more occupied with convincing herself she could sense the power emanating through the floor. "So, they never got to go to Ragaka'i?"

A grin sprouted on the king's face behind his storyteller's mask of painted wood. "Ha! You almost make me regret telling you about that. Two years you've been here, and I don't know if we've managed to go a single conversation without you bringing up Ragaka'i."

"Well, I want to go there and see the big giants walking around."

"You know you can't unless you're a dead king or in a dead king's honor guard."

She poked him in the knee. "Then you need to die quicker."

He guffawed and slapped the mat, thick claps sounding through the feast hall. "Or maybe you just need to go find some islands and become queen—" he leaned in and whispered "—then die." The king rocked back, roaring at his own wit. "Then our moai can be planted next to each other on Ragaka'i, and we can jump up and dance together as we please."

"No! Going when you're dead is no fun."

"How would you know? You've never tried." Before Qaffanngilaq could reply, he peeled off his storyteller's mask and spoke again. "I think it's time for you to go do your lessons. The meal, lamentably, is over, and I must once again take up the mantle of kingly duty."

Qaffa hadn't been living topside long enough to understand every word he said, but the essence didn't escape her. She groaned at the dismissal and made her way outside, squinting against the lancing light. Whether the sun was brighter up here than ice-side she couldn't say, but it was certainly hotter. She adjusted her woven skirt and plodded along to the knoll where she met with her tutor.

Her fingers slipped over velveteen blossoms and waxy fronds as she climbed the scrawling path through the volcano foothills. She hadn't reached a point in her topside tenure where she enjoyed it better than her homeland, but she had achieved normalcy. The fruits and meats they had for fare. The dark roughness of the soil. The amount of skin everyone displayed at all times. The lack of aurora. A thousand other details that insinuated themselves into her life. Almost she could call this place home.

The path leveled out for a stretch and off to the side rose the knoll of knowledge. She climbed it and found her tutor wasn't there yet. But she wasn't alone.

A man in a pure white parka with a tuuaaq crown stood down the slope to the sea below. He turned around as she summited the hill, revealing the blue-glinting candle in his grip.

"Qaffa."

She smiled and ran toward him, arms wrapping around his legs. "Daddy! You're here."

They stood a moment in embrace. Qummukarpoq pulled away and looked down at her. "Doubtless they're feeding you well. You've had no shortage of growth since our last visit."

The Nuktipik felt good on her ears and tongue. "Ariki Haka'atu says I need to grow fat like a real woman."

"The man has a way with words."

"That's why he's king. Is Nehenehe coming?" She glanced down the hill searching for a scrap of movement.

"Today, I am your tutor." He took out a tuuaaq candle

and passed it to her. Qaffa ran her hands over it with glee. "The last time we tried this gave me hope that you might become an angakkuq like your mother and myself. If you still lived with us, you would have begun your training in earnest. As it stands, I will give you what training I can today, then leave a candle with you."

Qaffanngilaq liked that idea very much. Qummukarpoq helped her get a flame going, and she set about becoming an angakkuq. Over and over her father cut himself and constrained her to seal the wounds until she'd long since wearied of the task. It was, he said, the cardinal competence in candle control. When caverns crumbled, when ice storms carved flesh, when bears rampaged, you could heal, or you could die.

That was well enough, but she wanted to conduct the aerial feats she'd spent her wee years watching her parents perform. Her spirit danced within the aurora, and her body yearned to join. Her father, however, would have none of it.

Diplomacy, apparently, was yet in its infancy, and the daughter of a foreign state soaring the skies on foreign magic might stir up untoward feelings in the Rapai'ian populace. Her father was very good at finding ways to say no.

"Notwithstanding," said Qummukarpoq as the day stooped toward sleep, "there is a talent you must develop before you can skywalk."

Qaffa was ears all over.

"I will allow you this, but only if you covenant with me to never tell your mother until you reach adulthood."

"Oh, no problem. I can keep a secret a thousand years." Anything for new magic. How hard could it be? She only saw Orluvoq a few times a year.

"You realize that you can only keep a secret to yourself?

Tell one other and the world will hear. You mustn't tell your patron the king, nor your tutor, nor any of your island friends. They will talk without thinking, and your mother will hear. She hears all the news that comes through Sulluliaq. Can you keep a secret thus?"

She was longer in the thinking this time around. Eventually she gave a nod. "Yes. I can keep a secret." Right?

"Do you recall, before you ever left the castle, hearing the first rule of being an angakkuq?"

"Don't eat the tuuaaq."

"Precisely. And did anyone ever tell you the first rule of being a tirigusuusik?"

"Uh…" No. Not a soul had breathed a word.

"The first rule of being a tirigusuusik is *always* eat the tuuaaq." He broke off a crumb from a baton of tusk he held and offered it to her. "I am tirigusuusik. Your mother is tirigusuusik. And you will be tirigusuusik. The queen would have you never touch the blue flame. But you and I both know you are destined for things greater than orange can provide."

Qaffa held the speck of narwhal tusk on her palm and watched it as if it might blow her arm off. Orluvoq had gone to great pains to instill a fear of the tusk within her. It needled her hand, riled for her to drop it. She didn't. That might crack the island right in half.

"There is nothing to fear. You've been working with tuuaaq for hours. It's the same substance you now hold. It hasn't changed and neither have you."

"But…" Her hand quavered.

Suddenly the king seemed tall as two men. The meager light bent around him, swaddling his form in a cloak of carrion hues. Hoar encroached white over the balmy hilltop. His voice threatened from every angle. "Qaffanngilaq, daughter of my blood, tirigusuusik expectant, heiress of the ice and all that lies below. Your king commands. You will partake. You will ascend."

Her face ran wet with tears as she quailed before the floating man. Slowly, with no further provocation, she raised the crumb toward her mouth and tipped it inside. A long while she held it on her tongue. A glance at the king's face ended the long while, and she gulped it down, clutching at the ground for support.

Qummukarpoq's feet touched down, and his voice came from somewhere above her. "So it begins.

20

Plague had never dwelt with the Nuktipik people. Not in body, not in speech. A fever came, sometimes it stole, but always it left. Twenty years ago, when the first Rapai'ians visited the ice, they brought with them fever. It descended, it worked its schemes of rapine and death, and it didn't depart till evicted by angakkuq and quarantine. For the first time, the Nuktipik people knew plague.

"Will I carry the burden of ice above me or of loves lost beneath me?" was the byword of the heart. Clans spurned merchant ships as if they ferried demon hordes. Timeless feuds liquified to senseless slop in fever's crucible. Igloos traded warm and laughing bodies for cold and moaning winds. A child's last cough echoed for leagues unheard.

Yet theirs was a hardy stock. An irrepressible breed hardened through untold generations in a furnace of shadow and ice. When winter's hand smothered them, its calluses of privation grinding them into the crust, they held their breath until the tyrant tired of its sport and left. Then onto frostbitten feet they pushed their aching bodies and again took up the long walk. When two decades ago the new scourge plague at last lifted its hand, they found they could not stand, yet forward they faced and began to drag. The long walk became the long crawl.

As she assessed the girl before her, Orluvoq reflected on the benefits and blemishes of the decades since the first opening of Sulluliaq, the tunnel to the sky. The Rapai'ian girl could have been sixteen. Nothing striking about her appearance. A bit on the pudgy side. The girl shivered as her body took its first tastes of the world below the sea.

Orluvoq clucked and shifted her eyes to the man beside the girl, presumably her father. "How many did you say are in your party?"

"Eleven, Highness," he said in passable Nuktipik. Though how much of an achievement was it to string together two intelligible words?

Orluvoq crossed her right leg over the left under her pure white parka. Even if she could ward off the chill with a candle, the ice throne was quick to brutalize her backside. "You'll have to send two back."

The girl bit both her lips to dam her tears. The Rapai'ian merchant's mouth compacted into a line as he tried to school his emotions. "Highness. Surely after coming all this way it would be—"

"Sir," Orluvoq cut him off. "I do not command because I dislike you or your people. I command because there is only one way to keep Sulluliaq from collapsing. If I let a hundred pass for the price of one face, it would only be a matter of months before none could pass. Am I understood?" Even with her tightening the passage exchange rates, it might not be much longer than months.

Moments passed before the merchant nodded his acquiescence. "Yes."

"Kiffar will help you send them back through, then connect you with your contract ship." Orluvoq gestured to an elderly woman, one of four attendants standing in the throne room, who accompanied the Rapi'ian man out.

At the room's verge, he turned. "I will be here for my daughter." The smooth walls simultaneously amplified the voice and drowned it in its own reverberations.

A pang tweaked Orluvoq's chest. "That is not suggested, sir."

He redoubled his stoutheartedness. "I *will* be here for my daughter."

The queen sighed, head bowed, and slowly rubbed a thumb across her brow. "As you wish." She looked up at the girl and nodded. "Come here, dear."

Apparently the girl understood enough Nuktipik to grok the gist. She approached the throne.

When one learns to walk, the accomplishment trumps all else. Twelve years on and walking is but one of life's presuppositions. Even so, the thought of losing it is cause for quaking. Twelve years Orluvoq had been exacting the beauty tariff. It no longer yielded her the same surety of strength and power, but losing it would mark a swift descent into weakness. She had been wrong. There was no better path, regardless of how steep the price of this one.

She took in the girl's worry-creased face, and remorse flakes fluttered around her heart. No better path. A delicious lie. She simply wasn't good enough to find a better path.

"I won't tell you not to worry, but I *am* told having your beauty taken doesn't hurt, if that helps at all." The queen slipped a shard of tuuaaq into her mouth. "It just feels extremely uncomfortable."

The candle on the arm of the throne blinked to a chill

blue. The girl began to weep. Perhaps tonight, Orluvoq would too.

Twenty years ago, plague descended upon the Nuktipik people, but it didn't assail them as a lone tyrant. Plague took the spirit from the body. The queen at the start of the world took the body from the spirit.

21

7 Years Before

The cold needled at Qaffanngilaq's alertness, pricking her awake then pulling her conscious thoughts out—until she almost toppled over and it stabbed her awake again. Four years since she'd last seen the ice, save for crystalline dreamscapes, and what had drawn her ten-year-old self back? Death. Death had called her down from the summered heights. What better way to honor the dead than to follow them the way of all bodies? Down. Descending between worlds. Surrendering what warmth life offered. Seeking the dark which cradles corpses.

The dark hadn't claimed the corpse before her entirely. Qaffa watched the aurora's light play across her grandmother's features. Kitornak's body lay in a sledge adorned in a hatchwork of scarlet and green, awaiting its delivery to the ice. This the ninth time with her grandmother would also be the last.

A clutch of mourners ringed the body, their bodies rigid in dispute. Contesting silent, or in tears, nature's malice in the giving. Every generosity it abundantly gave, later it rescinded. Pitch black hair uprooted by gray. Vigor and sprite eroded to crackling strain. Warmhearted mother snatched deep into ice. No matter how strong the boat, time would see it rowed to fragments and the diligent oarsmen drowned.

Heavy hollows weighed in Qaffa's chest, though she couldn't articulate why. Certainly, she ought to love her mother's mother, and she suspected she did. But she had memory of only four meetings, the most recent nearly half a life distant. Her love felt like trying to learn a salmon's dreams by playing its fishbone harp.

Perhaps it was in every glance she cast her own mother's way. Orluvoq, whom so many spoke of from the sides of their mouths as imperious and exacting, wept in body-wracking clenches. Qaffa had even heard some people call her a monster. When a monster weeps, what can the world do but dread?

Two singers held out their last notes, then retreated. Paarsisoq, the Watcher at the end of the world, stepped forward. The young princess stepped with him and held his hand as he spoke of his wife's life. It felt like something that fell under the purview of good granddaughters. She flexed her fingers inside her gloves, testing the confinement she'd grown unwont to.

Her gaze wandered across the candlelit faces of the assemblage perhaps forty strong. A heterogenous lot, as she gathered from the introductions earlier. Merchants, sailors, angakkuit, clan archons, the Rapai'ian prince Mahiahia. Maybe more. Either her Nuktipik was a little frost-rotten or some people cultivated accents specifically to avoid communication.

Her eye caught her father's. She only held the intense

connection a moment before glancing toward Nunapisu. She'd rather stare at that and slowly be overwhelmed by the acrophobic feeling that the end of the world would swallow her. Still, she couldn't but notice that his light glowed yellow tonight. He abided by Orluvoq's request that no blue attend the exequies.

Qaffa herself had no issue following her mother's demand that no tirigusuusik powers show themselves at Kitornak's funeral. Something about the blue flame disrespecting her grandmother's memory. Qaffa wouldn't touch the strange flame at all if it weren't for her father visiting her dreams to assess her progress.

"My wife was a lover of stories," said Paarsisoq. Qaffa tuned into her grandfather's voice. She too loved stories.

"She would want me to tell her favorite so that it might live forever and teach you as much as it taught her." He closed his eyes and sighed a plume.

"In the age of second names, there lived a woman called Mikit, the greatest runner the ice had seen. When dogs were still wolves, she ran alongside them. If they tried to turn her into fare, she would slap them on the nose and run until not even their howls caught her. Not only fleet of foot was she, but light of foot too. Her fellow clansfolk often spotted her running atop fresh fallen snow without a hitch in her step. It was even said she could dash across water without so much as a drop touching the top of her boots. Mikit lived a good life.

"In the same village lived a man named Erininar. He had no speed to speak of nor spryness of foot. He had the favor of the children, for he would often join in their play, but the adults gave him little more than squints and tight-lipped nods. He constantly gave gifts in hopes of gaining fellowship. No matter his efforts, and many they were, his clansfolk wouldn't warm to him. Erininar lived a lonely life.

"One day there came a traveler to their igloos. He spoke of a forest in the east that was haunted by ten demons: four ijirait, three kigatilit, two atshen, and one tariaksuq. There couldn't have been a more fraught grove of trees, yet if one could get past the rabble, a great treasure lay at the forest's heart. Something that would surpass even Mikit's sprightly running.

"The sprinter, loved by many, said she would go and test the woods, best the demons with her might. The village voiced a lively approval. In the morning, they saw their champion off and awaited her triumphant return.

"Shortly thereafter, unnoticed by any, Erininar, loved by none, left with a bundle for the forest east. If perchance the champion failed, he would run his trials and fetch the prize. If he never made the middle, at least he would die in a thrust of heroism instead of being shunned by his kin. And if Mikit achieved the treasure, no one would be surprised.

"For five days Mikit ran her best, taking occasion to stop at villages and ensure she was on the right path. On the evening of the fifth day, the tundra broke, and dark trunks of weathered pines formed a stretching barrier before her. She hadn't been to many forests, but she was sure she felt something darker than mere shadow dripping out from this one. Seeing no reason to test what spirits there might be in the pitch of night, she awaited daylight. Luckily, summer was dawning, and a few hours later she stepped past the first trees.

"Four ijirait. That was to be the first challenge. Shape shifting creatures bent on hide-and-seek and snatching children. They didn't worry her much. Mikit prepared her muscles for what they were made for then leapt into a mad sprint. A wild caribou intercepted her, bashing her with its antlers, and she went sliding through the snow. But of course, it was no caribou. She pushed herself to her feet to run away from the ijiraq's next charge, but it was nowhere to be seen.

"For two days she played the game of hunt and dodge with the four demons, retreating and circling back when necessary. Perhaps she should have been more worried at the start. At last, she came to a section of the forest where the black trees relented to gray. The second trial. Three kigatilit. Where the ijirait had loved mischief, the kigatilit loved violence. Faces like fishes full of glowing fangs, gangly limbs with arm-length claws spurting out. These worried her more than the last.

"But her worry soon proved to be folly. Though any unassuming person would freeze at the sight of a snarling mouthful of sharpened light leaping for their throat, it gave Mikit plenty of warning. She laughed at the kigatilit's grace-lessness as they hared and dove after her. Before she knew it, the surrounding trees changed color to the white of snow. The third trial. Two atshen. The spirits of murderers trapped in the permafrost with only enough power to emerge when they could smell human flesh. But what power it was, that boundless lust for blood! Now Mikit truly worried, for she walked the cannibals' territory.

"She spent half a day in a tree taking what sleep she could, then she descended and ran her best. As she dashed, the atshen exploded from the ground. Spirit vestiges of ice cores ripped up with them, clinging to their muddy-red, skeletal forms. The chase waxed brutal. The atshen had more speed in them than any of the previous demons, they hungered for her meat and bones, and Mikit had been running for days.

"Giant, white trees passed in a blur as she struggled to escape the atshen. They slashed through her parka once, twice. She would soon slow, and her weakness would only feed their power. One of the spirits got in a third slash, deep in her back, and Mikit went sprawling.

"She woke up an hour later. How did she wake up? She should be devoured. Looking around she saw that the trees were no longer white. They stood as ghostly shadows. She reached out to the nearest one and her hand passed through. The final trial. One tariaksuq. A creature of obscurity that dwelt in the spaces where shadows pressed against reality—sometimes. It could step into reality as it pleased, but merely looking at it would send it back to the in-between.

"Mikit didn't know how worried to be. There was nowhere to run to; the prize lay within this stretch of forest. And how could she run away from what she couldn't see? She certainly wasn't running back to the atshen without the help of the treasure. She slowly advanced.

"At the center of it all was an igloo built of the same transparent shadows as the trees. Barely visible in the center sat some object. A bone? The lack of demon so far set her unease, but she felt well enough recovered from the atshen that she decided to try the only thing she knew. Mikit sprinted toward the shadow house—

"—and passed right through. A shrill laugh echoed from the trees. She tried twice more, each time hearing the ridicule of the tariaksuq. For two days she attempted every method she could think of, but it only left her exhausted. She had no food left and had seen no game—or tariaksuq—since entering the shadow grove. Would she really die so close to the glory?

"As she lay in the dust-snow contemplating death, she

heard the crunch of boots. She started and looked up to see a man, and not just any traveler, a man she knew. The most ignominious character in her clan *here*. How had *Erininar* gotten past any of the demons, let alone all of them? She was about to ask when he called out to the woods.

"'Tariaksuq. Your watch is lonely, as mine has been my entire life. Come treat with me, for I would be brothers.'

"What was he *doing* talking to a demon? He would never—

"Something rippled in the air and a voice spoke from the closest tree. 'Brothers? You would be brothers with a tariaksuq?'

"'None other will have me. And,' he reached into his pack and withdrew a length of narwhal tusk. Where had he gotten *that*? 'I have brought you a gift.'

"A shadowy figure of a man appeared and lifted the tuuaaq from Erininar, then threw the stick into its body. 'I could use a brother like you. Come to my house and eat with me.'

"Together man and demon walked into the igloo. The tariaksuq picked up the shadow bone from the floor, and Erininar accepted it. Mikit watched feeble in agony as the no-name swallowed the prize she'd earned but couldn't touch. He vanished, reappearing an instant later before her.

"'How did you get past the rest of the forest?'

"'Once you find what the demons want, working with them is easy so long as you are willing to give.' He handed her some seal fat from his pack. 'Perhaps I will see you back at the clan, Mikit. If I ever decide to return. I can walk the shadows now. Go anywhere. It might be nice to find a people who appreciate me.' With that he vanished once more and the cackle of the tariaksuq echoed from the shadow trees.

"It is said that when a child finds a toy that was lost, or a new toy entirely, Erininar has smiled upon them. Perhaps in your time of greatest need, if you can reach him through the shadows, he will appear and give you aid."

Paarsisoq paused to let the story settle. "There are many meanings that can be interpreted from this, but my wife's favorite was this. If you place all your confidence in one ability, the day will come where you break yourself on your own strength. You may find your own meanings, but in Kitornak's memory, tell the story of *The Ten Demons* to your children. With that said, I think the time has come." He stepped back and Qaffa followed.

At last, the speakers had finished their lores. The singers had finished their lays. The mother of the high north, who had given second lives to more than a score, was hefted from the sleigh, a man to each corner of the caribou hide. They laid her form upon the crust and stepped into the crowd of vigilants.

Nature trimmed the grievers' watch with garlands of disquieting hush. Minutes lapsed without a scratch save keening from constricted throats. Then, as bells from heaven drifting, minced a delicate tintinnabulation. Combing fingers white and clear clicked their way across the hide; found the body, found their mark, and began their careful climb. A strew of diminutive clinks prickled Qaffa's ears as the ice consumed her grandmother's flesh. Its queerly systematic spread saved the face until the end.

For a single, lucid moment, Kitornak lay in regal respite, draped in the white shared by queens and tundra. Then the veneer of ice clothed her face in its pall. The queen Orluvoq breathed a ghastly whimper as the body began to sink. It took longer than Qaffa would have guessed, but within minutes her grandmother's barrow was a featureless swatch of snow at the end of the world.

Her feelings seesawed inside her. Sorrow, curiosity, confusion, fear, indifference, contrition, back to sorrow. How could she know what to feel after witnessing that?

The adults converged into smaller circles and murmured amongst themselves. With no one else her age around, Qaffa found herself drawn to the edge, woozy at how big nothing could be. Though they both stretched boundlessly, the black was so unlike the ocean. No sway, no sound, no spirit, no body. Nunapisu was naught but a name. She tightened her grip around her candle and toyed with the thought of sticking some tuuaaq in her mouth for greater control. But no, she didn't like the sensation, and wouldn't dare her mother's disapproval.

A presence at her side floated into her perception. Heartbeats stumbled over each other racing into her chest. She'd known this moment would arrive.

"What does the void say to you today, daughter?"

A shiver oozed across her shoulders. "At the end of it all, there is only darkness."

Qummukarpoq lifted a white-clad arm toward the aurora. "What then is that?"

"Arsarneq." She watched its languid waves roll. "The heavenly light."

"And what is this?" He tapped her candle.

She stared at the glimmer in her hand.

"As angakkuq," he said, "you have the heavenly light wherever you tread. You carry a flicker of the end with you always. If you truly master it, you never need fear it."

Qaffa looked to the aurora's inscrutable provenance and the blackness that birthed it. "A flicker of the end? So, I hold a piece of darkness in my hand, then when I burn it, it puts off light? I don't know if I like that."

"Is it dark in your head?"

The question put her off balance. "I think it might be?"

"And yet that is where your spirit lives. Is darkness bad?"

"Darkness is..." *Scary*, she almost said, but that wasn't what the king wanted to hear. "No?"

"Your eyes fill with light, yet your head remains filled with darkness. How then can your spirit know what your eyes know?"

"I don't know." It all muddled dark in her head now.

"Light casts shadow, unless it touches nothing. And of what use is light that evades? In order for sight to happen, light must stop. And where light stops, shadow begins. What light asks, shadow answers. For you to see, light must die, yet would you wish your sight to cease?

"By your words, the tuuaaq you hold is born of darkness. As angakkuq, you destroy the darkness to birth forth light. You say you do not like this. Herein you confess that you value darkness more than light. But I vow to you, Qaffanngi- laq, you need not fear the dark. This shall not be my resting place, and with proper schooling, neither will it be yours." He gestured once more at the strip of green light in the sky. "That is where we shall take our rest."

Some time had passed since her last such lecture from the king, and Qaffa's head was a whirl of pinging darks and lights.

He faced his shoulders to Nunapisu, marking a shift in conversation. "When you looked at your mother tonight, what did you see?"

She grimaced. "She's been hurt really bad, but not in the way you can touch."

Qummukarpoq walked around her. "There is that which

can be saved once broken, and that which can only be saved before it breaks. Hearts, it seems to me, know nothing of restoration, only scarring. Your mother's heart could have been saved before it was broken, but now it will scar and hurt till she herself is laid upon the ice."

"That's terrible!" Qaffa's heart panged for her mother. "Can I... can you help her? You're the best angakkuq ever."

The king transfixed the void with his gaze. "No, Qaffan-ngilaq. This is not the type of thing that can be saved once broken."

Her words melted like flakes to flame. Nothing to be done. Her mother would roll in torment until her days fell dark forever. The thought pressed. Qaffa crouched down and hugged her knees. "Then why didn't you save her before she broke?"

The silence that came after somehow both stretched and bent back on itself. Finally, the king spoke. "Your grand-mother was old for one of the Nuktipik. Sixty-three. But with the proper application of candles, she could have easily had twenty more years. Could have seen you return to the ice a full-grown woman resplendent in power. But to do so would have taken more than the pale yellow of blandly burning tuuaaq. Only the skills of a tirigusuusik could have preserved her, and your mother so loves to pretend to limit her use of the blue flame."

"So... Mama could have saved her? But she didn't, and now she's sad?" That didn't sound fully right, but her father wouldn't lie to her. Or, more appropriately, he didn't need to.

"She could have done many things, including save her mother. However, she only did one. It is the domain of curious children to speculate on what could be, and the domain of piteous elders to speculate on what could have been. Do not follow the folly of the old who never gathered wisdom. Think instead on how you can affect that which is to come."

Something seemed a tilt off, nevertheless the words puckered on her heart like some far-flung betrayal. Her mother could have saved her own mother, but she chose death. Life on the ice was bitter and fierce, Qaffa knew that exceedingly well after spending so much time in the easy sun. It was all the more necessary to stick together and help where possible. Not leave your own mother to wither body from spirit. She hadn't truly embraced the blue flame in the two years since Qummukarpoq had first instructed her on it. But if it was the only way...

"What should I do?" she asked her father.

He turned to her. "You must touch the things to be avoided. You must become tirigusuusik."

Memories of the king burning with a tainted dark while profane blue sleeted through her spirit. Half-hearted struggles with the tuuaaq herself. Shame of concealing her dabbling from her mother. It all creaked in her mind like a single tree tipping in a windless cavern. She bent her head and shrank her voice to the size of a snowflake.

"I will."

22

ORLUVOQ

S he dreamt of ice. Why would she dream of aught else? That same primordial ice she had first beheld twenty years ago when Nalor had guided her spirit here to the Warren of Immortality. That same scent of dead ages feather-thin in her nostrils. The shut-in sense of stolid stretches of ice heaped above her head. The quibbling cloud of spirits hemming her every side.

It almost felt like home.

Orluvoq knelt with one hand in her lap and one on the clear, green stone, thumb running across a line of runes. *Kitornak*, she said within herself. Unlike her first visit, she could read every name inscribed in the catacomb. Sometimes she did just that, but none weighted her breath as heavily as her mother's. It seemed like Kitornak had been the only woman she had never taken anything from. No, Kitornak had given freely.

A surge of introspection washed through Orluvoq. Here she knelt in her pitiable sanctuary of folded dreams, biding her time until reality summoned her back to ravage anew. Though she didn't look a day over a sultry twenty, her spirit ached with the weariness of having lived a hundred lives. Perhaps in order to take from someone's body, you had to sacrifice a portion of your spirit. Maybe that was why tiri-gusuusit tried to live forever. When they died, there wouldn't be any spirit left. Just a beautiful body and a name to curse.

Perhaps that was why she liked coming here. It reassured her that some modicum of spirit resided still within her.

She stroked her mother's name again. "I'm sorry. I should never have left you." Lured into darkness by the faintest of lights.

And now, in spite of her best efforts, Qaffa was being pulled adrift by the same cold light. Why had they even sent her to another land twelve years ago? A pure start. A clean snow. That's what Orluvoq had wished for her.

But the tusk reached farther than her imagination. Merchants hauled their goods whithersoever clients called from, and more than meager portions of narwhal tusk made their way to Ariki Haka'atu's domain. Apparently, a daughter of the ice couldn't resist the song of her mothers' sky thrumming in her blood, so the blue flame made a stage of her daughter's hand.

She had disdained the first reports two years ago, feared the reports of yesteryear, and grieved every report she heard today. Qaffa had found the path—or had it found her? Did the hardest path reach for the strongest people? Or was it merely the lot of the weak to stumble onto the roughest way? Not that it mattered when it befell one you loved. Both resulted in equal pain.

The queen's attempts to reach Qaffa through the dream yielded no success to speak of. Some way, somehow, she would pluck her daughter from this path of descent. If she had to travel up topside herself, or bring Qaffa under her watch down here, or—

No. Best not to follow that thought any further. The two resolutions she'd named each came with attending complications, though, and most of those revolved around the king. Could she find any way around that bulwark?

The press of spirits shifted and Orluvoq looked behind her. In the shadowed corridor stood a man possessed of no outward menace. But Orluvoq knew better.

Nalor stepped forward with a twinkle in his eye. "Fancy bumping into you in a venue like this. You just stopping by to gather some interior design ideas? Finally got fed up with the 'castle austere' aesthetic?"

A part of her pained at seeing the man who had led her path into the azure depths. She smiled. At least he was a reprieve from her usual life. "And why would an old scab like you show up to somewhere this holy?"

"A scab? That's when your body works to stop itself from bleeding out. I'm not nearly so useful." He walked toward her on soundless feet. "And you are beautiful as ever. I'll have to get your skin care routine sometime. Pit sweat and blubber, was it?"

She rolled her eyes over a genuine smile. "Yes, I stole it from you."

He laughed, sounds of his amusement pinging round the cavern. "Do you sharpen your wit on your husband, or have you gained humor all on your own? Imagine how grand our romp twenty years ago would have been had *both* of us been funny."

Her smile faded to a wan strain. "The situation was funny enough for me. A, what, five-hundred-year-old man sending a girl of eighteen on a quest of rapine and horror, all because he was too ugly to get what he wanted? I've laughed about it for years."

"Five hundred? Such a tawdry sum. I wasn't even ninety."

That caught her interest. Twenty years of efforts to discover her husband's age had all fizzled, but she had worked out that he was no more than two decades Nalor's senior. That slotted Qummukarpoq somewhere in his hundred twenties. Old codger.

Orluvoq shuddered. He would have been over a hundred when Qaffanngilaq was conceived. She shuddered once more for propriety's sake, even if his body hadn't looked much past forty then.

"Anyway," Nalor continued, "I had rather hoped you'd be here. It's been, what, three, four years since our last talk? How are you holding up?"

She was almost touched that he asked. "I destroy girls for gain. My husband will brook nothing else. I have nerve pain down my left backside that won't be healed by candle. And my only daughter is tainting herself with the path of tirigusuusit."

"But you do live in a castle," said Nalor thoughtfully.

"You've been angakkuq for too long. You've kept yourself warm with the candle so many years, you've forgotten how humble people live."

"What do you mean by that?"

She placed her mother's stone down and stood. "In a normal igloo, you heat the air with body and breath. The ice of the walls keeps the warmth of people in and the chill of winter out. You think we have enough people here to heat a *castle*? And don't even get me started on all these windows. Whoever built this oversized igloo deserves a dunk in the sea."

"You might be onto something there. Should I start doing fasts from the flame to remind me of common concerns?" He chuckled to himself. "Maybe you just need to take a little time and dream of somewhere warmer."

"You know what you've never told me?" Her hands found her hips. "How did you know what would be past Qilaknakka? You talked about warmth and all the ice being gone before Sulluliaq was ever opened."

"Oh," he flapped a hand, "just a dream I had."

The evasiveness pulled a sigh from her. "And what have you been doing up there since? No Rapai'ians ever make mention of you."

"Not every island is Rapai'i." He leaned into an eyebrow. "Speaking of our island friends, I am ever so curious to know, how comes your husband's moai?"

"Are you asking about its current state, or the method they'll use to ship it here?"

"Let's go with the current state of the moai."

Orluvoq put some of her distaste into a shrug. "One month is what they say. However, there might be... complications."

"Fright of frights. Complications hauling a several ton rock through the ocean? Impossible."

"Even more impossible when Sulluliaq crashes in on itself and becomes just a memory in the face of Qilaknakka."

He raised an eyebrow with unusual interest. "Oh? Is this your plan for getting back at your husband for forcing you to seize beauty?"

Orluvoq's cheeks warmed. Even if she'd entertained the idea in the past, her spirit was far too deviant to stop taking now. And Qummukarpoq's wishes were far better followed than dismissed. "Nothing so brash. And I don't *seize* beauty.

Not since your introduction to the practice, at least. I take what is given. But what is given is given less and less these days, and my body leaks beauty quicker than it ever has. If no one comes to Qilaknakka within two weeks, I fear Sulluliaq will close."

It felt good to breathe the words into open air, even if it was to just one person beside her husband. It wasn't the sort of thing a queen voiced to her servants, nor was a queen's failing beauty the sort of thing servants voiced.

"I assume the king knows?"

"Oh, yes. He won't let up about it. He wants me to skywalk to the north, enter a village, and demand a royal offering." Qummukarpoq's wishes may be better followed, but there might still be a chance she could shift the object of *that* wish.

"And shall you?" Something dark glinted in Nalor's eyes.

"I... will do what's best for the people."

He studied her awhile before speaking. "You rose from orphan to powerful angakkuq queen, yet you are bitter over your station."

"Bitter over being forced to do what I hate for twenty years? I must be the pinnacle of unreasonable."

"You've never enjoyed *any* benefits?"

She rubbed her tongue against the ridges of her hard palate. "The king commands, so I must obey."

"It is Qummukarpoq's fault, then? Your bitterness?"

"Nalor. I want to be strong. I want to do right. Maybe once he gets his stone, I'll have the opportunity."

Nothing left to crawl for, yet his hand kept her prone. All the strength she had gathered along the way amounted to nothing beneath that hand. One month more and she could wriggle out from under; finally take up the search for a better path. Maybe even stop taking beauty.

"Orluvoq. Let me tell you something that, ironically, took me years to learn. You can't awaken someone who is feigning sleep."

"Exactly! He *knows* what is right, but he has decided that his will is straighter than what is right." That stultifying phrase described Qummukarpoq with compelling accuracy. In his overassurances, he dragged her down with him.

Nalor tapped a finger against his chin. "Are you patient enough to hear a story from me?"

"I believe I have time."

"Most excellent." He cleared his throat, no more than an affectation in the dream. "In a certain clan there were two women who had babies only days apart. The clan knew it couldn't provide for any more mouths at the time, so when the first bore her child, they asked her to surrender it to the ice. She, having great love but being pragmatic and devoted to her clan, assented and laid the babe to sleep in Nunapisu's cradle. Sadness gripped her, but such is the way of things.

"When the second bore her child, the clan asked her the same, as she knew they would. Unlike the first, her emotions overpowered her devotion to the clan, and she pleaded until she prevailed upon them to let her keep the babe, with the agreement that she would always be last to receive food.

"Watching the other woman's child live, the first woman mourned her decision for the rest of her days. Years passed, and the child grew into a mighty hunter that single handedly saved the clan from certain starvation one winter. The second woman rejoiced in her decision for all her days. For the actions of the two women, where did the responsibility lie?"

"The responsibility lies with the entire clan," Orluvoq said on instinct. "Even a child knows that."

"Then why was the first woman sad?"

"No one in a clan rejoices that they have to lay a babe on the ice. But she wasn't only part of the clan, but the child's mother beside."

"You describe the typical depression that hits such a surrendering mother; the weight of yielding to the clan. You fail to mention that when she laid her babe on the ice, she had no choice. So she said. And when she had no freedom, she had no responsibility. But her clan sister soon proved that sometimes a mother's word holds more sway than a clan's. Her guilt was writ clear as blood in snow, and her remorse stretched to Nunapisu's pit. Contrary to what she'd always known, it had now frozen sharp into her spirit that the weight of yielding surpassed the weight of defiance."

Orluvoq held a frown that had been forming. What was Nalor trying to say here?

"But that's not the only interesting question to come from the story. The second woman took responsibility from the clan—or perhaps exercised the responsibility she'd always had—and twisted herself, her child, and even her clan into great risk. When even a child knows to follow the clan's decision in leaving behind those that can't be cared for, why would this mother choose something so reckless?"

"Selfishness." Orluvoq gave the answer any Nuktipik person would, but her heart didn't fully feel it.

"Or was it love for her child and hope for all his possibilities?" Nalor reached out and put a hand on her shoulder. "Remember these two things. You can't scrape away responsibility without scouring away choice. You can't melt risk without evaporating possibility."

As queen, Orluvoq had grown accustomed to withholding a response when it suited her. But now response was withheld from her. She had no choice but to not respond, yet still felt responsible for being responseless. He had always been adept at that. Finally, words came to her, even if they erred on the side of graceless.

"And what of all your wrongs?"

He frowned and drew back. "Cast your gaze back one hundred years, name an action of mine, and I will claim it. Show me the bite, and I'll show you the teeth."

She returned the frown. "Claiming your wrongs does not make them rights."

"Neither does avowing they belong to someone else."

Orluvoq studied the wall. Meeting his eyes could wait for another time. Frail of her to do so when she had held face with so many merchants and dignitaries. But where they saw only the dour witch queen, he saw past to the medley of fragments that made up her spirit. The chaos that still awaited a master puzzler. The weight she still hadn't found the strength to lift.

Nalor drew in the breath that preludes farewells. "Nevertheless. Your father misses you terribly. A visit wouldn't be amiss. I hope we meet again soon. Perhaps at the end of the earth, even. Until then."

She winced at the reminder of the pain she'd given her father in exchange for his love. As Nalor disappeared, the cavern air swirling in his subtraction, that statement of his tossed around Orluvoq's head. *You can't awaken someone who is feigning sleep.*

He had been speaking about her husband.

Right?

23

QAFFANNGILAQ

6 Years Before

Qaffa screamed and harrowed up black soil with her fingers. Her hands itched to fly to her leg and force the bone back together, but the current pain sickened her enough as it was.

"Qaffa!" Ka'emu shouted and slid down the tree adjacent to the one that Qaffa had occupied until a few seconds before. She thudded into the dirt, pushed aside a branch of orange and purple flowers, and looked down at the damage. "Oh! Ah—Qaffa! Oh no! Your leg!"

"Ka'emu." Qaffa gritted her teeth and spoke between sobs. "Calm down. Help me."

"Okay. Okay. Sorry. Sorry. What do I do?" Ka'emu's tears flowed as though she were the injured one.

Qaffa pillaged her brain for any hints from her tutors on what to do for a broken leg. The answer usually amounted to: *find someone with a big moai as fast as you can.* "Go get some of the matatoa who didn't go on the war raid with the king. They can help fix it."

Ka'emu half-bent and stretched her arms as if to pick Qaffa up, then she stood back up and put her hands to her mouth. "I can't carry you. Qaffa, please don't die."

Qaffanngilaq moaned as a swell of pain masked her mind. She tore flowers and fronds up by the roots. "I know. I know. Go get someone. Hurry."

Ka'emu made a shapeless whine. "Who should I get?"

"Anybody! Hurry!"

"Okay, okay!" Ka'emu took one last horrified look at the newly angled leg and set off running down the mountain, batting the undergrowth aside. Even at that pace, it would take the girl half an hour to find anyone.

Qaffa laid her head in the dirt and resigned to wait. With the agony throbbing up from her leg, she feared that the next funeral she attended would be her own. Would her mother insist on a Nuktipik burial, like her grandmother's last year, or would her family come topside for a burial beneath the sun? No, Qaffa didn't have a moai yet. She would have to go to Nunapisu. Funeral on ice it would be.

In the midst of her wallowing, a recollection sprung into her mind. She had tuuaaq.

She fumbled at her sealskin satchel, casting reprovals at herself for taking so long to remember, and withdrew a candle. Over the past year since her oath to become tiri-gusuusik, she'd been acclimating herself to the yank and yaw of the narwhal's tusk. She'd certainly grown more accustomed to its wiles, but she had little appetite for it. The way it crooked her spirit into something else.

None of her apprehension followed the candle today. She stabbed the wick with her teeth and chipped off a generous flake. Within no time at all, the frothy warmth of Arsarneq prickled her organs, and she began to float. Or, she thought so.

If she'd had any presence of mind, she might have attempted windwalking. The tuuaaq ensured she had little mind present. A distant cry—perhaps from her knees—told her she'd taken too much. At some point, a brace of wild boars trotted by and worked their bristly snouts back and forth over her. She made desultory attempts to shoo bugs away.

After a stretched amount of time lying supine, a rustle of bush and a chatter of voices alerted her to the presence of humans. A face stippled with tattoos appeared over her. He smiled down through the bushes.

"I'm glad I didn't teach you how to climb trees, daughter of the ice. I don't know if I could stand the embarrassment."

Qaffa gave a dreamy smile and waved at the matatoa.

"Oh, thank heavens. You're not dead." Came a second voice.

She turned to see Ka'emu. She had run all the way to... wherever, just to bring friends. What a nice girl. Beside her stood another matatoa, so denoted by the moai hanging from his neck. Qaffa wanted a moai.

"Why would I be dead? I'm just lying down. Have you never heard of, um, lying down?"

"Dead people often lie down, Qaffa." Ka'emu bit her lip.

Oh. She was right. Qaffa would have to remember that. "Does that mean I might be dead after all?"

"It might mean exactly that," said the matatoa over her. "We'll have to carry you home for a proper burial, eh?"

Qaffa nodded. "Okay. I think I'd like that." She let herself be hoisted and attached to the back of the overlarge man. This was comfortable. She might have to die again soon.

"I'm holding you and Paga'a is holding your leg." Her mount pointed to the other matatoa.

Qaffa wrinkled her brow. "He is? But he's not even touching me."

"With his moai, you silly chicken."

"I hope I get a moai soon," said Qaffa.

They set off and she settled into an agreeable state of watching the colors of life pass by. A score or two of trees into it, she realized she had a captive audience. Or she was a captive audience. Either worked.

"Hey." She tapped her ride on the shoulder.

"Huh?"

"You know any stories?"

"Stories? How about the time my toenail grew sideways, and a quarter of my foot turned purple?"

"No, I mean good stories. Like about where islands come from, or the evil warbird that swallowed a volcano."

He looked back at her and grinned. "Ah, that kind of story. Well, since you mention the warbird, have you heard 'Midnight Blue Egg'?"

"Um..." She could remember as many as three things right now, one of which being her own name. "Should I have?"

"You should consider yourself lucky to hear it from such a wondrous storyteller as me first. A pity I didn't bring my storyteller's mask. Now, let's see." He readjusted her and cleared his throat.

"In the most fleeting of times, for they are now the most gone, was an island called Mahu. The people gorged themselves endlessly on anana fruit and pig meat until they grew fat and happy. They did not know sailing, so they sat in their tree shade and poked fun at each other until they felt it was time to sleep.

"After one of their beloved sleeps, they woke to find the most curious thing on their shores. An egg taller than a man and striped up and down with smokey trails of dark blue. Nobody had ever seen an egg bigger than a fist, so they scratched their heads at what to do with this one.

"Some said it had been laid by a giant, man-eating bird while they slept, and that they had to push it into the sea lest the bird come back and kill them all. Others argued that if a killer bird *had* left it, pushing it into the sea might only anger it more.

"Some said it was the spawn of some giant leviathan of the deep, and that they needed to drag it further onto land so that it would die when it hatched. Others argued that if it *was* the lost child of a sea monster, it might hatch and call out in distress to its mother, who would then come and lash their island with her tentacles. It seemed there was nothing they could do.

"Their oldest grandmother said it had come to them, so they should bring it up on the land and care for it as one of their own. Some were uneasy with the idea, but all eventually agreed if there was any circumstance that called for his wisdom, now was it. But there was one even older than her.

"They looked to the sky and asked the sun what he thought they should do. The sun bent down and gazed at the egg for hours before settling back into his sky. The people all wiped their sweat away and gulped in cool breaths. Asking the sun was never without price.

"When the fire in the sky finally spoke his judgment, he said only two words. 'Burn it.'

"Some were quick to agree. They needed to get rid of this evil as convincingly as possible. Others grumbled that of course the sun would say that. Whatever bird hatched from there would block out the sun wherever it flew, and he was a jealous ball of fire. Still, the people of Mahu could make no decision.

"The contention grew until slaps broke out between sides. People began sleeping on different sides of the island. Spears that had only tasted the blood of beast were turned on man. Before they knew it, the island of Mahu was at war. Augurs were consulted. The appropriate sacrifices slain. Promises inked onto skin in fresh tattoos. New war masks carved. Long-haired priests convened in the middle to shake freshly painted gods at one another and shout their opponents down with threats.

"After many battles, the side who believed in destroying the egg succeeded in capturing it. First, they beat it with clubs. It would not crack. They struck it with flint knives. It would not chip. They surrounded it with wood and ignited an all-consuming fire. It remained the same soft white with stripes of dark blue. Finally, the chief of the egg breakers declared they would push it into the volcano. They would do as the sun had originally told them.

"Battle after battle they fought their way up the mountain, for the egg keepers still believed they should let it be. The closer they got, the hotter it became. Everyone was tired from standing watch while others took sleep in the shade. Everyone was weary from the endless fights. At long last, they found themselves at the volcano's mouth and sent the massive egg tumbling into the fire below.

"The mysterious egg smacked into the lava and slowly sank in. The egg breakers gave a mighty roar. They had triumphed! From the other side, the egg keepers wailed their sorrows.

"But the mourners and the gloaters soon found themselves trading tones. A white and blue oval bobbed to the surface. Not even the volcano itself could destroy the egg. The breakers clutched at their faces and burned their gods while the keepers laughed lustily and set to feasting on pork and bread fruit.

"As the fires of the keepers crackled, the breakers set to work. They would see the egg broken, no matter the cost. Through much travail they heaved heavy stones up to the rim of the volcano and pushed them in, angling for the egg. But nothing they could muster would fall far enough toward the middle to hit their mark. The egg remained untouched.

"They needed something longer.

"In a stroke of inspiration somewhere on the border between madness and genius—perhaps a whisper from their new gods, perhaps a twist in a sacrifice's intestines—they brought forth their hatchets and began to carve a long column from the inside neck of the volcano itself. The work was hotter than asking the sun for advice, and it felt harder than the egg's shell, but they knew it was the only way they could be safe.

"They slept, cut, slept, cut, slept, cut, taking every spare chance to bask in the shade, until at last they had carved far enough down. They chopped the anchor ropes and let the pillar fall. End over end it tumbled until it struck the egg dead on. The breakers let up a loud whoop. Three cracks wrapped around the egg. One more direct hit ought to finish the job.

"Fueled by success, they slept and cut and slept and cut again, their excitement so great that they decided to carve their chief's face into the stone. Their work didn't go as swiftly this time. The keepers sent waves of attackers now and again to stymie their progress. But the work went, and after many sleeps, they were finally ready to unleash their weapon.

"On the day of release, the keepers attacked them from below with everything they had, sending spear after spear at the breakers. They replied with furious defense as the stonecutters made the final cuts. In heat like fiery death, the stonecutters in their harnesses made the finishing crack and separated the pillar's base from the volcano. The men above swung hatchets and severed the binding cords. The rock began to fall.

"The breakers hooted in jubilation. The keepers wailed in despair. As its top passed its base, the stone suddenly halted.

"Confusion hopped from person to person until they noticed the chief holding out his hand. Slowly, the rock raised up above the lip of the volcano and came to rest on the edge. One by one, both keepers and breakers dropped their clubs, obsidian-edged swords, and shark teeth knives and dropped to their knees. This chief of breakers, he was more than a chief.

"He stood next to the carving of his face twice as tall as him, looked it up and down, then looked to the matatoa all around. 'I don't know what moves in this stone, but it now moves in me. Now we end this.'

"The people gasped as he raised off his feet and floated over the volcano's mouth. He thrust his hand down in a mighty gesture and a loud crack ricocheted up. The egg was no more.

"The volcano erupted, but not with fire. Darkness poured out, billowing greater and greater. Even the stoutest matatoa turned and ran down the mountain. It was not enough. The darkness swept the island and rushed toward the ends of the sea until even the sun cried out and fled for the marvel of it.

"The people of Mahu hid until, hours later, the darkness finally left. When the sun returned, he bent down to the island and shouted at their foolishness. For hours and hours he chastised them until they were sure they would perish. No shade would block the heat of him. Then the darkness returned, rolling across sky and sea. The sun saw it coming and fled.

"Twice more the cycle repeated until it seemed to the people that things might be that way for some time. They began to call the hours of sun 'day' and the hours of dark 'night'. In the darkness when the sun wasn't bellyaching, the egg keepers took up the responsibility and heaped their own whining on the breakers and the chief. On the fourth day, when the darkness had retreated and the sun came out to shout once more, the chief decided he would have no more of it. He faced the sun and shouted back.

"'Do not come at us to shout. We do not alone own the island. The trees flourish. The swine forage. The volcano grumbles. Why then should it go against reason that you might have to share the sky? We will hear no more of your complaints.' With that, he called upon the stone that they called moai and pushed the sun higher and higher away from the island. It complained the whole way and shouted that it would return.

"So, the people cut more moai. They built boats that they might travel far and multiply their moai, and thus we find ourselves the people of Rapai'i, of Marama, of Moko-mae, and many more. We nod to the darkness as our ally, but we know that the night will come when night does not come; when darkness fails to cover the ocean. When that eternal day arrives, the sun will wage its final war, and every moai bearer will be called upon to defend the islands against its fiery face."

"Wait," said Ka'emu. "He moved his own moai? I thought moai couldn't work on themselves."

"Shhh," the man chided, "you're ruining the story. Maybe back then they knew secrets we've forgotten."

Qaffa patted her matatoa on the shoulder. "You're sweaty."

"It's the sun. It senses my moai and wants to fight me." He and the other matatoa laughed. Qaffa wasn't coherent enough to figure out why. Before she could, her mind wandered lost in scenes of the legend and the rhythm of the trot.

QAFFA WOKE the next day coherent enough to figure out that she had broken her leg, and that shunted her straight into a sour mood. It was the exact type of thing her mother would have told her not to do. Then again, she had been on something of a rebellious crusade lately, all at her father's behest. Except for the leg situation. He probably would have admonished against that as well.

A trio of scrimmaging flies ported their buzz around the room, whirring near her face too frequently for her tender royal temperament to cope with. The king would have called them properly large flies. The kind that would lose in a footrace. Ariki Haka'atu was always urging her to get properly large, as a woman should be. She looked down at the leg she'd mismanaged. Seemed there would be time aplenty for devoting to food.

Someone or another with a moai had apparently cajoled her bone back in line, but moai could only set things up for healing. It was left as an exercise to the body to work out the rest. She picked at the brace made of staves and some durable leaf which her tutors would have sighed in disappointment that she couldn't identify. A minute in and she was already weary of the next two months—two weeks with the right amount of orange tuuaaq flame.

She polished up her best listening ears and pointed them at the doorway of her palace room. Surely nobody would mind if she nipped off for a moment. The king was off on some war knocking heads about. She had to execute his will in his absence, and how could she expect to heal like a proper woman without a supply of pristine air and sunshine?

She rolled tenderly off her mat and braced her weight with her hands. Now it was just a matter of—

She nearly collapsed sick from the bolt of pain that came with trying to stand. Her breaths cycled quickly as she waited for her gorge to abate.

A different plan, then.

With walking descended into utter penury on the scale of good ideas, it seemed only one other option for locomotion presented itself. If she kept her fouled leg off the ground just so... Yes, there it was. A picture of poise. She embarked on a shuffling crawl toward the door, one foot held behind as if it refused to follow. One check to ensure she had her sealskin bag on her, and she was out into the hall.

After sneaking past a cohort of armed guards—does it count as sneaking if they point at you and call you a smelly crab?—she finally dug her fingers into soil and lavished sunshine upon herself once more. Where to go from here? The half-cloud sky presaged mud. She and walking weren't on the best of terms, but the crawling hadn't been exactly chummy either. Perhaps she'd get better results from windwalking? Her hand floated toward her bag.

"Qaffa?"

She looked up to see an eleven-year-old girl approaching the palace. "Good morning, Ka'emu."

"What are you doing?"

"Me?" Qaffa glanced at her leg. "Just out for a walk. You?"

"Coming to see you, of course!" She flapped her arms in exasperation. "Mama keeps turning me away, saying come back either when you're awake or when lunch is ready."

"How about we skip lunch and go on an adventure?"

A grin split Ka'emu's face. "I was hoping you'd say that. Only..." She gestured vague concern at Qaffa's freshly set limb. "Where will we go?"

"Let me think." And as she thought, a dastardly plan struck her with the force of a mountainside hitting a falling girl's leg. Out of pure respect for her mother, she almost cast the sordid strategy from her head immediately. Out of nervous respect for her father, she entertained it like a visiting dignitary. And perhaps it was.

"How about we go see the swine herd?" she said.

Ka'emu snorted a porcine response and helped her to her foot. Qaffa acted the parasite to Ka'emu's host, slumping against her friend as they shambled off toward the hillside pens.

An arduous trot later, they entered the air stenched with the color brown and leaned up against the fence, calling their favorite creatures by name. A spare few rolled from their muck and sniffed their way over to the perimeter. The girls' primary target, however, couldn't be inconvenienced to make the trip from belly to legs.

"Pupu!" they shouted with manic gesticulations. But the prized pig taller than any man gave them only combinations of side eyes and flicked ears.

"Do you think they're ever going to eat him?" said Ka'emu.

"Probably waiting for Haka'atu to get back from his war."

"Maybe." Ka'emu pointed toward the pig handlers' shack. "Rarapa says it's probably too late to eat him. It would send the herd into a frenzy if their 'guardian' disappeared."

"We can send the herd into a frenzy right now." Qaffa mummed jumping into the thick of things and received a laugh from her friend. Bracing herself against the pen with one arm, she reached into her bag and withdrew a candle.

"What is that for?" Ka'emu voiced her usual hesitancy toward the foreign magic.

"I think it might be able to help my leg."

"I thought you didn't like using it."

Qaffa waved a hand in frustration, unsure how to explain the contradiction that dwelt within. "Yeah, well I don't like having a broken leg either."

She tipped a paring of tuuaaq into her mouth, then fumbled with firemoss until the wick caught flame. She watched the orange gnaw at the air as she waited for the narwhal tusk to ripple in her blood. When its call rang her fabric like the setting sun igniting clouds in vermillion magmata, she hesitated.

If she pressed on, she would stray further from her mother than ever she had. Though she may live in a foreign land, it was always her dole to return to the ice. But here she poised to wander into a foreign land of the heart, and who could say whether the path back could be conquered?

Qaffa forced a bridge between the tuuaaq in her body and the tuuaaq in her hand. The air chilled. Ka'emu backed away. Like a lush landscape painted on a dying leaf, the blue flame's beauty was hedged in the melancholy of its impermanence and the decay over which it glossed. But beauty it had, nonetheless. Qaffa swallowed at something in her throat and faced the herd.

She had already selected her target twenty paces back. A pink beast of medium stature with a brown blotch marking its left flank. She had never learned its name. Not that that would matter. It would be fine. At worst, it would have a broken leg. At worst.

Two weeks with the orange flame? Make that two minutes with the blue.

She reached out with the power of the flame and began a work that, between her father, her mother, and herself, would only make her father proud. The pig squealed and darted around the pen, fomenting bedlam until it collapsed. A sinew of euphoria entered her—where precisely she couldn't tell—and streamed into her leg. Chip by chip, the damages redressed themselves. A laugh escaped her lips, elatedly blind to the pig's malforming legs. Ka'emu spoke some reproof, but Qaffa had no ears for her.

When finally her leg called no more for draughts from health's sweet cup, she doused the flame and her connection died. With a boundless smile across her face, she reached down, unwrapped the brace, and settled weight onto her leg. In her joy, she laughed and awarded herself a frolic, a gambol, and then a skip.

"It worked! I can't believe I did it." She bounced over to Ka'emu and took her by the shoulders. "Let's go play somewhere else."

"Uh, Qaffa?"

The daughter of the ice finally noticed that her enthusiasm didn't echo in her friend. Qaffa's spirits tinted a shade darker. "What is it?"

Ka'emu pointed to the victim mired in squalor and

injury. Qaffa took in the beast's crooked legs. Not leg. All four had ambiguated in direction and color, a spew of entropy where order once had stood. The animal wheezed as it lay on its side. Qaffa pressed a hand against her mouth.

"I didn't think... It wasn't supposed to be like *that*. It was supposed to be just *one* leg." Tears threatened to wash away her joy. Had her father said something about this? *To gain a finger, you must take a hand.* It was too difficult to remember all his teachings, especially when most were filtered through dreams.

Ka'emu touched her on the arm. "We should leave. Before anyone sees us here."

Qaffa nodded and they ran, but the running had lost its savor.

4 Years Before

Q affanngilaq climbed onto a black nose of a rock hooking out above the surf and fussed until her bottom found a comfortable perch. Terror overtook her momentarily as she found an unreasonably rotund saltwater millipede taking up an arm's length of rock next to her. After an undignified screech and flinging of the worm into the sea, she looked ahead at the man whose head bobbed atop the water and gave a gawky grin.

"Greetings, Qaffa," he said.

"Hello, Puneki." She pushed a clump of hair behind her ear. "How are you?"

The man looked down to his arms, each of which were anchored fast to king-size stones on the ocean floor far below. "Bad. And you?"

"Oh, good. Just good. They still feed you?"

"No, I have to catch fish with my toes and hope I can eat it without any sharks catching the scent," he joked.

"Why don't you kick the sharks and eat them too?"

"There are too many, and I've never been much of a dancer."

Qaffa giggled. Something about the prisoner always captivated her. Probably the puzzle of how he could be bound for years in the ocean and maintain levity.

"So," said Puneki. "It's been too long since your last visit. I lose track of time so easy out here. What are you now, twenty-eight?"

"I'm thirteen!" She kicked at the water.

"It hasn't been fifteen years? Strange. Feels like at least twenty." He let his legs float up so he lay on his back, arms stretched into what must be a painful position. "What brings you out here? Couldn't resist my charming stories for one second more? You've brought a knife and are finally going to free me?"

"Ka'emu is supposed to come back from the ice today. This is the closest spot to see the ship coming up." She had spent plenty of daydreaming time spinning iterations of her reunion with her friend after more than a month below.

"Oh, so I'm just an eyesore marring your beautiful ocean view, is it?" Puneki spat an arc of water across his torso.

"Well... I was also maybe wondering if you could tell me 'The Heavenbound King' again." She put her hands together in supplication.

The prisoner barked a laugh. "You and that island. There are other stories, you know."

"But none of them are as fun."

"You mean, 'None of them feed my irrational obsession with Ragaka'i.'"

She smiled her fakest smile. "Wow, Puneki, you are so insightful. I wonder how many insights I would learn if you told me 'The Heavenbound King.'"

"You didn't even bring a storyteller's mask for me to

wear." He heaved a sigh and shook his head, but a smile trickled across his lips. "Just for you, girl, I will take some time out of my inundated schedule and tell you the tale, yet again."

Qaffa squealed a vote of affirmation, followed by a shriller sound as she noticed the millipede tessellating its way up the rock again. Taking out a candle and sucking away its life tempted her, insidious little creature. She instead dispatched it with an overhand pitch, farther this time, wiped off her hands, and turned her attention to the prisoner.

"In this wide ocean, man may set foot on any island save two. Ragaka'i and Nanaka'i, the havens of the dead. The only islands that sit before the wall of cloud that reaches into heaven. As has been known for thousands of years, if you live a good life, your spirit will enter your moai when you die. Carve well your moai, for in life we may wear masks for any occasion, but in death you wear one mask alone. If your moai face is shown love and given arms and legs, you become a pa'ina, to walk as though alive. But what good is it for the dead to walk among the living? The dead cannot understand the living, for they are dead, and the living cannot understand the dead, for they are living. No, in this it is wisdom that they are sent to an island of their own.

"But restless are the dead, for they cannot sleep. In their itching unrest, they tilt back their stone faces and gaze into the holy heights. The garden of gods where every spirit yearns to roam. Yet how can the common dead from Nanaka'i surmount the skies? They cannot jump as tall as a man, let alone summit the uppermost cloud. If you served under a good king, he will await you on Ragaka'i, and you can ride to heaven upon his back when he jumps. So, the common dead build their boats and make the pilgrimage to the isle of dead kings. Serve well your king, for in life you may be mischievous and slothful, but in death you will be banished back to Nanaka'i.

"There was once a man named Hokoho, a friend of seven kings. A man dissatisfied with the idea of waiting till death to find heaven. He wanted to see it in the flesh, not in the stone. But none of the other leaders knew that he himself was a king, for Hokoho played the beggar with the battered boat. The metanesial vagabond, sailing from isle to isle in search of an impossible goal. The tattoos that wrapped his body were not so extravagant as a typical king, so most assumed him a disgraced matatoa, wounded in some clash to never fight again. But Hokoho wasn't disgraced. Not yet.

"Only the eldest kings did he befriend. Before them in their courts he came, knelt in panting obeisance, and proclaimed, 'Ariki, oldest and wisest of kings, I come before you today to pray for wisdom that only you can give. I, Hokoho, have lost my moai and cannot go to heaven. What might I do to leap above the clouds?'

"Many years he presented himself, and the kings came to endure his petitions with fondness. In a world where they had to answer for sickness and hunger and war, what was one battle-addled matatoa with an innocent question? Many answers they gave, and always he answered the same. 'Thank you, Ariki. Your wisdom is great. I will think on this.'

"One by one, the venerated kings went the way of all bodies and their moai were taken to Ragaka'i. After each had passed, Hokoho made secret journey to that island of dead kings. He found their moai peeking out of the ground and made his recitation once more. 'Ariki, oldest and wisest of kings, I come before you today to pray for a boon that only you can give. I, Hokoho, have lost my moai and cannot go to heaven. May I ride with you when you jump above the clouds?'

"Every time the answer was the same. 'Hokoho. What you ask is no boon. The land above the clouds is not for the eyes of the living. I will not carry you to heaven.' Every time, anger burned within Hokoho's heart, but he gave the same answer. 'Thank you, Ariki. Your wisdom is great. I will think on this.'

"With every passing king his desperation grew. The new kings were too young and would outlive him. If he couldn't achieve this, he would be locked in stone forever like the rest of them.

"Finally, the day came when the seventh king died, and Hokoho followed his funeral catamaran to Ragaka'i. He waited a day and a night and a day as the honor guard half buried their former king's moai, then rushed forward as soon as they were small on the horizon. Once more, he posed his question.

"The seventh king waited as patiently as only a stone could, then made his reply. 'Hokoho. What you ask is no boon. The land above the clouds is not for the eyes of the living. Yet all these years have I known you, and you have asked but one question that all yearn for in their stomachs. I will tell you not to go, but if you ask once more, I will permit it.'

"Burning this time with elation, Hokoho spoke his question for the final time. 'May I ride with you when you jump above the clouds?'

"'You may. I will jump in five years, when more of my subjects are with me.'

"Five years to the day, Hokoho beached his boat on Ragaka'i and ran to his heavenbound friend. Around the massive moai scuttled thousands of knee-high pa'ina, all jostling for the choicest spots. Upon Hokoho's approach, the ground began to rumble. The king began to stand. With a yank and a tug, the seventh king pulled great arms of soil and stone from the earth. Those braced against the ground and pushed out a body, and soon legs kicked to the surface. Hokoho gawked at the colossus, well taller than twenty men. The small pa'ina went into a frenzy, clambering all over their erstwhile king.

"When they had more or less sorted themselves out, the massive pa'ina stooped down and held out a hand. 'You may turn back now, Hokoho,' he said.

"'No, Ariki,' answered Hokoho. 'I have lost my moai and cannot get to heaven. I must ride with you when you jump above the clouds.'

"'Very well.' The king lifted him up, then great knees were bowing. Hokoho looked up the wall of clouds that stretched without end. Could this massive pa'ina really scale that in a single bound? Judging by the lack of other kingly moai on the island, he supposed it must.

"The giant pa'ina of the king released its energy and jetted into the sky. The clouds passed by like he was falling into a dream. The wind picked at his face. Darkness crept across his vision. But for the first time in years, Hokoho was happy. Before the heavenbound kings reached their summit, blackness took Hokoho entirely.

"When next he woke, he heard joyous sounds. A rapturous commotion abounded around him. Quickly he opened his eyes to see. All he saw was darkness. Again and again he tried, but the black would not dissipate. Hokoho was blind.

"He cried out, adding a single, mournful keening to the gaiety all about. A voice broke into his weeping.

"'Hokoho, why do you cry?' It was the seventh king.

"'Ariki, oldest and wisest of kings. I, Hokoho, have lost my eyes and cannot see heaven. What shall I do that I might see?'

"Great sorrow lay upon the seventh king's voice when he spoke. 'Oh, Hokoho. I tried to warn you. The land above the clouds is not for the eyes of the living. You are permitted to stay, but you may not enjoy.'

"Bitter tears spilt from Hokoho's dark eyes. He chased back and forth, seeking the joyous sounds but never drawing any nearer. A gleeful exclamation, a bubbly laugh. He stumbled forward, fingers grasping at nothing. As he staggered toward a merry commotion, his foot stepped onto thin air and he found himself falling. Heels, head, heels, head, over and over until consciousness left him.

"He awoke to the slosh of waves around his ears, sand in his nostrils, and darkness still in his eyes. After a few minutes of blundering around, he realized he was back on Ragaka'i. He eventually found his ship again and set sail to find his home islands. It is said that if you come across a blind man sailing the open sea, you must sail away as quickly as you can. For if you look into his eyes, you will see things not for the living and fall blind into the ocean."

Qaffanngilaq basked in the ambiance of the story's end, quivering slightly at the thought of finding a lone boat bouncing on the open sea, manned only by a man who cast eternal darkness wherever his gaze landed. She wondered if perchance she found the fallen king, could she take the blindness from him? Were those the types of things one could siphon off with tuuaaq? She'd have to ask her father.

She thanked Puneki for the tale. Then, as always, she asked, "What did you do to end up a prisoner here?"

And as always, he replied, "I capsized heaven."

"But no one else has seen it fall. I've asked."

"Well. I capsized *someone's* heaven," he said into the surf.

The timeworn answer slid off her. She had always assumed him a murderer, evinced by the heavy tattooing marking him as a matatoa high of rank, but she needed more clues. She set herself a different tack. "Did you have a good life before you did whatever it was that landed you here?"

Puneki doused his face in water. "Very. But I fear I could only learn that by coming here. I was never satisfied with the thought that all the little days that came and went, those were life. I reached for more and more, and by degrees, life became the reaching. Greatness, I knew, lay behind the teeth of the hound, within the caverns of the shallows, beyond the hiss of the moon. With time, reaching came perilously close to grabbing, and fear distilled in the souls of mighty men regardful of my rise. They, too, turned their lives to reaching—reaching for me. Before I could grab, I was grabbed. Cast low. Bound. Punished for aspiring to be more."

She stared at his inked face for a blink's space. "That's it? I don't think you actually told me anything. My father said, 'There are those who tell a thousand truths with but a single lie, and those who tell a thousand lies to hide a single truth.' I think he was talking about you. You're so evasive." It was the fifth time she'd used 'evasive' since learning it yesterday.

He grinned and shrugged at his fetters. "Given my current position, I'd wager I'm the least evasive man in all the islands."

Her brain toiled over a retort when a glint from the horizon speckled her eye. She pushed up to her feet and pulled a candle from her sealskin bag. "I have to go. Thank you again for the story."

"Come back soon. Bring something to drink. We can

play dice. Give each other symmetric scars. Plot against the king."

Qaffa slipped a crumb of tuuaaq into her mouth and sparked a blue flame, its flicker difficult to discern against ocean and sky. Below it, she saw the millipede clicking its way up the rock again. Weary of the thing's solicitations, she summarily sucked its life into her and watched its curling husk plash into the ocean.

"Well," said Puneki. "Not something I expected to see today."

She ignored him and stepped into the air. Her damp hair sparred with itself as she picked up speed. Phalanxes of waves marched by beneath. The boat grew in stature. Ka'emu was back! Qaffa couldn't wait to kindle her friend's envy recounting all her talks with the Marama prince during his weeklong visit. Or to make it known that the matatoa Rava'apa had eaten nineteen sweet potatoes before stretching his belly. Or to see what curio her parents might have shipped topside to her. Hopefully the boat's freight included a few sticks of tuuaaq.

She reached the twin pontoon vessel and let herself down, stumbling as she made traffic with the deck. Father would have given her a stern glare for the botched landing. Mother would have given her a stern glare for the skywalking. Qaffa smiled at the crew of fifteen, reminding herself that she shouldn't steal their memories of her graceless landing just because she was a buffoon. She should do it because she was a princess.

But no. It would take her too long just to excise the memory from one of the crew, let alone the ship's full complement. And *maybe* it was like Ariki Haka'atu said. Just because you can crush a thousand ants with a step, it doesn't make you any better for doing it.

"Hello." She snuffed her candle. "I'm looking for Ka'e-mu." It shouldn't take tuuaaq and a moai to find her.

Passengers, some still removing their parkas, flashed each other shaded looks. Two thumbed toward the stern where Qaffa spotted a bundle of furs huddled in on itself. She skipped forward and put a hand on her friend's shoulder.

"Ka'emu! Guess who came while you were gone."

Ocean noise filled the gap as Qaffa waited for an answer. The hunkered-down girl didn't move.

"Ka'emu?"

But Ka'emu kept her silence, and in the keeping she forced it on the world.

How could she stand to be smothered in all that outerwear topside? She obviously needed some assistance remembering the nature of the sun. Qaffa reached over the boat's side to the garland of bird feathers and plucked one out. She stuck it around her friend's hood and wiggled it across her nose.

"Ka'emuuuu," she teased.

Ka'emu slapped her hand and shrieked. "Stop it!"

Qaffa drew her stinging hand to her chest. She struggled between returning anger for anger and attending to her friend's obvious distress. "Sorry. I... You should take the parka off. It's hot. Ka'emu?"

Now Ka'emu moved and gave a continuous response. Small shakes and hitched sobs.

Qaffa returned a hand to her shoulder. "Hey, hey. What's the matter?"

"J-j-just go h-home, Qaffa. Go." Ka'emu wouldn't lift her face from the crook of her arm.

"No, I've been waiting for you for a month. What's the

matter?" Qaffa tried to pull her friend around. Ka'emu wrenched her shoulder away.

"I'm not t-t-talking to anyone a-a-again. Lea-leave, Qaffa."

"I'm your friend. Let me help. What's the problem?"

Ka'emu's breathing got heavier. "What's the problem? Your mother. She's terrible. I hate her."

Qaffanngilaq's brow knit patterns of bemusement. "My mother? What could she—"

Qaffa didn't need to finish the question. The realization stabbed into her gut like flutes of ice. She had been so stupid. What other reason would a pretty, young girl like Ka'emu be doing on a trading voyage?

Ka'emu swung her head around, pulling back her hood. Qaffa cringed backward, hand flying to her mouth. The face before her *was* her friend but bred with mongrel deformations and pariah perversions. It pained and pinned her eyes to look at.

"Ka'emu... You're—"

"A demon."

So *stupid*. How could Qaffa not have realized? She would have made every protest when the trip was being organized. They would have listened, too, she being the princess of their country of destination. Her hands wavered for comfort, and nowhere offered solace.

"I'll figure out a way to..." She trailed off, thumbing the candle in her left hand. *To steal your beauty back*, she'd been on the cusp of asserting. Only, that wasn't wholly possible. The stealing part might be a cinch, given that she had some more time to cultivate her skill with the blue flame. Transferring further to Ka'emu, though. The tirigusuusik way catered far more closely to taking than giving. "I didn't realize it was this bad. That thing my mother does."

Ka'emu ignored the second statement entirely. Glinting hope pierced her red eyes. "You can get it back? Get *me* back?"

Gutstrings tremored in Qaffa's belly. Could she really instate a vendetta against her own mother? Mere minutes ago, the question would have landed on her in a grotesque splay of tentacles and slime. Mere minutes ago, Qaffa only knew of her mother's gruesome side the way a tree knows the ocean: a body of undrinkable water viewed from a distance. Now she knew of the monster Orluvoq the way a tree knows the ocean after it is felled, carved, warped into ship beams, and forced to drink the salt for the rest of its days.

And yet. Even if she were to forge enmity in her heart, she could only ever hope to provide retribution. There could be no recompense. She again assessed her friend's foul features, not daring to wonder how she looked beneath the parka. Perhaps retribution would suffice.

Something cold formed in her chest. Not the hot of animosity. Not the ire of thundering kings. A placid feud she offered berth, to carry to her mother's feet and cast it in her face. She would take back what was taken. Steal the starlight from the queen. And should the channel Sulluliaq torrent into naught, so much the better for the generation growing tall.

Qaffanngilaq laid her hand again on Ka'emu's shoulder and looked into her eager eyes. "I can try."

F eigning sleep. Had she truly been feigning sleep, letting reality dance impiously before her closed eyes, muttering assurances that any defilement she made was but a vagary of dream? That if she could not see a better path, it was because one could not be found, not because she dared not open her eyes?

Nalor's poison of yestersleep, so effortlessly trickled beneath her skin, had worked its needling sermonry. She'd thought herself strong for her command of the candle, but she'd been soliciting impotence all along. Of course she could walk no other path when permanently genuflecting before the king.

The time had come to cast off her feigned slumber. Soon her new path would be found, with or without Qummukarpoq's approval. But tonight, there was another who'd fallen victim to her pretend slumber.

Qaffa.

Orluvoq lit a candle, cycled through several deep breaths, and strode out of her room on the upper floor.

Emeraldine fillets cut from Arsarneq's hide skittered

through the castle's halls. In winter's deep, the auroral gleam was all that did betoken night. Window by window, the prancing flickers followed before her as she stepped. Toward the chambers of her husband. Toward a fear of mighty grip. The tuuaaq taper in her hand, it glimmered with a mundane orange. The icecraft walls about her sides, they stole the hue and cursed it cold.

He would not suffer her compunctions; merely left her to her griefs. Their daughter's drifting vexed him nothing. For his folk he hadn't a fret. So on she walked. On to face the music he disclaimed.

The king at the start of the world was not a man to be hectored. Every lash of her tongue she laid upon him left her sucking blood. And however harsh his integument, his angakkuq aptitude yielded even less. Doubtless even now he sensed her approach. Her assault would have to be quick.

She stopped her walk outside his door, guarding what presence she could with the tusk. Surely he felt her. If he spurned sleep, as was his wont, then already he'd seen the breath of her candle sighing orange around his fishskin door. If she dared reach out with angakkuq threads, doubtless he'd rebuff and snare her in blue. He who broke demons with scarcely a thought would varnish her will in his and fold her to a crookback serf.

She reached.

The days of chest clutching would be numbered in retrospect only, in one matter at least. Her angakkuq fibers quested through the door and met their mark. Her heart fluttered, for he lay on his bed without so much as a stub of candle spitting life. Quick as the wind smiting the naked, she pushed into his head. Nimble and thorough she worked her craft, drowning his cognition in draughts of vision, just like she used to do for the sailors thirty years ago.

When he seemed good and intoxicated on lurid illusions of tusk and desire, she stole through the doorway to prove her his sleep. The body lay supine still in its parka of white. Breaths swelled the chest in constant cadence. Eyes bobbled beneath lids, snatching after details the mind dredged like spice.

The king at the start of the world was under her spell. Time to turn her candle blue.

She walked to the window, stepped up on the sill, then bracing a foot on impalpable air, she stepped into the sky. Far beneath, the sea muttered to the shore, but its petitions were soon supplanted by the rushing of wind. Its salty tang dried to the scent of pure frigidity. She angled for Sulluliaq, that hole of pitch black faintly smoldering with Arsarneq's green.

Up the tunnel she skywalked while gathering her wits, toward the land of a hundred kings. Toward the garth of smoking islands. All that lay before her must be accomplished before her husband woke, for once his dormancy abated, he would seek, and he would find.

Out the tunnel's maw, across the drowsy waters, above the sandy beaches of Rapai'i's prime island, and into the palace of Ariki Haka'atu. The guards on watch passed eyes right through her, blessed in shadows as she was. Tenderly, with tuuaaq-damped footfalls, she let her candle fall orange and stalked into the royal halls.

The first room she chanced upon, she spied a woman asleep within. The dark concealed the sleeper's face, but the body's shape evinced enough to know the woman was an islander. Some relation of the king? A servant would likely not be allotted private quarters. Orluvoq stepped into the room.

For a moment, she forgot her breath. Every quarrel twixt

her and Qummukarpoq could be here laid to rest. She would no longer be the willful wife. He could belay his hounding words, his dialects of pique. A mere month more she needed endure, then let Sulluliaq thunder shut. Here lay the solitary offering that would bridge the weeks. Her finger itched toward the tusk to break her off a flake.

She cringed back in disgust and snapped into the present, cognizant of every sweaty drip the sultry air had pulled from her. Forthwith away from the sleeping shell and back into the hall. She reasserted her grip on her sputtering mind. The void had called, and she had been ready.

As always.

But, however much beauty begged to be taken, she only answered when it was given. Helping someone in their choice to get hurt preserved more of the spirit than hurting them for your choice alone.

Away she walked from her faltering and past a dozen rooms. It had been long since she'd visited, but she knew her path and found her destination. She pushed through the freshly plucked banana leaves hung across the doorway and into the chamber.

On a woven mat, leg slashed silver by the sickle moon, slept Qaffanngilaq, her wayward daughter. The true reason for her excursion tonight.

Orluvoq made to awaken the girl but stopped. The nub of tuuaaq she'd picked off in the other room still tickled her palm. In this scrap of time she'd stolen, she needed to impress upon her daughter that this was the wrong path. What better way to teach Qaffa the black side of the blue flame than a practical application? Sow in her the fear of its contaminations through pitiless emphasis. Orluvoq popped the tusk into her mouth.

With a thought and a push, her candle burned from

orange to azure. The island swelter balked at the light incongruous with nature, and Orluvoq's parka felt pleasant once more. She uncurled her angakkuq threads and probed for her daughter's face, tipping off the ground to cluster closer.

As tendrils met skin, Qaffa's eyes flew open. She opened her jaw to scream but produced only a gurgle. Orluvoq, face only half an arm away, smiled.

"Hello, daughter. If you weren't having a nightmare, you are now."

She began to pull, and Qaffa's face warped like drifts driven wild by wrestling winds. Skin peeled from flesh, and the mask of Qaffanngilaq shuddered upward. On the verge where beauty would start to trickle, Orluvoq stayed her tugging. She suspended the moment, attended by Qaffa's beggarly attempts to fill more than her uppermost lungs.

When she deemed an impression had been made, she abandoned the threads and swerved up to her feet. Qaffa's face clasped back onto her head, and the girl broke into sobs.

"Wh-why would you d-do that? Why? What ha-have I done? How much did you take?" She pressed her hands to her face.

Orluvoq frowned at the islander accent on her own daughter's tongue. "I took nothing. Tell me, why do we call it tirigusuusik?"

Qaffa didn't answer, so Orluvoq repeated the lesson her daughter hadn't retained yet. "It is an old word meaning, 'a thing to avoid'. When I first burned blue, I had no idea of the grief it would bring me. If I could go back, I'd tell myself to never leave my home at Nunapisu. But *you* know the evils at play, so why do you seek to become a thing to avoid?"

Qaffa had regained some composure during the

polemic. "I'm as old as you were when you became tirigusu-usik. You've left me to make my own choices for more than ten years. Why now, when I'm fully capable of making my own decisions, do you decide that you need to come—come *attack* me?"

"Because I thought you were better." Orluvoq damped their voices with the candle to avoid unwanted attention. "I thought you would *know* having grown up around it. I didn't believe the things I heard about you for years. But now I'm here, and you're denying nothing except my wishes."

Her daughter stared for several incredulous seconds. "I *didn't* grow up around it. You never told me anything the first six years of my life, then I was banished away here. I've grown up around unthinkable power, all the moai here. You know if they wanted to descend upon us, they would wipe out the Nuktipik people? What else could I do but reach for as much power as possible?"

Orluvoq noted they twain had spoken nothing concerning Qummukarpoq. As if by continuously casting aspersions at each other they could solve the issue entire. She could place some due fault on—

No. She halted that thought. It profited her nothing to shunt all blame to her husband, else her whole journey was vanity. She sighed.

"Yes, I can see that. I've spoken in anger. I haven't been the steadiest of mothers, and I can't fix that in one night. But please listen to my words. I have walked the path you're on, and it has only brought me misery."

Qaffa spoke, and her voice was small. "It's because of the blue flame that you had me."

And then Orluvoq's parka wasn't enough. The chill of freshly sworn blood covenants on winter's bleakest night stood her body hairs on end. Words caught twice in her throat. To agree was to accede that good could come of tiri-gusuusik. To deny was to discard her only daughter. Finally, she spoke, and her voice was smaller. "Just because there is beauty in tragedy does not mean a woman should seek tragedy."

Qaffa took her time gathering up a response, speaking slowly as the words came to her. "There is an animal here called kekepu. You've seen pigs? Kekepu are smaller than that with a larger snout, and their coat is striped white and black. It has been a tradition for centuries to argue whether kekepu are black with white stripes, or white with black stripes. When someone good does something bad, people refer to her as a white kekepu. She may have black stripes, but she's white underneath. When someone bad does something good, she's called a black kekepu. Just because she has white stripes can't hide the fact that she's black underneath.

"I think you and I view the blue flame differently, mother. You think it's a black kekepu, and I think it's a white one. You think it's tragedy with stripes of beauty and should be avoided. I think it's beauty with stripes of tragedy, and I say just because there's tragedy in beauty doesn't mean a woman shouldn't seek beauty. Say, doesn't that about sum up the motto of your life?"

Orluvoq's brain stopped except for one petite chunk keeping her composure lumped together. Since when had Qaffanngilaq been so infuriatingly astute? Orluvoq had truly let too much time slip between visits. Enough of her brain restarted for her to have and quell the thought of sucking Qaffa's voice from her body.

"I understand your eagerness. But imagine you stocked food for winter, then told your children you were going on a trip, and you died a day into your journey without them knowing. They would laugh at all the abundance and waste their way through it in weeks. For those weeks, they would only see the beauty of no rules, all play, and endless food. When starvation and death finally hit them, tragedy would have the last laugh. I've been doing this for longer than your whole life. You're not old enough to see that this truly is a black kekepu."

"Not old enough?" Qaffa threw up her hands. "I was old enough to get sent away from my parents at six because of the blue flame. Old enough at thirteen to see my friend get her beauty and future sucked away all so some adults could swap fruit. Old enough to see that you're just father's toy because of the blue flame, and that you've ruined your life due to it. But just because you've failed doesn't mean no one else can have a chance."

Orluvoq recoiled. A daughter's words shouldn't be able to pierce a mother—let alone a queen—with such brutality. The entire venture suddenly seemed unaccountably burdensome, and she wanted to beat a retreat home and sleep. Perhaps even feign sleep.

"I'm sorry I'm not the mother you deserve. But this..." She raised her free hand, then dropped it. "No, no excuses. I will let sorry be sorry. But I will still ask you to consider my words with real intent."

Qaffa looked her in the eye. "After you, mother."

A taste like blackened snow oozed into Orluvoq's mouth. The Rapai'ian fug dazzled her dizzy. The parka choked her body like a pelt of wet flame. "Sleep well, Qaffanngilaq. I must return to the place where the world begins."

She whisked through the banana leaf door, tiptoed on shadows past the guards, and skywalked toward the locus in the ocean that would swallow her away from this humid hell above. Down the green-tinged tunnel, into the bitter cold that didn't soothe enough of her discomforts, and down to the castle below. Mind too scattered to extend her senses beyond herself, she lighted into her room ignorant of the presence already there.

"Back so soon?"

She started, eyes flying to the blue flicker in the corner. Muscles knotted down her front. "I come as I will."

He didn't honor the lie with a response.

"She denied you, didn't she?"

Twenty years and his perspicacity still left her off-kilter; how her designs lay transparent before him. No, 'Did you not find the Rapai'ian weather agreeable?' Or, 'How is our daughter?' He sliced through all the blubber and lanced the heart of it.

"She is considering things," Orluvoq replied. "Eighteen is a tumultuous age."

"You fear that she isn't your daughter, hasn't been for years, and never will be again."

Tiaavuluk. No one cared a whit for her tonight. In fact, the last time she'd felt human warmth was when her father visited two years ago. She cursed herself again for leaving Nunapisu.

"Why do you hate me so?" Her voice trembled.

"I do not hate you, wife. I—"

"You just love yourself so much that the outcome is the same."

The moment stretched into pregnancy. The underglow of blue cast the king's face into caricatures of villainy. Orluvoq's stomach did a pocket-size dance. Had she just silenced Qummukarpoq?

At last, he moved, pausing at the doorway. "Sulluliaq must be open when the moai is complete. You will take beauty within two weeks."

The prospect of having this conversation again now

wilted her, so she let him walk away unanswered. The muscles down her chest and stomach relaxed.

Failed. Again.

Why? Why had every move she'd made to find strength in the last thirty years only left her more helpless? Rejoining her clan, besting tuuaaq, gaining beauty, conquering the blue flame, becoming queen, rescuing her daughter. It seemed that any crutch could be weakness, even a crutch that would be called strength in any other light.

She sought sleep, but the muscles around her stomach hadn't relaxed as much as she'd thought.

So, she pretended.

The Nuktipik were not a people much given to war. Winter's inclemencies tolerated little save barest survival, and summer's pleasantries brooked only a scrape above that. If your clan of thirty only had six strong hunters and your hunters must double as warriors, it wouldn't be long before your clan of twenty-seven only had three hunters.

As Orluvoq sat on the not quite comfortable ice throne listening to a woman explain why the queen needed to interfere personally in a clan dispute turned bloody, she wished she had been a better student of the islanders' warmonger ethic. But more accessibly, she wished she could dispatch a detachment of Rapai'ian matatoa to go and knock some sense into these people's heads. That would be much simpler than working it out herself. A canny ruler delegates.

"And how long did you say these... troubles have been going on?"

"For three weeks when I left to come here. So, unless

they've reached a truce, then about a month." The woman nodded, more to herself than to Orluvoq.

"Total losses on either side?"

"Well, you must see. They started with a clan of fifty-two, and us of thirty-nine. They've always encroached on our territory, but this time they *stole* raw kills that our hunters had brought down. So, we—"

"Total losses?" Orluvoq didn't need to hear the story a second time.

"When I left, we were down to thirty-four and them to forty-six." The woman gave her self-affirming nod.

Orluvoq sighed. The inertial aspect within her ached at the thought of skywalking north, but it would be good to get away from the castle—and Qummukarpoq—for a while. Maybe she would even stay a few days to make sure things remained quiescent.

"I will go forth, if not tonight then the following one. We will see this conflict resolved, or else Nunapisu will soon have eighty new bodies."

"Thank you, thank you," the petitioner said, bobbing her head each time and wiping at her eyes.

As an attendant stepped up to direct her out of the hall, the king strode through the doorway with a girl in tow. The three attendants and the one petitioner all bent at the neck in obeisance.

Qummukarpoq spoke as he walked to the middle of the hall. "I will fulfill this entreaty, wife."

Orluvoq bridled her surprise, giving only a genteel nod. "If it is your wish, husband." She burned to ask what the girl was here for, but a putrid feeling in her gut told her she already knew.

He gestured and waited for the petitioner to be led from

the hall. "Now. You will take this girl's beauty." He placed a hand on the girl's shoulder and steered her in front of him. She couldn't be more than seventeen, and her loveliness would go unnoticed by none.

Olruvoq's spine stiffened toward paralysis. She wanted to flout the call to vampiric action, to instead hunt her new path. But after last week's failure with Qaffa, how could she hope for anything besides fumbling? The path lay yet afar off. Besides, she had consumed the beauty of hundreds, and what was the weight of one more?

Or. There was perhaps one avenue of defiance. A thread of strength in a tapestry of helplessness.

"What is your name, dear?"

"Kukkujuits," the girl mumbled, eyes only staying on the queen for brief periods, then returning to the safety of the floor.

"And how did you come to stand before me today, Kukkujuits?"

"The king..." Kukujuits stopped with a minute glance backward.

"Speak freely. I have required it."

"The king, he, um, he came to my village last night, woke me in my bed, and said I had to come with him. I couldn't say—well, it was the king, you know? I didn't *know* that he was taking me to you, but..." She bit both lips.

"I see. And now that you are here, do you offer your beauty of your own free will? You know it serves to keep Sulluliaq open and trade flowing between us and Rapai'i and the other islands."

The girl faltered, repeating the word "I" four times before moving to the next word. "I will do... what must be done."

Orluvoq's eyes shifted to her husband. "You ask treachery of me. This girl had no choice but to come, and she absolutely does not want to be here."

"No girl has ever wanted to stand before you." The king stared tense serenity at her. "From the thousands of clans to the thousands of islands, not a one has approached your feet with relish. Blandishments and threats from kith and kin are all that bring them here. And after hundreds of offerings, you blanch before this one because *I* have brought her instead of her father?"

Orluvoq's vitals prickled as with morning frost. The king esteemed the subtlety for naught, so it would do no good to attempt a defense of her position. "I will wait for a willing woman to come before me. Kukkujuits, you have nothing to fear from me. Unless you'd like to declare your willingness in plain speech?"

The girl shook her head from side to side as though beset by hypothermia.

"Then you are free to go." Orluvoq motioned to an attendant to show her out of the hall, and Kukkujuits took a few jittery steps backward.

"Go nowhere," Qummukarpoq commanded, eyes still on Orluvoq.

The attendant vacillated, throwing a glance to the queen. Kukkujuits' hands took to wrestling each other.

"The kings above tax their people plenty," said Qummukarpoq. "This is no different."

"They tax material goods," said the queen, "not the very bodies of their peoples."

"Not so. The people have no material goods save they first expend their bodies in some way to acquire them. Physical possessions are but a manifestation of bodily sacrifice."

"But strength rejuvenates. Beauty does not."

"In the end, nothing rejuvenates."

Orluvoq couldn't help but roll her eyes. "What a heartening philosophy. Act on every evil inkling, for death erases all."

Qummukarpoq adjusted the crown of tusks on his head. "If it is true, your appraisal of how much it heartens is immaterial. You can deny the winter is deadly because the mere intimation treads on your feelings, but doing so will get more than your feelings trodden on."

Orluvoq shifted in her seat. "So you believe it?"

The king's gaze sloughed pressure onto her like fat cut from narwhal bones slamming snow. "I live it."

She had known he'd say something in that mold. He maintained a supposition that his stock was more elevated than those he came in contact with, and that his angakkuq prowess would carry him to some inverted, celestial Nunapisu heedless of death's timetable. At the same time, he knew that her usage of "evil" had substantial overlap with his usage of "expedient", and she in turn knew therefore not to take his statement at face value. Twenty years of even an aloof marriage left the occasional indelible impression.

"Well, I do not." She returned the gaze as best she could. "You speak of taxes. I do not like your taxes. They would take away a woman's birthright simply because she's unfortunate to be born under your rule. When merchants and emissaries come to breach Qilaknakka and travel Sulluliaq, we charge them a fee to keep the passage open. If they do not wish to pay the fee, they need not use our services.

"And look. That is exactly what they've been doing the past several years. Fewer and fewer of them see the value in the price, save those islanders addicted to tuuaaq, and most of them have run out of girls they can convince to make the trip with them. We are a dying fashion that you're trying to force back into popularity."

She didn't add that nearly everybody from Nunapisu to the far isles held her in contempt, nor that this entire endeavor had been a massive exercise in neglect of their daughter.

A tuuaaq craving clipped her with an oblong, hollow twang. She wrung fists within her gloves to direct her thoughts to a bit of violence instead. Funny how she could go months without sparing a thought for the stupefacient stuff, even when taking minute doses, only for it to pounce on her at the least leisurely of times. Sometimes she wanted nothing more than to find Ikingut, her old ship's angakkuq, and repay him for the tuuaaq he gave her three decades ago.

"I will explain that which you ought know by now," said the king.

It rankled a little that he didn't appear even a little rankled at her harangue.

"Sulluliaq exists so that the Nuktipik might gain a moai. The instant we saw their power, we saw the path to our vanquishment. We are outrivaled, and that must be amended. They might have shown us peace these twenty years, but their lust for war will eventually turn toward our depths. And when it does, I will be stationed here at the portal through the ocean sky to dissuade them with the power of a moai-bound angakkuq.

"Until then, we must show constancy in maintaining this rent in Qilaknakka. Any breaking of the treaty will see us accused of subterfuge and the agreement annulled. Enjoy it or despise it, the world became bigger when we opened Sulluliaq. So, if you think it evil for me to secure the future of the Nuktipik people, then evil I gladly sew into my life. You are obviously content to spare one girl when every child of the ice could perish under the unopposed assault of the islands and their thousand kings."

Orluvoq held his gaze, but her insides felt no less desiccated for it. She wanted to stand and revile; to aim a righteous finger at his miserable gnarl of a spirit and reprehend him into decency. She could nearly feel the juices running across her tongue and down her chin from the delicious bite of denying him his megalomaniac wish. And she *should*. Unless she needed five more minutes of feigned sleep…

But she couldn't. Because he wasn't completely wrong.

As she wrestled with the wording of a logical denial, Qummukarpoq placed a hand on Kukkujuits' shoulder and steered her in front of him. "Orluvoq. Do your duty as queen of the Nuktipik."

Orluvoq examined the girl and found her no less or greater than any of the countless others she'd siphoned youth from. It was Orluvoq who was different. She wanted to purge from her this numbness. Now that the appendage came sizzling back to life, it nettled like an onslaught of subdermal teeth jabbing for freedom. She'd either have to let it painfully revivify, else roll back on top and smother it insensate.

Smothering struck her as the more attractive of the two options. The weight of failure. The sleet of her husband's argument. And one additional fact scampered by with every third thought.

She was getting ugly.

Merely having the thought irked her, but the implications rattled her, and that irked even more. She was still comelier than most—well, *all*—thirty-eight-year-olds. More eye-catching than any eighteen-year-old, even. But she could feel her stolen beauty fading. The same miniscule, back-of-the-face sag that had first whittled at her twelve years ago, the only time she'd ever let Sulluliaq shut.

She looked at Kukkujuits again. What was the weight of one against hundreds? What would it hurt to wait until the moai rested in the castle to finally cast aside helplessness? She placed a hand above her pocket and felt the bulge of candles within.

"Husband," she said at last. "I will do my duty and keep the tunnel open. But I, myself, cannot bear to forcibly take any girl's beauty. Bring me one who is willing. Bring four past their prime. So long as they are willing, you will find that I am also willing."

What was the weight of one against hundreds?

Enough.

The king briefly looked to an attendant, but they had all relinquished their beauty years ago. He fixed his regard and all its weight upon Orluvoq for too many cold heartbeats. She distantly noticed that he held no candle.

"I will make it so." The king turned in a swooshing of white and paced out of the hall.

Tension ran from Orluvoq's torso, and she succeeded in not exchanging any looks with the attendants. They shouldn't know her true heart. She instructed that Kukkujuits be provided for. The girl reminded her too much of Qaffa. Thinking of which, she should appeal to Nalor to see if he could go topside and complete the work she could not.

Orluvoq left her throne and stumped through the halls, trying to work out the rest of the tension. Her beggar's victory felt empty. The people of the ice weren't the only ones with access to great power. If Sulluliaq closed, the islanders wouldn't accept silence and mystery. They would sail out with all their greatest moai and forge Sulluliaq anew

—or something cousin enough to transverse. What, then, would her thawing morals and new strength be worth? And what would they have cost?

A new path. A new price. If the better path cost the world, was it really the better path?

Most flowers looked dazzling, smelled delightful, and tasted pathetic. That had been one of the first bits of woodcraft Qaffa picked up as a six-year-old on Rapai'i. Most flowers, however, didn't include the puati.

Qaffa nudged aside woman-sized leaves and pliant, arm-thick branches as the forest sucked her deeper in search of a puati. She'd only seen its pink and orange flourish of anatomy four times, being allotted a single petal on each occasion. It always hit the tongue and melted into a mellifluous muddle more pleasurable than any fruit.

Often, foragers would seek for three or four days before finding a single puati. Qaffa had only been at it two hours, but she felt victory lay just around the next fern. Not that she would mind if it took four days. Puati was always worth it. And the time might help cleanse her spirit.

Floes of resentment and bewilderment bumped their way around her heart. Her mother's visitation of a week ago still had sufficient claws under her skin to reagitate at every unwary move.

What right did the queen think she had? Leave Qaffa to

flounder about for years of youth, then come and impose rule once she was old enough to decide for herself? Orluvoq should have tried that long, long ago. Not that father would have let her. Qaffa evaded considering what blame was her father's portion. It disagreed with her much more than focusing on what her mother—

She slowed as a subliminal buzz leaked up her neck. She was being followed. Likely some tree cat. She'd been walking too long for a human to have trailed her. She should have been probing out with tuuaaq to make sure of it. No better time to remedy that than now. Her hand reached to her sealskin bag to arm herself with a candle.

Something cracked across the back of her head and she pitched to the ground. The scent of unwashed sea witch exploded between her eyes and vented out her nostrils. She groped around the forest floor for the candle, pleading for her vision to recalibrate. A blurry woman's form reached down and snatched up the tuuaaq taper.

Addicts. Of course. If anyone would track her through miles of jungle just to get a fix, it was addicts. She needed to regain her wits before they started searching her for more.

Too late.

A man without a moai rolled her over and pilfered her bag of the remaining candle. A woman with a far too obtrusive lower jaw shoved grimy hands into any weave of Qaffa's clothing that might conceal a candle. She threw off Qaffa's every attempt to push her away.

"Two?" her pinched voice demanded. "Two's all you got?"

Qaffa's rubble brain was returning to grooves and paths. "It's all I needed. I can get more if we go to the palace."

The woman scowled, bottom lip folding over the top.

"No. You'll just get us killed. Two it is." She looked to the man. "Kill her."

That shocked Qaffa's brain back into paths and grooves even quicker. She tried to raise up to her elbows, but the woman leaned a knee against her chest.

The man looked from side to side. "But Kinoki, I already gave her a real big bonk. I don't want to do no killing. We got the tuaku. Let's go."

Kinoki's demeanor darkened to nightshades and she cuffed him across the ear. "How dumb? How dumb are you? We let her go and she goes straight to Ariki Haka'atu, then he'll be after us with aaaallll the power of his moai. Do I gotta say it again?"

He rubbed at the side of his head. "No. But I... She's not so bad, right? She's the ice princess. Maybe she can just go home to the ice instead?"

"Amomo!" Kinoki's eyes bulged. "Do it now! She's a tuaku burner."

Amomo stared down at Qaffa a long time, and she poured all the pleading she could back at him. Then he finally looked down at his tuuaaq spoils, said, "Okay," and reached for her throat.

Qaffa's mind mainly registered incredulity. Just moments ago, she'd been raging against the eidolon of her mother. Now here she was, on the side of a volcano, about to get choked to inexistence by a reluctant, sluggard murderer.

Hands closed on her throat and husky fingers closed off her air and circulation.

"Excuse me."

The pressure relented. It took Qaffa a moment to realize why the voice had been so out of place. It wasn't that it was coming from a fourth person, nor that that fourth party had somehow found them leagues from humanity under dense overgrowth.

The voice had spoken in Nuktipik.

She craned her neck to see a man in a reindeer hide parka, standing in the forest as if he had stumbled upon them during his afternoon stroll. Other than his dress and skin, one thing was off. Beneath a full-sun sky, he held a burning candle.

"What did you say, tuaku burner?" shouted Kinoki.

"I, of course, can't understand you," answered the Nuktipik. "But I suggest you let her go."

Kinoki drew breath to yell at him again, then turned to Qaffa. "What's that tuaku burner saying?"

"He wants you to let me go," Qaffa croaked in Rapai'ian.

"Well tell him we ain't letting go of anything." Kinoki clutched the stolen tuuaaq to her chest.

Qaffa looked at the newcomer and spoke in Nuktipik. "They're killing me for tusk. Help?"

A smile widened his cheeks. "Gladly."

She hadn't noticed him take any tuuaaq, but a chill thrilled through her as his flame flipped from orange to blue. The addicts raised their arms and crouched in defensive stances.

"I don't like this, Kinoki," said Amomo.

"Shut up! Knock that candle away and you can snap him in half."

"But he—"

"Shut up! Do it!"

Amomo took one step toward the tirigusuusik man before a tundral breeze swept past Qaffa and the addicts slumped to the ground, spitting up gurgling sounds. The Nuktipik man floated forward, toes skimming the undergrowth. Qaffa finally succeeded in sitting up, and she scooted away from the proceedings.

"What shall it be?" mused the tirigusuusik, hovering above the pair. "Sucking your lives clean out of you is the most obvious, but almost *too* obvious. Voices? No, that leaves you a little too free. Ah, I've got it."

The addicts' spines arched rigid while their hands quaked. Sliver upon sliver, their eyeballs bulged like a hen adding to its brood. Then one by one they popped out, tethered to their brains by gory cords. Qaffa scooted even farther away, sickened by the vivisection but more shocked that the tirigusuusik could leech from two people at once. Almost she begged him to spare Amomo, but the words never made it to her tongue.

The two layabouts twitched like half-mashed beetles while ethereal ribbons of blue issued from their vacated sockets. The wispy blue stopped, and the Nuktipik man released his hold. Four plops brought their eyeballs back into their heads. Blinded. Amomo moaned. Kinoki screamed.

The tirigusuusik reached down and grabbed Qaffa's candles from where they'd fallen, then floated over to her and offered a hand. "Hello, Qaffanngilaq. I'm Nalor."

She stared at it. "Who are you and what are you doing here?"

"My story is of little consequence, save for the fact that I am what you are not."

"Ugly?"

He grinned. "Powerful."

Qaffa considered the two addicts still wallowing in the dirt. She took the hand. "So, you're here to teach me? Did my father send you?"

"No, he didn't. But I have met both him and your mother.

Time is too short for me to get into any practicals today. Would you be interested in a story?" He set his feet on the ground and began to walk away.

Qaffa paused, looking back at her blinded attackers, listening to Kinoki curse everyone in the vicinity.

Nalor turned back and followed her hesitation. "What do these two mean to you?"

"The man," she said. "He can be better. He deserves better."

"If you say so." Nalor gestured with his head. "Talk with me, I won't be terribly long, then windwalk back to your home and get some matatoa to come with you to get your 'friend'."

Qaffa gave one last look, then reasoned that even if Amomo had been bashful about it, he *did* try to kill her. He could suffer for a while.

"So, what story do you have?" she asked after explaining what sort of flower she'd been hunting.

"Have you ever heard 'The Warrior Children'?"

"It's a Nuktipik tale?"

"Aye."

"Then no. The Rapai'ians have something close to that though."

"Maybe someday I'll get to hear that one from you." He breathed in the forest's earthy odor. "In a time more than ten generations distant, there were two clans."

"Only two?"

"Don't get smart on me, girl. I have halitosis and I know how to use it."

Qaffa's Nuktipik upbringing had, sadly, left a gap where there ought to be a definition for halitosis.

"As I was saying, two clans. I'll call them Hare and Bear, for their names have been lost."

He paused and Qaffa knew that lost names should feel weightier, but she didn't reverence names the same as her parents.

"Both lived along the ocean shore and fished the waters and hunted the snow fields. When the sun drooped low and daubed igloos gold, their old men sat along the strand chewing the gristle and speaking of ancient heroes. When winter devoured all, their old women huddled together and worked their crooked fingers, spinning narwhal guts into nets.

"Two hours' sailing to the south of either of them rested an island girt in green sea and robed in iridescence. Feathered in trees and dappled with lakelets. Once a summer and once a winter, each clan was allowed a day's hunt to snare the moon fox. A sprightly beast whose coat shimmered gold and echoed silver, then shimmered silver and echoed gold. A nobler garland could not be found among the Hare nor among the Bear.

"For years they practiced their ways, so conjoined yet always separate. But there came an ill-omened winter where one among the Bear, a certain Valappaa, waxed disdainful of their customs. Five summers and six winters he had failed to fetch himself a moon fox sash. While winter smothered silently, he conceived a second raid.

"Six nights he hunted on the island with two fellow Bears as coterie. When they returned home with their kills and braggart's grins, the people of Bear denounced their sin. However, they made no demands save that Valappaa and his hunters could not wear their prizes around the Hare clan.

"But Valappaa was a man of no small pride. He would not set aside his new ornament and wore it across his puffed-up chest before their sister clan. The Hare, well galled, demanded that Valappaa and his friends cast their moon fox furs into the sea and never hunt on the haven isle again. The Bear did not take well to this. You can bring every accusation against your own blood, but as soon as an outsider does the same, they have brought an accusation against you.

"For the first time in their long friendship, war broke loose.

"After the first bloody battle where more than a dozen died on each side, the Hare held council. They needed to ascend to warriorship before the Bear, else the Hare would become rare. After long talks that amounted to little more than puffing mist, Noqarti, the clan angakkuq, stepped forward.

"'I have a way we could become warriors and never lose another life to the Bear.'

"'What is it?' they demanded.

"'Have you ever heard of tupilaq?' he asked.

"And so, he told them of an ancient practice among angakkuit, long since forbidden, wherein the candle worker could reanimate a corpse and bend it to his will.

"'Have we not heard of this?' they said. 'Is this not the bluebodies of which you have spoken in the past?'

"'Not so, my brothers,' he said. 'Though both must need the flame of blue, an angakkuq has full control over a bluebody, but he can only puppet one at a time. An angakkuq has only basic control over a tupilaq, but he can make as many of them as he has candles. After I wake the body, I put a candle in the chest, and it will fight for us until the flame is gone.'

"With greedy smiles and a meal of caribou heart, they made the pact to do all in their power to help Noqarti, their angakkuq, to field them an army of tupilait. Narwhal after narwhal they felled from the sky, collecting tusks. Every

battle-slain man corpse they kept from being claimed by
Nunapisu. A constant perimeter of guards they established.

"When the preparations had been made, Noqarti sent
the first of the tupilait lurching for the Bear. No one liked
their tendon-tense movements, but a handful of observers
trailed behind to behold victory. The living Hares came
back cackling with two fresh bodies in tow.

"'They died like sick fish,' said one who had been there.
'Seven or eight of them in one go. They hacked down the
tupilait eventually, but that just means we didn't have a
single loss. We were able to grab two of theirs to make new
tupilait with.'

"The Hare celebrated their great victory with an all-
night repast and dance, dancing until they began collapsing
where they stood. They only left one guard out at a time, for
the Bear had been subdued for a good while. Or so they
thought.

"In the wee hours before Arsarneq had withdrawn from
the sky, three angry Bears hitched dogs to sled and stole
across the snow fields. They stormed the halls of the Hare
igloo and brought slaughter in their visitation. The fest-
worn Hares roused a sluggish defense and ended their
attackers, though not before eight Hares lay slain.

"The next night Noqarti sent the bodies over in tupilaq
vengeance, but the Hare were in for a nasty surprise. The
Bear sent tupilait of their own.

"The battle raged for well over a month, until the sun
poked its nose above the horizon and began its banishment
of winter. Each clan suffered losses more grievous than any
they'd thought they could bear. They'd fortified their igloos
and thrown up battlements of ice thicker than a man is tall.
But what they'd done best was die.

"Down from a hundred twenty each to no more than

thirty per clan, food had become scarce. Not that the fish in the sea, the caribou in the field, nor the narwhal in the sky had dwindled in number. All the best hunters had been turned to tupilait. The Hare clan gathered in council once more to uncover how they could end it all before their extinction.

"'I have one suggestion we have not tried,' said the angakkuq Noqarti.

"'Tell us, tell us,' they demanded.

"'When I make a tupilaq, I must place the candle in its chest, as you have seen. It then follows a simple instruction until the candle burns to naught.'

"The clansfolk nodded along. This was why they had made the longest candles possible.

"'Any candle would last twice or more as long if we were to make a child tupilaq.'

"They all sat in glum silence at his revelation. More than half their number were children. It made sense that at some point the young must start contributing to the clan's survival. But wipe out children down to the last and the clan had no survival. In the end, the clan decided to try it with the sickest child, one who wouldn't last more than a week. It was no different than giving a babe to the ice for the good of the clan.

"So, they sent a dead child to terrorize a wounded people. Small in stature, poor in spirit, not a frolick left in its bones. In its chest, a candle burning. In its hands, two seal bone knives. Round its neck, a moon fox sash. Over the bulwark, into the igloos. Through the halls and into rooms, shuffling, swinging, and impaling. Breaking seagrass left for drying. Slicing gutstrings stretched for sewing. Finding hearts in covered chests.

"Before they stopped it, six had died. Six the Bear could

not afford to lose. No one had expected death to wear a child's form, so no one had countered it until far too late. They mourned their dead, then sent them forth as tupilait, including two slain children.

"For two more weeks their battles raged in tuuaaq-fueled tableaus of carnage. Raid after raid with tupilaq after tupilaq until the Bear clan angakkuq was slain. That left four survivors of the Bear clan, all children, and four of the Hare clan, one of them a child. Heavy was the price of three moon fox skins.

"They say the only thing worse than winning a battle is losing one. Perhaps even worse than losing is when there is no victor.

"Of the four surviving Hares, the two old women griped betwixt themselves, saying how it had all been Noqarti's, the angakkuq's, fault. Deciding they'd rather perish than have their survival abetted by the angakkuq butcher of the Hare, they crept to his room one night and opened his throat. The last blood of the war had finally been shed.

"The Hare, having spent their future on clash and fray, took in the children of the Bear. Yet how could they call themselves either Hare or Bear? Both clans had achieved decimation. Neither remnant would survive without the other. They cast aside the ancient names and chose anew, one to forget the days of blood and death. The two women and their flock of four children petitioned another clan for aid, and somehow, they weathered the next winter. To this day, their descendants can be found on the ice by the sea."

Qaffa spent a few moments sorting her spirit out in the unsettling denouement. The stories of the ice. They were nothing like island tales. "They live on to this day? What is their clan name?"

Nalor waved a hand. "It is neither Hare nor Bear."

She frowned. It felt as though if she missed something apparent to those more conversant in Nuktipik. "Is there a grander reason you chose this story? Or do you tell it to every girl you meet?"

He stopped walking and looked her in the face. "It is a warning. Your mother wishes for you to never touch the blue flame again. I cannot bring myself to give the same counsel. However, I can say this. Know what you hold. Know where you stand."

She nodded slow as a setting sun. "I think I understand."

"To Noqarti, every problem required a tirigusuusik solution. He forgot there is more to life than flames of blue." Nalor pushed back a giant leaf and Qaffa gave a squeal of surprise.

She rushed forward and plucked the tuapi flower by the stem, careful to not let its nectar reservoir drip loose. She drained some into her mouth and let her eyes roll back at the gush of sweetness.

"You should visit your grandfather soon."

"What?" Qaffa's eyes snapped back forward. "You know everyone in my family?"

"I knew Paarsisoq before your mother did. He would appreciate a visit from his only granddaughter."

She looked at him for the first time in earnest and realized his age defied discernment. "Who are you?"

He smiled. "I'm just Nalor. But I've got places to be, and so do you. I believe you'll find someone waiting for you back at the palace. Perchance we'll speak again, Qaffanngilaq."

In a blur, he windwalked between a stand of trees and out of her life. He hadn't even tried the tuapi.

❄

Qaffa dropped out of her windwalk and took the remaining paces up to the palace at a dawdle, basking in the burned hues of the falling sun.

"Qaffa," said Tikai, a matatoa doorguard. He said it like all Rapai'ians, never starting the word far enough back in his throat. "An important messenger came for you while you were away. You'll find her just inside."

Qaffa nodded her thanks and passed into the feast hall. In spite of Nalor's hint, she couldn't suppress the mild surprise at seeing her second Nuktipik person for the day. The woman noticed her enter, then pressed herself up from the mat where she sat eating cold ti root. Beside her sat the Rapai'ian prince, Mahiahia. Qaffa's counterpart who had lived with her parents as she had with his.

She blinked surprise. "Mahiahia, what are you doing here?"

"Princess," the Nuktipik woman said, preempting the prince. Qaffa had seen her in the ice castle before but couldn't dredge up a name. "I'm glad they found you. The guards sent someone looking hours ago."

"My hunt finished. I came back on my own. What is your message?"

"Your father requests your presence at Qilaknakka, and he no longer requires Mahiahia's presence."

Qaffa's heart clenched faster. She hadn't received a summons in years, yet this one sounded uncomfortably final. "And when shall I meet my father?"

"Tomorrow."

"Tomorrow." They usually gave her a week's notice. "What occasion can I expect to be attending?"

"King Qummukarpoq did not say. Apologies."

Bile nattered in her stomach. The queen would call her back on such vanishing notice to attempt further dissuasion from the blue flame. A king-sent summons for an occasion-less occasion? She'd rather face another set of addicts.

"I will do as my father commands," she said, hoping she remembered the correct form for 'command'.

"Then, if it pleases you," the messenger reached down to retrieve her parka from the mat, "let's go."

"Tonight?" Visions of Amomo stumbling around the forest bumped through Qaffa's mind. "That would be most inconvenient."

"I can't force you to come tonight," said the messenger. "But if you're not there when the king expects you to be, he very well may come collect you himself."

Qaffa spun through the possibilities. By far the least frightening was comporting herself according to her father's demands. Sending a few matatoa out after Amomo wouldn't be so bad. He *had* tried to kill her, after all.

"Let me gather some things from my room, then I'll leave with you."

Orluvoq, queen at the start of the world, wore white on the day she was to obey the king. Not that her wardrobe contained much else of late. Some king long since committed to Nunapisu had fancied white vestments, and no king since then, seemingly, had the authority to supersede that preference.

Her feet and hands would know no rest. Qummukarpoq had brought his willing sacrifice to the castle the night before. Orluvoq's impulses drove her to avoid the girl's face through the long hours. Almost she had taken a blindfold to her eyes from the offering's arrival until the siphoning's end mere minutes from now. Evils unseen were evils unreal, yes?

But that wouldn't do. Looking the brave girl in the face was the victim's due. As she sucked away the pearl dust and withered the ermine softness of the girl's countenance; as she crumpled the fluting heartsong and hacked with age's heavy blade; the smallest recompense she could muster was an eye unblinking and a mind unforgetting.

She paced around the throne room floor, a tic her servants hadn't heretofore seen. In muttering tones, she chastised herself. Why fear that which she'd made a profession of? Like the times in hundreds before, this would start and end the same. She'd grow pretty, the girl would fall grim, and Qummukarpoq would have his game.

It was, she knew, because the more she evaded change, the more she ensured that she could never change. To the strong came yet more strength. From the helpless was taken what little strength they had.

No, this wasn't evasion. This was one final farewell. The duty she owed to the folk of the ice. She'd take from the willing to furnish with peace. She'd safeguard the clans with a decadent shield. And when she'd discharged this duty she held, she'd slacken her grip and welcome the fall.

Qummukarpoq entered the hall.

She steadied on her feet, a gentle hand on the throne's white back, a leaping heart within her breast.

"Orluvoq."

"Husband."

"I trust you're ready?"

She dropped her chin in a nod. "You'll hear no complaints from me."

The king turned and called through the doorway. "Come."

Orluvoq's glove tightened on the chair back as a girl stepped through the door, her footfalls scraping up to the queen's ears.

"What is the meaning of this?" Orluvoq demanded, eyebrows reaching for each other. "She should not be here."

"Being a ruler isn't easy."

The girl came to stand beside him, eyes pointed at the floor.

"We agreed on a willing participant. You can't convince me that she's had a change of mind."

Qummukarpoq turned a fraction of his gaze to Kukku-juits, the girl he'd brought two days before. "Her? No. She's just here to remind you what could have been had *you* had a change of mind. Or, more appropriately, had you *not* had a change of mind."

Orluvoq's cheeks bunched around her eyes in bemuse-ment. "What?"

The king turned once more to the doorway. "Come."

The doorway darkened. A girl stepped through. Within Orluvoq, revolt broke out against ribs.

Qaffanngilaq.

"No." The word grated out like the raking of bones across tundral crust. Her empty stomach seized like a sack of drying rawhide.

Qaffa, garbed in a new white parka, walked forth to stand beside Kukkujuits and the king. "Mother."

"Qaffa. You shouldn't be here." Orluvoq's speech ran quick across her tongue.

"Why not?" A certain defiance underlined Qaffa's chin.

"Because you are my daughter, and I say so." Orluvoq knew the injunction came across trite, but the moment didn't permit her to think of anything truer. The scene that had played behind her eyes for eighteen years manifested in corporeal horror. The little needle of pathos that always prodded her to ask, 'What if this was my daughter?' She stared at the girl—the woman—before her. There was no longer place for 'what if'.

"Am I not also his daughter?" Qaffa pointed to the king.

"What have you promised her?" Oluvoq asked Qummukarpoq.

"He hasn't promised me anything," said Qaffa.

"What threat—"

"And he hasn't threatened me either," she broke in again. "He asked."

Orluvoq's world reeled and yawed. Love never went far without pain following. She placed another hand on the throne to levy more of her weight. There lurked a lie behind it all. A bait and switch? Angakkuq emotion manipulation? If she chewed, she would bite the bitter core devised by Qummukarpoq.

"And you agreed?" Orluvoq asked.

"I did."

"Qaffanngilaq, how could you agree?" Orluvoq knew that at some point her shock would render into anger and fuel her with convictions. She could only hope the transition would snap in the next minutes, not days.

"How could anyone agree? You seem to have been perfectly content to take anyone these past twenty years. Which means you'll accept anyone, even when they don't want it, but you'll reject your own daughter when she gives herself freely. Yes?"

Nothing would lock together in Orluvoq's brain. *Why* would Qaffa agree to anything approaching this? She wouldn't.

Correct?

Or had Orluvoq crafted a paradigm in her head over two decades that couldn't hold up under the friction brought by a daughter raised by foreign hands? She needed to distract the conversation so she could churn through the mess. She swung a hopeless gesture at Kukkujuits.

"You've kept this girl and brought her in just so you can taunt me. Is that the sort of action fit for a king? You've brought her to watch our family contend, then to spread word of it to her clan and all the ice."

"Firstly," the king's voice cut in, "there is none but I who can decide which actions befit a king. Secondly, do you really believe I'd let her watch the royal drama then return home with her memories intact?"

Kukkujuits' eyes widened.

"No," said Orluvoq. "I don't suppose you would."

"She is here to illustrate the price of duty. Had you observed your obligation two days ago, the price would have been her. Delaying duty till today has incurred a debt."

Words pooled on her tongue to ask Kukkujuits if she wouldn't reconsider. Deeper down wound the darksome urge to fall upon the girl unwarned. Qummukarpoq had come blowing war upon his trump. She could sidestep his careering and lame him in one swoop. One last unexpected, rapine act.

Unless.

A nightwind chill percolated through her stomach. Unless that was the exact stratagem he drove. Present the choice she'd passed on, juxtapose a more daunting choice, and force her into frantic action to reclaim the choice she'd rebuffed.

It was all a calculation to erase any progress she'd made absolutely. To shush her in her stirrings from feigned slumber. She couldn't burgle this terrified girl. But neither could she accept the offered beauty from her own daughter.

It was all so... ugly.

"Orluvoq," said the king. "Not many days hence, Sulluliaq will close, and we won't have a moai. You gave your word. Now uphold it." He put a hand on Qaffa's shoulder and moved her forward.

Whatever plan the king had laid, he'd cued Qaffa in on at least some of it. Orluvoq doubted the king would bat an eye if she did as he said and laid into Qaffa. He'd already taken that into account. But how would their daughter feel if Orluvoq really chose to drain her instead of a stranger?

She opened her mouth. "I..."

"Mother, get it over with. My nerves aren't exactly quiet right now. We can chat after all this stupid tension is gone."

Mouth still ajar, Orluvoq's eyes wandered to Kukkujuits, who looked up. Something cognizant registered in the girl's face. Kukkujuits wrapped her arms around herself and threw her gaze to the floor. She knew.

Integrity dictated that Orluvoq stride forth and reduce her own daughter to a jagged shambles. Nature howled against duty, demanding she march to the stranger and suck her dry of pulchritude. Her gut told her to vomit so the pain would pass for now. Either would do. Both would do. Anything to make it pass.

Her hand slipped toward the candle in her pocket.

Addicted to tuuaaq at eight years old. Slave to beauty at eighteen. Never a season in her life where she could rise in her own strength. Always the itch. Always the worry. Always failing. Always broken. Always hiding. Always waiting. Waiting for a better path to find her. Waiting for a master puzzler to arrive and banish her chaos. Waiting, because the veil of helplessness convinced her she could do nothing greater.

Her hand stopped.

"Orluvoq," said the king.

"Mother," said Qaffa.

Daughter and father spoke in unison, a demand and an entreaty. Orluvoq answered both the same.

"No." Once again, the word grated out. "I will be beautiful no more."

No? Had her mother really just said that? After a spell of confusion, Qaffa's insides bubbled with unexpected warmth. She didn't want the warmth. She'd come to this hall to see a vendetta fulfilled.

"You won't do your duty?" asked the king "You will leave the Nuktipik unguarded?".

"A duty you created then imposed upon me?" asked the queen. "You fulfill it."

Qaffa's jaw dropped. Whose mother was this? Surely not hers. She cast a quick eye to her father, searching for a hint at the next step. He'd alluded to this possibility when he'd debriefed her last night but had only supplied vague instructions. Qaffa hadn't given the idea much credence anyway.

"If you forsake this duty, then its honor is no longer yours."

Honor? No honor pertained to her mother's position.

"Why does duty look so much like evil?" said Orluvoq.

The king's hand brushed the pocket where he stowed his candles. "Never have I warped your emotions to the tusk. Always has it been your choice to take. You would do well to remember that such is not assumed, but permitted."

Orluvoq's lips thinned, and her hand hovered over her own candle pocket. "Try it."

Qaffa's jaw opened and didn't close. Was this indeed her mother? The monster Orluvoq? The weak-willed instrument of the king who sucked beauty as readily as breath? This woman beside the ice throne stank of none of that. This woman was... strong.

His hand drifted to his side. "No. I am fed full with your snivels and mewls. The honor shall be given to another."

"Another may take my place."

"You mistake me, Orluvoq." The calm ice in her father's voice shivered Qaffa. "There is no time for another to simply take your place. They must also take the honor endemic to your station."

At this her mother hesitated, a single line of worry creasing her flawless face. "What does that mean?"

"Sulluliaq can only be opened and stay so if Arsarneq's light is channeled through a perfect vessel, as we have discovered. Anything less and the construct will break. We lack time, and the world lacks talent for another to rise up and do as you've done. Except for one, that I know of." He turned to Qaffa, and she briefly met his eye. "Qaffanngilaq. You must become the perfect vessel."

The world contracted to a very small point, grabbing all things hither and thither and rolling them into one. Steal beauty. The king had just commanded her to steal beauty. And not just any beauty. Her mother's. Steal her mother's beauty. Take from the maw of the fatted beast. Her breaths plumed quickly, limned by rays from the morning sun cutting through the hall's high windows.

To steal what had been stolen once. Did that undo the wrongs, or did it just make you twice the thief?

"But you'd have to be married to me to keep Sulluliaq open. The most beautiful woman married to the most powerful angakkuq." Qaffa took a step aside. "I can't marry my father."

Qummukarpoq gave a single shake of the head. "That was just the slogan to make it more enticing. I reasoned it would prove far simpler to keep a wife by my side for decades than some capricious woman. The only requirements are my strength and your lack of blemish."

"But..." Why was she hesitating? Was this not the woman who had gruesified hundreds? Had she not earned a humbling? Had Qaffa not spoken feuds of blood against this very woman? Where now the fire? Where the javelin in the furled fist?

The picture her father had painted last night had stained itself too deeply on her mind. Primarily, trick the queen to take from the village girl. Prove that she couldn't change for all her preaching.

Failing that, force her to take from her own daughter. Oblige her to live what she had done to countless others. After being leeched from, Qaffa would leave the room, take beauty from the village girl, then skywalk back to Rapai'i.

Failing that, the king had bidden Qaffa follow his lead and asked if she would obey his command. She had agreed, not imagining any such thing would actually come to pass.

Qaffa couldn't quite say which she'd preferred. The first supplied that Qaffa herself didn't have to do any leeching, while the second would likely hurt her mother on a more personal grade. Neither mattered now. Only the third existed, and it torqued a gray fear into her.

"Is it really a daughter's place to correct her mother?

Could I not just take from her?" Qaffa motioned to Kukkujuits.

"You are not ugly," said the king. "But this girl doesn't have enough external perfection to take you to the pinnacle. Drink where the snow is clearest. You'll likely need both though."

"Qummukarpoq, this is insanity." Orluvoq strode down from the dais, hand in her pocket. "You can't force her to work the blue flame, especially not on her own mother."

Chill streamed over Qaffa, and a blue flame flickered in the king's hand where no candle had been seconds before.

"I have already told you. Nothing I do today includes forcing our daughter. She's here by agreement."

A separate pinch of cold and a pop of azure burst to life in Orluvoq's hand. "I know about your invitations and agreements."

Qaffa found her hand grasping a candle. Kukkujuits broke into tears. The two attendants ran to a corner and crouched down, arms around each other. The thick castle walls ate more light than a normal igloo, so even at this, one of the brightest points of the day, enough darkness abounded for the king's and queen's breath to be tainted blue from below.

"What game shall we play, wife, you and I with candles blue?"

An arm's length separated the two. "We play the game where I leave, and you don't see me again."

"Qaffanngilaq," said the king. "Light your candle after the manner of the tirigusuusik."

Qaffa did as she was commanded, nibbling on a flake of tuuaaq and waiting for her flame to cool.

"You two can have your Sulluliaq," said Orluvoq. "You can stay and wrangle helpless thousands. Dine with a different island king each night of the week and stroke your moai together. As for myself, I am finished."

A measure of indignation mingled with Qaffa's head havoc. How could her mother think to just drop her duty and leave the land to fall? To close off the only route to Qaffa's true home? To abandon her just moments after choosing her?

Then a plan began to simmer and swirl in her head. Perhaps duty was not always a straight line one must walk.

Orluvoq turned to her. "I'm sorry I haven't been a better mother. When these times are past, I'll seek you again and see what amends I can make."

The queen windwalked out the room.

Or, she tried to. The king hadn't made a move, yet she went sprawling across the slick floor. He turned and slowly took the eleven steps to stand over her while she twitched and gagged. Qaffa wanted to be uplifted by an air of satisfaction, seeing her mother in the same position she'd been put in just a week prior. All that stirred within her was revulsion.

"Qaffanngilaq. Come here."

She did. The space between her and her mother could have been leagues.

"Now," said the king. "Take your mother's beauty."

Her mouth went dry like sand in a fire. "I've never actually tried on anything but animals."

"It's not so different. Perhaps a little more resistance at the start."

Qaffa looked down at the beautiful, struggling form of her mother. "Can you show me? Maybe do just a tiny piece?"

The king stared at his daughter. "Whatever I take could endanger our entire purpose."

"Right, sorry." She tried to keep her breathing in check.

"Um, then maybe just take it to the point right before and hold it there so I can see how you did it?" She really didn't think her heart should be beating so quickly.

"That is reasonable enough." Qummukarpoq turned his attention to his spasm-wrought wife and levered his will inside of her face.

Qaffa took a step back and watched the ghastliness. A turn-sick vapor floated through her head and chest. Instinct goaded her to intercept the king with her own act of candles. But as Nalor had taught the day before, not every problem requires a tirigusuusik solution.

Trying to summon every tip she'd ever been given by a matatoa, Qaffa swung her free hand like a stone from a volcano and slammed it into the back of her father's head.

The king of all the world let out a concussive grunt, stumbled over his tortured wife, dropped his candle, and crunched against the ground. Qaffa stabbed out with her angakkuq threads and set to draining him of consciousness. He struggled to his hands twice before one final collapse.

She shuddered. Now they were going to have to steal Kukkujuits' memories for certain.

Orluvoq's face slapped her in the face, then she turned and watched her daughter drain her husband into a heap on the floor. She blinked. That was one to remember for certain. A quiet moment hung in the hall. She looked to Qaffa.

"Did you... kill him?"

Qaffa's grip wouldn't stop shifting on her taper. "No. No, just consciousness. A lot of it. I'm not an expert, but he should be out for days."

Orluvoq staggered to her feet and stumped toward her candle. "I'll admit, you had me deceived. What exactly was your plan after incapacitating your father?"

"We need to flee to Rapai'i. Hide with Ariki Haka'atu. He and his matatoa will protect us until Sulluliaq closes. I think I can even convince him to not give father the moai."

It was a fantastic plan, barring her aversion to the heat. Powerful though Qummukarpoq might be, he couldn't outdo a whole unit of matatoa plus an islander king. "Before I decide anything, one more important question," Orluvoq bent down, grabbed her still lit candle, then looked to Qaffa in the half light, "why?"

Qaffa hesitated. "Why what?"

"Why save me? Why not just take my beauty and move on? It seems like you'd have been happy to do that a week ago."

The girl with ice blood and island skin bit her lip then spoke. "I realized that I had been thinking of you all wrong. You're like the man who cheated his way into heaven, then when he got there, everyone could see heaven but him. You've taken all this beauty, you've worked great magics, you've changed the world for two different peoples, and yet you see none of it. You live in the belly of it, and all you see is darkness."

Again, Orluvoq couldn't repress how impressed she was at the excess keenness her daughter possessed. "Well. I'm glad you looked deeper. I don't think we should stay here much longer."

"Should we, uh..." Qaffa pointed at the king. He looked so relaxed compared to his usual posture. "What should we do with him?"

Orluvoq swung her head to her daughter. "Were you going to say, 'kill him'?"

"Um..." Qaffa swallowed. "Well, that's how the matatoa like to do it."

"No." Orluvoq sputtered air between her lips. "No, no. I may not hold any love for him, but he hasn't done anything that deserves death. At least in the past twenty years, to my knowledge. He's just very difficult to be alive around."

A tension evaporated from Qaffa. "Okay. Good. What about the rest?"

The queen rushed over to her attendants and laid consoling words in their ears.

"And this village girl?"

Orluvoq looked to Kukkujuits, who had transformed into a sobbing wreck, and she knew her daughter was speaking of taking her memories. "What's done is done. If what's done is known, so be it. Kukkujuits, boats will come. The soonest one should be tomorrow. Tell them the queen commands you sail north with them."

"Do you need anything else?" Qaffa asked her mother.

The queen went to stand by her daughter. "No."

"Let's go then."

Dread sunk into Orluvoq's stomach. The very air weighed heavier around her.

"Mother? What's wrong?"

"I can't go to Rapai'i yet."

Confusion marked Qaffa's forehead. "What? Why?"

"Your grandfather. If I leave and Sulluliaq closes, I leave him to die alone. He deserves so much better." Worthless was she if her final salute was but a gust of pain in exchange for his life of love.

"We can't go stay out there! Anywhere on the ice and father can find us, and I don't think I'll be able to pull another move like that on him."

"No, we'll go get Paarsisoq and take him through the sky wall," said Orluvoq. "I will carry him on my back from the world's end to its beginning and beyond."

It was a stipulation most foolish. She knew how poorly things could go. But she had found a new path, and she would pay the new price, no matter the pain. Besides, Qummukarpoq needed at least one of them. His worst would come in the form of emotions bent to the tusk and beauty force feeding.

Qaffangilaq, just a finger shorter, stared at her mother a

long while with pursed lips. At last, she nodded. "Let's go get Grandpa."

A light that had been so long darkened awakened inside Orluvoq. The light, she reckoned, outshone the foolishness. She smiled and wrapped her daughter in a sweet embrace. "Oh, Qaffanngilaq. Welcome home."

THE GOING HAD BEEN slow until night fell, or at least as slow as windwalking goes. Once Arsarneq slithered into the heavens, mother and daughter climbed the heights and traversed its gleam. Sometime in the wee hours, they espied the breach where white became black forever, and they descended to the ice.

"I hate to wake him, but you can't choose when emergency calls." Orluvoq walked into the igloo she had called home for a decade. A draft of sinuous homesickness found the breaches in her spirit, and she had to clutch her stomach as she approached the bundle of blankets against the far wall.

"Dad?"

She shook the lump.

"Dad?"

Qaffa pushed through the door, and a frigid gust showed its teeth.

Orluvoq shook the blankets again. This time they stirred.

"What? Who is it? Who?" Paarsisoq rolled onto his back and blinked against the candlelight.

"Hi, Dad."

He stared beneath brows dropped low. The longer he stared, the more Orluvoq wondered if he had gone into his dotage. Then the brows flew up and moisture pooled in his eyes. "Orluvoq! You've come back! You've come back."

He struggled out of his furs, sat upright, and took her in his arms. The queen at the start of the world couldn't keep her eyes from overflowing.

"I'm back," she whispered.

They held onto each other almost as long as they needed, then she drew back. "Dad. This might sound ridiculous. I haven't come to stay. I've come to get you. *We've* come to get you."

"We?" He looked past her for the first time.

"Hi, Grandpa."

"Qaffanngilaq!"

Orluvoq moved and watched the show of hugs be repeated. After a dehydrating number of tears had been shed, she spoke again.

"I apologise for showing up in the middle of the night, but we really do need to go. We'll explain on the way."

"Go? This is my home. I will die here, likely within a year or two. It's of little use for me to transplant myself somewhere new now."

"Dad." Orluvoq took his hand. "Qaffa and I have to go live on the islands, and we're not coming back. Sulluliaq will close soon. You're the only family we have. Please come. We couldn't bear to leave you here to die alone."

The Watcher at the end of the world furrowed his ancient brow and sank into ruminations. As he thought, Orluvoq realized the self-centered nature of this maneuver. Who was she to yank an ailing old man into an entirely different world just to make her less sad? To think she could undo years of neglect by tearing him from his work and home and forcing him into an unbelievably hot clime?

Paarsisoq dipped his head in a nod. "I love you, my daughter. I will come."

Her heart broke.

He was far more than she deserved. "I love you too."

"Uh, Mama?"

Orluvoq turned to her daughter's voice, surprised to hear a name other than 'mother'. "What?"

"Use your candle and feel toward the aurora."

Orluvoq's blood slurred gelid in her veins. She quested out into the air and felt his tug.

The king of the Nuktipik and all the world in the sky above. Qaffa's spell hadn't held.

He was coming.

He was here.

Like shadow aflame, like maelstrom electric, coursing cruelly came the king. Shod in fury, right foot chopping. Shod in rancor, left foot slashing. Corridor of light primeval bearing spoors he coarsely carved. He a livid, albine arrow loosed to gore the world on vengeance. Loosed from its eternal start to its eternal end to end.

There beneath him prowled the black, the space where earth ought have a jaw. And on the ice before the blackness, sensed he him his wife and daughter. Vile ingrates, bloodborne blight, flyblown minds all puckered with valor. Never in the breadth of time had there been known repugnance so utter. Never in the depth of time would there be known chastisement so final. They would quake and they would fall, for Qummukarpoq had come to call.

Incandescent arced he earthward, broke his truck with Arsarneq. Blazoned white and searing flume betwixt the ice and the aurora. As his feet engaged with snowpack, flakes gushed out in convolutions, crackling o'er the lonesome igloo, scattering down the final forever. With three steps he reined his motion, then called toward the lowly abode.

"Hateful wife and spiteful daughter, walled in ice to screen your shame. Scurry forth and bare your faces, beautiful, inimical. Hark and hasten lest I conjure dismal spans of fiery scourges. Lest I flail into the igloo, boil you from the earth's white surface."

Tinseled green with heaven's light, he breathed thickly waiting, waiting. No more waiting, he contorted power from the candle blue. Coiled and twisted might enough to rend the very atmosphere.

Running came the women from the igloo's mouth like hares affrighted, clutching at their azure flames as though they two could break his ire. He released the power in his angakkuqly hold, yea, the king let it evaporate and pierced them with his gaze alone.

"You have courted cowardice, consorted with the craven's course. Duty lies a path untrodden in your fickle, icy hearts. You have sought this unlit pit to bury all your disrepute. There will be no word of it, for I have come to take your youth."

Orluvoq scowled deeply from the darkness of her hood. "You have been a beastly husband from our union's earliest inklings. Mirthless void behind your ribs, which you tend with zealous care. Wherefore should I listen to you sternly lecture over duty, when you've spat upon your duty toward your wife and only daughter? You are but a charlatan, your cloak of white hides black within. And though you take from me my life, your Sulluliaq will yet die; die within your grasping fingers, die with moai yet unborn."

Qummukarpoq would hear no further, so he tapped the tusk again, drew him out a length of power, struck toward the women twain. More than flesh he met in answer, angakkuq reprisal flared. Mother, daughter, heaving outward, met the onslaught blow for blow. Bristling with majesty they turned aside his every thrust, held at bay the wizard lethal, crowed into the gelid air. Almost then they heroes were, fated to be framed in lores.

But the king was no mean shaman, no frail top-snow thawed by dawnlight. Years a hundred he had moiled, bottling thunder in his bosom; peddling to both mind and body provender of bitter blue. Inchmeal peeled he back their breastwork, darkled he their feeble luster. Terror spoiled their manful war cries, pitching toward a rancid shriek. Fingerwalking came his magic, youth and vital spirit ware.

As his essence slapped aside theirs, nighed to feasting on their skin, from the black of Nunapisu billowed up a cloud of flakes. O'er the verge a man came dashing, bearing down upon the king. Qummukarpoq broke from his bout and leapt to heights, his feet a blur. On his heels the man came nipping, buoyed into the sky by azure. When the threat of three had minished quickly down to one, the king unbarred his mouth and shouted harshly to his tracer.

"Who are you to give me chase, me the king of all the world? You are but a sordid knave who hides in pits, a worthless cur. Hie back to your native abysm, lest your spirit I deprive you. Lest I take your empty body, place it neath me as a footstool."

"I am Nalorsitsaarut," the man exclaimed above the wind. "You stole from me my father's name. Stole his name from all with ears. Turned him into ghostless bones; blacked his spirit into soot. You should have found another son. One whose mind forgets to echo. You marked me, an echoes' steward. You are now mine for the venging."

Hot waxed wrath in the king's cold chest, in the king's old flesh burned a new unrest. He would not grow flighty when a brash pretender posed in challenge, pressed the trump of ultimatum glibly to his lips and sounded.

"I remember well your luckless father and his nameless corpse. Well do I recall your haste in showing me your back and running. Not a breath you breathed in yore times could have much as grazed my coat, and years a hundred notwithstanding, you are yet a blundering urchin. Bid your body dear farewell. You are now mine for the taking."

Sharply turned the king about, ate another cleft of tuuaaq, turned the chaser to a rout, harried him with cords of power. Cloudless night air gnashed them sharply in its cold and crystal teeth. With aplomb this so-called Nalor cuffed aside his every inquest. Noble wonder gripped the king, gawping at the low-born's craft. He would brook no vulgar shaman besting him in matters blue. From his coat he took a taper, lit it off the shrinking stub, hurled his fury toward this Nalor, hurled his body in the wake. Far below the ice fields halted, yielded for th'eternal chasm.

"Visions you have sought in thousands, sought to plumb the future's depths. Fainly you are future's voyeur, yet each viewing brings you woe. Not a one has shown you conquering, casting me to sightless hell. I, the angakkuq superior, need no visions for to know. Merely coming, you have fallen, made abyss your soulless bed. You are mine, o son of the voided. To your father I return you."

Qummukarpoq unleashed a torrent, seeking purchase under skin. Filaments of tuuaaq power pierced defenses, found their mark. Foolish Nalor flagged in earnest, dropping through the sky like sheet hail. Smile curling onto lips, the king careened in hungry chase. Down from heaven and its river. Past the earth plain and its snow. Nether into rank perdition. Falling into black infinity.

To the wall of Nunapisu Nalor stumbled through the

air, goaded on by glee-strung driver, prize-drunk river, prime of shamans brought to bear. Scrape and crack of feet on wall the void behind them swiftly swallowed. Sightless, atavistic gazes stared unblinking at their steps, while spirits in their legions doubtless crowded closely watching on. King and coward, feet a tumult, ran the dead toward oblivion.

"Now you see," the king declared, "your witless vengelust has undone you. Past the dead you speed your course, for your place is not among them. No interment is your lot; yours is of the silent pit. Whilst I break you e'er so finely, I will chase you into it."

Qummukarpoq kept lashing, lashing. Nalor, though, had found new strength. Not the strength to curb the onslaught, but to dodge beyond its reach. Oaths and witch-words spat the king as fervor lent he to his pace. If the man should not here perish, never could the king know sleep. Aggravation found his tongue, loosed his jaw and bounded forth.

"Wherefore do you naught but run? Came you not to measure candles? Have you trowed that once you saw that vicrt'ry wasn't sure, you could turn about and sue for peace and have it for your glutting? I am finished with your weak, invertebrate display. And now we see, twixt you and me, how kings contrive to play."

And while he walked with wind and sky, with corpses and abyss, he whisked a strand of power high and linked it into Arsarneq. That verdant foe with violet frills which reigned amidst the sky, he had treated with its taming times enough to bend it at his beck. From the vacant bowels of shadow roused the king great machinations. Arsarneq waned from its realmway, slumped into the frigid pit. Corpses in their limpid barrows cracked their eyes as light blazed past; light illuming horrid secrets tucked beyond the frozen bodies.

Nalor saw the falling brilliance, saw his doom in fleet descent. Frenzy fed his every gallop, reason left alone to fend. Qummukarpoq let sound a cackle as refulgence cut toward them. What mere man might him oppose when all creation's river bowed? Cataclysm was his scepter poised to strike with subjugation. This pretender ought to number his remaining sovereign breaths.

Then the light was swathe around them, soundless green cacophony. Larm of wind and footfall patter smothered by auroral strait. Thick with power pulsing round him struck the king out once again, sent his threads a-seeking Nalor, lancing for the—

Choke.

Motion faltered—was arrested—and the king made not a quiver. Reached he for his threads of power, could not squeeze more than a trickle. Something waggled in his gut, a baleful eel of ice and fire. In the black beyond the world, fear engorged his belly taut.

Nalor swiveled on the wall, walked toward him, steps uncaring, with a gesture sent the candle tumbling from the old king's hand. How malefic then he seemed, his visage flush with fiery emerald. How portentous then his gait, striding forth with wrath and menace.

"I am Nalorsitsaarut. I have come to venge my dead. All the ice will soon forget the names you've borne and deeds you've bred. First from you I take your name," and the king felt something shift. Particles of memory eviscerated from his mind.

"Then I take from you your candles."

Tuuaaq tapers tore from pockets, flew to Nalor's open hand.

"How?" the king begged in his wonder. "Whence is your supremacy?"

Nalor gave no voice to answer, looked instead into the wall. Qummukarpoq gazed quickly after, gaped and stammered at the sight. There where ought be smooth and glassy had been torn an aberration. Height of man, a hollow lay where elsewise should have stood a corpse. But he marveled not at thoughts of bodies breaking free, for behind the hole there stretched a stone, a towering face with eyes to see. Here abreast the blackness cased in clear, undying ice, yes, here there was a moai standing watchman o'er the void.

"What?" The king looked back to Nalor. "How has come this stone so yonder? Do you taunt me with my moai here before the ever-drop?"

"If this stone were yours to bind, why would I then hold you tightly? Next, I take from you your moai." Nalor cast a wilting gaze. "Never shall you see your rock nor feel its power touch your bones. Never shall you conquer kingdoms. Never shall you capture thrones.

"Last, o king of all the world, I take from you your precious life. And as your body falls forever, it will dwindle down to atoms. When the form of you is not a whit more than a scattered wraith, then your spirit and your name will join with you in dissolution. Hie you hence, o wicked man, and take with you your plague. This I vow, you won't be missed. Now I commit you to your grave."

Gravity reclaimed the king, and he reclaimed his limbs. Madly lashed he every way with eyes lurch-lurching like a beast's. Auroral light he left behind along with all the world above. Wind beat sharply in his ears, inside his hood, against his bones. With no candle giving heat, all was coldness, all was madness. Not a place to rest his eyes save on the green and glowing ribbon.

So, he watched the band diminish, the band whose roots he was to roam. Soon it was so slight and yonder, blinking nearly made no difference. The wall he could no longer see. Not see nor touch nor hear nor hate. He closed his eyes and held himself while shivers rippled through his frame.

It was so dark.

It was so cold.

Bellies to the ice, heads peeking out over Nunapisu, Orluvoq and Qaffa looked at each other.

"Did you feel that?" asked Orluvoq.

Qaffa nodded. "Something's changed."

Qummukarpoq and Nalor weren't so far down the cliff as to be invisible, but they didn't present an abundance of details either. Two little figures in a floating lake of green. But that had changed, and now there stood only one little figure upon the wall. Distance obscured, but it took only seconds before the queen and her daughter knew that the aurora was shifting up. The figure was coming for them, and with it Arsarneq.

"Is that... father?" asked Qaffa.

Orluvoq tapped into the glim in her hand and probed toward the advancing shadow. Identifying individuals at a distance had never been her highest of proficiencies, but after two decades, she knew within a heartbeat whether a person-shaped feeling was the king. A loping grin spread across her face.

"It's not him. It's Nalor."

Qaffa let out a whoop, and the two of them stood and backed from the edge. Arsarneq made a rumbling growl as it climbed toward its seat. It cascaded billowing refulgence up and upward, down and forever. Drafts of puissance affluxed over them, sloughing up from its ascent. Then the silence of the river, the passing of the aurora itself. Always Orluvoq had sought out the sky's light. Now *it* found her and enshrouded her in its tripartite calm, the unperverted essence of name, body, and spirit.

Arsarneq sailed past queen and princess, leaving them tottering on their feet. Orluvoq caught her balance and gawked. Near Nunapisu's verge rested a tremendous pillar of stone on its side—the largest stone she'd ever seen—worked to the cast of a Nuktipik's face. Before the pillar stood Nalor, candle burning cooly in his hand. He saw her and broke into a grin.

"Oh, now this is just fun. Seeing each other at the place we first exchanged names? You make me feel like I'm eighty-three again."

The green gloss continued to fade as Arsarneq flew higher.

"Nalor. Is my husband..."

"Dead?" he walked forward, checking his parka for debris. "No. Will he be in a few days when his body is completely dehydrated? Sounds likely."

A few lethargic feelings nudged each other around in her head. None came to the front. Qummukarpoq was no more. That ice shelf ever hanging over her had calved off and missed her by a hair. But had he really *deserved* to die? She decided to be happy for the moment. After twenty years, every path was open to her once more.

"*You're* here?" Qaffa pointed an incredulous finger. "Who *are* you?"

"I am Nalorsitsaarut. But you may, at last, call me Puigor."

Far above, Arsarneq settled back into its groove and the light evened out.

"Alright, Puigor." The word worked its way out of Qaffa slowly. "How did you get a *moai*?"

"I asked." He twisted his lips into an impish smirk. "Though it did help that one of the kingdoms up island-side thinks I'm the god of the underworld."

"What?" said mother and daughter.

He chuckled. "I've been sending bluebodies topside for many decades, but I couldn't go myself until you and our falling friend opened Sulluliaq. Once I manifested in person, rather than just one of my 'servants', I suggested they construct me the biggest moai they could manage. And as you can see," he waved behind himself.

Qaffa began to make demands about which islanders, but Orluvoq cut her off. "That's fancy and all, but how did you get *that* thing *here*, much less down *there*?"

"I learned that for whatever reason, the kings have a terror of a time trying to fly their own moai for any distance. I reckoned pairing with the candles I could do better, but I couldn't bet everything on that. Flying *down* Sulluliaq was one feat, but perhaps the easiest stage, as it's more just falling. Getting it here to Nunapisu, on the other hand. That, I feel, is worth the best cut of whale meat during summer's longest feast."

"And how exactly did you do that?" Orluvoq kept wondering how she could have missed a giant obelisk of rock sliding through her greatest matter of stewardship.

"Timing and panache." He twiddled his fingers inside his gloves. "When the ice takes bodies to Nunapisu, it doesn't leave behind the clothes or the trinkets. I learned that so long as things are positioned right, the ice will take any object."

"But... where did you leave the moai to get taken by the ice?"

"Beside your castle."

Orluvoq scrambled her head from side to side. "You *what*? How? I never saw or sensed you."

"It was only earlier tonight, after Qummukarpoq had left the castle."

Numbers streamed through Orluvoq's head. "But how did you skywalk here faster than the king?"

"Orluvoq." He gave a single chuckle. "I was *with* the moai and dead body. The ice pulled me here."

The queen reeled. Never would she have thought to travel the world by hugging a corpse and playing dead. "Who did you kill?"

"No one. They had already died. One of my, ah, followers. I wouldn't have had to do the burying part had I known that it's quite easy to carry the moai once you're in Arsarneq, as I've just discovered."

"But this all seems overly complex," Qaffa injected. "If you had a moai and are an angakkuq, why go to the trouble of doing the fight all the way out here? You could outmatch my father at the castle."

Nalor's lips pulled into a humorless grin. "Though I just fought a battle, I am no warrior. Haka'atu is jealous of his portal to the ice world, and he has an alliance with the king and queen. How do you think he reacted when I rode right up with a massive moai and dropped into Sulluliaq?"

"He probably mustered every matatoa on his islands and chased after you," said Qaffa.

"Brilliant girl. Must take after your mother. Yes. Ships were already dotting the horizon when I fell down Sulluliaq.

If I tried to fight the battle at the castle, I'd have an army of trained matatoa hot on my neck, the most feared angakkuq in the world to my front, and me completely untrained with the moai in the middle."

"I see." Qaffa pondered a moment. "But it's taken you how long, and now you're stranded out here with a moai? What are you going to do with it?"

"The plan was always to take it back topside. As I said, using Arsarneq will make that much easier. There are certain things I want to explore. Things about heaven. Let's hope I don't end up blind." He winked.

A frown had set into Orluvoq's features. "I think I understand how you did everything, but I still don't understand why. What is Qummukarpoq to you?"

"First, did you never consider what would happen to *you* once he was able to work the powers of the islands and the ice in concert?"

The frown pinched. "What do you mean?"

Nalor's easy demeanor hardened. "Second, he killed my father by stealing his name from everyone who'd ever met him. He stole my name from everyone but myself, thereby almost killing me. He's crossed many others, none who could defend themselves. At last, I have defended us all."

The knives of Orluvoq's brain trimmed and dressed the proclamation. Her voice came out cool. "So you had me marry the man you considered a monster just to get revenge?"

His brow froze into one solid furrow. "Not revenge. Justice."

She pushed tension into her jaw and stared him down. "You've had me throw more than half of my life into Nunapisu's pit all in search of justice for one man?"

He met the stare. "I did what I thought was expedient. If

I require to be brought to justice of my own, then so be it. But I have, at last, fulfilled my duty."

"Expedient. Expedient is just one of evil's masks." She waved a hand at her face. "Trust me."

"If duty must wear one of evil's masks, does it cease to be duty?" He narrowed his eyes against the world's end breeze. "The difference between evil and justice is a question of who strikes first, not a question of who never strikes."

"Who struck first, me or you?"

The night wind purred through the fur of their hoods, giving voice to the chill while Nalor gathered words. "At times, the difference between duty and justice may also find itself to be a question of who strikes first."

She let her wrath heat her insides without melting anything. Twenty years. Twenty years he had thrown her to hardship for the sake of his revenge. She did not much care whether evil or duty lay beneath the mask. She was quite finished with masks. "I do not like your justice, Nalorsitsaarut. Perhaps it would be expedient if you left."

Nalor weathered her gaze for a time, then he nodded. "As you say."

He stepped toward the moai carved in effigy of him and yanked on Arsarneq. The aurora responded to his call like a dog to its name. The snow grew lambent with vapors of green as the light descended. It hit the tundra and clamped all noise to nothing.

Nalor looked down the tunnel of light. His soft words lanced straight to her. "Goodbye, Orluvoq. And thank you."

Arsarneq lifted from the ice at the end of the world and bore Nalor heavenward. The sounds of breezes and far off animals returned. Orluvoq suddenly felt as though she had loaned out three warm hearts and they had all returned to her frozen and cracked. She sagged.

Qaffa inserted herself beneath her mother's arm and they tottered toward the igloo.

"The path of obsolescence," said Orluvoq.

"The what? I didn't grow up here, you have to use smaller words."

"That's what Nalor meant." Her eyes hung wide. "Your father always intended to reach a point where he no longer needed me. The plan was to try and combine candle and moai to control Sulluliaq. Then he could get rid of me."

Qaffa glanced at the queen. "Well, he's gone now."

"So he is."

Inside the igloo felt like the thing Orluvoq had been craving for decades. Home. The stability of her first parents. Boundless security provided by the small bounds of walls. A mass of strangling helplessness split from her spirit and drifted toward her abysmal husband. She fell to her haunches and dropped her head into her hands.

"What was all that, Orluvoq?" asked Paarsisoq from his blankets. "I've never seen Arsarneq act so wild."

"Remember how I said we needed to leave?" Orluvoq slid over to him and took his hand. "You go back to sleep. I'm staying."

Serenity in a smile wandered onto Paarsisoq's face. "She always said you'd come back." He looked on her awhile then let his eyes slide shut.

"Mother? Er, Mama?" said Qaffa.

Orluvoq turned to her daughter.

"How long do you think until Sulluliaq closes?"

"A few days. Why?"

"I love you, I think, but this is not my land. I would feel forever lost if I were cut off from the islands. I—I want to go back."

"Sulluliaq will close. You will never see the narwhals in

their pods again. Never hear a tern cry, telling you the sea is close. Never slay a bear in combat and wear its white pelt in honor. Never smell the ice. Never touch another candle. Never see Nunapisu and all your ancestors. You know this?"

Qaffa bowed her head. "I know. It is much to give up. But it is not who I am."

Orluvoq, still on the floor, reached out and touched her leg. "Then go, my daughter."

Qaffa looked up and smiled. Were those tears? "Thank you, Mama. If it's alright, I think I'll go tomorrow night."

Orluvoq smiled back, already laying plans for her last day with her daughter. The first full day of walking a new path. "Tomorrow is perfect."

EPILOGUE

Qaffa walked into the burning afternoon sun, quickly hopping off the palace flagstones burning under her feet. She had been gone under a week. Was she already so weak to the heat?

Ariki Haka'atu stepped out after her, tattooed hands laced atop his belly. "Look at that. Not a single rain cloud has come to greet you. What did you do to offend them?"

She turned to him and planted her hands akimbo. "Maybe it's *you* they don't like. How do I know you didn't do something to anger them while I was gone?"

He boomed a laugh, eyes swallowed in squints. "Maybe you're right! I haven't been eating enough and the clouds are offended that I do not appreciate the harvest they give us."

Qaffa smiled. It was good to be back. "I'm just glad I made it back."

The king gestured over his shoulder to the ten or so honor guard with him. "My matatoa say that your ocean tunnel is all closed up. Looks like you have to stay here forever, princess. If that's the case, you're going to have to get a lot better at eating properly."

She knew she'd been cutting it close trying to get back topside, but if Sulluliaq was shut less than a day after her return, she'd been risking more than she knew. "Be that the case, I'll be eternally grateful for your hospitality. However, the volcano's still thinking."

He'd taught her the saying. One could never say how many years—or days—until the volcano exploded. To always live like it would erupt tomorrow wasted everything you could be.

"So it is, so it is." He stepped off the flagstones. "Well, shall we see if it works?"

Qaffa tried not to look too eager as she skipped up to the massive cylinder of stone lying in front of the palace.

"Like I said, we made it for your big man, but he never came by to pick it up." Haka'atu reached up slapped a thick hand against the moai. "You might be able to bond with it since it was made for your blood relation. If you can, it's yours."

Excitement shivered off her. She'd gone to watch the stonecutters work on it many times. She knew its exact measurements—just slightly less than Haka'atu's.

"So, what's the trick to making it work?"

"You have to make it see your spirit." The king floated up to stand atop the rock.

"Why does it matter that it was made for someone in my bloodline?"

"If it's not close enough to your body, it won't recognize your spirit even if it sees it."

That sounded eerily familiar to the body, spirit, name belief of the Nuktipik. Qaffa would have to think about it more later. For now, she placed a hand against the long, gray stone and exposed her spirit.

The response inundated her immediately. She stumbled

back, mouth hanging wide. A colossal bar of energy sat before her like a second sun, and all she had to do was reach.

She reached.

Qaffa exploded up into the sky, wind and wind and sunshine chafing past as she flew. She laughed to the heavens as she rushed into their bosom. As the surrounding air chilled, the bar of energy dimmed until she knew she could go no higher. Full of smiles and childlike delight, she dove back to the palace.

The king waved a hand and the matatoa broke into applause as she landed. Qaffa performed three over-indulgent bows. The two things Qummukarpoq had said that opening Sulluliaq required were a powerful angakkuq and a perfect vessel to pass Arsarneq's light through. If moai really were analogous to bodies, what more perfect vessel could there be than one carved over twenty years? Might not hurt to sneak in an occasional visit to her mother.

"Of course, I am happy to have you here," said Haka'atu. "But a woman with a moai that proper needs an island of her own. Ariki Qaffa. How do you like the sound of that?"

Visions of a peck of land somewhere in the vicinity of Nanaka'i, Ragaka'i, and the wall of cloud that ascended forever upward gushed into her head. How difficult could it be to poke around a little yet avoid becoming a Hokiho successor?

She smiled. "I like it very much."

THE WATCHER SAT at the end of the earth; she sat at the start of the sky. Today she watched errant flakes of snow drift over the edge in glittering gusts of chance. It was one of the many beauties her eyes would never tire of, their ambling drift shimmering before a backdrop of inexhaustible darkness. Because she was a lucky woman, that wouldn't be the only beauty she saw today.

Orluvoq turned from Nunapisu's edge and walked to the igloo that she once again named as home. She'd quested out as far as candles would allow. No one was coming, whether to bring company or to throw themselves into nullity. That was fine, as far as she was concerned. She had somewhere important to be.

The Watcher ducked into the igloo, lit a mundane candle, and walked over to the bundle of blankets against the far wall. "Dad?"

Paarsisoq stirred in his bed. "Eh? Thought you could sneak up on me, Orluvoq? I've got the nose of a bear and the rump of a bear."

She laughed in spite—because?—of the confusing analogies. "Oh, I would never dare sneak up on you."

His eyes remained closed. "You couldn't anyway, with a face that beautiful. I'd see you leagues away."

"Dad..." Nearly a year she had lived at the end of the world. A year more resplendent than any since childhood. Nevertheless, a year for time to start finally catching up to her face and body. She'd had relative success turning her gaze outward and finding beauty inherent in the world, but she couldn't quite escape her shriveling skin.

He knew what she'd done. What she'd been. The multitudes she'd hurt at the start of the world while he tried to save them at the end. The ugliness of her spirit. He called her beautiful anyway.

Paarsisoq coughed and Orluvoq reached to brace his head. After the fit had subsided, he gave a thin smile. "I'm not all I used to be, my dear. Not all at all. At all at all."

She knelt beside him. "You're strong. The strongest man I know."

Paarsisoq's breathing labored toward his next sentence. "She always knew you'd come back, you know. 'Our Orluvoq,' she'd say. 'She's such a good girl. She'll be back here, you can mark me.'"

"She knew me better than I did. I just wish…" Orluvoq trailed off. How could she possibly expound all that she wished before her father fell asleep again?

"Don't think on that now. You're here. You know, you haven't hit forty yet. My life didn't even begin till I was almost forty-five. You'll be fine. You'll be fine."

His breathing got heavy, then steadied. Asleep. Orluvoq treasured the moments of lucidity. It seemed she'd have to wait till tomorrow for another. She pressed her hands to the floor and began to rise.

"Thought you could sneak away on me, Orluvoq?" he said with eyes still closed.

She fell back to her knees. "Oh, I would never dare sneak away on you."

"Do me a favor?"

"Anything."

"Hold my hand. No gloves."

Orluvoq peeled off both gloves and reached under the blanket to cup her father's hand.

"Now. Tell me your fondest stories of Mama."

Not quite expecting that, she filled her lungs with cozier air than the castle had ever offered and broke into a maundering recounting. He nodded along, laughed when he could, and squeezed her hand with what drops of pressure he could muster. Sometimes the stories ferried him out of consciousness. Orluvoq kept up the narration, and always her voice ferried him back awake.

As the words poured out of her, a resonance mounted within. A small, contented hum laden with gratitude for this man who had taken her in a second time. Who had decided that every person was good enough to be his brother or sister. Who spent his life at the world's black end catching those who would fall. Who, amidst all the responsibility he had found for himself, claimed her as his own daughter.

Tears flecked her vision. She let them flow, uncaring of the hitch they sometimes injected into her voice. The hours rolled by and the girl spoke softly to the father of days long past, carrying them both to fair and pleasant pastures of the mind. To joy-enameled seasons with her lovely mother. To laughter-sodden winter nights between this very igloo's walls.

After tales in their multitudes had taken them well into the night, for the first time in days, Paarsisoq's eyes cracked open. Orluvoq's dry voice caught, and her story tumbled into silence. "Dad?" she asked.

Eyes glinting from the igloo's single candle, he held her face in his gaze; his gaze which suddenly pierced through the nigh lightless room.

"So beautiful," he whispered.

His hand gave one final squeeze, then he breathed no more. Orluvoq's tears poured as from an endless field of melting snow, but the thrum of gratitude that pulsed through her body entire could have lifted her off the floor.

"I love you," she said.

Pain followed the love, as always. But this pain was different.

It was beautiful.

The candle reached the last of its wick and guttered into darkness.

AUTHOR'S NOTE

You finished my tome, for which I plaster you with thanks and pandering. Before you evanesce into a cloud of paisley and sapphires and withdraw your readership to warmer climes, I must impose one thing upon you. The internet is a fraught place, full of basilisks, ne'er-do-wells, and search algorithms. In a rosy-cheeked author's struggle against these titans of opposition, the silverest bullet I can discharge is a cornucopia of reader reviews, particularly the doting variety. If your benevolence so moves within you on this holy day (the day of your finishing *Orluvoq*), I importune you to galavant to the realms of Amazon and Goodreads and scrawl your screed. Make known your passions red and undying of your love for *Orluvoq*. Pen a manifesto, so that all might be enlightened and taste the same joy you did consuming this novel.

This book was a beast of process to get across the finish line. Back in 2016, I had an idea for a novella, and that became Part 1, finished January 2017. I was going to publish it and be done, but I realized it could be grander with Parts 2 and 3. So, I set about writing those and finished in

December 2019. Beta reader feedback and rewrites took the next half a year (blame my day job). Then I got overzealous about artwork, and the book is more copiously illustrated than your average fantasy novel. If you didn't notice, there are a few sections written in poetic meter (parts of 16, all of 31, plus a few paragraphs here and there). I encourage you to go back and read those out loud to get the full effect.

I'd like to thank Isaac, Mom, Dad, Robb, Zack, Cooper, Steven (who narrated the audiobook), JJ, Hannah, Crystal, Keller, Luke, and my editor Austin Gragg. Can't not mention the incredible artists as well: Abel Klaer (the cover, where Qummukarpoq pulls the aurora down through Orluvoq), Davide Edoardo Cassano (young Orluvoq at Nunapisu), Luke Wilmitis (narwhals in Arsarneq), Jonathan Elliot (young Orluvoq fights a bluebody), David Michael Wright (teenage Orluvoq steals beauty from Sinngup), Allen Hinrichs (young Orluvoq stumbles upon Nalor working blue candles), and Arina (the chapter headings).

Maybe someday I'll write the sequel, *Qaffa*, which follows Qaffa and her adventures in the Rapai'ian heaven above the cloud wall. But for the time being, *Olruvoq* is a standalone novel. It was a very prose-intensive process, which takes longer than windowpane prose. If I wrote a sequel, I would want the tone and prose to match. For now, I'm going to focus on other projects.

Speaking of which, my next release is a satirical short story collection about university in a fantasy world. If you're interested in getting an advance reader copy, contact me through social media.

If you want to experience *Orluvoq* again, I encourage you to pick up the audiobook, narrated by my brother Steven. He smashed it.

Again, thanks for reading, and please leave a review!

Until next time.

Check out this other crap I wrote.

Young adult duology about a kid who gets caught in a lucid dreaming gang war:

The Oneironauts 1: Schools of Thought
The Oneironauts 2: These Apparitions

Novelette about a guy who makes plagues for a living:

A New Plague

Satirical short story collection about the horrors of higher education (coming late 2021):

The Jewel of Tusco

https://www.bennyhinrichs.com